My future is not bright—I don't need her to tell me that.

"What do I need to do?"

"Burn."

I shake my head. "We walk alone in Death, and Ella's already there. I can't burn."

"You must. Or your sister is lost. Death will keep her."

"I can't! The rules—" Panic hits, and my thoughts race across all the ways this could go wrong. If my lifeline tangles with Ella's, she'll wander aimless in the deserts of Death with nothing to guide her beyond the Horizon. So will I. Or we'll get trapped in the veil like Haylea did, and the Gilded will be sent to cut us free. We'll lose all sense of who we are and why we're there—we'll fade into fog and mist, insubstantial except for our hunger, which we'll turn toward the veil.

The Spinner watches my panicking with a light frown. She shakes her head. "Break the rules, Penny."

I stare at her. Why is the Warden's pet telling me to disobey him so blatantly? Is it a test? To see where my loyalties lie? "No one will help me." My voice is a croak.

"Burn alone." She sounds mildly exasperated. "You must find Ella. It is vital that you do."

"I..." I want to refuse. Burning alone—it doesn't bear imagining. The Spinner's eyes soften with *sorry*, but there's no sympathy, no pity, only a resigned certainty. And for some reason, it makes me trust her.

Who is she, this girl with midnight shining in her gaze? Who was she before? But I don't ask those questions. "When?" I whisper instead.

She smiles softly. "Tonight."

Tonight, I Burn

Thorn Witch Trilogy: Book One

Katharine J. Adams

orbit

orbitbooks.net

Cover design by Lisa Marie Pompilio
Cover art by Shutterstock

Author photograph by Tara Lemana Portraiture

Orbit
Hachette Book Group
1290 Avenue of the Americas
New York, NY 10104
orbitbooks.net

First Edition: November 2023
Simultaneously published in Great Britain by Orbit

Orbit is an imprint of Hachette Book Group.
The Orbit name and logo are trademarks of Little, Brown Book Group Limited.

Library of Congress Cataloging-in-Publication Data
Names: Adams, Katharine J., author.
Title: Tonight, I burn / Katharine J. Adams.
Description: First edition. | New York, NY : Orbit, 2023. | Series: Thorn Witch trilogy ; book 1
Identifiers: LCCN 2023010371 | ISBN 9780316551816 (trade paperback) |
ISBN 9780316551977 (ebook)
Subjects: LCGFT: Fantasy fiction. | Novels.
Classification: LCC PR6101.D36327 T66 2023 | DDC 823/.92—dc23/eng/20230404
LC record available at https://lccn.loc.gov/2023010371

ISBNs: 9780316551816 (trade paperback), 9780316551977 (ebook)

Printed in the United States of America

LSC-C

Printing 1, 2023

For Tilly & Noah
Burn bright
xxx

Prologue

The Tale of the First Witch Queens

On a dark and stormy night, the kind of night most people shutter their windows against, the smallest of flames burned on a clifftop. A girl cradled it, fuelling its ember with stolen magic. Four others stood beside her, and their magic was stolen too, contained in the crystals that hung around their necks.

The girls' skirts cracked in the gale, damp hems snapping against their calves while rain needled their skin and bruised their flesh.

It had been simpler, before magic came. No one died, no one aged, no one fought. Magic walked hand in hand with Death and it awoke evil in the hearts of men.

Death smelled of dirt and rot and silt in a desiccated stream. When the first villager grew sick, it was chalked up to an unfortunate mistake. Then a second and a third fell ill. Skin betrayed age and fingers creaked with the passing of years. Memories faded and wits dulled. People exhaled and never breathed in.

"Where did they go," the survivors asked the gods in their

prayers, "when their eyes turned to glass and their hearts ceased to beat?"

The Sorcerer replied, "Death."

"How do we stop it?" they prayed.

The Dark Mother replied, "Give up your magic."

But magic is seductive. And men have always been inclined to bargain with Death. So they began to whisper, to plot and scheme. They turned to potions and herbs and necromancy. When they failed, they turned to *her.*

To Death they must make a sacrifice. Such was the word of the elders. A girl, young and vital, full of power and life. An excellent bargain. She wasn't inclined to agree.

The other covens did the same–chose a girl and named her their saviour.

But the girls did not want to die. Alone, the girls begged the gods for mercy, and their gods replied, "Divide magic and we will crown you as their queens." The Sorcerer gave them a knife, so sharp it could cut the air in two, and the Dark Mother guided their hand. The five girls listened and agreed. They stole all the magic and ran.

Together, they faced the sea and the storm they'd summoned. They could have thrown magic to the tousled seas and peace might have returned. But the gods had offered them crowns, and power is a difficult thing to resist. So, they joined hands and reached for the storm.

They drew it down and down into their hearts until lightning sparked in their eyes and the sea rose in a great standing wave above the cliff. Rocks trembled and shook. The wind softened into a silence that swept down the hill. All around them the world began to burn.

Death roared a warning from beyond the veil.

The girls laid the stolen magic on the ground, a pile of sparkling rainbow crystals that contained all the magic in all the world, and with the Sorcerer's knife and the Mother's hand, they divided it. Five piles of magic crystals shone in the light, red and blue, green and yellow and purple.

Ember, storm, tide, ore, and thorn.

The girls returned to their covens to claim their god-promised crowns.

In the burnt and bleeding grass they left behind, there lay—a crystal black as midnight; one rainbow bright; and the Sorcerer's blade stuck deep into the ground.

Chapter One

A witch will burn today.

This time it isn't me.

This time I'm lighting the match.

A coven of witches should have a more efficient way to start a fire; with magic at our fingertips, sparks should fly with a wave of our hands. Regrettably, we don't. My coven and our thorn magic is bound entirely to Death. And the ember witches don't like to share. Not with us.

The first strike of the match-head against the box fails. Sparks fly and wink out as they fall. The second strike catches and gutters down to a tiny orb of flame before flaring, pale wood curling black as fire consumes the matchstick.

My sister catches my eye. She's the one who should be trembling; she's the one about to be burned alive on the Warden's orders. But Mila's been walking in Death for years. She's the oldest of the three of us, the Thorn Queen's heir. She gives me a superior smile, the kind of smile she'd accompany with a flounce of her hair if her hands weren't manacled to the iron stake behind her. "Penny, you're going to burn yourself if you're not careful."

A low chuckle ripples around the coven. Twelve of us laugh.

I don't. It isn't funny.

I drop the match, right into a little pile of straw set at the base of the pyre. It catches without hesitation, and *that* is courtesy of the embers.

I wish there was an easier way—a way that didn't feel so needlessly brutal. But leaving a body behind rather complicates the whole thing. I'm not sure it's even possible. Spell books state that burning is the most effective method of crossing the veil if we want to return, but then again, the spell books we're allowed to access are all preapproved by the Warden or his council of sadistic old men. At best, they're watered-down versions of the truth. And I know everything in Halstett is a lie.

Mila's smile wavers, falters a little. Reforms.

Pain is coming. She knows it. She's done this before. But tonight is my first time lighting the pyre, and my oldest sister is the first witch I burn.

Smoke wisps around the straw, wraith-like fingers rising to clutch at her ankles.

Her bare toes press into the platform in a tiny movement of unease. We all feel it, linked as we are. Ella slips her hand in mine, a sisterly gesture, a squeeze of solidarity. "Breathe, Pen," she murmurs. "It's going to be fine."

Then, the chanting starts, ancient words that open the veil between Life and the cold plains of Death. The low hum of magic builds in my ears, and I join my voice to theirs—words I learned as a child, words I wished I'd never have to say. Yet I've repeated them each night since we were brought to Halstett thirteen years ago.

I didn't want to be a death-walker. But I am. And as Grandmother says, we can't fight the truth of who we are, only choose what we do with it. Not that we have a lot of choice. Imprisoned within the Colligerate walls, those with our particular power have two paths: serve the High Warden as a death-walker or become one of his soulless Gilded army. There's no in-between.

Grandmother reaches for my hand, her eyes flashing with a glint of the queen I haven't seen since the Gilded tore us from our village. She was respected once—an ageless beauty who fearlessly guarded Death from those who sought to defy it. Now, her gnarled fingers ensnare mine and the circle around the pyre closes. Warmth prickles at the soles of my feet, though the flagstones beneath them are cold as winter ice. The scent of singed cotton clogs my nose and throat. Mila begins to burn, her feet blistering, smoke rising from charring skin, and searing heat claws at my own.

Still, we whisper; still, we chant.

I watch my sister die and it's eerily like watching myself. With our colouring so similar and only a few years between us, Mila and Ella and I used to be mistaken for one another. Until they began to walk and the light began to fade from their eyes, their skin grew dull and paler, their bodies somehow diminished. Auburn hair flickers with fire, and I lose the line where Mila ends and the flames begin. Her silver eyes squeeze shut. Her fingers dig into the post she's bound to.

As my sister burns, we burn with her in spirit. We're stronger together. Every moment is shared, divided by thirteen. I wonder how bad this would be alone, without a coven to ease the passing.

Mila doesn't scream. No one does. Death for us must be quiet and emotionless. Screaming wakes the dead; fear summons fog-wraiths hungry for destruction.

Pain lets us pass.

With a soft sigh, Mila is gone.

My sister is dead. But it's a routine patrol, a walk along the borders between Life and Death. She won't go deep. Thorn witches rarely go far from the veil. She'll be back by morning. Then, tomorrow night, we'll do it all over again. It's a vicious life, a brutal one, slowly stealing a part of our soul each time we walk. Still, it's better than being Gilded. Anything is better than that.

In two days, it is my twenty-first birthday. And I will be ordered to burn for the very first time.

The ritual demands that the witch who strikes the match stays to undo the empty manacles and ensure the veil closes behind the witch who burned. Not having come of age, I don't sense the veil yet, so Ella takes on that role tonight. A light frown creases her brow as she nods, confirming Mila has passed without incident, and I gingerly release the manacles. They clatter against the stake accusingly, and I wish I'd been more careful. Ella's still frowning while I place the key neatly on the low wooden workbench in the corner and wipe the ash coating my fingertips against my shift skirts.

The chamber allocated to our burning is deep beneath the Colligerate wing we are told is our home. Vents draw in the cool autumn night—and filter the smell of burning flesh from the smoke when it rises up the chimney and into the sky, ensuring our regular demise does not disturb the Warden's evening stroll.

Ella wrinkles her nose, freckles twitching. "You've got Mila's ash on your ankle."

I snatch a checked cloth from the bench and scrub. I long for a bath, a small consolation—a piece of privacy and quiet. I can slide under the water, close my eyes, and pretend I am anywhere but here. I wonder if that sense of comfort will fade, once I walk. When I step into Death for the first time, which fragment of my soul will I leave behind?

Ella pulls the cloth from my hand and there's an odd glint in her eye that I don't like at all. "Pen, I need a favour."

"What kind of favour?"

She rubs her elbow, pressing a thumb into the crook of it, thinking her way around a problem like she used to when Mother set us potion tests. Then her frown clears to a calculated satisfaction that sharpens her eyes. "Remember how we used to sneak out?"

My heart sinks as my hope of a bath floats away. "You mean, when we were little and the worst punishment we faced if we were caught was a rap on the knuckles. Yeah, I remember. Why?"

"I left something in the library." Ella bunches up the cloth and shoves it back on the bench.

"We can't get into the library," I protest as she pushes me out the door.

"We can." She hurries a bit faster up the stairs and down the passageway, past the doors to the baths.

"What's so important it can't wait until tomorrow?"

"A book."

I huff with frustration. "Fine, be like that."

Ella halts so suddenly, I barrel into her back. "I'm not lying."

She most definitely is. "Just being economical with the truth?"

We're by the entrance to the Thorn Coven's wing, an arched door made of grey, polished wood. Gold studs mark a pattern of diamonds that reflect flickering lamplight, and there's a keyhole to which our coven has never seen a key. I'm not sure it's ever been locked. Beyond it lie the Colligerate hallways.

Ella's silver eyes sparkle, bright with challenge, and she's the sister she was before she first walked, when we used to sneak out all the time. "Scared, Pen?"

"No." My answer is reflexive, not a well-thought-out response. Going to the library after the curfew bell rings is a terrible idea.

"So you're in?" Ella's tone, the way she raises an eyebrow daring me to back out, makes it feel bigger than a trip to the library.

I shrug. "Someone probably needs to keep an eye on you. Who knows what trouble you'll get into on your own."

Ella grins, flashing white teeth and dimpling her cheeks. "Stay close. Once the curfew warning rings, we have precisely ten minutes before the next round of the guard."

Before I can ask how she knows, Ella slips out, leaving me no choice but to go after her.

The bell sounds as the door clicks shut behind me. The hallway lamps dim in response to the warning, ember magic burning low in glass-scalloped sconces set high up the walls. Night hangs outside the windows, creeping over the sills as the chime reverberates through flagstones and drifts up to ceilings the lamplight can't reach. When the next bell rings, anyone in a corridor without permission will be at the mercy of the Gilded, and the Gilded and mercy don't mix.

The buildings that make up the Colligerate compound are perched high on the peak of a hill right in the centre of Halstett's fortified city walls. A second wall circles the foot of the hill, and a third rings the Colligerate itself. I think it was a sanctuary once, a place of knowledge and learning before the Warden criminalised the truth and bent history to flatter his image. The library tower is in the very middle, seven corridors spread out from it like the spokes of a spiderweb. Each coven has its own spindle, five wings with a tower at the end.

The sixth corridor is wider, more extravagant, a gold-carpeted path to the Warden's luxurious palace where he keeps his consort wife and his pet prophet locked away. It's heated in the winter and cooled in the summer, that corridor. The three of us sisters, Mila and Ella and I, used to hide behind the tapestries when the cold of our own wing turned our fingers numb. Aunt Shara caught us one day, wrapped in fabric and giggling. She taught us a lesson, one we didn't forget in a hurry: She took us to watch the next trials, showing us precisely what the Gilded's punishment would be if we were found out. I still remember the sound of blood dripping to the courtyard flagstones, the shock in the woman's eyes when she saw her finger on the ground.

Yet, here we are again, out of bounds. Holy Dark Mother, Ella should know better than this. So should I.

She slows and holds out a hand behind her, twitching a finger to send me closer into the wall. We're at the circular juncture where the spokes of the Colligerate meet. If we're caught anywhere, it's most likely to be here, near the seventh corridor, which leads to the courtyard outside the Gilded Barracks and the amphitheatre that houses the eternal fires.

I hate those fires and so does every other witch I know. Halstett is built where the veil is thinner, and where the fires burn is the thinnest place of all. Magic creeps from Death into Life there. It scratches our skin and crawls down our lifelines like carrion beetles scuttling into a corpse.

Hidden in the shadows between lamps, we listen. It is utterly silent, amplifying the quiet thud of my own heart in my ears, the movement of cotton against my ribs as I inhale, the soft wheeze we all get after a burning as I breathe out. Ella squeezes my hand once. A signal to wait, stay still—don't breathe.

Boots sound in the distance, along with a male laugh and a deep-voiced reply. I imagine the palace guard are spiders creeping along spidersilk, hunting their prey. I hope it's the guard and not the Gilded.

As we huddle close, I can smell the smoke clinging to us. If the Gilded catch that scent on the dry Colligerate air, their attention will swivel in our direction, and once they begin a hunt, their quarry never escapes. The Gilded can manipulate lifelines and control consciousness, holding prisoners aware as they punish at the Warden's command. In their hands, death is a distant hope. An impossible dream.

The boots turn a corner and fade into the quiet of the night, and we run the rest of the way to the library.

Ella has had some bad ideas over the years, but this is one of the worst. In the shelter of the library entrance, I hiss in her ear, "What now, genius?"

"We go in." Ella pulls a ribbon out of her pocket, black velvet tied with a bow to a key the length of my pinkie finger.

My eyes widen. "Where did you get—"

"Don't ask, and I won't lie." She's so sure of herself, so determined, and it's infuriating. I hate getting half a story, and she knows it.

Her tone softens as she sees my scowl. "I'll tell you a secret?"

A secret? She's reaching if she thinks a promised secret will convince me. If she's reaching so far, she needs me more than she's letting on. "It'd better be a good one."

"It is." She pauses. "Please, Pen?"

Reluctantly, I nod, and she unlocks the door.

We step together into the hushed library quiet. I close my eyes, savouring the smell of books. Even the air is respectful here, a gentle reverence that would not be out of place in a church or temple. It's also the only place in the whole Colligerate where the Warden and his Gilded do not step foot. Here we are safe, free of the Warden's demands. For a while, anyway.

Ella slips a hand into mine and takes a lantern from the hook by the door. With a tap of one finger, she activates the ember spell in her lantern, and light pools around us, illuminating the library reception desk, an island of warm-polished cherrywood in a sea of black-and-white checked marble floor.

The library belongs to us all.

And some of us belong to the library. Reading is a faith requiring suspension of belief in a shrine of knowledge and imagination. Stories feed my soul and words are sharper than knives if you know how to wield them—and how to listen.

Here, magic cooperates even if the witches who wield it do not. The covens hate one another, Grandmother says, and I've never seen evidence to suggest she's wrong. Our villages were divided by forest and water and vast expanses of wilderness. We came together only once each season for the coven leaders to sit in council and to barter magic in times of peace. I don't know how it was in times of war. The only war I ever knew, we lost. History has a nasty habit of erasing lost people from its pages.

But the covens refuse to be erased. Ore magic is woven into the stones of the library tower, shimmering in the moonlight and making the impossible spiral of stairs and landings a magnificent reality. Ember magic glows softly in the dormant lamps that circle each landing. Storm magic shines in the glass windows, filtering the light of the moon, and tide magic hums quietly in the vents, pulling the moisture from the air to preserve the ancient tomes. Only thorn magic is missing. Not even the library welcomes Death.

The stairs alternate black and white as they curve up the circular library tower. Nine floors rise into the darkness above. We listen and pray we are not listened to by whatever shuffles books about on the shelves in the night. When we hear nothing, Ella gives me a little nod, and quietly we climb the stairs to the first floor where spell primers live and small witches cluster when their lessons are done. We tread carefully, light footsteps barely making a sound on the semicircle landing that takes us to the next flight of stairs.

On the second floor, the shelves are lined with fairy tales, so many it might hold all the fairy stories ever written in all the world. Each spine is a dark rainbow shade and it's the closest we get to full colour. I wonder if they know, the Warden and his council, that the library defies their colour restrictions. Maroon and bottle-green and midnight-blue leather all embossed with silver and gold take on a brightness they never had before the laws came into force. If the leather bindings are precious, the pictures inside are priceless. I used to wish I lived in a fairy story. Now I wish I had a little more time before I walk in Death and lose fairy stories for good. Mila walked for a year before she lost all joy in painting. One day she put down her brush and never picked it back up. Ella took a little longer. She still loves the library but never reads for fun anymore, and I can't face the idea of slowly losing my hiding place in the pages of a book.

As we get close to the stairs, we tiptoe, Ella and I, holding tight to each other's hands. Miss Elsweather, the overseer of literary pursuits, has her rose-embellished office on this floor; if she's working late and catches us, justifying our night-time wanderings to her will be almost as painful as trying to talk our way out of it with Grandmother.

Ella speeds up on the Third, pulling me faster, and I don't know why. This is the dullest floor; I spent most of today on my knees at the foot of these bookcases, reorganising the military history of the High Warden's rule, inaccurately documented in untruthful detail. Each book is a dreary shade of brown, the titles stamped in black ink, and no one ever comes here except the occasional palace guard and librarians on cleaning duty. My sister is jumpy, glancing down each aisle between the books, and I don't think she breathes fully until we reach the Fourth, where the spell books permitted to the covens' general use stand on neatly dusted shelves.

There are gaps in the books here. Series missing volumes. Tomes missing chapters. Those pages that survived the Warden's censorship have lines crossed out in heavy black ink. Books awaiting censorship are still whole and perfect, locked safely away from us in the censors' offices along the back wall. The offices are connected directly to the furnace by a chute topped with a steel lid. The Warden's dull-eyed clerics work there in the daylight hours, taking words from books and throwing them away. I hate this floor, filled with what could have been and what we should have known. The rough-ripped edges of torn-away pages are a wound in our magic that's unlikely to heal.

The air is heavier on the fifth floor. The dark becomes darker, denser. Shadows sharpen and tables take on nefarious angles. Bookcases shiver as if they hold more than neat lines of books. Mythology, legend, and the history of spell craft live side by side on the Fifth; there are no labels on the shelves, no filing system to organise them, the books are left where they fit best; a decorative edition of *Ballads of the Wayvern Spine* sits beside *Advanced Techniques in Pyromancy*, and an old, broken-spined copy of *The Epidemiology of Magic* leans drunkenly against a shiny hardback of *Notable Storms of the Western Seaboard*, which appears unread.

I try to slip my hand from Ella's, but she tugs me toward the stairs. I've never been above the Fifth. Only more senior librarians than us are permitted access. Last time I was caught in an alcove I wasn't supposed to be in with a book I wasn't permitted to read, I was banned from the library for an entire moon cycle, and it was quite possibly the most effective punishment I've ever received. But my reluctance is more than fear of repercussions. I do not want to disturb what resides in the upper floors. Ella tells me it's nothing, but we all know something is there: something made of magic and spell craft, or caged by it.

Fear trails a chilled finger down my neck, and I can't take another step. "Ella, stop. Please. Whatever game you're playing, this is too far."

She's pale, even in the warm light of the lantern. "You want that secret?"

"Not this much."

Ella huffs, lets go of my hand, and leans back against the banisters. Moonlight outlines her hair silver and reflects off green gilt on book bindings, looking for all the world like tiny eyes watching us from the shadows. "This is big, Pen."

I lean beside her so the banister presses against my spine. "Define *big*."

"I've . . ." She falters.

I nudge her with my elbow. "I'm not going up another step unless you tell me why."

"I just need you to hold the light."

"Why?" Holy Dark Mother, she's infuriating.

Ella laughs nervously as she turns toward the stairs to the Sixth. "I've met someone." She swallows. Grins. And runs.

"Damn it, Ella!" I whisper. I can't let her go up there alone. And she's got the light. I take a breath and then hurry after her, skipping every other step, trying to ignore the rules I'm breaking. "Wait! Who did you meet?"

We run around the sixth-floor landing. I have no idea what books this level holds; none of the books seem to have titles on their spines, and there are no labels anywhere, no writing, just a curious flicker of light that keeps changing colour from green to orange, purple to pink, and back to green. And I have no desire to investigate; I don't want to be here at all.

Ella comes to a stop on the Seventh, panting slightly. No one goes to the Eighth. Above that is the Ninth, and whatever hides there is enough to keep the Warden away and stop the Gilded from entering. I once asked Miss Elsweather what was concealed there, and she answered that knowledge is like fire: safe in a wintertide hearth, but devastating in an inferno. Knowledge turned a continent into a wasteland outside of Halstett's walls and took our home with it.

But whatever it is, I hear it sometimes, a soft murmur of my name that scuffs down the elevator shaft when I'm loading a book trolley at the bottom.

The Seventh is filled with dusty tomes, padlocked shut and chained to the shelf. Dust is caught along the panelling and it smells different here. Drier. Less book and more magic. Maybe this is where the spell books that were too powerful to be destroyed by the Warden's magic purge are hidden. I look at Ella, who's staring at the number seven embossed in gold upon the ebony-panelled wall.

A small spider rests on a little web it's woven in the number, its eyes sparkling green in the odd light. It's brighter here—or darker farther up. I can't quite tell.

"Stay here," she says in a voice that crackles like rice paper.

"You can't be serious."

Ella tries to hand me the lantern, but I'm not taking it. If I take it, she's going higher, and she can't. She shakes it in frustration, sending shadows dancing down the spines of gilded books with elaborately scripted, illegible titles. "Hold the light. I won't be long."

"You are not going up there! The last person—"

"Didn't come back?" she finishes. "Lies meant to scare us."

"They did come back?" I saw the silver coven sash they recovered when Skyla vanished. They said the stairs to the Ninth were wet with ink.

"Penny, please." I realise suddenly that Ella doesn't want to be here any more than I do.

"Just tell me what's going on," I say, my eyes intent on her face.

Ella picks at the freckle on the inside of her forearm absently, her attention on the darkness at the top of the stairs. "You don't want to know."

"If this is some dare..." I leave the accusation hanging even though I'm fairly certain she wouldn't be so foolish. "We're too old for this nonsense."

"Fine." Ella unfolds her arms and squares her shoulders, and it makes her look smaller. "I shouldn't have involved you in this in the first place."

"Involved me in what?" My voice rises.

The elevator clangs. Once. We both freeze, listening to its echo. The silence afterward.

In the apex of the library, the darkness is cut with a stuttering green glow. A faulty elevator light? They do that sometimes. The magic is old, the spell work complex.

In the book-muffled silence, Ella leans close to whisper: "A gear settling?"

I swallow. "Must be." I don't sound convincing.

She shoves the lantern at me. Everything in me is screaming to grab my sister's hand and run, down the stairs, out the library, back to the relative safety of the Thorn Wing. Instead, I take the lantern and mutter, "If you're not back by the next bell, I'm coming after you."

Ella squeezes my shoulder, nods, then turns and runs up the stairs before I can change my mind.

Her shift seems to melt into the shadows as she reaches the next floor. Even when I lift the lantern higher, I can't see her. I can't hear her either. No footfall on a stair, no thud or shuffle. Nothing. It's as if she vanished into thin air. I count my breaths to keep myself steady. The next bell will ring soon—sounding curfew this time, not a warning.

Green light sparkles on the next landing, my lantern bouncing off a spell book or a green glass inkwell. Whatever it is, it's unsettling. I blink hard and tap on the lantern to dim it. My hand shakes, and the light snuffs out, plunging the library into a darkness so solid it presses on my nerves.

Above me, glass smashes. The lantern slips from my hand.

Ella gasps.

My heart pounds so hard I feel sick.

I drop to a crouch, frantically feeling for the lantern. I can't get to the stairs without the light and I need to get to Ella. My fingers scrabble over nothing and I want to scream.

I squeeze my eyes tight shut. Inhale once. *Smell a rose*, Mother says when the walls of panic start closing in. *Blow it away.* I exhale and snap my fingers. The lantern blinks on at my feet, warm light illuminating a crack in the glass and Ella.

She stands at the bottom of the stairs, staring straight at me. Through me. Her eyes are wide and glazed, her lips slightly parted. Silently, she holds out a hand, and I take it and tug her away, too scared to speak in case it's not Ella that answers. I've read too many stories with monsters disguised as friends, watched too many gildings steal my family. I can't lose Ella. Not like this.

All the way to the ground floor, Ella is silent. Not one word as I hang the lantern on the hook and pull her out the door. She locks it, pockets the key, and hand in hand we tiptoe from shadow to shadow, darting into an alcove when we hear voices coming from the corridor to the barracks. Her fingers are ice-cold, but they're beginning to tremble—and any sign of life is a relief.

We don't stop until we reach our rooms, and I whisper: "You're not hurt?"

Ella's expression doesn't change as she shakes her head, but her fingers are still trembling.

"How far did you go?"

She doesn't answer, just stares at me, her eyes slowly regaining their focus, but slightly off in a way I can't quite put my finger on.

Worry nibbles at my thoughts. "Tomorrow, Isabella Albright, you are telling me everything."

The use of her full name, the one Grandmother uses when she's angry, startles her, and finally, finally, *Ella* reacts. A frown furrows her brow. "I can't." Her voice is raw. "I can't. This is bigger than me."

I worked that out around the time the lights went out. But I don't want to push her too hard tonight, pale as she is. I nudge her gently on the arm. "You promised me a secret, and so far, all you've told me is that you're secretly seeing someone. Tomorrow, you tell me who they are and where in this forsaken place you met them. And what exactly you're going to do when Grandmother finds out."

"Deal," Ella replies. She turns to go into her room, then pauses. Her expression is more serious than I've ever seen it. "I'm sorry, Pen. Tonight was a mistake."

"Els," I say, my throat tight with worry. "What's going on?"

"Nothing," she says quietly. "Everything is fine. It will be fine." She kisses me lightly on the cheek, then slips away and closes her door, leaving me alone and bewildered in the hall.

Ella is playing with fire. Death-walkers like us are forbidden love. We might be tempted to intervene in Death's plans if our lovers were to die. Instead, a death's head hawkmoth is tattooed on our shoulders, a permanent reminder of our duty to protect the veil between Life and

Death. We're told it's a badge of honour, a symbol of our supposed freedom. I called bullshit on that when I was fourteen and got a clip round the ear from Grandmother. A tattoo and an oath is better than being Gilded like the rest of the silver-eyed witches. We're the last death-walking coven, the last thorn witches with our own free will even if we can't exercise it.

This place is a prison, but to suggest as much is a punishable offence. We're "honoured guests." We cannot leave. But I still dream of more, of green fields and blue skies, picnics in the sunshine and stolen moments in a twilight-gloamed forest sparkling with fireflies. I long for *home*, the home I still remember: our village on the edge of the woods with the dancing stream winding through the centre.

But that place is cinder and ash now, the forest a wasteland. And our coven is the Warden's private defence against Death. We guard against angry souls resisting the pull of the Horizon on their lifeline and fix any damage they might cause.

That is the truth of why we're here—why we weren't gilded with the other death-walking witch covens when they rounded us up and brought us in. Everyone has a lifeline, an invisible cord stretching from their chest, winding through Life and leading beyond Death's final Horizon. Everyone except the Warden. His is bound to the veil, his life fuels it, and if he dies, the veil will harden into a wall no soul can pass. The living will be unable to die. Their souls will vacate their bodies and become fog-wraiths and the dead will devour life.

Responsibility for the veil should be his. But the Warden is wounded, his health faltering. So, we pay for his mistakes every night with our burning.

My grandmother's magic keeps him alive. The Thorn Coven is his shield.

The High Warden is our gift to the people of Halstett: an immortal tyrant who cannot die.

Chapter Two

The next morning, there's a distinct chill to the sunshine and an unseasonable haze of frost on the inside of the windows. It's still not quite light when I crawl out of the warmth of my bed and dress hurriedly. I'm braiding my hair with clumsy fingers when there's a light knock on my door.

Before I can answer, Mila pokes her head in my room, and I'm torn between annoyance at the intrusion and relief my sister returned from Death unharmed. I settle on confusion. "Why are you up so early?" Grandmother insists we spend the entire morning in bed to recover after a burning.

"Carlotta was on collection duty."

"So what?" I tie a black ribbon around the end of my braid and shove it over my shoulder. Already, wisps of my red curls are escaping, and I need to tame them with bobby pins before I can be seen at breakfast.

"She's indisposed this morning. We're going instead."

"Both of us?" Collection duty is normally a single-witch job.

Mila smirks and sets a wooden box on my bed. "It's in the city."

I'm so surprised I accidentally stab myself with a bobby pin. I've done collections before; registering children born to witch families and gathering a drop of their blood is one of the Thorn Coven's regular duties and part of the reason the other covens have a special level of dislike for us. But I'm not supposed to be allowed outside the Colligerate walls until I turn twenty-one. Grandmother's so overprotective, I wasn't sure I'd even be allowed out then. My world narrowed down to the spiderweb of the High Warden's Colligerate compound a few days after my eighth birthday.

Mila takes the bobby pin from my hand and fixes the curl for me. "Don't worry, Pen. I'll keep an eye on you, and we'll have an escort. It'll be fine."

I scowl, half at her patronising reassurance, half at her mention of an escort: An escort means Gilded.

Mila's smirk widens. Clearly, she intends to be utterly insufferable this morning. "You have to get used to them sooner or later. We work together."

She's right, of course. The Gilded work with us on both sides of the veil. Their death-walkers are capable of crossing too, whole regiments of them. The mechanism is different, the damage to the veil catastrophic without a thorn witch around to repair it, but even Death is not safe from the Gilded. Mila continues, "It'll be like old times. It's been ages since we did anything together, just the two of us."

I shove the last bobby pin in. "It's hardly just the two of us with a bloody escort."

"Ignore them."

"Gathering blood wasn't really something we used to do in the village."

"Not quite like old times."

"And we have to come back here when it's over."

Mila's face falls. "I thought you'd be pleased. Grandmother took ages to convince. You're always hinting you want to see the city outside the Colligerate walls and it's your birthday tomorrow." She rolls a little plaited bracelet up and down her wrist. It used to be pink and white. I made it for her when I was ten. She made a green one for Ella, and Ella made a yellow one for me. When the Warden banned colour except for our uniform sashes, we dyed them black with ink stolen from Grandmother's desk rather than remove them. Ink rubbed off on our wrists for weeks afterward, but we still wear them. Mine is tucked under my cardigan sleeve.

Maybe Mila really isn't intending to be all difficult, and it's me being prickly. "Sorry. I'm just tired."

Mila raises an eyebrow. "I'm sure you are."

My heart trips over itself. Does she know about my and Ella's misadventures last night? I study her face, but nothing seems amiss. Still, these days, I can't be sure which Mila I'm dealing with: my sister, or the Thorn Queen's heir.

"Wait till you walk, Pen. Then you'll know what tiredness really is."

Relief courses through me. She doesn't know.

She keeps up her chatter all the way to the main corridors, all the way through them, telling me how her walk went last night—just facts, there's no story in her words—and I listen as long as I can before my mind wanders off to the ninth floor and what might actually be there.

My favourite theory is that the most powerful grimoires are contained there. In the Warden's purging of magical items, he ordered them destroyed and the books refused. He ordered them thrown in the magical fires in the amphitheatre, but the fires spat them out unharmed. He ordered them torn apart by the strongest of his soldiers, but the bindings were stronger. Ordered them buried, and the earth refused to settle on their covers. Drowned, and the sea floated them back to shore. In desperation, the Warden banished them to the Ninth and sealed it with a spell that can never be undone. He has never stepped foot inside the library again.

I like that story; the idea of a bookish rebellion makes me smile.

The idea of what Ella might want with a powerful, illegal grimoire, however, does not.

The main entrance to the Colligerate is normally only used by the Warden's council, the men who underpin the foundations of his office and agree with his every word. These are stairs for the wealthy, each white tread polished to a shine that reflects the low-gathered clouds overhead. In the courtyard is our transport, a gleaming black harrier carriage. Gauzy white fabric curtains two sides, there's a footplate at each corner for our Gilded escort, and the driver's seat is right in the middle of the roof.

A swamp harrier sits on each corner. Four massive birds with talons the length of my forearm watch us approach with disdain in their glossy black eyes. Their wings are silver and black, feathers sheened a glorious blue, and their span is easily twice the height of the tallest Gilded. They are harnessed, their razor-sharp beaks are held shut with a golden band, and a storm witch is perched on the driver's seat between them. The blue of her coven sash matches the birds' feathers, and in her hands rest shimmering blue ribbons attached to the harriers' harnesses. She eyes Mila and me with as much disdain as her birds.

Two silver-uniformed palace guards hold the anchor lines at the front, their eyes on the ground. Two Gilded wait for us beside them, gold breastplates shining in the cloud-filtered morning. These are the Warden's creatures, his self-made and soulless army who have no will but his. Gold-gauntleted hands clench on the hilts of their swords. The left sides of their faces are masked in gold, rigid and glittering. None look upon the Gilded's faces. We might see familiar eyes behind their golden half-masks. Empty eyes with no trace of the person they used to be, the circles of magic around their irises darkened with flecks of grey. I don't look, but the chill of their gaze lifts the hairs on the back of my neck.

My father is Gilded: a fact we must never acknowledge out loud. Last I saw him, he was being dragged away, unconscious.

Mila was mistaken if she thought any part of this trip would be fun.

One offers a hand as we approach, a stiff and twisted charade of a gentleman handing a lady into a carriage, precisely like a picture in a book of stories I read last week except that one had swans to guide it and no gold-masked brutes with death-blank eyes to make sure she behaved. I'd laugh at the ridiculousness of it, but sparking the Gilded's displeasure risks my fingers and I'm rather attached to them. Instead, I clamber in unaided.

The Gilded who offered me his hand slides the curtains into place and grips the handle on one post. It's dark inside, and claustrophobic even with the gauzy curtains wafting in the faint breeze.

Mila sits on a black-lacquered bench facing backward, shoves the collection box under the seat with one foot, and pulls a notepad from her pocket. "It's all right to be nervous. I was terrified the first time. But it's perfectly safe."

Irritation prickles at her patronising tone. She's worse than Grandmother at treating me like a naive little girl. "It's not my first ride."

She pats the back of my hand. "It is."

"We arrived in a carriage exactly like this one, me, you, and Ella. Have you forgotten?" Mila frowns, honest confusion on her face, and pulls her hand away. I wish I could take it back. I meant to tease her, not point out a memory she's lost to Death.

Our escort steps onto the footplates, two guards to the front, two Gilded at the back, and the carriage lurches upward. A rush of a downdraught from the harriers' wings sweeps the curtains inward. Fabric clings to my neck and face like a shroud, and it takes an awful minute to untangle ourselves. The storm witch on the roof chuckles and whistles a command, and the whole contraption jolts and shudders. Then, the swamp harriers' wings ease into a steady beat, and we tip slightly as we move toward the Colligerate gates and through them.

I want to pull the curtains to one side and look out, but I don't dare with the Gilded close behind us, so I settle for watching the world pass by in glimpses through the gauze instead. Already, I can taste the air outside the Colligerate walls, see the city of Halstett spread out and reaching down to the sea. There's salt on the breeze. I miss that scent, and so many others: the leaf-littered forest outside our village, the damp mist blanketing the shore, the clean tang of a retreating tide.

Inside the Colligerate we are surrounded by smoke and metal polish and stone. My one reprieve is the library scent of beeswax and books. And of course, Mother's poison garden. I always believed the compound's walls were slate grey, but outside the jagged battlements and narrow archers' windows are plated in gold and the Colligerate shines like a beacon in the morning light, marking the highest point on the landscape for miles around. The hill it stands upon is bare, no soil, no vegetation, no leafy forest or dew-coated meadows. I thought maybe there would be farmland here, tucked into the shelter of the walls, but there is nothing.

We pause, waiting for access through the lower wall gates into the city, and I look down at my hands. These walls, with the bodies hung upon them, I do not want to see.

A scratch of pencil on paper makes me start; it seems so loud, loud enough to draw the Gilded's attention. But when I risk a glance, they're occupied with the harriers flying just a little too high. Mila writes in soft pencil on a fresh page in her notebook: *I need help. There's too many.*

I frown. Too many what?

Mila traces a line down her nose and rests a hand on her cheek, a sign for the Gilded we came up with as children.

My frown deepens.

The escort, there's too many of them. He's nervous, she writes in perfectly rounded letters, each precisely the same size as the next. I've always been a little envious of her handwriting. Mine looks like a pigeon tap-danced across the page with ink on its toes.

I mouth the word *Who?*

Mila rolls her eyes and scribbles: *The Warden! Do you need me to draw a picture?*

I huff, snatch her pencil, and gesture for the notebook. Mila gifts me with the most beautiful of scowls as she passes it over, and I scrub out the word *Warden* first. If we're caught writing about the High Warden of Halstett, we're risking more than a finger or two. I write carefully *What the hell?* and hand it back.

Cover for me, Mila writes. *I've got a message to deliver.*

She passes me the notebook, and I write: *Who to?*

Mila gives a wry smile, an actual sisterly smile. *Grandmother's supplier.*

Is there even a child?

Born last night, Mila writes. My eyes widen; normally we wait until babies are a few months old to register them. *Can you distract them or not? She needs gingerweed for Carlotta and a new shipment just got through.*

Gingerweed grew in the forest near our village but refuses to acclimatise in the cold desert left behind the Gilded's wave of conquest and destruction. Even Mother can't get it to flourish in her glasshouse. We rely on the black market to manage our moon cycles and fertility. It gives us a small measure of control over a life where everything is decided for us.

I write two words on the notebook Mila nudges into my lap: *Of course.*

Our cousin Carlotta has been through a lot in the last year. Her sister, Haylea, died horribly last winter, tangled in the veil after an encounter with a fog-wraith in Death. Her mother never recovered. You'd imagine a thorn witch to be well acquainted with Death. It's different though, when someone you love crosses the Horizon, passing the point of no return. Haylea's accident devastated us all. I still miss her bitterly; for Carlotta it has been so much worse.

We've lightened her load, relieving her of the worst of our duties—not the burning, even our grandmother the Thorn Queen can't protect us from that—but Carlotta has a steady supply of sugared almonds and her pick among our other daily tasks, and I saw drawing pencils in all the illegal colours of the rainbow on her desk the last time I was in her room.

Mila thoroughly scribbles out our conversation and tucks the notebook back in her pocket. Her hand wraps mine, hidden by our skirts, and I wonder if she knows how I'm dreading tomorrow's burning. I am the most reluctant thorn witch in the history of our coven, Grandmother says. She used to say it fondly with a gentle tug of one pigtail when I was little, but recently it's become an insult. A failing that cannot be allowed to continue.

I hold tight to my sister's hand as the carriage flies through wide streets and into the city centre, glad it's Mila with me today and not an aunt or cousin. Glad I got to see beyond the Colligerate walls before I burn for the first time.

The streets here are lined with silver flags, looped like bunting along glass-windowed shopfronts. A cobbler displays a single polished and perfectly heeled shoe on a shining stand, a haberdashery holds artistically stacked bolts of cloth in every imaginable shade of grey, and a dairy storefront is packed with huge rounds of waxed cheese brought in from over the seas. The best of the imports are reserved for the Warden's tables; some are sold to the merchant families that live in the fancy district closest to the foot of the hill. The leftover scraps serve everyone else.

The carriage slows as we pass a statue of the Warden, raised on a plinth and plated in gold. He is stunning in his re-creation, chiselled muscles and wide shoulders and strong jaw. I catch Mila's shudder, feel ice crawling down my spine. The statue shows a man who's met the end of multiple centuries, yet no years line his eyes or crease his brow. He was perfect and horrible in his never-ending vitality until his sickness. We've never seen him without his golden mask, and I wonder if he still looks the same behind it.

We come to a smooth halt in front of a shop with a black hat in a small glass window and a sign that reads: JOLTS AND VARA MILLENARY SUPPLIES. APPOINTMENT ONLY. TRADING REGISTER: 72/21. Another statue looms in the street right in front of it: the fabled Sorcerer carved from polished yellow stone, so lifelike the fringing on his robes ruffles in the wind. His nose is thin-bridged and his eyes set high. They are completely silver, his eyes. No whites. No pupils. He stares at me as one of the Gilded guard opens the carriage curtains wide.

Mila whispers, "When I give you the needle, drop it."

I nod and follow her into the shop. Inside, the closeness of the air is stifling. Row after row of hats line the walls, in shades that range from nearly black to almost white. No pattern, no feathers, no adornment. No colour.

Disappointment hits unexpectedly. I wasn't hoping for a riot of bright, happy rainbows, but I was hoping some shreds of colour might have remained out here. A pink ribbon, perhaps. A green satin trim or a purple silk flower.

Up the stairs at the back of the shop, we find a tiny room with a woman seated on a low couch, her baby asleep beside her in a cradle fashioned from softwood. She's a witch. I blink at her in surprise, and she stares right at me. Her dark hair is caught back in a grey gingham band, sweat sheens her brown shoulders, and her shift is plain grey wool. Once Mila and I have squeezed inside, there's barely space for a single Gilded to follow as well.

The mother's eyebrow hitches when she sees Mila, then her eyes skip straight to the Gilded blocking the doorway. She leans forward, shifting slightly to put herself between the baby and us, and tucks one perfect little foot under the crib blanket.

Mila pulls her notebook out, all business and no nonsense while I'm still blinking at the mother. How is she a witch? How is she not sworn into one of the Colligerate covens or forced into a gilding ceremony? How has the Gilded not noticed? The telltale emerald ring around her irises gives her away. She's a tide witch. Mila jabs me hard in the ribs with her pencil, and I jolt to attention and take the notebook and the pencil.

"Family name?" she asks.

The mother answers softly so as not to wake the baby. "Vara."

"Child's given name?"

"Marylin." The mother spells it out so I can write it down correctly.

"Gender assigned at birth?" Mila asks.

"Female." The baby stirs, stretching one tiny hand out to clasp its mother's finger, and opens its mouth in a little circular yawn.

Mila drops her voice. "Eye colour."

The mother's jaw tightens. A muscle twitches in her cheek. "Green."

We all exhale at that. Green is a safe colour. Occasionally a child is born with unexpected silver in their eyes, and for most silver-eyed witches, there is no future worth having. There's no hiding it either, the magical mutation that allows us to walk in Death.

"Green," Mila repeats, not checking as she should. I look quickly at the Gilded, but his back is to us, blocking the doorway and any hope of exit, should any of us decide to attempt an escape. I write it down carefully, forcing my hand to remain steady.

"History of magic in the family?"

The mother shakes her head. "Not since my great-grandmother. None of her descendants have shown any signs."

It's a lie. A blatant one. This woman who is rocking her child's crib so gently could conjure a waterfall down the stairs fierce enough to wash our Gilded escort out the front door.

Mila glares at me as I stand gaping. "Write it down, Penny." I do, and she holds out the needle she brought with her.

I take it.

Drop it.

Mila curses, loudly. "Damn it all, Penny! Where's the spare?"

I feel the Gilded's attention; his chilled gaze frosts the back of my neck, and I don't have to entirely fake being scared and sorry. "I don't have it."

"Well, what are you waiting for? Go and fetch it!" Mila winks, and I hurry down the stairs and outside into the fresh air.

The Gilded follows me all the way to the front door. The carriage stands right where we left it: palace guards holding the anchor lines, the second Gilded standing stiffly to attention and watching the storm witch, who's plaiting the reins in her lap. She doesn't move as I walk steadily across the cobbles, but her eyes slide to me. Her fingers twitch. The bird closest to the hat shop spreads its wings wide and launches itself into the air.

The downdraught knocks me sprawling backward, right into the Gilded behind me. The guards shout, clinging to the anchor lines as the carriage pitches. Gold-gauntleted hands grab my shoulders. Cold fingers dig into my skin. My heart squeezes tight. But the

Gilded pushes me aside and lurches past to grab the carriage. I watch from the doorway as he leaps onto the carriage footplate, weighing it back down. The storm witch waves the reins around and shouts apologies from the roof. I swear she gives me half a questioning smile as she settles her miscreant bird, smoothing its ruffled feathers. It twists its head to stare right at her, beak to nose, and she scratches it gently, right between the eyes.

The carriage steadies on the street as the guards tighten their anchor lines, and the Gilded step down, keeping one hand on the handles at the back. The biggest Gilded turns, and I drop my eyes to the street before he can see me watching. "Enough," he barks at the driver, who's apologising for the fifth time. "Get what you need," he orders me.

They watch over my shoulder as I search for the box Mila left under the seat. In the commotion, it's slid sideways and wedged itself in the back corner so I have to climb right inside and scrabble around on my knees to pull it out. I fumble with the catch on the box and make a pretence of rummaging through the contents, reorganising the array of tiny glass tubes, small, sharp blades, and packets of needles, buying Mila as much time as I can until one of the Gilded bangs a hand on the carriage roof and I jump clean out of my skin. He says something I can't hear, but his meaning is unmistakable. What time I can afford Mila has run out.

I grab the box and hurry back up. Mila and the mother have not changed positions at all, but a tiny inclination of her head tells me she's done what she came here to do. She slips her hand in her pocket, pats it closed, and holds out a hand for the box.

There's nothing left but to prick the baby's perfect little heel, collect the tiniest drop of blood in a thin glass vial, and leave the new family behind. I wonder as we climb back into the carriage where the father is and why he wasn't at the mother's side. I hope she has someone, a husband, wife, or partner to share the burden of bringing a child into Halstett and the cost of hiding her magic.

"Not a word," Mila whispers once we are airborne again. "Not to Ella or anyone. Promise."

"Not one and no one," I reply, using our secret vow of silence from childhood without thinking.

Mila flushes pink, and I give her a stiff smile as the curtains fall back into place. Mila running mysterious errands involving tide witches in disguise is confusing. That Grandmother condones it makes no sense at all. Mila never breaks the rules, and Grandmother never stands against the Warden's laws. It seems Ella isn't the only one keeping secrets.

Chapter Three

The two rules of Death hit me in the face as I take my seat at the dinner table. They're carved into the black marble wall of the coven's dining hall directly above where my grandmother sits at the head of the table, each letter a foot high and outlined in silver.

Rule one: Always walk alone.

Rule two: Never look back.

Unbroken and unbreakable.

Beneath them, a glass case contains the coven crystals, a sparkling array of pink and purple gems protected by Grandmother's wards.

Our lives are bound to those carefully polished stones. They anchor our lifelines when we walk in Death. Everyone's lifeline feels different. Mother's is normally gentle like a warm hug, but today, it's crinkled and sharp as she takes her seat at Grandmother's side. Grandmother's is clingy, reminding me of the grass that needled seeds to my skirts back home. It's extra prickly this evening, matching the collar of silver thorns she wears at her throat. Mila's is like a hedgehog, sometimes soft and inquisitive, sometimes spiny and sharp.

No one else notices. No one should sense lifelines this side of the veil between Life and Death. But I feel them as a whisper of sensation against a single hair. An invisible trip wire that strings tight when my sisters walk in Death. And sometimes, I think Grandmother hates me for it. The first time I asked her about lifelines, I was five. That night, she sent my father into Death to create my crystal. She made me watch as they burned my father alive, my hand trapped in hers as the heat of his pyre parched my eyes and mouth. My father dying with a drop of my blood clenched in his fist haunted my nights for years; Grandmother's rage when he returned with an obsidian gemstone, grown from my blood in Death's sand, still does.

Behind her, the coven crystals sparkle softly in the evening light streaming golden through the window. Mine appears to be an amethyst, dark and deep like all the Thorn Queen's descendants. But it is fake. My true crystal, an obsidian gem, is unspeakably rare. And apparently coveted by the High Warden. I have no idea where it is, only that it's safe. Grandmother locked it away the day my father returned with it from Death, and I haven't seen it since.

Tonight, Grandmother is almost as stiff-backed as she was that night, and a frown shadows her eyes. A heavy white braid hangs over one shoulder, and her lips are a pale, thin line. Mother sits beside her, worry creasing lines around her silver eyes. Our mother is the most beautiful woman in the whole of the bleak and godless city we're misfortunate enough to live in. Dark hair frames her heart-shaped face, bound back with a silver band of delicate ivy, and freckles scatter across her cheekbones just like mine.

Her eyes are on the crystal around Grandmother's neck, a polished gemstone of deepest purple resting on her black knitted cardigan. She only wears it when she's been summoned to tend to the Warden's wound, which is happening too frequently of late. She'll go there directly after tonight's burning—Ella's burning—which explains her frown but not why she's directing it at my mother as if daring her to speak. I love Mother, so much, but I wish she'd stand up to Grandmother more. I wish I got to spend more time with her too.

"They've been arguing all afternoon," Mila says between sips of tea. "No one has any idea why."

Ella sets her fork down, leaving her dinner plate untouched. It's filo pie tonight, chicken in a pale creamy sauce with tiny spears of sweetcorn piled on the side. I don't know where our food comes from. It appears on our tables, but I've never seen a field or a farmer, and our trip into the city today only makes me all the more confused. I'd imagined crops tucked tight into the Colligerate walls where they cannot be seen from the coven towers, not a grey rocky waste with not a green thing in sight. The only animals in Halstett are the birds in the eyrie at the top of the storm witches' tower, Miss Elsweather's cat, Jemima, and the rats she keeps her to catch.

I don't even know where our meals are prepared or who prepares them. We're not permitted to speak to the servants we occasionally see in the halls; when we collect blood, their children are brought to us by the guards. When I asked Mother where the kitchens were, she gave me a vague nonanswer, and my aunts flapped me and my questions away. In all the years I've lived here, all the corridors I explored, I've never seen a hint of a stove or a laundry or an outdoor garden to grow the herbs like the green tarragon flecking the puddle of sauce that's congealing on my plate. Mother has her poison glasshouse attached to the workrooms, but it's for strictly controlled plants, not dinner.

No one seems to care how our clothing reappears clean and folded in our drawers, or how the fire gets laid—they only care that it happens. On the other hand, I've lain awake long after curfew wondering where our firewood comes from when we're told there's nothing alive outside Halstett's walls and there's no hint of a forest inside them either. Surely, it cannot be brought in by sea?

It's frustrating, knowing so little of the workings of the place we're ordered to call home.

Ella's not the only one who's lost her appetite. I wipe my fingers on my napkin, neatly line my fork on my plate, and glance to make sure Mother is still the full focus of Grandmother's attention before I say quietly, "You'll be careful?"

Mila skewers her last piece of sweetcorn and waves it at me. "Ella's always careful. She's never made a mistake. What's got you so worried?"

Ella jabs me with her elbow. "She's just nervous about tomorrow, aren't you, Pen?"

I glare at her. "I don't know, Els. Maybe it's more to do with last night?"

Mila chews and swallows. "What happened last night?"

"Nothing the Thorn Heir would approve of," Ella replies archly.

Some of the light in Mila's eyes fades. "Fine. Keep your secret. But don't come crying to me when you mess up." She scrapes her chair back and stalks out of the room, leaving me and Ella to clear away her plate to the trolley by the door.

"That was uncalled for," I hiss under my breath as we leave the dining hall behind, following Mila at a safe distance toward the stairs.

"Was it?" Ella gives me a sad smile. The more time Mila spends with Grandmother, the further apart Ella and Mila drift. I miss how it used to be, but I think Ella misses her more. "She's in Grandmother's pocket, Pen. If she knew where we were last night..."

"How high did you go?" I blurt out. Here isn't the place to ask, but I need the answer before she burns.

Ella glances over her shoulder, checking no other coven members are near. "Stop worrying. I only got as far as the Eighth. I'll be fine."

"How can you be sure?" More to the point, how can she be so damned calm about it? She's about to be burned at the stake, she might not come back, and other than picking at her dinner, she shows no sign of nerves. I don't know if I can match that. If I'll be able to walk calmly down the stairs to the Chamber of Flame and Smoke tomorrow. Sometimes, I'm so proud of my sisters, their bravery in the face of burning, what they sacrifice to protect Life from the fog-wraiths who seek to destroy it.

Sometimes, I think we should let Halstett burn, even if we're damned in the process.

The nerves of walking tomorrow hit full force all over again, and I wonder if my sisters conspired to keep me occupied. Was that what Ella was playing at in the library last night? She knows I'm scared, but an out-of-hours trip to the Ninth seems like overkill; a game of cards would have been a less risky way to distract me. Mila's room shares a wall with mine so I've no doubt she's heard my nightmares. I hear snippets of hers. But arranging a trip into the actual city? I'm not sure even Mila's privileges as Grandmother's heir would afford her that.

Mother seems to know everything about us three without being told—but she was more obvious with her intentions. She had me running errands all afternoon once we returned from the city and handed the collected blood over to Grandmother's safekeeping.

My legs ache from walking every square foot of the Colligerate at least three times over. I've been to each coven's wing and up each tower, delivering dried nightshade and belladonna for the potions and spells the Warden uses to pay for his overseas trade. I took a jar of something foul smelling to the Warden's wing, handed it to the Gilded guarding his door, and hurried away. Worst of all, she sent me to the barracks with a tincture for fever, which must have been for one of the palace guards as I don't think the Gilded have enough mortality left behind to get sick, and the paste for treating burns after the gilding ceremony.

The only place she didn't send me was the library, and I was glad of that. But it meant Ella was able to avoid me damned effectively until dinner. I pinch her as we reach the stairs to the chamber. "You owe me a secret."

Ella's fingers find mine and squeeze. "You have no idea."

"Did you at least find it... what you were looking for?"

"No."

"Don't go back, Els. It's not safe."

She tightens her grip on my hand, and the bones in my knuckles protest. "There's no point. I—" She swallows whatever she is about to say. "Stay off the upper levels, Pen. Promise me."

"I wouldn't have been near them in the first place if it wasn't for you!"

Ella snaps her mouth shut and nods toward the foot of the stairs. Mila leans against the chamber door, arms folded. The words *Flammae ac fumo* are written in silver flowing letters beside her, painted by my mother when the Thorn Coven realised this was it. This was our life. These words were the first attempt to make this our home. The sign nailed below reminds us it's not: NO UNAUTHORISED ENTRY, stencilled in red on white board.

Mila raises an eyebrow and says to Ella in the worst stage-whisper imaginable, "Did Pen tell you we went to the city today?"

Ella's eyes widen. She quite clearly had no idea. Which is unusual. Normally our duties are written on a piece of parchment and pinned to a board in the hallway, so everyone can see and anyone can find us, which is irritating or reassuring depending on how dangerous our task is or how many rules we're choosing to break at any one time.

Mila continues, loud enough for anyone to hear. "Collection duty. She did well. Two Gilded they assigned us. Last time it was one."

"Did they now?" Grandmother's voice floats down the stairs behind us, and Mila winces as the three of us press against the wall to allow her to sweep past. Silently, she unlocks the chamber door and holds it open. "Inside, all of you."

We obey like children caught stealing from a cookie jar. Heads hung, hands behind our backs, we arrange ourselves in a neat line in front of her and wait. Grandmother stands in the very centre of the Chamber of Flame and Smoke and asks Mila, "Two Gilded?"

Mila nods once, sharply. I can feel the tension in her shoulder where it touches mine.

"And yet, there was no mention of this in your report?"

Mila's mouth opens and closes and no sound comes out.

"I will see you in my office, Mila, directly after the burning."

The colour drains from Mila's face, and I want to squeeze her hand and tell her it will all be fine. Grandmother won't do anything to Mila. Not really. She's the precious thorn princess, heir to a broken crown.

When we were little, she was different, our grandmother. She was always a queen, the part of her that is utterly inflexible has not bent with our circumstances, but there was a piece of her that belonged to us, her granddaughters, and it was ours alone. I think that piece burned along with our village, the grandmother who made us hot chocolate and wrapped us in shawls with purple fringing and took us outside to show us the stars. She'd name the constellations and tell us their stories and sing us their songs, and we'd drift to sleep on her lap to the sound of her whispering magic into our dreams. That was before. Before we came here and everything got broken.

It's almost impossible to believe that the woman welcoming the other coven members into the chamber, about to watch her granddaughter burn, who tomorrow will set light to my birthday pyre, is the same one who soothed our grazed knees and gave us barley sugar. The witch checking Ella's pockets and hands and fastening black iron manacles to each of her wrists is the grandmother who oh-so-carefully sewed the eye back on my favourite dolly when I was five.

Thank the Dark Mother, tonight I do not have to light the match. Burning Mila was nearly impossible. With Ella, I would have failed. The task falls to Carlotta, and Ella smiles as our cousin strikes the match, a smile with sharp corners and brittle edges. Only Mother's tight grip on one hand and Mila's on the other stops me from crying out. I want to beg Ella not to do this.

Instead, I listen and feel and hurt with her. I take her pain and share it. I chant to open the veil, and tonight, I hear it answer faintly in the distance, soft like a waterfall deep underground. I want to slam it shut. I want to run and take Ella with me. Midnight grows nearer with each minute that passes, my birthday lies in wait just beyond, and tomorrow, I will hear the veil's roar in all its horrifying glory.

I send a silent prayer to the Dark Mother who made us all, who wove us lifelines to guide us and breathed warmth into our veins, that Ella will return safe from her patrol. I pray that whatever she is mixed up in that led her to the ninth floor of the library isn't as bad as it feels. And even as I silently form the words of my prayer, I'm not convinced there's anyone there.

The Dark Mother has forsaken us, like the Sorcerer whose statues stand in the city. If she was real, she'd help her children, shield us from the Warden and his tyrannical rules. If the Sorcerer existed, he'd protect the veil he supposedly created. The magic he gifted to us would help us escape.

I fear there's no one listening to our prayers and hopes and dreams—our pleas for a future better than this, better than being a coven of imprisoned witches chained to a tyrant we cannot allow to die. But I pray for Ella's soul anyway because there is nothing else I can do.

How the Sorcerer Anchored the Veil

The first shard of magic sliced through the roof of the Palace of Study and Prayer and hit the library. By some stroke of luck (or maybe divine intervention) the shard missed all the books, but it pierced the librarian's rosewood desk and drilled into the tiled floor, spiralling down and down, deep into the earth until it hit the bedrock of the world. And there it stopped.

In the dark beneath the soil it began to grow. A crystal slowly pushed the palace high above the city until it stood on a perfect symmetrical hill. Scholars examined it, philosophers debated it, storytellers wrote about it. Then the Sorcerer came. He pricked his finger and spilled a drop of his blood and the crystal began to bleed. Magic spilled from its edges and wove roots beneath the continents and seas. Crystalline threads of power connected mountains and streams, cities and shrines. It spread under every living place and every barren ground until a web of magic lay beneath every inch of the world. From the web, through earth and sea and air, the veil rose, invisible and impossible to defy, separating Life from Death. Dividing the living from the dead.

And so, the Sorcerer anchored the veil with his own lifeline to ensure it never shifted and protected it with blue flames so it never would fail.

The Day Magic Fell from the Sky: Myths for Under Twelves. *Approved by the High Council in the second year of the rise. Shelved on the second floor of the Great Library. Author: Elspeth Elsweather.*

Chapter Four

My birthday starts with the kind of silence that drips fear into my bones. Unease tiptoes along my nerves, sharpening each ring of the morning bell in the Colligerate clock tower. It crinkles against my skin as I crawl from my bed, shrug on my black cotton shift, and tie the silver sash that proclaims me a thorn witch. I fumble at the knot and need to redo it twice before I'm satisfied it won't snag Grandmother's attention with mismatched ends and snarls of silk cord.

I worry too much, Mother says. But something isn't right. I hear it in the footsteps walking down the halls of the Thorn Coven's wing, in the whispers smothered with the backs of hands, tones dropping as they pass my door. I feel it in the part of my heart tied to my sister.

Mother knocks on the door. Three raps. Light ones. Hesitant.

I don't want to answer. Answering will put a name to my unease. But it already has a name: "Ella," I murmur. Still trying to convince myself I'm imagining things, I snatch a ribbon from the dresser, hastily tie the end of my braid, and open the door.

"Penny?" Exhaustion stiffens Mother's greeting. She'll have sat up all night waiting for Ella's return. She always does when Mila or Ella are on patrol. Tonight, she'll wait for me.

Her normally straight shoulders are softened with defeat, silver eyes bright. The whites around her irises are fine-veined with red like crazed glass after a fire. "It's Ella," she says quietly, her voice strained, like she's forcing it past a lump in her throat. "Pen, Ella's late."

My own breath catches. "Thorn witches are never late."

It's entirely the wrong thing to say. The truth often is. But Ella should be back by now. She should have been back by dawn.

Mother's eyes sharpen, rosebud lips tightening into a thin smile that wobbles a little at one corner. "Nevertheless, Ella *is* late." I reach for her, but she backs away, anxious lines bracketing her mouth. "There's a gilding this morning. Your grandmother requires your assistance."

My heart skips and thuds into my diaphragm. "That's…"

"Ella's job," Mother finishes for me. "Seeing as Ella is no longer with us, that duty has been reallocated. Don't let her down. Not this morning, Pen."

I nod, mutter some kind of promise that I'll do my best as her words ring inside my head, over and over again: *no longer with us*. Mother thinks Ella is dead. Not late. Not in trouble.

Dead.

She isn't. She *can't* be.

Her crystal will tell the truth. Crystals can't lie. If Ella is still alive, rainbows will swirl in her crystal.

I snick shut my bedroom door and hurry in the wake of Mother's stiff-backed march to the dining hall.

Ella's crystal hangs beside mine, a deep pink hue to its dark-rainbowed depths. Faint swirls of silver mist curl and fold in on themselves inside it like smoke from our pyres.

The tension balled in a hard lump beneath my ribs eases.

Her lifeline is tethered to her crystal, flickering and unsteady but it's there. It flutters like a hawkmoth's wingbeat at the edge of my senses.

Mila glances at me as I slide into my seat, her eyes red-rimmed as if she's been crying.

Mila never cries.

Ella's empty place at the table gapes like it's lined with teeth, threatening to eat us alive if we pay it too much attention. She's in trouble, and there's nothing we can do to help her. In Death, we walk alone; to do otherwise risks our lifelines tangling, and tangled lifelines snap under the strain of crossing the veil. I wonder who made the first rule—how unbreakable it really is. Surely if we were careful...?

Mila slides my breakfast across to me, and the smell of sausages and bacon curdles in my stomach. I force myself to chew and swallow and a piece of bacon sticks in my throat. Helplessness hollows my gut, frustration jangling at my nerves as breakfast continues around me with no mention of Ella.

No plan.

Nothing.

My birthday forgotten, abandoned bacon cools on my plate and egg yolk congeals into an orange smear. Glancing from one defeated witch to the next, I clench my hands in my lap. "She's not dead." My voice comes out quieter than I intended, but it has the desired effect. The table freezes into a tableau carved from stone. I want to shrivel under the weight of eleven silver-eyed glares.

Grandmother slides her plate away and pulls her lace shawl around her shoulders to ward off the early-autumn chill drifting through the arched windows. "Not dead?" A challenge she issues with a warning in her eyes underlining it.

"Ella. Her crystal's still anchoring her. She's not dead..." I trail off. If I'm helping with the gilding, I have an entire morning in Grandmother's company. Maybe I should have done this alone, without the whole coven watching, so Grandmother didn't have her Thorn Queen status to maintain.

"Ella is lost. All we can do is pray she walks into the Horizon."

"Ella's your granddaughter!"

"So was your cousin," she snaps. "Pray that Ella does not make the mess Haylea did." Across the table, Carlotta scowls at the mention of her sister. Grandmother talks as if the coven is disposable. A commodity, not a family. The only person she ever really cared about was her son, and we don't talk about my father anymore. Grandmother shakes her head and smooths a nonexistent wrinkle from the tablecloth. "Ella is gone. She'll cross the Horizon by nightfall."

My mother flinches. Mila wraps her arms around herself, her knife dripping bean juice to the floor. Carlotta violently spears a mushroom with her fork. I clench my teeth so tight my jaw hurts: There's no return from the true death beyond the Horizon. We are told time and time again, before we even learn to strike a match, that we must never go near the light. Ever. Not until the end. Once a soul crosses the Horizon, there is no crossing back.

Despite her dismissal of Ella's fate, Grandmother's fear is palpable as she hands out the day's orders. Distrust sharpens her eyes when she comes to me. "You'll be assisting with the gilding this morning, Penelope. Afterward, you'll resume library duty with a smile on your face. Not one word of this *situation* outside our doors."

I sigh a little with relief. In the library, I'll have time to think without watching my back. I'll find a way to help Ella.

I rise to leave, but Mother stops me with a delicate hand on my wrist. The silver braided belt at her waist is untidily knotted and her narrow shoulders are stiff with tension. In Death, she can destroy a fog-wraith with one strike of a blade formed from magic and sand, banish them into the Horizon with a twitch of her fingers. Here, she seems fragile, as if she might break in a strong gust of wind. "Don't make it worse, Pen. Challenging your grandmother won't help."

I answer with more certainty than I feel. "Ella isn't dead."

"Penny..." Mother shakes her head, sorrow hazing her silver eyes grey. "Happy birthday."

"She'll be back."

I gently untangle her grip on my wrist, and hurry after Grandmother.

The Gilded Barracks leer over the courtyard with a broken-toothed smile of shuttered windows. The entrance gapes like a bony nasal cavity, the doors wider at the bottom than the top. Gilded are stationed to each side. Their lifelines scratch at my nerves. Unwieldy and brittle and serrated with vicious barbs—a reminder of their power.

I lower my eyes as I catch up with Grandmother and shadow her up the steps.

In the prescribed history approved by the Warden's council, the gilding process was devised by the Sorcerer as a horrifying method of controlling magical prisoners without the waste of execution. But with his Gilded creations, the Sorcerer handed the Warden too much power, and so, the Warden exiled him into Death. Banishing a deity makes the High Warden's reputation all the more terrifying, not that he needs it. But powerful as he is, he's just a man. A man who wrote the history books. Anything can be created with paper and ink; a tale written down is made real by the generations who consume it. I'm not sure if the Sorcerer of fairy-tale fame ever existed at all. Or how the Warden could have banished him if he did.

I think the Warden created the Gilded himself.

Before the poisoned wound threatened his lifeline and the veil, the Warden would have had the power to do it. So many witches were gilded on arrival to our new *home*, and there were no thorn witches here to help him back then. Not to start with. No *Sorcerer* then either. So it must have been him. Nothing else makes sense.

The doors creak open to the barracks, and I pace my steps across the entrance hall, back straight, knees steady. Show no fear. We're taught it shields us from fog-wraiths in Death. But it's a defence against the monsters this side of the veil too.

Across the entry hall, golden doors reach high into the cavernous ceiling. A shudder trembles behind my breastbone where my lifeline is rooted. The amphitheatre is behind those doors and the eternal flames burn in the centre.

I don't breathe again until I'm safely through the coven's work-room door. It's pitch dark in here until Grandmother lights a match and sets it to the wick of a lamp. The lamp flares clean and bright, illuminating the most pristinely white room I've ever seen in my life. Silver canisters line the shelves, alchemical symbols stamped into their metal. Callipers are already laid out on the worktop, and scales and weights glitter in the lamplight beside a line of scalpels, so sharp they could slice a soul precisely in two.

I've watched gildings before. We all have. A reminder, Grand-mother says, of what she saved us from. But I have no idea what to expect on this side of the process. Els was always tight-lipped on the work done with Grandmother prior to a gilding.

A piece of parchment is pinned to the wall with a miniature silver dagger so perfectly formed I wonder if spell craft shrank a real one. Names march down the parchment in Ella's delicate writing, their magical affiliation marked in Grandmother's hand beside it. Num-bers stand to attention beside each one. Black lines slash through the top three names. The fourth is today's recipient of the gilding: Aaron Edson—963—aged seventeen.

Grandmother drifts around the room in a whisper of black skirts and silver chains. She lays out a pestle and mortar on a wooden butcher's block, selects a canister from the shelf, and snaps at me to get the fire lit and wipe down the marble worktops, which are already gleaming to polished perfection.

They gleam brighter by the time I'm done, and a tiny fire burns beneath a cauldron no bigger than my fist, the worktop scattering reflected light around it.

Grandmother flashes me the briefest of smiles and gestures to a door at the back of the room. "Unlock it, knock four times, and we'll begin."

The door is split in two like the barn doors of our old village—but that's where the similarity ends. The iron in this door is smooth and flat, a product of ore witch manipulation. The crack between the two halves is barely visible and magic hums along the metal. Gingerly, I slide open the bolts, rap four times with my knuckles, and step back. There's a shuddering clamour of gears on the other side, and heat seeps beneath the doors.

Grandmother presses her hands into the worktop and the temperature plummets, frosting our breath like a dragon in a children's story. "Penelope, the bone if you would." She says my name as if it cuts her tongue to speak it, and hands me a small wooden chest before she sets to work, unscrewing the canister lid and delicately removing what seems to be a still-living hawkmoth pinched between finger and thumb. Its feathered wings tremble, its feelers curling tight into its fuzzy little head as Grandmother pins it still and measures it with the callipers.

I blink, not wanting to watch, unable to turn away. Grandmother hisses under her breath. "Penelope. The bone. Have you lost your senses, girl? Grind the bone!" She double-checks her measurements against her pinkie finger, her swollen joint preventing it from straightening properly. "Just one should do it. The smallest."

I think the hawkmoth dies as I turn my back and open the box. Three white-bleached finger bones lie on black velvet cloth. I drop the smallest into the marble mortar and inhale slowly, trying not to wonder whose finger I'm about to pulverise into dust. I shudder as bone grates against stone like a tiny human scream. By the time I've finished and fine yellowish-white powder fills the bowl, my ears are raw from the noise.

The scent of singed hair crinkles my nose, and I fight back a sneeze as Grandmother mutters a chant. The little hawkmoth is swallowed by a vile black tarry mess bubbling in the cauldron.

The powdered bone is next. It fizzes as it sinks and the black gloop slows, thins, and settles to a steady shine. A red spark jumps from the surface. And another, orange this time. The next is auburn as an autumn leaf. Grandmother's magic retreats and the temperature swings from too cold to roasting hot. Bellows wheeze in the room beyond the two-part door, and the scent of molten gold fills the air—bitter and metallic.

Sweat trickles down the dip of my spine and itches the inside of my elbows.

The cauldron fizzes like cherry wine as Grandmother carries it carefully to the door. "Open it, Penelope."

I hurry to obey. In the gilding chamber beyond, an ore witch clad in thick leather overalls bends over a crucible glowing white and green, and a mould is hung on the wall beside the forge fire—a half-mask that stares at me with unseeing eyes. I linger in the doorway where the chill of our workroom cools my back and wait for Grandmother to collect her things, ready to begin.

The ore witch's irises flicker, sharp and coppery. Sweat sheens her black skin and beads on an emerald embedded in her temple. An ember witch in a pale grey tunic stokes the flames, magic uncurling from her fingers like crystallized smoke. She ignores us as she takes the tiny cauldron. Normally, the covens keep to themselves. Ore witches with their metal-sheathed nails and teeth do not work beside the ash-marked Ember Coven. The eerie tide witches do not join forces with the storms. Thankfully, the gilding ceremonies are the only regular occasion where we're forced to work together inside Halstett's walls.

In the very centre of the room is an iron table with metal restraints attached in the appropriate places. I don't want to look at that table. I don't want to bear witness to this.

I don't know the boy they're gilding. But when I watch Grandmother slash through his name on the list with black ink, my heart aches for him all the same.

Grandmother lays the pen down and selects a scalpel. She gives me a pinched smile that doesn't touch her eyes. "Today, you may observe, Penelope. Next time, you will do more."

I don't want there to be a next time. I want Ella to come home. Grandmother's smile stays pinned in place as we wait in the sweltering gilding chamber. The sparkling tarry potion has been added to the boiling gold. The cauldron stands empty beside a crucible nestled in a furnace so hot the hairs on my arms curl.

Three Gilded march in through doors at the opposite end of the room to our workshop. A boy on the cusp of adulthood walks between them, his steps unsteady and his eyes glazed. His lifeline drifts limply behind him, slightly fuzzy like the body of the hawk-moth before Grandmother incinerated it.

He's one of the lucky ones. His family had money to pay for sedation and privacy—and cared enough to part with it. So many born with glitters of magic circling their irises are abandoned the first time they open their eyes. Only last month, Mila was unlucky enough to be allocated a seat at a public gilding. They did three that day. Two girls and a boy. No sedation. No chance to say goodbye—no one to say goodbye to.

Drugged and compliant, this boy—Aaron—doesn't resist as the

Gilded strap him down. I wonder if he's frightened, if he tried to run. They do sometimes, but they never get far.

"Watch carefully, Penelope," Grandmother whispers so softly her lips don't move. Her bony fingers trace the back of my neck and her lifeline pulses with the beat of her heart, all prickly bits and anticipation. "We've lost so many this way. One slip and they're no good to anyone." Her eyes turn distant. "They say there was a knife once so sharp it could cleave a soul precisely in two, its blade guided by a single thought, but it vanished along with the Sorcerer who forged it." She sighs. "More's the pity. It would make this process so much more efficient." Her fingers freeze on the back of my neck. I try to imagine such a knife, sharper than the scalpel in her other hand, which looks devastatingly sharp and glittering, and I fail pitifully.

Aaron is silent as the ore witch fits the mould over his face, screwing it in place to the table with a twist of one finger in the air. He doesn't flinch as the ember witch carries the crucible to his side and my grandmother joins the others around the table.

The ember witch catches me staring and raises one eyebrow singed through with three scarred lines. Her black shift is bound at the waist with a red sash, her hair shorn close to her scalp, and one earlobe is pierced with a flame-bright stud that winks as she turns to the ore witch beside her.

The ore witch grins and flicks her thumb, spiking her nail sharper. I hide my wince and fix my attention on Aaron—as if I'm uninterested, not intimidated.

In the heartbeat before the molten gold is poured into the mould, he meets my gaze. A single angry tear glistens on his lashes. Beneath the layers of sedation and pain relief, he's aware. Conscious and defiant. I wish I could do something to stop this. I wish I had no part in it. In this moment, right here, I hate my grandmother for what she has made us into: puppets enabling the Warden's regime.

Then Grandmother untucks her crystal from her shift and the deep purple at its heart darkens. She runs one bony finger down Aaron's chest, feeling for the notch where his seventh ribs join his sternum. His lifeline is attached between them. I feel it shudder as she pauses, stiffen as her blade rests against his skin.

One slice of the scalpel severs his free will; one tip of the crucible burns away his connection to his soul and binds him to the High Warden's control. Gold mixed with Grandmother's magic flows into the mould, bubbling and hissing, and the stench of burning flesh smothers the room.

His brutalised lifeline writhes and twists. Spasms and solidifies. I sense it sharpen, and barbs erupt along it like thorns on the stem of a rose.

As they remove the mould, the last tear he'll ever shed falls from his lashes and Gilded number 963 opens soulless, death-blank eyes. A perfect half-mask clings to his face in a vicious golden mockery of his features.

Aaron Edson is no more.

Destroyed as effectively as if they'd murdered him.

And I helped them do it.

Chapter Five

Grandmother orders me to wash and change into a fresh shift that doesn't smell of smouldering flesh and ruined lives. She stays in the bathing chamber as I obey in silence, handing her my shift to throw in the laundry chute, and huddling in the bath with my knees drawn up to my chest. All I can see is the boy's eyes, so chilled and empty where only seconds before was warmth and life. The gilding by its very nature is irreversible, a severed connection it is impossible to make whole.

I wish there was a way to undo it. I wonder if anyone has tried. I've never thought about it enough to care. I should have cared, but thinking of the Gilded reminds me of my father and it hurts. I care now. What if there's a way to bring our loved ones back, to restore the connection of their souls behind their eyes? My fingers dig into my shins so hard the half-moons of my nails indent my skin.

The way Grandmother kneels beside the bath, her knees creaking, I suspect she recognises which memories the gilding awoke. Her fingers are gentle as she unties the ribbon holding my braid and smooths a tangle from my hair. "Ella was the same the first time. It gets easier."

I'm not sure I want it to get easier. If this stops hurting, I'll be as much a monster as the Warden and the Gilded—as my grandmother is becoming. Each time she is summoned to heal the Warden she comes back with another thread of her compassion snipped away. Maybe Father returning would soften her. If we could reverse the gilding, maybe we could heal Grandmother too, and Mila and Mother, bring the life back to their slowly dying eyes. I wonder if the impossible knife Grandmother spoke of earlier is in the Warden's possession and he uses it discreetly, privately, to disconnect my grandmother from herself. It would explain so much about her that I almost wish it were true. But the idea of the Warden with that weapon at his disposal is chilling, even in the steaming hot bath.

Grandmother sees my shiver and rests a hand on my shoulder. "You did well this morning, Penelope. Far better than I expected, considering."

I'm not sure I want her approval either. I definitely don't want her in the bathing chamber with me. But arguing with Grandmother is as effective as talking to a wall. If I ask her to leave, she'll just stay longer.

She rubs a thumb gently across my temple, exactly as she did when I was a child curled on her lap in her rocking chair listening to my father tell stories by a blazing winter hearth. His tales coloured my childhood shades of spring daffodils and summer peaches and an impossibly vast blue sky. The smell of woodsmoke meant stories back then, not my coven's daily burnings. I still feel his stories, see the pictures he drew with his words in my mind's eye, but I can't quite touch them. When I remember, I taste the cookies my mother baked with Mila on a stove heated with ember witch magic. We bought it in a jar at the winter united markets and carried it home in a little boat powered by storm-magicked winds held in a charmed silver box.

Mila and Ella would sit by his feet on a reed mat my aunts had woven, and Haylea and Carlotta would creep across the herb garden that divided our houses to huddle under a blanket, their bare feet specked with dew and smelling of crushed mint and thyme. We'd listen to him tell stories of the witch queens a thousand years ago collecting scattered magic and working together to weave forests from deserts and oceans from sand. They painted the sunshine in the sky and hung the moon too, to hear my father tell it.

He drew such a fabulous picture of what once was, that for the longest time I believed it could be again. Now, I don't believe that idyllic harmony existed at all—how could it have devolved into this? Coven hating coven, witches held captive, a tyrant ruling over us all. Magic is a quirk of our blood, not a gift from a god.

Father taught me one truth with his fantastical stories on those long, dark evenings. He never lost any part of his soul when he walked, never lost the ability to dream, and he visited Death more often than most. I can't imagine him without that spark of life in his smile. But his gilding put an end to that. I wonder if his eyes turned as blank as Aaron's when it was done. I wonder if he was sedated—if Grandmother had the option of paying for his comfort.

My teeth clench with irritation as Grandmother tucks my hair behind my ear; I'm twenty-one, not twelve. Maybe when I walk in Death for the coven, she'll finally start treating me like the adult I am. "Ella—" she begins.

"She'll come back." I never interrupt her. No one does.

"Maybe." There's a trace of regret in her voice. Beneath the hard facade, she's still our grandmother. With a sigh that informs me that this conversation is not done, she finally leaves me alone. I shiver as the door clicks shut, glad to be free of her smothering presence.

When I close my eyes, the tear tracking down Aaron's cheek is seared behind my eyelids. But I couldn't have stopped it. I just did as I was told. What happened to Aaron was beyond my control.

According to the High Warden's doctrines, he was born to be Gilded. Trained for it. He belongs to the Warden, he always has. Ella though? Ella's fate I refuse to allow to be beyond my control. Quickly, I dry and dress, anxious to get to the library.

Today, the library silence welcomes me like an old friend. I exhale softly as I step inside, letting my breath carry away the tension in my shoulders, glad that the daytime library has lost none of its peace after our illicit visit the other night. Miss Elsweather sits behind the cherrywood reception desk: a short woman with skin clinging loosely to her bones and a dusty pallor, as if she too is a forgotten tome placed on an out-of-reach shelf long ago. She found me once when I was eleven, sandwiched between two bookcases, and she's watched out for me ever since.

Her scalp glints through her thin, curled silver hair, half-moon glasses balancing precariously on the end of a narrow nose as her finger runs along the page. She speaks without raising her eyes. "Second floor, Penny. Aisles thirty-seven to fifty-two." She shoves a bright yellow duster and a tin of beeswax across her desk toward me, and I stuff the tin in my shift pocket, twisting the duster in my hands as I head toward the second floor.

The tin of beeswax thuds against my thigh with each stair and the duster is twisted so tight between my fingers by the time I reach the second floor it twirls into spirals. I pause at the top of the stairs and lean out over the banister to look up. The Ninth is still hidden in darkness even in the midday sun. Windows form a line up one side of the library tower. The storm-spelled glass softens the daylight but does not stop it. Every other floor is visible, but the ninth floor is not.

I glance at the clock tick-tick-ticking above the arched doors. The coven will send word if there's news of Ella. Maybe she's back and someone's already on their way? But I'd know if she'd returned to the plane of the living. There's silence in my heart where my sister belongs.

I'm cleaning the bottom shelf of row thirty-eight when boots stamp to a halt on the floorboards by my cotton-skirted knees. Military boots. Spit-shined so I can see the reflection of my yellow duster flickering like flames as I polish.

"Death-walker Penelope Albright?" Loud words staccato in the silence, making me jump.

I look up into the darkest pair of eyes I've ever seen. A palace guard towers over me, one of the magicless branch of the Warden's military. A tattooed band of interlocking silver triangles circle her wrist, an indelible bracelet like the hawkmoth on my shoulder.

I recognise her. I think we're around the same age and arrived here at the same time, though with her being military and me magic we weren't trained together. That was when they were still rounding us up and bringing us in. Testing and separating us.

The strongest tide and storm witches form the covens housed in the Colligerate wings either side of ours. They too work magic to the Warden's command, controlling the wind, the currents, and the sea. Not one raindrop falls without the Warden willing it to be so, not one wave breaks without his approval. Their captivity created the desert; without their magic, in the wake of the burnings, the land returned to the sand from whence it came. The Ore and Ember Covens' finest were also given wings to call their own. Ore witches hollowed out our burning chamber, reengineered the Colligerate walls to the Warden's design. The embers make fire dance to the Warden's tune. They both help to create the Gilded.

Magic users who scored lower were gilded; hundreds of witches were added to the Warden's magical army while behind them our continent burned. Those who failed the magic tests but showed skill with a blade were forced into military training.

The rest, rejected by the military and without magic, were thrown into the streets of Halstett to find a living any way they knew how. I wonder how the tide witch above the hat shop escaped the Warden's shackles, and how many others slipped through the cracks.

A year ago, there were whisperings that the Gilded had burned the last village, that the Warden might send his armies to the distant lands across the seas, lands without magic, who trade sugar and tea and silk with Halstett in exchange for spell craft: the tides' magical mirrors, the storms' weather manipulation, embers' fire seeds, and ore's water divining rods made of quartz. It's difficult to believe the Gilded destroyed everything outside Halstett's walls in the war against witchcraft. We should have fought back sooner.

There must be some kernel of truth to the rumours, though. They don't bring people in anymore.

I wonder if the guard pities me as I kneel on the library floor.

I wonder if she knows I pity her.

She snaps her fingers. "On your feet, thorn witch. The Spinner summoned you."

Shit. What does the Spinner want with me? I swallow softly. "About Ella?"

The guard narrows her eyes. I shouldn't have said that.

I follow her down the library stairs and pause at the desk. Miss Elsweather squeezes my hand as she reclaims her duster and beeswax. "Everything all right? Where's Ella today?"

I force a smile. "I'm fine. Ella's late back from patrol. She'll be here tomorrow."

Miss Elsweather senses my lie, her lips pressing into a tight line. She's not a thorn witch. She's one of the few nonmagic, nonmilitary people who found a niche inside the Colligerate. I have no idea how she got her position or who she was before, but she knows about the thorn patrols, knows we either return with the breaking dawn—or we don't. "Be careful who you trust, Penny," she says, soft as the turn of a page.

I nod and hurry after the guard, who's marching away through the library doors without looking back.

Never look back.

Even the palace guard follow that rule.

The Spinner's door is brightly painted with red flowers dancing across green fields, blossom boughs dipping to a sparkling stream, and little houses with rainbow-hued doors and palm-thatched roofs dotting the banks. The witch beyond sees fate, spinning tapestries of dreams and embroidering visions in jewel-coloured silk. The colours are overwhelming after so long in a world devoid of it.

Two Gilded stand guard on the landing, one to either side of the Spinner's door, blocking the light from the lattice-worked window. To keep the Spinner in, I wonder, or to keep others out? They are armoured and armed as if there is more than the Warden's pet prophet behind the bright-painted door. His *curious thing*: one witch and her loom.

The Gilded give the guard a brisk nod and stand back at our approach. She knocks once at the Spinner's door and pulls me closer, restraining me to stop me running, I suppose, though I'm not sure how far she thinks I'd get. The Gilded would catch me before I hit the top step.

Footsteps tap toward the door and trepidation spills into the guard's eyes. Everyone fears the Spinner. The guards believe she manipulates the future and plays with the past. Where they fear interference, witches fear the truth of what comes next. Sometimes, it's better not to know.

The door opens, cardamom incense wafts into the corridor, and a metal-gauntleted hand shoves me into the Spinner's smoke-shrouded domain. In the centre stands the Spinner's loom, a massive and ancient piece of intricate machinery powered by magic. The warp is spun from nightmares strung tight across it. The shuttle flies back and forth with a relentless click and clack, its thread spinning reality from dreams.

I fight back a cough as a low chuckle shivers through the haze. A tall-backed chair dwarfs the Spinner, who perches on it like a scorpion sizing up her prey. Her eyes are black, so dark it seems the pupils devoured the irises and made a start on the whites for dessert. Silver-blonde sheets of hair hang around slim, black-robed shoulders, and a gold braid binds her robe at the waist. She's the same age as me, yet infinitely older at the same time. Delicate hands shift and draw patterns, guiding the loom's restless weaving, and the sway of wide sleeves reveals gold cuffs at her wrists—a sign she is property of the High Warden.

As I will be, if the Warden discovers our coven hides a black-crystalled witch.

I realise she's assessing me the same way, head to toe. The dance of her hands ceases, and the shuttle pauses its endless task.

"Penny." Her voice is so surprisingly normal I can't hide my shock. She smiles a sad smile. "Take a seat."

Words—normally my friends—desert me, leaving me to face the Spinner alone. I sit; I watch; I wait.

She gives a satisfied nod. "You have questions?" No. Yes. So many. "About your sister?"

"Ella? You know where she is? Is she..." *All right* isn't the correct question. She's obviously not, or she'd have been at the breakfast table this morning. I can't ask if Ella's dead—if she's dying—I can't bear that answer.

"She needs help to return." The Spinner's obsidian gaze unpeels the layers of my mind and reaches into my soul. I am laid bare before her, and her loom spills secrets of a future I don't want to see upon the floor. The silk darkens like night claiming the colour from the world at twilight.

My future is not bright—I don't need her to tell me that.

"What do I need to do?"

"Burn."

I shake my head. "We walk alone in Death, and Ella's already there. I can't burn."

"You must. Or your sister is lost. Death will keep her."

"I can't! The rules—" Panic hits, and my thoughts race across all the ways this could go wrong. If my lifeline tangles with Ella's, she'll wander aimless in the deserts of Death with nothing to guide her beyond the Horizon. So will I. Or we'll get trapped in the veil like Haylea did, and the Gilded will be sent to cut us free. We'll lose all sense of who we are and why we're there—we'll fade into fog and mist, insubstantial except for our hunger, which we'll turn toward the veil.

The Spinner watches my panicking with a light frown. She shakes her head. "Break the rules, Penny."

I stare at her. Why is the Warden's pet telling me to disobey him so blatantly? Is it a test? To see where my loyalties lie? "No one will help me." My voice is a croak.

"Burn alone." She sounds mildly exasperated. "You must find Ella. It is vital that you do."

"I..." I want to refuse. Burning alone—it doesn't bear imagining. The Spinner's eyes soften with *sorry*, but there's no sympathy, no pity, only a resigned certainty. And for some reason, it makes me trust her.

Who is she, this girl with midnight shining in her gaze? Who was she before? But I don't ask those questions. "When?" I whisper instead.

She smiles softly. "Tonight."

Book Sprites and How They Came to Be

In the time before witches, a time when magic did not brighten the world and Death was not a concept, the Dark Mother lived with the Sorcerer at the very tip of the Eastern Seaboard where the sun meets the sky each morning and the sea gives birth to the moon each night. Their harmony drifted gently across the world and painted the colours of dawn, and new stars grown from their happiness hung in the night sky. While the Dark Mother planted her seeds of growth and life across the worlds, the Sorcerer sat in the quiet and began to write.

He wrote of magnificent trees that bore seven types of fruit, of diamonds buried in mountain halls, and soft velvet moles that dug tunnels beneath the ground, and rainbows arching across the skies. The Dark Mother took his words and made them solid and real.

Finally, they made people. Little versions of themselves. And the Dark Mother watched over them, so carefully, dutifully, and lovingly, and the Sorcerer saw the adoration in her eyes and grew jealous. They fought. Thunder grew within the clouds, hurricanes swept across the seas, and the Sorcerer cracked a mountain range in his rage.

In his anger, he tore the world they'd made in two, divided it with a veil grown from beneath the land, and took half for himself. He scattered his magic from the skies and gifted it to the people to entice them to his side. But the Sorcerer forgot who had made him. The Dark Mother came before all other things. She cursed his half of the world, and it was cold and lonely and filled with sand. His pens were his only company, paper his only friend. So he created his own companions made of ink–shadowy creatures animated with his words–drew a bridge from Death into Life, and sent them to haunt the libraries, protecting books and truth and knowledge. And there they remain.

Mythology for the Masses: Tales of Creation. *Anon. Retrieved from the second floor of the Great Library.*

Chapter Six

Dinner is a quiet affair. Mist still swirls inside Ella's crystal, folding and unfurling, but the rainbows have dimmed and the deep rose-petal pink has faded to peach. Aunt Shara glances at it as she passes the warded glass cabinet to take her seat beside my mother at the table. Mila closes her eyes as if in prayer. I want to tell her she's wasting her time.

Our attention flicks to the crystals as we eat, watching for a change, a sign. I'm glad my crystal is fake, that the real one is locked away: If I burn tonight, no rainbowed mists will betray my crossing.

I can't believe I'm considering it. Grandmother will be furious if I defy the first original rule of Death. I've witnessed her judgement. I've seen her shatter crystals and unflinchingly hand over defectors to the Gilded. A death-walker with no crystal is like a boat with no mooring, drifting on the tides until we run aground on the rocks. Aimless and without purpose we wander, until our minds disintegrate and we become nothing at all.

But I'm her granddaughter—she won't do that to me, and Ella's life is worth her wrath ten times over.

Shakily, I scoop the last bite of cheese-and-potato pie into my mouth and push my plate away.

"Penny?" Mother hisses.

Shit. She's been talking to me and I didn't hear a word. Everyone's staring at me. Heat rises in my cheeks, starting at the bottom of my neck and flushing upward. "I'm sorry, I—"

"Wasn't listening?" Mother's tone softens. "I was saying, I'm sorry we had to delay your first walk."

I try to look disappointed.

Grandmother sees right through me, the same sharpness in her tone as when she ordered me to watch the gilding. "Penelope never wanted to walk. She's relieved."

"Not at Ella's expense, I'm not," I retort.

Grandmother's eyes harden. "You'll walk soon enough." She presses her lips together before she continues, "Ella was one of our best. She'll be sorely missed."

"She's not dead! We could go after her!"

The soft buzz of small talk at the table dies, just as it did at breakfast.

Mila shakes her head. "The first rule—" she recites, but Grandmother cuts her off.

"We know the rules." She's trying not to frown, but I learned young to read her moods and the slight twitch of her jaw betrays her displeasure. "The Spinner summoned you?"

I'm surprised it's taken her this long to mention it. I nod my head.

"What did she want?"

"Nothing." It's not an answer she'll accept.

"The Spinner does not summon people for no reason."

"She swore me to silence."

Grandmother gives up on her attempt not to frown. Her chair scrapes back across the floor. "Go to bed," she says softly, dangerously. "All of you. You and I, Penny, are overdue for a little chat. My office, first thing in the morning."

The coven rises, black robes swishing against the flagstones as we leave. Only Mother and Aunt Shara remain, seated on either side of Grandmother. At the doorway, I glance back. I shouldn't. It's a bad habit I'm going to have to fix if I'm walking tonight.

Mother puts her head in her hands. My strong mother, my invincible, unshakable mother, hitches in a breath and her shoulders begin to shake.

I turn and march away. Matches, I need to find matches.

My grandmother's office is on the fourth floor of the narrow tower at the end of the Thorn Coven's wing. Matches are held there, locked in a drawer. But locks are a minor inconvenience. My father taught me how to pick a lock not long after he grew my crystal, a padlock clutched in my five-year-old hand and a bobby pin in the other. Cherry blossoms danced in the breeze that day, lost to time like my father's face, but my fingers retained the lesson and I have a bobby pin tucked in my hair.

I don't risk a light. I do slip to the window and twitch back the curtains to glance outside. Night coats the Colligerate in frost-tipped silence. It should be mild at this time of year, but hoarfrost glazes the walls and ghosts the flagstones with glitter. The curfew bell rang an hour ago and no one walks the courtyards. Steel-toed boots march them; the palace guard patrol the Colligerate all night. I wonder if the city streets are patrolled too. If those outside the walls are as imprisoned as us.

Two guards pass below the window, silver breastplates shining in the lamplight, fading into the shadows between.

I'm not really out of bounds, but I'm not supposed to be here. I've seen people found guilty on weaker technicalities, so I watch until the patrol marches out of sight before letting the curtain fall back into place and hurrying to Grandmother's desk. My father would be proud at how fast the lock mechanism springs free. I take a single book of matches; anything more is likely to be missed.

I'm padding back down the stairs when I hear a hiss. A shallow whisper, "Who goes there?"

Shit! I can't be caught. Not with illicit matches in my pocket. If it's a Gilded, I'm lost—and so is Ella. Panic thrums in my bones but I choke it down. If I can convince whoever it is that I'm on an errand for Grandmother, I might just get away with it.

My heart skips and races as I round the corner. On the landing below, staring right at me, is the guard who escorted me to the Spinner. She leans against a door dressed in loose black pants with pockets in the side seams and a tight-fitting black sweater. Her hair is tied off her face in a messy bun. She's off duty. Recognition narrows her eyes. "You!"

She bars the stairwell with her body and folds her arms. Her build is slight enough that she doesn't take up the whole stair. If I judge it right, I might make it past, but while I was stuck in lessons on Death, lectured on fog-wraiths, and trained in magic, she's trained just as hard in the barracks—strength and endurance and swordcraft. She'll easily incapacitate me. I'm skilled enough with a blade—but I don't have one. The steel in her eyes tells me I'm not slipping anywhere. "You shouldn't be here."

I fold my arms, matching her stance, and pretend being a stair higher gives me an advantage. "You shouldn't be here either. You're not on duty."

We hear the sound of boots farther down the tower.

Indecision flickers in her features. A moment's hesitation where I consider turning and fleeing back to my grandmother's office, hiding and hoping. I could return the matches. Conceal the evidence. But before I have time to run, she grabs my arm in a vice grip and drags me sideways through the door she was just leaning against.

The snick of the key turning catches at my pulse and sends it speeding even faster. "What—"

Her hand clamps over my mouth. The point of a blade pricks between my fifth and sixth ribs on the left-hand side. One flick of her wrist and steel will pierce my heart. "Silence," she whispers. It's an order, but there's a hitch at the end of it.

She's scared.

She pushes me back into the wall, slowly releasing her hand and pressing her forearm across my chest. Her blade doesn't leave my side, and I don't fight her.

All I can hear is the sound of her breath beside my ear and my own, slightly faster. She smells of laundry soap and jasmine. She stiffens as the boots ring up the stone stairs and pause on the landing.

I blink in the dark. We listen to the footsteps fade, each thud of steel toes on stone quieter than the last. She releases me and steps back, taking with her the scent of jasmine and the point of her blade.

Light flares on the end of a match, and she touches it to the wick of a candle. A sooty flame hangs between me and her, highlighting the worry in her eyes. We're in a storage cupboard lined with shelves heavy with jars of herbs. A wooden box sits on the bottom shelf, labelled with my grandmother's handwriting: *matches*. I file that away for later; breaking into a cupboard is far safer than breaking into Grandmother's office.

The silence tightens. This looks bad. Really bad. For both of us. If she's caught fraternising with a witch in a cupboard, she'll be punished. I wait for her to speak first.

"Penny," she says. "That's your name, right?"

I don't answer, don't move.

She straightens, pins me with eyes that seem darker in the candlelight, and a tendril of black hair falls loose from her bun. It curls a little, seeming to dance in the flicker of the flame. When she speaks again, her voice is closer to the military tones of earlier. "State your business."

Habit makes me lower my eyes. "I was checking my grandmother had locked her office."

"And had she?"

I nod.

"And what were you going to do if she hadn't?" The guard's gaze slides over my hands, my hips, my waist. My pockets where no bulge of keys tugs at the fabric—where the stolen matches hide.

"Tell her so she could lock it," I say, steady and quiet, and force myself to look up.

She knows I'm lying. I know she's not supposed to be here. If she lets me go, she's handing me power over her. Information. Not a lot, but enough to make her pause. I don't know her name, but I know her number, her rank, and regiment.

"Summon the dark," she whispers. It's not quite a question, but she's asking something all the same. I shake my head in confusion, and she smiles stiffly. "We could use another thorn witch."

"Who could?"

She considers me. "The Resistance. They're extremely interested in your audience with the Spinner."

"Right." The Warden would stamp out any attempt at a resistance long before they gained a foothold. "I need to go. If I'm caught—"

Her smile hardens. "You've already been caught. I caught you."

I sharpen my own smile. "And that's why we're hiding in a cupboard?"

It's a huge risk. But it's enough to save me. For now.

She narrows her eyes, then unlocks the door. Peers out into the stairwell, and stands back to let me pass. "Get out of here. One word—"

Before she can finish, I'm fleeing on silent feet down the stairs. Down and down and down until I hit the bottom running and slip from shadow to shadow along the corridor, avoiding the pools of lantern light until I'm back to my room.

Relief hits me as I softly close the door. I'm safe here. It's barely big enough for a bed and a side table, but it's mine. Books are stacked under the bed in neat piles with their spines precisely aligned, and pictures I've drawn in charcoal and black ink cover the walls. Trees and birds and lakes and streams; a riot of broken memories with the colour removed. I miss the world. I miss the water and the light. I miss the colour most.

My hands begin to shake as I sink into my bed. The concept of a Resistance is too huge to deal with—people standing against the Warden? It's too much to hope for. A fairy story more fantastical than anything I'd find on the library's second floor. Hope takes up too much space in my heart, it takes root and swells.

What if it's true?

Then, my hope deflates like a pie crust pricked with a knife. The Spinner's words rattle around my skull: *You must find Ella. It is vital. Tonight.*

I curl my hand around the matches in my pocket, a talisman against fear, and leave my room before I change my mind because this plan is ridiculous. Down the corridor, down the narrow stairs, to the wooden door with *Flammae ac fumo* marked upon it.

I risk a light as I bolt the door. There are no windows in this chamber buried beneath the outside world. The pyre is laid, ready to set ablaze. I balk at the sight of it.

I've been so focused on what I need to do, I haven't really thought about how I'm going to do it. Facing the smoke-blackened stake, I discover it is one thing to decide to do something, and quite another to go through with it. Somehow, I need to chain myself, light the match, and chant the words alone without screaming.

I need help.

And the one person who might have helped me is the one I'm trampling on the rules to find: Ella.

I don't know if I can do this. I whisper her name, a talisman against doubt.

If I light the pyre first, it will be impossible to step into it, but striking a match with my hands chained is no easier, and I'm not risking Grandmother finding me in the morning, chained to a post in a room I shouldn't be in with contraband tucked in my pocket.

Fire first, that's the safest way, then chains, and pray I don't lose my nerve before I get the manacles tight enough that I can't escape. It's a plan. Not a good one, but it's all I have.

Before I can talk myself out of it, I strike the first match. It catches, gutters, and dies. The second, I wear away the red from the matchhead until all that's left is a papery stick. Frustration lights the third.

When I drop it into the straw, hungry flames lick along dry sticks and twigs. With no burning tonight, no one is on cleanup duty in the morning. If everything goes right, I can imagine myself here when I pass back through the veil. Cleaning and re-laying the pyre will be simple in comparison to this. Fear screws into a tight ball beneath my ribs; I'm shaking so hard I can barely pick my way around the rising fire to step onto the platform. Holy Dark Mother, whoever made the rules for crossing into Death had a sadistic sense of humour. I manage to snap the first manacle around my wrist just as the last of my courage disintegrates. Steel clicks tight and there's no going back. I left the key on the table by the door.

Panic drowns my heart. What if I fail? What if I forget the words?

What if I'm not strong enough to pass the veil between Life and Death alone?

The iron platform heats beneath my toes. Smoke thickens the air.

I cough and whisper the words that will let me pass. They stick in my throat like the lump you get before you cry.

Fire bites at my ankles, eating me alive. Heat blisters my lungs with each breath.

But magic runs into my blood like iced water as I reach for Death and the misted veil parts beneath the pressure of my words, precisely as the books said.

The hem of my dress catches fire, and I whisper as my skin hisses—and I burn.

I burn.

I burn.

Pain is all-consuming. Never-ending.

A scream wells in my lungs. I swallow it back.

If I scream, I'm lost—and so is Ella.

What have I done? I can't survive this alone. A roar fills my ears. I squeeze my eyes shut. And I see it: the border between Life and Death. Grey mist waterfalls from so high above it has no beginning, into an abyss so deep it has no end, so close I can reach out and touch it. And there's a gap, big enough to slip through.

I just need to step.

First, I have to untie myself from my body and leave it to burn. But souls don't like slipping from the mortal coil—they like bodies, they like life. My soul clings tight. So do I. My fingers clutch at the post. One of my nails snaps below the quick and I barely feel it. I fight the urge to open my eyes. If I open my eyes, the gap will slam shut, and I don't have the strength or the time to chant again.

I tear my soul out of my body with a noise like a log split in two; a dull thud and a sharp crack. The veil is cool, a soothing relief after the fires of my death, and an overwhelming urge fills me, to look back at my burning body, to say goodbye.

I squeeze my eyes shut.

Don't look back. Don't look back.

I take another step.

Chapter Seven

I blink in the dim light of the afterlife, pausing on the threshold between Life and Death. Stillness surrounds me, inside and out; my ribs move without air filling my lungs, and my heart lies heavy against my diaphragm, a dead weight relieved of its duty. The familiar thud of my pulse is unsettlingly absent.

When I inspect my hand, the nail beds are a soft pink, but the faint scar on my palm—a reminder of a lost fight against Mila in training—is smooth and absent, my skin wiped clean of my past.

I thought I knew what to expect of Death, but no amount of reading could have prepared me for reality. Books describe Death as quiet, but the silence is so complete it has a curious sound of its own; a small high-pitched hum of nothing. Chapters detail the landscape as a barren desert of grey sand and the air as cool and still. But the grey has hues to it, a rainbow with the colour subdued, the stillness shifts without a breeze, and scents are threaded on the air—pine needles and moss and new-fallen rain—memories of the souls passing through.

It is a hollow place of echoes and unfulfilled dreams. Timeless, ageless, and unchanging. Quiet clings to my skin, a welcome caress of absence that means those crossing the veil tonight accept their end. Newly dead souls pass close by. An old couple shuffle hand in hand, their steps strengthening as they walk. A young woman with fair hair cradles a scrap of a child and a small girl skips behind them, her dress silken mist around her. She flashes me a smile, and hollows carved beneath sharp cheekbones suggest starvation ate her alive.

I watch them walk steadily toward the Horizon shimmering in the distance, white light transforming the grey dunes to silver waves, watch them vanish, and check my tether to Life. The ghost of my crystal hangs around my neck on a silver chain, my lifeline attached, and I exhale softly with relief. I'm anchored, the other end attached to my crystal in Life.

So far, I've managed to do four things right—I burned without screaming, opened the veil, untied my soul with no help, and kept my lifeline anchored. It's a good start.

But it's just a start.

The veil sparkles into the distance in both directions, a silent waterfall woven of mist, each thread fluid and shifting. If this was a sanctioned walk in Death, I'd turn left and keep the veil close, inspecting it for damage until dawn broke in Life. I'd maybe deal with a lost or reluctant soul, sending them across the Horizon where they belong, for not all souls walk placidly onward to true death. Some need a nudge to stop them giving in to temptation and looking back.

If they do, they solidify into fog-wraiths, and it's the Thorn Coven's job to banish them. I really don't want to discover how that process might differ from the descriptions in books tonight.

I picture a black uniform like the off-duty military wear, and fatigues replace my shift with a flicker of magic. It feels good to finally use it. I wiggle my toes in the sand, cool and damp like the riverbank in our village at dawn. Forgoing shoes, I drop to a crouch and hastily sketch a curved dagger with my fingertip, hold its image in my mind, and with a second flush of magic, the weapon forms, solid and real beneath my palm.

Appropriately dressed and armed, I focus on the missing piece of me that is Ella. Her lifeline stretches away from the veil and into the distance, invisible and faint like a hawkmoth's wingbeat in an empty room. I follow it, though leaving the veil behind is utter recklessness. I tread carefully, slowly; if our lifelines tangle, we'll both be lost.

Ella's lifeline flutters. The vibrations echo in the silent chambers of my heart, and then I'm running. Feet pounding through damp sand, hair flying loose behind me. I should have tied it up, off my face. At the thought, my hair twists into a heavy braid down my back and I smile. In spite of the pain it took to cross, there is comfort in the freedom of being here.

It shouldn't be a surprise—every book on death-walking I've ever read says thorn witches need Death in the same way an ember witch needs a flame; we are lost without it. For the first time in years, it feels I am found.

Ella's lifeline guides me onward, on and on and on through an unchanging sea of grey sand. I pause to get my bearings—careful not to look back over my shoulder—and scan the Horizon, assessing the slow drift of souls. All are soft and wispy, none solidifying or old...but a shadow darkens the sand dunes. A patch of something in the nothing. I blink and rub my eyes. A mirage? My mind playing tricks? A pack of undead wraiths racing toward the veil? Toward me? But I've done nothing wrong. I haven't looked back. Haven't shown doubt or fear.

My heart jolts in my chest as if it forgot it isn't needed here. My grip tightens on my dagger. I should have drawn a bigger weapon, sharper, more fearsome. I'm out of my depth on a rising tide.

Carefully, I move toward the dark patch. It's not retreating, not approaching. It is stubbornly still and definitely real. With each step closer, it solidifies. Materialising stone by stone, until a black fortified building stands a hundred yards away.

I pause again, resisting the urge to drop to a crouch and make myself small, and stare at what shouldn't be there. Black walls rise straight out of the desert. Green shimmers beyond them and towers rise above the green, a shine of red pinnacles topped with tattered black flags. A building in Death. Trees behind walls. I pinch myself hard on the arm and bite back a squeak. Whatever this is, it's real. It's not something I've created with my imagination and magic.

There's no gate in the walls. No entrance or doorway. No way in. And Ella's lifeline goes straight inside, threaded through solid black stone. My head spins with the impossibility: walls that cannot exist, Ella trapped inside, the door that isn't there. The brashness of the green haze of leaves on the other side—of life in Death.

A scream ripples over the walls, stirring the sand at my feet. Ella's lifeline twists and trembles.

"Ella!" I shout her name, then clamp a hand over my mouth.

My tether to Life snaps taut, a warning. Dawn approaches in Life and my time in Death is up.

I want to run to Ella. I want to hammer on the walls until they let me pass, rattle the stones with magic planted in the sand. If I could draw the right thing, summon it into existence, I could create my own doorway. But I need to act with caution, not desperation. I need to be clever, not impulsive. I have no idea what's inside, and rushing in could hurt Ella more. And I don't have time, not tonight. Reluctantly, I turn away.

A second scream follows me as I run toward the veil.

"Don't look back," I whisper to myself as Ella's screams fade. But I want to.

The mists roar as I approach, and I mutter the words to let me pass. This time, the veil is not cool as silk on my skin, it is sticky like molasses straight from the pan on the stove. Wisps of dark and light cling to my fingers and clutch at my throat, encircling my wrists and waist. I've done something wrong; I must have. Panic clenches my muscles and the absence of my pulse tears through me like iced water.

Death does not want to let me go.

Home, I need to go home. I hold the word in my mind and, step by agonising step, claw my way back to life. My lifeline vibrates with the strain, and pain skewers deep in my chest. Without thinking, I wrap my hand around it to relieve the pressure, and for one flicker of an absent heartbeat, my lifeline winks into sight, black and sparkling. I blink in shock, and it vanishes.

I shove through the mist and fall. Into the dark. Back to Life, leaving Ella behind.

Chapter Eight

I forgot. We're supposed to imagine our beds as we step back to life, and in my panic, I forgot. Mother's soft rebuke whispers through my dreams as I wake with dust tickling my nose: *Panic and you are lost, Penny.* I panicked and I nearly was. I still might be; I'm on hard floorboards, not in my bed. This is not my room.

It's pitch dark here. The air is heavy with decades of disuse, but beneath it lies the familiar scent of leather and paper and beeswax.

Books.

I'm in the library.

This is bad—but not as bad as it could be.

A spark of green pinpricks the shadows to my left. Another twinkles to the right. There's a soft noise, like the turn of a page. It's a figment of my imagination. It has to be. I scramble to standing and something tugs at the hem of my shift. I flinch, sending a stack of books crumpling to the ground, and jump so hard my heart slams against my ribs. Shadows scatter across the floor into the bookcases and the darkness lifts a little.

If my lifeline was tightening, that means dawn is breaking. I need to get to Miss Elsweather's office where spare keys are kept and back to the Thorn Wing without getting caught.

Pinpricks of light shine through the dark, emerald green and most definitely not my imagination; they blink, illuminating the number eight painted on the wall and the sheen of polished banisters. I'm at the foot of the stairs to the ninth floor. What was I doing, thinking of the Ninth as I crossed? Why here?

Something whispers my name as I scuttle down the stairs, begging me to return, to look back.

Ella was lost after trying to visit the Ninth. I can't afford the same happening to me.

Veering off on the second floor, I slip into Miss Elsweather's office. The library keys are kept in the top drawer of her desk and I snatch one up and run down the final flights, taking two steps at a time. Guilt prickles, but I'll sneak the key back tomorrow and hope she doesn't notice.

Grey dawn fades into a hollow blue sky outside the arched windows as I silently race down the corridors. Six bells sound from the Colligerate clock tower. The palace guard's dawn patrol will round the corner any minute. I make it back to our coven's wing with the last chime echoing in my ears. When the door thuds behind me, I sigh with relief and hurry to my room. I wasn't caught. No one knows I went into Death, alone, and now I know where Ella is.

My heart pounds as I curl into my bed and bury myself in the eiderdown to warm the chill clinging to my bones. I don't expect to sleep, but I'm exhausted and it drags me under quickly. For once, it's blissfully free of dreams.

I wake to dark hair tickling my cheek and my mother's worried face hanging over me. She straightens as I open my eyes. "Are you sick?"

"I... No?" I grasp for more words, but none come.

"You missed breakfast." It's a gentle demand: Explain yourself.

"I'm sorry, I..." I hunt for a believable excuse, but my mind is blank.

"Get up, Penny. Someone broke into the chamber last night, and your grandmother is out for blood. She wants to see you." Something akin to suspicion deepens the fine creases around Mother's eyes, and I try to hide my horror—that I forgot to clean up the ash of my burning. How did I forget such a simple detail? Mother shakes her head and turns away. "Be careful. She's also healing the High Warden this morning."

Mother and Grandmother are the only witches trusted to tend our faceless overlord's wound. Few in Halstett wish for immortality. Death sings a sweet song in the starving back streets. If the Warden dies, there will be no escape. No way out. No end. For anyone.

So we keep him alive. But we cannot heal him. And as he grows sicker with the mysterious ailment we are forbidden to discuss, the veil sickens with him.

I push the eiderdown off. "Ella? Did she—"

Mother cuts me off with a sad shake of her head. She's given up, I can tell. I want to tell her everything I did last night, give her hope. I settle for a hug, burying my face in her shoulder and breathing her in: lily of the valley and sweet peas. She's been in her glasshouse. I hope she wasn't alone. Gently, she smooths my curls with her fingers. "Get dressed, petal. Don't keep Grandmother waiting."

She leaves, and I climb gingerly out of bed. My stomach growls in protest at skipping breakfast, but otherwise, I feel fine.

I walked in Death. I broke the first rule and nothing terrible happened.

I dress quickly in a black cotton shift, long-sleeved and hemmed to skim the floor, and tie my silver belt. A breeze carries ice-cold mountain air in through the cracked-open window, so I snatch my cloak from the back of the door. Tying my hair back with a black ribbon, I hurry to the Thorn Queen's office. It never pays to keep Grandmother waiting.

Grandmother is seated at the desk I broke into last night. Her eyes sharpen as I approach. My mother stands quietly in the corner, and Mila sits by the window, arms folded, her expression suggesting she's already been questioned and passed with flying colours.

Grandmother gestures me to her side. Her hair was the same red as mine and my sisters' once, but now it's faded with age and bleached white by her walks in Death. "You are pale, Penelope." She looks me dead in the eyes. "Where were you last night?"

I was expecting this, prepared myself for it, but lying to Grandmother's face is almost impossible. So I deflect. "Mother said someone broke into the chamber."

"They had a key. Whoever set the pyre aflame left that key on the table." Grandmother watches me for a reaction.

I give her none. "Did they break anything?"

"They broke the law," Grandmother replies. "Whoever it was crossed the veil."

I try to make my eyes wider without overdoing it. Grandmother's eyes narrow. I'm horrible at this. "But what about Ella? Is she..." I glance desperately at Mother, at Mila. "Is anyone hurt?"

"No, Penelope. They are not. But there *was* a fluctuation in the veil last night, which has the Warden requiring my presence this morning." Grandmother purses her lips, gives me one more piercing stare, and releases me.

I want to sag with relief. If she suspected, I'd have to explain about the walls and Ella's scream. And it sounds ridiculous, even to me, who saw it. There are no buildings in Death. There might be beyond the Horizon, but none who pass there return to share those secrets.

Grandmother dismisses me with a wave of her hand toward the door. "Go and eat. We saved you a breakfast plate."

"My duties? The library?" A shiver crinkles down my back as I think of the whispering lights near the Ninth.

Grandmother shakes her head. "The Spinner summoned you."

Mother pushes away from the wall. "Again? Mother, that's unheard of!" I hate when she calls her *Mother*. It feels too familiar, as if they're not just related by Mother's marriage to Grandmother's son.

Every one of Grandmother's sixty-eight years is clear on her face as she answers, "I'm aware of that, Agatha. I have no say in the Spinner's orders. As long as she keeps weaving the future, the Warden indulges her fancies. Any word against her, and eyes will swivel in our direction. Penelope is drawing quite enough attention without me ruffling the feathers of the Warden's little pet." She frowns at me, as if confused why I'm still here. "Go! There's a palace guard waiting to escort you. I refused to spare you until the eleventh bell, so you have fifteen minutes. It's pancakes."

"Pancakes?"

She shakes her head and waves again at the door.

The luck that kept me out of trouble with Grandmother doesn't last. The same guard waits in the corridor, the girl who locked us in the storage cupboard. I dare not look at her for fear of what I might see: Resentment that I know her secret? Concern that I might tell? A threat of what will happen if I do?

I follow her through the gleaming marble corridors that will turn glacial when winter arrives in full force. The covens will freeze, huddled around fires that do little to warm our magnificent rooms. All of it makes a mockery of us.

As I hitch up my skirts to take the stairs, the guard says quietly, "Thank you."

She's taller than me, just enough that I have to tilt my head back to meet her eyes. I shrug, not risking a real answer.

"You didn't tell," she tries again.

"Neither did you." Leaving no room in my tone to invite conversation, I drop my gaze. It's midmorning, the halls are bustling with people, and she's taking too much interest in me. I can't afford to be noticed.

The sound of steel-toed boots against stone, an approaching patrol, snaps her to attention, her head straightening so fast a tendon cracks in her neck. Eyes front, shoulders back, her gait hardens, and I realise how far she'd slipped from military-precise movements as we walked.

I clasp my hands in front of my skirts as two Gilded march past. Obedient, both of us, and for a single surreal moment, it feels we're performing in a play for entertainment.

But no, this is brutally real, the consequences deadly if we break the rules. Which begs the question: Why is she speaking to me at all? What makes it worth risking the skin on both our backs?

We pass into the Warden's carpeted wing. The Gilded here are hand-picked for their monstrous size. Loops of gold braid swirl around the shoulders of their black tunics, gold breastplates polished, blades at their hips.

The guard steps forward alone to exchange quiet words with the Gilded. He glances at me, pupils constricting in silver irises. His gold half-mask shimmers as he raises one eyebrow, and goose bumps slide down my arms.

"She'll see you now," the guard says as if I'm the one requesting the audience, not summoned at the Spinner's whim.

The door creaks open, and I'm shoved inside again. I stumble angrily; I'd have stepped in compliantly if they'd just waited.

The curtains are drawn, leaving the room dark, and incense clogs my throat. My eyes sting and begin to water. How does she bear it in here, locked away from the sun?

"I like the dark," her voice rasps from a corner.

The loom clicks and clacks, weaving, always weaving.

My question comes out too loud. "Don't you miss the sunshine?"

The Spinner chuckles as she steps out of the shadows and goes to perch in her chair. She's less like a scorpion today and more like a snake hanging from a branch, mesmerising prey with hypnotic eyes.

"Ironic, isn't it? Even bound to Death, you seek the sunlight, and I, bound so tightly to Life, take comfort in the dark." It feels like a question with no right answers, so I don't provide one and glance awkwardly around her room to avoid meeting her eyes.

Trinkets are lined on the shelf in the alcove beside the fireplace: a silver box with a tiny keyhole, a sapphire-blue book with the title stamped in gold letters, and a porcelain shepherdess wearing a lilac dress.

The Spinner follows my gaze, a smile softening her features, fingers lightly dancing all the while. "You don't look?" She nods to the loom, jewel-bright tapestries unreeling from the end of it. "Why?"

"It's meant for the Warden, not me."

"A well-trained lie. Why, Penny? Why do you not look, when others would sell their soul for a glimpse?"

"Do you let them?"

"Sell their souls? Oh, they sell them, but not to me. I don't deal in souls; I deal in lives. Why?"

I shake my head. "I don't want to see."

"Yet you took my advice and walked in Death." The Spinner slips from her chair, all angular limbs and black floating silk as she drops to kneel beside the weavings of our lives.

"I didn't."

"Another lie. Death clings to you. You walked." Fabric runs through her delicate fingers. It looks soft as butter. She folds it hand over hand, searching, and holds it up for me to see. "You saw this?" She pats the floor beside her, and I kneel, but I still don't look. I can't.

Undeterred, she describes it, a black-walled manor in a sea of grey sand, a building that shouldn't exist.

Reluctantly, I nod.

Her sigh is soft as the kiss of a butterfly's wing. "You're going back."

"I—" I falter. Part of me itches to tell her what I saw: the green mist of summer trees above black walls, an oasis in the bleak landscape of

Death. I want to tell her how Death has its own heartbeat, how it pulsed through the sand beneath my toes. I want to tell her I heard Ella scream.

"I don't know who has her," she answers, though I did not ask. "Behind the walls is shielded from my sight." She rises to her feet and offers a hand. I take it, and her cool fingers wrap around mine, sending an unexpected flutter through my veins. We're close, she and I. So close, I can smell layers of spring sunshine and primroses beneath the cloying incense. Her eyes deepen into a midnight sky, star-flecked with silver around dilated pupils. I could drown in her eyes. Never resurface for air. Never want to.

I'm so confused. The first time I came here, I expected a monstrous creature cuffed by the Warden's power, and I've found a girl who takes my breath away, as attractive as the guard in the tower last night. The Spinner inhales slowly as if she's breathing me in. I wonder if she smells grave dirt and ash.

"Lilies," she says. "Lilies and winter nights laced with woodsmoke."

Is she reading my mind? Oh, Holy Dark Mother, what if she heard me thinking she was attractive? Or monstrous? "Can you stop doing that?"

She recoils like I slapped her and slips back to her chair. "You walk again. Tonight."

My temper flickers at her demand. "Burning alone—you have no idea what you're asking. I need help and no one will stand against the Thorn Queen."

"You did, Penny. Cast your net wider. You've hidden for too long. We need your sister." The Spinner leans back as if the strain of my company is exhausting. Pale hair streams to her waist; a tendril falls across her face and catches on heavy lashes. I feel bad for snapping. She seems so young and vulnerable. That could be part of her illusion. The Spinner is the Warden's creature—but I would never have burned last night without her. She's given Ella hope. Maybe this girl with midnight in her eyes could be a friend. Maybe she needs one as badly as I do. I've never had a friend outside the Thorn Coven before.

"I'll try," I say. "But if I get caught..."

"Tomorrow," the Spinner says, her mouth twisting into a wry smile. Sadness wells in her pitch-dark gaze. "Come back to me tomorrow. I'll send for you."

I swallow, trying to word my response carefully. "You're drawing attention to me. If I stand out, walking will become impossible."

Her voice takes on a sing-song tone as if she's reciting a poem. "Together, we are strong. Divided, we fall. We were strong once, Penny. He divided us all." The Spinner glances at her wrists banded by wide gold bracelets that control her magic in the same way the golden half-masks control the Gilded. Less brutal; still effective. One witch is easier to force into submission than a legion. "My name was Alice. The Warden took it away. Don't let him take yours. Keep it safe, Penny." She closes her eyes, black lashes fluttering onto her cheeks, and doesn't open them again. She looks to be asleep, but her fingers still dance, and her loom clicks and clacks as my dreams weave into silken nightmares.

"Goodbye, Alice."

I knock lightly on the door for the guards to release me, and her contented sigh bids me farewell.

I'm going to walk again. Tonight. But how? The Chamber of Flame and Smoke is now out of bounds: As I was eating my pancakes, I heard the muttered conversation that Grandmother has set sealing spells upon the door. No thorn witch is permitted to walk until Ella returns or the light in her crystal dies. They'll give her another day to cross the Horizon, maybe two like they did with Haylea, then, they'll send in a Gilded hunting party to banish her, and a thorn witch will be ordered to repair any damage. Haylea's loss is a wound that has not healed. It still hurts to think about it. I miss her horribly.

The veil must be protected at all costs, but I can't let the cost be Ella.

I can bring her home. I just have to find a way to burn.

Chapter Nine

After lunch, library duty is a blessing and a curse. If my walk in Death had been sanctioned, I'd be on strictly enforced bed rest today. I'm beginning to understand why. Grit scrapes my eyes, and I've fought three yawns in the last ten minutes. My fingers tremble with tiredness as I stack books on a trolley to return to the third floor.

Silver trolley wheels catch on the rickety elevator, and I swear under my breath. As I shove it hard with my hip, it clatters into the cage, spilling books to the floor in a flutter of leather and creased pages. Tears prickle as I drop to a crouch and try to smooth the damage, restacking the books neatly, wincing at the dog ears caused by my impatience. The door, a concertina of interlocking metal, slides silently into place even as I yank it shut with me on the outside. Ten buttons line the wall, numbers marked in worn silver paint. I send it to the third floor; a backward letter *C* is all that remains of the number three.

A light hand lands on my elbow.

Miss Elsweather flashes me a smile. "You need a cup of tea."

"I can't. I just sent a trolley up to the third floor."

She taps a young librarian on the shoulder, a dark-haired boy I don't recognise. He startles. Fear haunts his eyes, cheekbones sharp in the hollows of his face. I wonder where he's come from. I don't ask. Sometimes it's better not to know. Miss Elsweather speaks to him quietly so I can't hear, and he scurries away up the stairs.

"He'll rescue the books," Miss Elsweather says. "Work can wait five minutes."

Two panes of frosted glass take up most of her office door, OVERSEER OF LITERARY PURSUITS printed on a plaque between them. Inside, her kettle emits a thin whistle from the wood burner and steam billows out the half-open window.

She waves me to a stiff-backed gold chair that saw better days last century, and busies herself pouring water into a white porcelain teapot.

"So," she says, pushing a saucer into my hand. "Is it the visit to the Spinner that's left you looking like Death chewed you up and spat you out? Or is it something else, Penny?"

Tea splashes into the saucer as I sit straight in surprise. "I just slept badly."

She raises an eyebrow. "There's help available, should you decide you need it."

"I... thank you?" I try to hide my confusion. I've always liked Miss Elsweather, but I suddenly have no idea if I should trust her.

"Ella was an asset to the library."

I take a sip of tea and it burns down my throat all the way to my stomach. I hate her talking like Ella is already lost. Even Mother has forsaken hope. But she's still tethered to her crystal—I checked at breakfast and again at lunch. Her lifeline is fading, thinning, but there.

I do need help. And Miss Elsweather has never let me down. I take a breath, consider a moment longer, and then say, "I found her."

Miss Elsweather regards me steadily over her half-moon glasses. She doesn't seem at all surprised. "You walked."

I stare at my tea. "I need to again, but Grandmother's made that impossible."

Miss Elsweather slides open a drawer, rummages through it, and presses her palm flat on the table. "Finish your tea and back to work." She slides her hand across the wood and something scrapes against the surface. "Keep the library key. Ella was searching for something, Penny. If you happen to find it, let me know. Summon the dark."

My eyes widen. The palace guard said the same last night in the cupboard.

Miss Elsweather gives me a knowing smile and leaves in a waft of lavender and grey cotton skirts. A piece of parchment rolled into a tube lies on the table where her palm was.

Lost in thought, I drink the rest of my tea before it gets cold. I hate cold tea. Then, I unroll the parchment and a silver vial clatters into my saucer. It's warm to the touch and topped with a metal lid, not the normal cork stopper Grandmother uses to seal vials. A rose is engraved on the base in the faintest of fine black-tarnished lines. I slide it in my pocket next to the key. A sketched map of the library is marked on the parchment. There's an X drawn where I'm sitting in Miss Elsweather's office, and behind it, where there should be a wall, the image of a staircase runs deep underground.

Across the middle of a small room at the bottom of the stairs, she's written *Burn me*. And I wonder if she means the note—or myself.

Each forkful of rice at dinner sticks in my throat. Ella's crystal has faded since lunchtime and her lifeline is little more than a frayed thread. She's drifting deeper. If I don't find her tonight, she's lost.

If there was the tiniest chance Grandmother might bring Ella home, I'd tell her everything and face the fallout. But she won't. The fire that burned in the hearts of my coven guttered long ago. I try to reconcile the woman seated beneath the rainbow of our crystals with the Thorn Queen of my childhood, who ruled over all the covens of the Eastern Seaboard. She was magnificent then, seated on her throne of thorns, an obsidian crown sparkling upon her flame-red hair. Now she clings to what authority the Warden allows her.

The best option I have is to investigate the room marked on Miss Elsweather's map and pray the vial in my pocket is a path into Death. The pyre in the Thorn Wing is the only Colligerate-approved method of crossing the veil, but there's more than one way to burn; poisons that sear from the inside out and potions that incinerate blood in veins. I hope Miss Elsweather gave me precisely what I need.

Because my only other option, the only other place to burn, isn't an option at all. The eternal flames in the firepit in the centre of the Gilded Barracks.

I'm the last to leave the dining room. Mother pats me on the shoulder as she passes and drops a light kiss on my hair. "Get an early night. Staying awake reading until all hours won't help Ella. You look exhausted."

I force a smile as I wish her good night. It sounds a little like goodbye but she's too distracted to notice.

"I love you," she says, and with her eyes fixed on the case of crystals, she could be talking to Ella or me.

"I love you too," I whisper as the door shuts behind her.

Night's chill stretches along the corridors, defying the warmth of the lantern light. Shadows dance across the walls like broken marionettes with their strings half-cut. The clock tower chimes out a warning. Two hours past curfew. If I'm caught outside the Thorn Wing, I have no excuses, only an ill-gotten key and a silver vial to incriminate me further.

Boots sound around the next corner, the palace guard patrolling the hallways, and I slide into an alcove. My breath echoes in my ears, my heart thuds against my ribs, loud enough to wake the dead. But the boots fade into the distance without coming closer. When they've disintegrated into silence, I run the rest of the way to the library.

The key turns with a soft little snick and the doors open soundlessly. I creep inside, wishing I could make myself smaller, less visible. No lamps are lit in here. No candles burn in the windows. The library is shrouded in darkness. *Shrouded.* I bite my lip. The word conjures images of nefarious creatures protecting forgotten tomes smothered in dust and crumbling with time.

As I look up, a light flickers on the Ninth, pinpricks of green against the dark. A second sparks on the Eighth. A third on the Seventh.

They wink out at the same time.

I'm frozen between fight or flight. Saving my skin or finding Ella.

For Ella. I repeat it like a benediction. Before I can falter, I run, clutching at the polished banisters and stumbling up the first stairs.

Penny. My name rasps around the dust-moted midnight library.

I miss the last step and lurch onto the first-floor landing. The light on the elevator pings on. The arrow points to the number nine. At the top of the library, doors grate open and shut. With a whirling clatter, the arrow on the elevator creaks to the number eight.

An emerald glow lights the whole ninth floor, shining eyes peeking through the banisters. A cold sweat breaks over me and I move faster up the stairs. I'm hallucinating. I have to be.

I make it to the second-floor landing as the elevator arrow twitches to the number five, and race to Miss Elsweather's office, my breath gasping. I slam her office door as the elevator scrapes open, and my name crawls through the gap beneath it as I fumble with the key in the lock.

The green glow creeps up the frosted glass and I brace my hands flat against the door expecting the handle to rattle, but there's just my name whispered, quiet as the turn of a page, over and over again.

Maybe the Gilded Barracks would have been better than this. At least I know what sort of monsters the Gilded are.

Heart still pounding, I turn my back on the whispers and tiptoe across the rug to the bookcase where the staircase was marked on Miss Elsweather's map.

I press books and pull them off the shelves. But nothing happens. I bang my hands against the bookcase in frustration. Something has to happen; I can't go back into the library where the green light is brightening by the minute. I can't burn on Miss Elsweather's office rug either.

I run my shaking fingertips along the shelves, following a carved line of thorny stems to a rose in full bloom. One rose petal feels smoother than the rest, more polished. I press it and the entire bookcase swings outward. An abyss yawns behind it.

A sigh creeps beneath the office door and the light snuffs out, plunging me into darkness. The door creaks. I unscrew the vial, tip its contents down my throat, and step into the dark, pulling the bookcase shut behind me. I miss the top step and stumble.

Fire hits my veins as I fall.

My skin smokes as I hit the bottom of the stairs.

I barely manage to gasp the words to part the veil before my throat is scorched shut. As my body crumbles into ash, I tear my soul free. Glass shatters in Miss Elsweather's office, and the paper-dry rasp of my name follows me into Death.

Chapter Ten

I died too quickly. Shock clouds my senses.

I itch to look back.

I drop to a crouch, dig my fingers into the cool sand, and listen to the desert, forcing myself to focus. The abrupt silence of my heart rings too loud and I sense nothing. No lifelines. No Ella.

Finally, I feel her, a mothwing flutter in the distance. Her lifeline is fainter tonight—disintegrating. I should draw a weapon or change my clothes, but my hands are trembling too hard.

I clench my fingers deeper into the sand, and freeze. Dark grey tendrils ripple out from my hands in an intricate spiderweb of darkness. Fear races down my spine, and they deepen to ebony black. I've studied pictures of this in textbooks: Fog-wraiths wake beneath the sand.

I am frightened, and Death has smelled my fear.

The web constricts and flares, flooding the desert with shadows, and a broken-edged screech cracks the silence.

I fly to my feet, wheel away from the veil, and run, following Ella's lifeline deeper into Death.

If my heart still beat, it would be pounding. If I needed to breathe, my lungs would be begging for air. But Death is many things and sometimes it is kind. Sometimes it is merciful. Here I can run and run without my muscles protesting. My black skirts blend with the sand, and the red of my hair, answering my plea for invisibility, fades to a dusty hue.

I scramble up a dune, and towering black walls rise from the desert beyond. I slide down and they grow taller as I close the gap. Rocks dot the sand, and I skip around them.

The dunes shift as I run; they rise and fall, concealing my flight.

Sometimes Death is deceptive.

The ground lurches, and I pitch forward. Quicksand swallows my hands to the wrists, sucking and clinging as I pull them free. Fog unpeels from the sand, clamping like fingers around my ankle. I prise it off with a shudder and shoot to my feet.

Sometimes Death is hungry.

Dark shapes rise from the desert—human shapes, bent and angular. Sand clings to fog-wraith limbs erupting from the dunes. I meant to sneak up on the manor, circle the perimeter, and find a way in. But there's a gate, huge and caged with a portcullis, its points driven deep into the sand. Knocking on the front gate should be a last resort. Now, I throw myself on the mercy of whoever—whatever—is beyond the walls.

I rattle the portcullis gate.

Sometimes Death has a plan.

The gate shudders upward as the fog-wraiths close in. Bony fingers clasp at my dress. I should have drawn a weapon; I should have thought this through. Fabric tears as I duck under the gate, and it slams shut, saving me and trapping me with one clattering thud.

I want to look over my shoulder at the fog-wraiths. I've never seen one before outside of an encyclopaedia colour plate.

Don't look back.

Fear keeps me pinned on my knees as footsteps approach. Black polished riding boots halt by my hands. I attempt to rise, to meet my fate, but pain slams into the back of my skull and everything goes black.

Sunshine wakes me, streaming in through a wide-open window. The brightness burns my eyes, and when I try to sit, the room rocks and sways. I'm in a parlour; apple-green armchairs sit beside an unlit hearth, lilac flowers meander across the wallpaper, and a vase of scarlet roses stands on a low table. I must be dreaming. Colour and light overwhelm me, and I squeeze my eyes shut.

I'm still in the same room when I open them. Pollen whispers on the breeze dancing though silver-veiled curtains embroidered with roses. This isn't a dream. Dreams don't smell nice. Dreams don't hurt, and my head aches.

I inhale slowly as I try again to sit, and pain skewers my skull so hard, a whimper slips free. A low voice freezes my efforts, a male voice, mild curiosity strung through his words. "I'd lie down a little longer if I were you. You took quite a knock."

"You hit me!" My head throbs in time with my heart and confusion tangles my thoughts: I'm in Death, my heart should not beat. My crystal is cool against my chest, and when I reach for it, my lifeline is intact.

"I'm not in the habit of hitting women." The owner of the voice approaches, his boots eerily silent on velvet carpet. A broad-shouldered man, silhouetted against the window. "The blow to the back of your skull was courtesy of a fog-wraith and a rather large stone." In a single, fluid movement, he sits on a low chaise longue, one arm thrown out across the back, idly swirling a glass in his hand. He's not much older than me, dressed impeccably in a black shirt tucked loosely into dark pants, rolled-up sleeves exposing muscled forearms. Silver swirls curve like bracelets around his wrists.

He's the most perfect man I've ever seen. If someone asked for a diagram of male beauty, I'd paint a picture of this one.

How is he here? No one lives in Death, no one has a parlour here with rose-embroidered curtains! The only person able to live in Death was the fairy-tale Sorcerer who created it. And I don't believe in him... or I didn't.

It's impossible. Thorn witches can't have patrolled Death for years and not seen so much as a ripple in the desert to indicate such a powerful being resides here. Yet no one has seen this manor before either.

His eyes meet mine. Dark eyes. Dangerous. A slow smile spreads across his lips.

I realise I'm staring and my cheeks flush hot. "Thank you. For letting me in."

"It would've been rude not to. You had no less than seven fog-wraiths in pursuit." His gaze slips to my lips and trails down my throat, lingering on my crystal before snapping back to my eyes. There's something off about him, an absence I can't put my finger on. "Tell me, what inspired you to bring the undead clamouring at my door?"

I sit up, ignoring the splitting thud in my head and the spin of the room. "I'm searching for my sister."

"Ah, that would be Isabella?" He takes a sip of his drink without taking his eyes from mine. *Danger*, screams the corner of my mind responsible for my survival. "Isabella made an unfortunate mistake. I am feeling benevolent, so I'll allow you to see her."

I shake my head. "Ella doesn't make mistakes."

His smile sharpens to a tight line. "Isabella looked back, and you know precisely what that means. Don't you?"

The second original rule of Death broken. If a soul looks back, they twist into fog-wraiths; if a thorn witch looks back, Death owns us completely—forever. We cannot cross the Horizon; we cannot pass the veil. "Let her go."

He laughs a dry and bitter laugh. "Is that the best you can do? You find your sister held captive inside a manor that should not exist, in Death of all places, and your first push is 'Let her go'! Oh, Penelope. Isabella told me about you. When you appeared on my doorstep, I expected at least a little entertainment, but this... this bores me. I thought your *High Warden* would send someone intriguing. A girl with a spark, not some vapid waste of my time."

"I'm not vapid!"

"But you are a waste of my time. Get out."

I tilt my chin, stubbornness stamping on fear. "You said I could see Ella."

"I changed my mind."

"No."

"No?" He rises to his feet, and I force myself to mine as he stalks toward me. We meet in the middle, him towering over me, dark and formidable, all chiselled muscle and piercing eyes; me, refusing to cower. I didn't risk the Thorn Queen's wrath just to be sent away. I didn't burn myself alive, alone, twice, just to crumple beneath his glare. I force steel into my spine, and wait.

The depths to his eyes are terrifying, inhuman, black as Alice's but wild as the sea after a storm. My stomach clenches. If he's the Sorcerer, the actual Sorcerer who supposedly created Death and was banished into it, he could turn me into dust, or a wraith, or worse.

With an exasperated sigh, he grabs my arm and turns me toward the door.

Struggling is futile. Probably dangerous. I fight anyway, twisting to ram an elbow in his ribs. "I'm not leaving without her."

"Then you can stay here with her." He holds me out of range, his grip tightening as he frog-marches me into an airy hallway with white curlicues of plaster decorating the ceiling. Glittering chandeliers scatter rainbowed sunlight across pale yellow walls.

I jerk my arm, trying to break free.

My back hits the wall. His hands plant on either side of my head, trapping me, stilling me. "So, you do have fire in you." His voice is lethally soft. He smells of rain and dark chocolate and bitter almonds dipped in brown sugar. "When your sister showed up at my door, I thought she was the one. But your Warden, it seems, sends me another." There's a gleam in his eyes, sharp and cunning. I flatten my spine against the wall; there's so much of him, so little of me. His presence is overpowering and intoxicating: I want to shove him away and lean into him all at once. Instead, I stare right back at him.

Who does he think I am? Why does he think I work for the Warden? Why hasn't he disposed of me yet?

"Very well, Penelope. You have my interest. I uphold the laws of Death, and your sister broke those laws. A life is forfeit. One of you can leave; I'll let you decide who."

I don't have to think. Ella's lifeline won't last the night, mine is strong; I have time, Ella does not. I made it into Death on my own, I can make it back out again. "Let her go."

Half a smile greets my answer. "You won't escape, if that's what you're thinking. She tried."

Of course she tried.

"Why do you assume I work for the Warden?"

He raises an eyebrow as he straightens, one finger twitching toward my crystal before his hand falls to his side. "Because the Warden likes games, and you two are precisely the kind of game he likes to play." Stillness settles across his features as he waits for my response.

"I don't work for him." I swallow and lay my cards on the table, hoping my assessment is right. "I hate the Warden. Whoever it is you think I am, I'm not. I just want to take my sister home."

"A life for a life," he says. "That is the law. The rules of Death are nonnegotiable. Yet it seems you have broken the first of them and not been made to pay the price." His pause strings us both tight. I watch the flickers of calculation behind his gaze.

He leans closer and his words chill my neck. "Thirty nights." His thumb runs down the side of my throat and follows the path of my chain, stopping just shy of my crystal, and ice trails in the wake of his touch. He's so cold. "We make a deal, you and I. Return to me, Penelope. Every night for thirty nights, bring me information on the Warden and his court. I'll have your soul as collateral. You break the second law—look back as Isabella did—and your soul is mine. You miss a night, you are mine. At the end, if you want to leave and never return, I'll set you free."

"You want me to spy on the court?" My throat is dry as dust.

He smiles, and fear eats at my gut. "I want you to spy, as you so inelegantly put it, on the Warden."

"And Ella?"

"Ella is free as soon as you agree to my terms."

I'm dealing with a demon—and he's asking me to spy on worse.

I nod, aware I'm walking into a trap, not bargaining Ella out of one, praying this man isn't the Sorcerer. "Thirty days is Samhain." He can't be the Sorcerer. Can he?

"Is that a problem?"

I shake my head, heart pounding. "An observation."

It sounds like he chuckles as he turns away. He leads me to an office, lays a piece of parchment on a mahogany desk, and in elegant cursive writes the terms of our deal and holds out a knife. I stare at it blankly.

"Those who deal in death seal their word in blood. If you're having second thoughts, I can keep Ella? Though, I've grown quite attached to her. Watching her lifeline fail will be almost distressing."

Bastard. He's backed me into a corner; the cruel upward twitch of his lips suggests he knows it.

"I have a question." I have lots, but one answer is all I need for now.

"Then ask it."

I bite my lip, watching him carefully. "Who are you?"

He presses the point of the knife into his thumb so the pad indents, but the skin doesn't break and he's still staring at me. "Who do you think I am?"

I exhale shakily, wishing I hadn't asked. But I can't make a deal if I don't know who I'm making it with. "You're in Death."

"Is that another observation or an answer?"

"The... Sorcerer was banished into Death?" I brace myself. I want to close my eyes. Instead, I stare at his hands, at the knife, at his thumb, and wait. His hands are so clean, his nails so perfect.

"Was he? I've been in Death for a long time and never seen the Sorcerer wandering around. If I had, I'd have invited him in for tea. It can get terribly lonely here."

I blink at him in surprise, but his face is perfectly composed. Is he mocking me? "So the Sorcerer is... he's real?"

He nods. "I believe so, yes."

My head is spinning. I'm not sure what to think. "But you're not him?"

"No, Penelope. I am, most decidedly, not the Sorcerer." His answer sounds choked. As if he's laughing. I glare at him, but his expression hasn't changed. He's still not smiling, just looking at me as if I'm an interesting bug he'd like to catch in a jar and examine.

"How can I be sure?" I ask.

"Tricks and lies invalidate contracts, and I think you'll find this one particularly effective in its binding."

I search his eyes and find nothing there to indicate he's lying. "You haven't answered my question. Who—"

"No," he says, cutting me off. All trace of laughter is gone. "I haven't." He spins the knife so he's holding the hilt and twitches his fingers, indicating I should give him my hand. "Isabella's lifeline is fading."

I still don't know who he is, but I know who he isn't. It has to be enough, for now. "Fine." Reluctantly, I stretch out my arm, and he takes my hand gently. He's careful as he pricks the side of my wrist with the point of his blade. A bead of red swells and wobbles, and he guides it to mark our contract. Silently, I watch him do the same.

Two ruby-bright lines swirl around each other to form a curlicued letter *M* caging a letter *P* written in what is most definitely my handwriting. The ink of our blood shines as it dries.

The parchment is rolled and in his pocket before I can blink.

He hands me a handkerchief to press against my wrist, opens the door, and gestures for me to leave with a wave of one hand. "Down the hall, third door on the right." His fingers catch mine as I brush past. "Take tomorrow to rest. Your thirty days start the night after."

"Thank you..." My words die. I have signed away my soul and I don't know the name of the one who bought it.

"Lord Malin," he fills in the gap of my goodbye as he releases me. "Good night, Penelope. I very much look forward to your first report."

I turn to ask how I'm supposed to get my sister out of the manor.

But he's gone as if he was never there.

Ella lies on a four-poster bed plucked straight from a fairy-tale picture book. Death has sucked the colour from her. Her hair is the palest of strawberry blondes fanned across lilac pillows, skin as white as the parchment Lord Malin wrote our contract on. The little braided bracelet Mila made circles her wrist. When I take her hand, it's limp and cold, and the crystal around her neck is hazed with cracks. Her lifeline is faded, the softest of wingbeats in the stillness. I call her name and shake her shoulders, but she doesn't stir or open her eyes.

On impulse I press my fingers to her wrist, searching for a heartbeat. Relief floods me when I find one; confusion floors me when I remember where we are. My own heart thuds inside my ribs, forgetting it should be still. The air whooshes from my chest as the enormity of what I've done hits me. I can't breathe back in, and my lungs burn for air.

I shouldn't need air. I'm dead.

A rough tap on my arm jars me back to my senses. Strong hands stand me straight and wrap a cloak around my shoulders. Lord Malin doesn't speak as he scoops Ella into his arms and strides away. I hurry in his wake, down the stairs and out into gardens overflowing with scarlet roses and archways heavy with honeysuckle.

The portcullis rises as he approaches, exposing damp desert dunes where everything is dead and cold. On the threshold, I falter, unwilling to step away from the flowers and the colour and the scent of summer. Reluctant to leave this haven of life in Death and return to the half-life of Halstett.

He speaks quietly as we walk through the dunes. "I can only take her to the border. You'll have to get her through the veil yourself."

"I'll manage."

He looks at me, an odd quirk to one eyebrow. "I have no doubt about that."

Silence falls between us, barbed and uneasy. Ella's head rests limply against his chest. We need to hurry; she's nearly out of time. If her crystal shatters, her anchor will be destroyed, and she'll die, irreversibly this time. I'll have no choice left but to send her beyond the Horizon. I'm playing a game I am unlikely to win. Everything seems utterly impossible, the odds stacked against me. No thorn witch has walked in Death so often for so long.

Malin watches me watching him and amusement lifts the corners of his lips.

Ella stirs as we approach the veil, the roar of mists rousing her. When she opens her eyes, her silver irises are tarnished grey. Confusion flickers across her features when she realises who holds her, switching to fear when she sees me.

Malin sets her on her feet a few yards from the veil. I wrap an arm around her back, hook my hand under her shoulder, and together we stumble toward Life.

"What did you do, Penny?" Ella's whisper is hoarse.

"I came to find you."

"You don't understand." Her knees buckle, and I stagger under her weight. "I was trying to protect you from this."

"Hush, Ella. Save your strength. It's all fine."

"Oh, Pen." Her voice is a near sob. "What have you done?"

I don't answer. Instead, I chant the words to let us pass and pray the crack spreading right down the heart of her crystal doesn't fracture it in two. I focus on my bedchamber, my bed with its bright patchwork quilt hidden beneath a steel-grey blanket, my pillowcase embroidered with stars. And I whisper to Ella to do the same.

The Witch Who Looked Back

When the girl was born, her future was set. She was a princess. The only princess. Heir to the Thorn Coven's crown. But no future is as solid as it might have you believe. No fate carved so deep it cannot be changed.

The second rule of Death, however, was carved deep enough that she should have known better.

Don't look back. The warning was written on the walls of the village, on the steps of the shrine, and in the tiny schoolhouse on the edge of the forest. They chanted it each morning when the school bell rang; it was in their nighttime prayers. They were warned when they made sacrifices to the Dark Mother at her altar or the Sorcerer at his. And still, they played Grandmother's Footsteps, creeping up on each other in the shadow of the trees, a game they'd learned from an ember witch child at the markets.

The girl should have known better. She was, after all, the daughter of a queen, and a death-walking queen at that. The girl grew into a woman and the woman into an uncrowned heir. All was well as well could be, until the day she took her throne. For the first time, the girl crossed into Death. As she burned, she remembered the rules. She remembered not to look back at her body as she left it behind, to look forward as she stepped into Death, to focus on the future instead of the past. She walked along the veil, she walked back, as the ceremony demanded.

She faced the veil, relieved her duty was done, and said the spell to step through. She smiled and took a step.

Behind her, something screamed.

She stumbled, half in Death, half out.

She should have recognised it for the temptation it was—the call of Death's desert pronouncing her queen. Startled, she glanced over her shoulder. The witch, who should have known better, looked back. The veil roared and snared her in its clinging grasp. Her lifeline solidified into stone and crumbled into dust. Her crystal shattered. And like that, she remained, half in Death, half out, until she faded into the nothing from whence we all came.

Cautionary Tales for Young Witches. *Approved by the High Council in the eighth year of the rise. Shelved on the second floor of the Great Library. Author: Emily Whimler.*

Chapter Eleven

This time, I get it right. I wake in my own bed as dawn breaks and the space in my heart where Ella resides is warm again, filled and whole. But there's a black splotch on my wrist, right where Lord Malin pricked me with his blade. It looks like a rosebud, petals closed tight.

My stomach grumbles. Two nights walking in Death without sleep have taken their toll, and creeping out of bed takes more effort than it should. Dressing feels like I'm wading through quicksand. I shrug on a woolly grey cardigan over my shift as I make my way to the dining hall, tugging the sleeve down to cover the mark on my wrist.

I find my mother and Mila red-eyed with relief by the dining hall doors. Mother wraps me in a hug and holds me tight, and I breathe in the honeysuckle smell of her hair. In her embrace I can forget the night, the bargain I made—the man I made it with.

Happiness radiates from her as she gives me an extra tight squeeze. "Ella is back. She came home."

"I know," I reply, and she holds me at arm's length, worry clouding the joy in her eyes. With a shake of her head, she leads me down the hallway, cracking the door open to Ella's room. Ella still sleeps, pale, so, so pale against grey sheets, but she's alive and she'll recover.

Grandmother is absent at breakfast. Mila whispers between spoonfuls of porridge that she was summoned to a meeting of the elder witches before the High Warden. She left with the dawn bell and doesn't know Ella is alive.

When she returns, her face is granite-hard, her gaze roaming across the coven, lingering too long on me. Ella is still confined to bed and Grandmother vanishes into her rooms, only to reappear with her face somehow harder than before.

She pulls Mother to one side, and I hear her say, "Nothing! She says she remembers nothing, Agatha. She's lying. I will not have this rocking the foundations out from under us." And with that, she throws me a glare and stalks from the room.

I wait, listening to the murmurs of unease flickering around the breakfast table and tracing Grandmother's path through the corridors and up the tower stairs. When I'm sure she's in her office, I leave the dining hall before Aunt Shara hands out the day's duties. For the first time in my life, I don't want to be assigned to the library. Miss Elsweather will have questions about her broken window. And the clang of elevator gears and the paper-dry rasp of my name still echoes in my ears.

Tucked away in the coven's workroom that adjoins Mother's greenhouse, I find the list of ingredients we're running low on and wander through the doors into a wall of hothouse humidity. Normally, I hate the heat, but with the memory of fog-wraith fingers still chilling my skin, the itchy prickle of moisture-filled air and the soft quiet of carefully listening plants is balm to my raw nerves. I've been jumping at everything this morning. Hardly a surprise, considering my lack of sleep, but it's irritating, the jolt of shock every time a door shuts too hard in the distance. Mila dropped her knife twice at breakfast, and the second time, I nearly leapt out of my seat and threw my spoon at her.

The greenhouse is Mother's place. The doors are marked with an elegantly painted silver sign, *THESE PLANTS WILL KILL*, and she's painted tiny blue wolfsbane flowers in a border around it. Inside, it is darker than a room made of glass should be. It's bigger than the greenhouse should be too. Poison ivy creates a shady tunnel down the centre and rows of plants branch off from the main path at unusual angles. A hundred varieties of poison grow here, heavying the air with toxicity. Pink oleander blooms beside azaleas, snake's head fritillary next to deadly nightshade, each plant in its own little sphere that provides it the perfect conditions.

Mother spent months and months perfecting the spell to create the spheres when we first arrived. When she succeeded, her collection took root from seeds she convinced Grandmother to request from the Warden. And the Warden allows her to tend her poisons, believing she searches for the cure to heal his ghastly wound. Now, Mother could gift a thousand different deaths, each one beautifully unique and terrible. But she does not have the volume of ingredients we'd need to stage a coup.

Even the entire greenhouse wouldn't make a dent in the Warden's Gilded army. Nor will Grandmother allow Mother to risk the veil by poisoning the Warden himself. It's a regular argument. A vicious one.

I frown as I brush my fingertips against a jessamine flower, wondering at Mother's difficulty growing gingerweed for our cycles. I wonder if the Warden allowed Mother the seeds for her poisons, but refused her request for gingerweed—that us having control over our bodies is more concerning to Halstett's council than an entire hothouse of fatal flowers and lethal leaves. I'm too tired to examine the uncomfortable nature of that thought, and the fresh-trimmed laurel bush is making my eyelids heavier and heavier, so I pick five of the freshest golden trumpet flowers and leave the heat of the greenhouse behind.

Trumpet flowers are exactly what they sound like, long golden petals curving out around a central stamen. White latex oozes from the cut stems, and I set them in a neat little line of small glass jars on the windowsill to catch it as it drains out. Later, the flowers will be hung to dry and the latex sent to the Ore Coven to mix into the molten gilding gold.

I wash my hands afterward, carefully cleaning beneath my nails, and settle to a quieter task. Perched on a stool at a knife-pocked wooden table, I fall into a steady rhythm of picking the leaves off a bundle of dried red perilla and sealing them in jars.

I'm finally feeling relaxed, writing out a row of labels, when there's a rattling sound by my ear. My heart collides with my ribs. Ink smudges across the paper as I spring to my feet.

Mila waves a bunch of perilla at me, seeds rattling like an angry snake. She tosses the dried leaves on the table with a smile. "Jumpy this morning, Pen?"

"Only when irritating older sisters sneak up on me."

"You're supposed to be in the library." She slides back a stool and sits on it with all the grace of an empress ruling over a glass city.

I perch beside her and snatch up my ink-splotched label.

Suspicion sharpens Mila's smile. "Where were you last night?"

"In bed."

"You weren't."

"And how would you know? We're not allowed out of our rooms after curfew." The label crumples in my fist, and I stare at her. Her eyes are hard. Mila's learned well from Grandmother, plays of power are a skill she'll need when she takes over as coven queen. I'm not sure why she's trying it with me. It might infuriate Ella, but she can glare at me all she wants.

She bites her lip, and her eyes soften. It's unexpectedly painful, seeing her fight between her responsibilities as coven heir and just being my sister. "I had a nightmare."

Her admission takes me by surprise. We never talk about our dreams outside the safe confines of our bedrooms in the night. "How bad?"

"Awful." The light dies in her eyes. "I can't shake the feeling something terrible is about to happen."

I hand her a sprig of red perilla and slide her a jar. "Careful. You start saying you're getting *feelings* and you'll find yourself locked up beside the Spinner."

We pick leaves without speaking, and silence settles, the most companionable silence I've heard in a long time. Out the window, clouds scud past the tall towers rising from the highest point of Halstett.

The Tide Coven's tower stands on one side of ours, white marble decorated with gold swirls forming waves and currents up the circular walls. They work their magic from an open platform at its top, where they can see the coastline, controlling the sea's ebbs and flows at the Warden's command. Envy prickles. It's been so long since I saw the sea.

The Storm Coven's tower stands on the other side, midnight black adorned with grey clouds and silver rain. A pinnacle at the top guides the storm witches' weather working into the skies.

I shake my stem at the window. "Don't you wish we were more like them?"

Mila pauses, frowns. "In what way?"

"No Death. No crystals. No fog-wraiths." I shrug and pick another flower. "They get a great view; ours is pretty abysmal."

"We're the Dark Mother's favoured ones. Walking in Death is our sacred duty. To wish otherwise is to defy her will." Mila recites the coven-approved propaganda and flicks a perilla flower at me. It bounces off my arm. "Yes. Every single day. I hate it, Pen. You think it's bad for you? Imagine being the Thorn Queen's heir—always having to say the right thing. Do the right thing. And you and Ella—you're so close. She barely talks to me anymore. It used to be the three of us against the world. Don't you remember? What happened?" She blinks hard and crushes the leaf she just picked.

I don't apologise, but I feel awful. "Halstett happened. It's thirteen years since our village burned, Mila. We came here; we grew up." Of course I remember, though. I remember Ella covered in itchy bites when we strayed too close to the marshland at the estuary mouth, and how Mila spent an hour dabbing camomile tincture on every single one. I remember losing a game of jump the stream and landing in murky water, and Mila and Ella jumped in too, so I wasn't the only one in trouble when we got home, covered in mud to our knees, our skirts soaked and dripping on Mother's clean floor.

Once, Mila got tree sap stuck in her hair, and Grandmother ordered it cut short. We snuck out that night, stole every candle from the Thorn Shrine, and buried them to spite her. Mila took all the matches and threw them in the stream, and Ella and I set the entire store of ember magic free of its jars. It danced like fireflies over the marshes, and we clung to one another's hands, barely breathing in case someone noticed. The coven had to use tinder and a burning glass to cross into Death for a week, and Grandmother took to carrying a book of matches in her skirt pocket at all times. We never got punished for it; she did get particularly difficult about which magic supplies we had access to afterward.

Mila chews on her bottom lip. She's trying to decide something. Her sprig is a bare stalk by the time she finally leans closer and whispers, "Ella's in trouble?"

I might feel bad, and I hate being stuck in the middle like this, but I'm not telling her Ella's secrets. I shake my head. "No idea."

Weariness laces Mila's frown. "The veil is failing. The Warden's getting desperate—so is Grandmother. I know you went after Els."

I remain silent.

"Pen?" Mila brushes her fingers against my wrist, begging me to deny it.

I can't. "Does anyone else know?"

Her shoulders slump at my confirmation. "What do you think?"

I think that the whole coven probably suspects. But no one knows for certain—except Mila, now—and none will point fingers as long as we stay quiet.

"Keep your head down. If the Warden finds out you broke the first rule of Death and survived it…" She trails off, swallows. "He'll demand to see your crystal. Grandmother will hand you over if he does."

"I know." Mila's right. Keeping my head down is precisely what I need to do. Unfortunately, I've got thirty nights of treason to navigate.

I've never felt so utterly alone. How am I going to cross the veil with no help for an entire cycle of the moon? What if next time the midnight knock on my door isn't my sister after a nightmare? I want to curl up in a ball and pretend this conversation never happened. To pretend last night didn't happen.

Quietly, Mila tidies up the workbench, leaving no trace of our occupation except ten neatly labelled jars lined precisely on the shelf. When she's finished, she rests a hand on my shoulder. "Ella's been asking for you. After you've seen her, you should sleep. You look like death. I'll cover for you; say you've got a headache or something."

"You won't tell?"

"I'm your sister," she replies simply.

It's not until I'm knocking on Ella's door that I realise Mila didn't really answer at all.

Ella is sitting up in bed, a spell book open on her lap, red curls shining around her grey-nightdress-clad shoulders. Her room is exactly like mine—the bed in the same corner, the nightstand set with a glass of water and an oil lamp.

She marks her place with a bookmark I made for her birthday a few years ago, a cherry tree embroidered with the last of my stash of coloured thread before the Warden issued an edict banning it. It's frayed at one end with use, the silk stitches slightly grubby as if she's rubbed her thumb over them too often. We used to play under the cherry tree in our village as children, Ella, Mila, and me. Played in the falling petals every spring and danced in the moonlight at the blossom festival to celebrate the shortening of the nights and the strengthening of the veil.

The spell book slaps onto the nightstand with a thud that informs me Ella is furious. "Sit," she says softly. Ella this angry is almost as terrifying as the man in Death with a stake in my soul. Last night has taken on a nightmarish quality in the light of day, or maybe that's my mind trying to save itself from falling apart.

Ella hisses, "What were you thinking?"

I perch on the edge of her bed, and she shuffles her legs over to make room. "I was thinking: My sister is in trouble, and no one is doing anything about it. Did you expect me to sit here and do nothing?"

"That's exactly what you were supposed to do! I was meant to protect you, Pen, not the other way around." Ella's eyes spark, silver catching fire. "How did you manage it?"

I tug my cardigan sleeve down, hiding the black mark on my wrist. "Miss Elsweather helped."

What little colour is in Ella's cheeks drains. The spark of anger in her eyes fades into worry. I want to tell her it's all right—she's safe, that's all that matters.

"Shit." Ella never swears. "Holy Dark Mother. They've been pushing for you to join for months."

"Who has?"

"The Resistance. I've held them off, but after the stunt you pulled, I've been ordered to bring you to a meeting tonight."

"The...the Resistance is *real*?" Shit! The guard who caught me in the cupboard wasn't lying. And Miss Elsweather's offer of help suddenly makes sense. They used the same words: *Summon the dark.* "And you joined?" Ella nods. If she didn't look so damned fragile, I'd shake her. Or throw something. "Damn it, Ella! Grandmother will eviscerate you!" Right now, I want to eviscerate her! How could she keep this a secret?

She sighs and shakes her head, red curls tumbling around her shoulders. "Someone has to stand up to the Warden. You have no idea what he's trying to do!"

"Enlighten me, then," I snap.

"I can't!" Ella rubs her arm, wrapping her fingers around one elbow in an odd gesture.

"Who ordered you to bring me to a meeting? How did they get a message to you?" I glance around the room for I'm not sure what. Our windows don't open wide enough for someone to climb through and deliver Resistance orders. I suppose someone could have thrown a note? Or... another thorn witch could easily come in... "Who else is involved?"

"No one." She blinks. Ella always blinks when she lies. It hurts more than it should.

"Right."

Ella reaches for my hand. I snatch it away, and she winces. "I'm sorry."

I shrug and we fall silent. The silence with Ella is all sharp corners and brittleness. Everything is upside down. Mila worrying; Ella angry. I'm too scratchy with lack of sleep to deal with this.

Ella watches me carefully, her hand resting on my knee. "How many times did you walk?"

"Twice," I mutter.

Her eyebrows shoot up. "Alone? No wonder you look like Death just spat you out."

"You don't look much better yourself." I pause, debating my next question, remembering Lord Malin's accusation. Ella doesn't make mistakes. If she did, her involvement with the Resistance would have been noticed long ago, and she hid it even from me. I was shocked enough that she'd met someone and not told me. I never thought she'd keep a secret like this. It almost cuts too deep to hurt. I consider revealing the bargain I made—she'll hate that I made it to save her—but I hold my tongue. "You didn't look back, did you?"

Ella shakes her head.

"What happened?"

"How did you get me out?" she counters, as unwilling to answer my question as I am hers. Then she grabs my wrist, pulls me into a hug, and whispers into my hair, "Thank you."

"I love you," I reply, inhale the lilac and cindered-honey scent of her, and untangle myself gently from her arms.

Her lifeline flutters, an invisible mothwing caress. "You'll come to the meeting?"

"Do I have a choice?"

"None of us do. Not really," she says. "I tried so hard not to drag you into this."

My anger drains away. Ella looks lost and pale, and I see her as she was in Death, laid out on the bed, still and quiet. "I think you've dragged Mila into it too. She knows what I did."

Ella stiffens. "She knows Miss Elsweather helped?"

"No, not that. But she knows I came for you."

We look at each other for a long moment until Ella breaks the tension and pats the bed beside her. I climb under the covers and we curl up together like we did when we were children. We had our own beds, the three of us sisters, our own rooms, but we never used them. Exhaustion clouds any sensible conversation Ella and I might have, so I ask her the question that's been burning since I woke in Death to find a beautiful, impossible man staring at me. "Who is he, Els?"

"I don't know." She curls a little closer and her fingers catch mine. I hear her swallow. "I thought at first he was the Sorcerer..." She trails off.

"He's not," I whisper. "I asked him."

Ella tries to smile. "Of course you did. But did you believe him?" I nod, and she exhales shakily, suddenly unsure. "He is real? There was a man? You saw him?"

"He's real." *Horribly real*, I add silently. And so was the contract I signed. I squeeze her hand, trying to be reassuring, and her eyes narrow. "Shit, Els! How has no one ever seen that manor before? How did you end up trapped inside it?"

She tries to shift away a little, and my grip on her hand tightens. "I can't."

"Can't what?"

"Tell you anything else. Not until after the meeting. Once they've met you properly, I'll try and get permission to tell you everything. Promise."

I open my mouth to insist she tells me right now. But she looks so tired and sorry, I don't have it in me to argue.

"It's fine, Pen." Ella shivers, taking the reassurance out of her words. "I'll make sure it's fine. Just stay away from the manor. If you see it again, don't go near it."

Goose bumps spread down my arms as I lie: "I won't."

Ella says with forced brightness, "I owe you a secret." And I let her put it to one side, glad she's not asked more about Malin, relieved I haven't had to explain the deal I made—desperately worried about Ella and her involvement in the Resistance.

Tucked under my sister's eiderdown, holding tight to her hand, I listen to her story. She met him in the Resistance, he is kind and funny and safe, they've been together months and she thinks she might be falling in love—she's so relieved to finally tell me. And

I find I'm not resentful she kept this secret. This is hers and his. She tells me they snatch minutes together on the third floor of the library, which explains why she behaved so oddly by the military history books the other night.

A piece of the puzzle clicks into place. "So that was why we went to the library! What do the Resistance want on the ninth floor?"

Ella clamps a hand over my mouth. "Shut up."

I unpeel her fingers, shift so I can see her eyes, and whisper, "It was them, wasn't it, that sent you up there?"

She nods. Sighs. "Later. Ask all your questions at the meeting. I can't tell you anything more."

"Why did you join? You can tell me that."

She shrugs. "We're dying. Every time we burn, a little piece of us doesn't come back. If I'm dying, I want it to mean something."

"We're protecting Halstett. Keeping Life separate from Death."

Ella raises an eyebrow. "You don't truly believe that?" I stare at her blankly, and she sighs again. "Well, I was protecting you."

I wrinkle my nose, confused. "You mean us."

"No, Pen. Just you." I want to ask more, but her eyes are drifting closed, and she adds, "If you don't sleep soon, you won't have any sensible questions to ask at this meeting."

I sit up, and Ella's eyes open; her face falls. "Don't go."

"I'm shattered, Els. And so are you."

"Stay," she says. "Please. I don't want to be on my own."

Neither do I. "I missed you."

"I love you too," she replies.

We drift to sleep hand in hand, and I dream of burning. I dream of roses and manors and dark-eyed lords. I dream of Alice weaving an image on her loom: me on my knees before the Warden, bound with cuffs of gold.

Chapter Twelve

An hour after curfew, Ella knocks lightly on my door. I fasten my cloak, pull the hood up to cover my hair, and try to settle my nerves as I step out into the hall. I've barely had time to process that the Resistance exists. That they could organise in secret—and right under the Warden's nose . . . it all seems so utterly unbelievable.

And if anyone discovers Ella's involvement . . .

"This is too dangerous, Els," I hiss under my breath as we creep out of the Thorn Coven's quarters to meet the Resistance.

Ella huffs a laugh and tucks a loose curl back beneath her hood. She's relaxed and there's a confidence to her movements as she hurries me along the night-dark corridors, slipping from shadow to shadow. "It'll be fine, Pen."

I purposefully misunderstand. "If we're caught—"

She cuts me off with a squeeze of my hand. "We won't be." She pats her pocket. "I've got the palace guard schedule right here—names, times, and ranks—and the Gilded are all with the Warden."

When the High Warden discovered Ella's miraculous return, he sent his Gilded to sweep the desert in Death, an irregularity that will keep Grandmother and Mother busy until dawn. The Gilded might be capable of crossing the veil in greater numbers than us, but the serrated barbs on their lifelines leave tears that require the thorn witches' more delicate magic to repair. Their patrols are the only occasion thorn witches are permitted a quicker passage into Death through the eternal fires in the barracks. It's exhausting work, repairing Gilded damage. Mother will take the first part of the night and Grandmother the second. They need their wits about them, their senses sharp. If they miss one damaged thread in the veil, the world around us will burn. The Gilded couldn't hold off a swarm of fog-wraiths for long. They might protect the Warden, get him to safety, but undefended, the ragged population of Halstett would be decimated in hours.

Ella drops my hand in the shadow of a monstrous statue of the Warden, his face covered by a gold skull mask staring down from the shadows of the arched ceilings. Four threads trail from one massive fist: fire and ice, stone and air. One representing each coven. A symbol of the High Warden's ultimate control over all witches. A fifth thread of obsidian black coils above the statue's head, symbolising the Thorn Coven's supposed freedom. Another winds around it clear as air and sparkling with rainbows—no one knows what that one's supposed to mean.

Ella presses a whorl on the heel of the statue's boot, and the wall behind unlatches.

That the Warden's statue conceals the path to the Resistance is deliciously ironic, but meeting in the catacombs beneath the Colligerate seems ridiculously obvious: an underground organisation meeting literally underground.

Tunnels filled with centuries of the dead swallow us whole as Ella seals us in. Torches flicker at even intervals into the distance, flames reflecting on dusty femurs and humeri arranged in alcoves along the walls. A spider lazily spins a web between time-bleached ribs, and another hangs in the centre of an empty eye socket.

Ella speaks softly as she hurries us deeper into the dark. "The Resistance don't know what happened in Death. Don't tell them. If they ask, let me handle it."

I'm still not sure what happened to her in Death, and I haven't told her what happened with Lord Malin. "I won't say a word."

"If only," she replies. Her fingers run along walls carved into the bedrock of the city and lined with the bony resting places of Halstett's forebears. She's guiding us by touch not sight. We turn a corner and the dust-riddled air turns to ice, piercing through my shift and clamping my jaw shut so my teeth strain to chatter.

"The tunnels are warded." Her grip on my hand tightens. She tugs me into a dark as thick and choking as smoke, pulling me around corners I can't see. Inky shadows conceal the skulls in their alcoves, hiding their fleshless grins. Not seeing makes walking past them worse.

"Swallow, Penny." Ella's whisper unpeels the dark, or maybe we just turned another corner. I lost my sense of direction a few turns back. I swallow and the darkness lifts. "Not much farther."

"Who spelled that?" In spite of the hideousness of the frigid dark, that ward was impressive.

"Ore witches wove storm witches' magic into the quartz in the rock. It's a beautiful spell." Ella explains as if it's the most normal thing in the world, ore witches working with storm witches. I open my mouth to question but she stops, one hand pressed flat on what seems to be a solid wall. She leans into it, and warm orange light slices apart the dark as a door swings open.

This is it. I'm about to meet the Resistance I believed was an empty dream of rebellion against a tyrant. It seems more impossible than walking into the pages of a fairy tale, that this is real, a secret society, a stand against the Warden. Ella tugs me inside. Silence greets us as the door shuts, candle flames dancing in the draught.

I blink in surprise.

I expected a gloomy collection of figures robed in black, assassins and cutthroats and vagabonds in a cave in the dark. I didn't expect a primly proper tea table in the middle of a mausoleum so huge it inspires hushed voices and bowed heads. A civilised afternoon tea in the middle of the night.

A tea party in a tomb! I clamp my lips over a giggle.

Light cascades from an intricate iron chandelier suspended in midair. Alcoves line the white granite walls, a black marble coffin resting in each, guarded by grimacing stone creatures. A single ornate coffin sits on a marble dais behind the tea table, candles dripping wax down silver candelabra balanced on its lid.

Ella's shoulders soften as she glances at the witches around the table. Mine tense. I've never seen witches from all the covens sitting together voluntarily. I know it happens at the elders' meetings with the Warden, it happened before we came here, at the gatherings of the witches' council, and we work together at the gildings, but...I thought the covens hated one another. I thought the other covens hated us.

A storm witch with pale curled hair smiles at Ella, and a tide witch, her features shifting like ripples on a lake, gives me a welcoming wave. An ore witch with an emerald the size of my thumbnail embedded in her temple twirls one finger in the air and magical quartz veins wind through the rock and across the door, sealing us in. Precious stones sparkle in the crook of her elbow and the side of her wrist as she sips tea from a porcelain teacup decorated with lilac flowers.

She stares at me, her head cocked slightly to the side, one copper nail tapping an uneven beat on the white lace tablecloth. The ore witch from the gilding, I realise. I offer her a tiny smile and she grins unexpectedly. I recognise the ember witch sitting next to her from the gilding too; three scorch marks slice through one eyebrow, her dark hair cropped short.

The table is set with finger sandwiches and little pink and yellow cakes topped with crystallized sugar on a tiered porcelain stand. With a jolt I see my cousin Carlotta is here too, absorbed in picking apart a sandwich, crumb by minuscule crumb.

And Miss Elsweather presides over the spread. "At ease, Ella," she says with a wave of her hand. "Sit down for goodness' sake. We kept it small—safer that way. Penny, I believe you've met Evelyn and Beatrice before."

Evelyn, the ember witch who hasn't blinked since we arrived, acknowledges my presence with a brittle smile, and Beatrice, the ore witch, gives me a cheery wave.

We take our seats, and Miss Elsweather continues the introductions. I'm hopeless at remembering names unless I see them written down. I wish they had badges. "The tide witch dripping water all over my floor—I do wish you wouldn't do that, dear—is Sybil, and the storm witch is Gail. Her mother had a wonderful sense of humour." She chuckles sadly. "Tea, dear?"

Steam rises from the spout of a pink teapot, and Carlotta hands Miss Elsweather a cup and saucer painted with pale green leaves.

Evelyn, the ember witch who still hasn't blinked, turns on Ella. "You're sure she won't talk?"

"Now, now, Evelyn." Miss Elsweather's reprimand is paper soft, unsettlingly similar to the whisper in the library last night. She peers at Ella over the half-moon glasses balanced on her nose, lips pursed, creasing the skin around them like a broken book spine. "He's not here, Ella. Neither is she."

Ella relaxes a little at the reassurance I don't understand. "Penny is not joining."

Miss Elsweather pushes her glasses up her nose with one finger and pours a cup of tea. "We'll let Penny decide that, shall we, dear? Sandwich?"

"We've eaten." Ella sounds so unlike Ella, hard and uncompromising, that any contribution I might have made to the awkward conversation dies before it reaches my lips.

"I'm sure you have." Miss Elsweather props her elbows on the table, steeples her fingers, and stares at Ella. "Straight to the point, then. In spite of my help, Penny's recent *misadventures* opened a can of worms I've kept nailed shut for over a decade."

"You helped her!" Ella says.

Miss Elsweather regards her levelly. "I did."

"You *promised*—"

"Circumstances changed." Miss Elsweather is all stick-insect angles as she slides first my cup of tea, then Ella's across the table toward us, the tablecloth crinkling in a bow wave of creases. "Penny brought attention to herself. You're out of time, Ella. She must decide and soon."

Steam laced with honey and camomile drifts from my cup. "Decide what?"

The angles of Miss Elsweather soften and she's back to the librarian helping a cautious reader choose a new book. "To help the Resistance. Or stand against us." She lays the rose-etched vial from last night on the table. "Do you know how difficult it was to explain a broken window in a library?"

"Did you know your elevator is possessed?" I shoot back.

Miss Elsweather raises an eyebrow. "The elevator?" I nod, and she sighs. "You're a loose thread, Penny. One tug and the whole Resistance will unravel. Either weave yourself into our *organisation*, or they'll snip you free."

Ella inhales sharply, her teacup juddering in her hand. "You wouldn't."

"It's not my decision. Carlotta informed us that Penny broke the first rule of Death and survived. She crossed the veil with you already there. Or is Carlotta mistaken?"

My cousin withers under the glare Ella throws at her. My heart squeezes.

Ella shakes her head and Miss Elsweather says softly, "Then we need her. You know we do. With Penny on board, for the first time in years, we have hope."

Ella snaps, "She doesn't want to join!"

Miss Elsweather's face turns to stone.

I wish I'd refused to come. I've made enough life-changing decisions recently; bound my soul to a mysterious lord to save my sister and agreed to spy on the faceless tyrant holding Halstett in his rotten fist. "A hope at what?"

Ella sets down her teacup and pinches me hard on the thigh.

"A hope at disposing of the Warden," Miss Elsweather says bluntly.

"You can't kill him! The veil—"

"I'm well aware of his link to the veil, and we have no intention of killing him. Not until we've cut his lifeline free of his Guardianship. Have you heard the stories of a particularly elusive knife? Who owned it? Created it?"

"The Sorcerer's knife?" It's not a stab in the dark; Grandmother mentioned the Sorcerer's knife at the gilding. Charmed, she said. One thought guided the blade, so sharp it can cut a soul in two.

Miss Elsweather gives Beatrice a nod. "Tell her."

Ella swears, loudly. "Bea, don't you dare!"

Beatrice gives her a wry smile of apology. "It's too late, Els. The minute you brought her through the wards in the tunnel it was too late."

I have no idea what they're arguing about. Ella's hand slaps into the table, setting the teacups jumping and clattering in their saucers.

"Enough, Ella!" Miss Elsweather's rebuke bounces off the coffin behind her.

Beatrice turns copper eyes on me and recites as if she's making a report, "The Sorcerer had a crystal once. Like you thorns do, but it was black as a starless midnight and so powerful it contained half of all the magic in the world. The Dark Mother had one too, a clear crystal filled with the hues of the rainbow that held the other half."

I try not to frown, not liking where this is going. If they know about my crystal...

"The knife," Evelyn says, unsmiling. "The Sorcerer used his crystal to create it. The Warden stole it. Then he used it to slice the Sorcerer's lifeline away from the veil and banish him into Death. Forced to work against its creator, the knife shattered."

Beatrice nudges her under the table and shakes her head before taking over. "The Resistance is trying to reforge the Sorcerer's knife. We have been for years. Since all our magic comes from the Sorcerer, we figured out it takes a witch from each coven to re-create it, but every attempt so far has failed. Gail's mother died during our attempt last year. So did your cousin Haylea." My eyes fly to Carlotta at this mention of her sister, but she refuses to look at me. "The spell we're using is a copy, and we have no idea of the original source, nor access to it. But we think something's gotten lost in transcription."

I look at the women around the table. "You all believe the Sorcerer from the storybooks is real?"

Miss Elsweather delicately puts down her sandwich. "Of course he's real, dear. He's as real as you or I. Why on earth would you think otherwise?"

Lord Malin said the same last night. I still have my doubts. "I... You think the Warden banished the Sorcerer?" She nods, utterly serious. "But... a sorcerer that powerful couldn't be banished by a man."

Most people would be shocked at the insinuation that the man revered as a god in Halstett is, in fact, mortal, but Miss Elsweather doesn't bat an eyelid. "I assure you, Penny, most stories about the

Sorcerer are true. More true now than ever, some might suggest. I understand your reluctance to believe in what has been gone since well before your lifetime. But finally, his strength is returning. Only a few nights ago, his power rippled through the veil."

I blink, trying to slow the spinning in my head. I crossed the veil a few nights ago. If the Sorcerer is real, and Malin said he's not in Death, then where is he? If his power is rising, what does he want? Miss Elsweather is watching me carefully, thoughtfully, and I need to say something, anything. "You're trying to reforge a knife made by the legendary Sorcerer with five witches?"

Evelyn sneers. I'm not sure what I've done to piss her off. "We have more than five witches. This isn't the whole Resistance, *thorn witch*."

I blush, immediately feeling stupid. Of course it isn't. I should have realised that. "How does this involve me?"

Ella blinks. She's about to lie, and there's a silent warning underlining her words: *Don't react.* "The original spell to forge the knife should be in the Sorcerer's Grimoire. We think it's hidden in Death along with a crystal dark enough to work the magic. The more thorn witches we have hunting, the more likely we are to find it."

The Resistance don't know about my crystal. I keep my face blank, hiding my relief.

"With the knife reforged, we can slice the Warden's lifeline away from the veil and put another in his place," says Miss Elsweather. She lays a little silver vial on the table, flicks it so it spins, and changes the topic of conversation so fast my head spins with it. "Maybe we need to be clearer on the dosage. That would have killed you five times over at least, dear. It must have been excruciating."

"It was quick." Five doses? If I'd known that, I'd now have five nights of crossing into Death relatively risk-free. My heart sinks.

Miss Elsweather continues steadily, "If you happen to come across the Grimoire on your travels, we only ask that you pass the information on its whereabouts to Ella."

What she's asking is quite clearly bigger than that. Ella turns paler, but she gives me a tiny nod, indicating I should agree. "If I find it, I'll tell her."

Miss Elsweather flicks the empty vial across the table and I catch it. I almost miss the sad smile she gives Beatrice.

Quartz light dims with a wave of Beatrice's hand as she rises and reaches for me.

Ella grabs my wrist, knocking my cup from my fingers. "No!"

Miss Elsweather takes another sip of tea as if we're discussing the correct shelf order for the encyclopaedias. "Don't be so dramatic, Ella. It's merely a safeguard to ensure she doesn't talk. We're not forcing her to join."

I stare at the stain of my spilled tea seeping across the tablecloth as all eyes fix on me: Carlotta's and Ella's silver-sharp, Beatrice's copper-bright. Blue sparks ring Gail's irises and Sybil's glitter a deep and depthless shade of ocean green. They wait silently for one of us to speak.

Evelyn clicks her fingers and my back heats as fire races along Beatrice's quartz veins sealing the door.

"Fine!" Defeated, Ella pulls me to my feet and turns me to face the coffin behind Miss Elsweather. "I'll do it myself. I'm sorry, Pen."

I shake my head at her, confused. "Do what?"

"Make sure you can't expose the Resistance." She gives me a small smile. "It won't hurt."

Beatrice snorts and adds, "Much."

Ella scowls in response.

I don't resist when Evelyn takes my wrist, thankful she chose the opposite arm to the one Malin marked as she rolls up my sleeve and tightens her grip, her skin too hot and too dry against mine. Ella makes a nick in the crook of my elbow with an excruciatingly long pin. Beatrice summons her ore magic and the scent of sulphur creeps through the air. The stone coffin lid ripples and swirls, and an indent pierces the marble with a puff of bone dust. We watch a single bead of blood trickle from my elbow and into the dip in the stone. Lord Malin's words ring in my thoughts. *Those who deal in death seal their word in blood.*

"Promise, Penny," Miss Elsweather says, not moving from the table. "Not one whisper of the Resistance outside these walls to any except sworn members of our little organisation."

"Not one," I confirm. What's one more promise? After the deal I made with Malin, this is nothing. The hole in the coffin lid yawns like a gaping mouth, and my blood vanishes, leaving a black dot on my skin, which could easily be dismissed as a freckle. If only Lord Malin had been as discreet. If only Ella had told me about the Resistance sooner. If only I hadn't used five nights' worth of poison to cross the veil once.

If only... There are too many ways to finish that sentence. Far too many. I run through them while the others finish their tea. They fall into the easy chatter of friends, and Ella relaxes as they talk about people I don't know until all that's left of the cakes are crumbs and the little sandwiches have all been eaten, and Miss Elsweather dismisses us.

Evelyn pulls the tomb door shut behind us. Carlotta hurries away before I can speak to her, head down, shoulders hunched. Gail and Sybil link arms and vanish into the tunnels, heads bent close in conversation. It's bizarre, seeing witches from two different covens so friendly.

Beatrice catches my wrist. Coppery nails scrape my skin. "Welcome to the Resistance, *thorn witch.*" Her fingers tighten hard enough to bruise my bones, clashing against the brightness of her smile.

"I didn't join," I point out.

"You will. When you find out where the Sorcerer hid his Grimoire, they'll make sure of it."

Ella elbows me in the ribs in an attempt to shut me up. Beatrice's grin warms when I don't. "And why, *ore witch*, do you think I will?"

"Because," Evelyn answers in Beatrice's stead and twirls one finger in the air, dancing fire along the quartz-veined tunnel. "We saw it." And then, a parting shot as she disappears into the dark. "Be grateful the Warden doesn't see what we do."

Chapter Thirteen

Midday the next day sees me shelving books on the third floor. After the whirlwind of the last few days, I should be glad of the comforting ordinariness, but I'm no closer to finding information on the Warden to take into Death. I'm no closer to a plan to cross the veil tonight either.

When the palace guard marches into the library, I say a silent goodbye to my lunch. With Alice once again shining a light in my direction, it's only a matter of time before the High Warden notices me; I might as well whisper goodbye to my freedom too.

Alice is quiet as I enter, she doesn't uncurl from her oversize chair to greet me. If anything, she curls tighter in on herself, her fingers weaving absently in her lap, the shuttle on the loom keeping time. I want to throw the curtains wide to wash away the shadows hung beneath Alice's eyes. Instead, I perch on the window seat and peek through the gold-fringed drapes.

Below, the courtyard stretches to the Gilded Barracks, its chimney spilling smoke from the eternal fires into the low-clouded afternoon. An ore witch crosses in front of the steps, her yellow sash lifting in the light breeze. Her finger twitches, her eyes shimmer copper-bright as she bows her head and skips out of the path of two

Gilded on patrol. A flagstone lifts, one Gilded boot catches, sending him stumbling, and the witch's shoulders tremble as she hurries away. I think she's laughing. The Gilded aren't. He watches her until she's out of sight and bends to inspect the flagstones before marching back inside.

I don't know what to make of this tiny act of rebellion under a smoke-veiled sky. An act that could cost her a finger or worse. I can't imagine taking that kind of risk for such little gain. With a shudder, I let the curtains fall. Maybe keeping the curtains shut is Alice's way of ignoring the constant reminder of the Warden's power. Maybe she hates him too.

She exhales, stirring the incense-clad silence into eddies and whirls. "He's everywhere." Alice's lashes sparkle as if she's been crying, but her eyes are clear. I'm not sure she realised she spoke aloud. "You found Ella."

"You knew I would."

To my surprise, she shakes her head. Her hair is not spun from silver silk today; it's threaded with tangles and catches on her fingers when she tucks a strand behind her ear. "The future keeps splitting. The Warden doesn't like it when it splits. You make it split, Penny, and it's getting harder to hide." She's exhausted, fragile, not the defiant Alice of last time I was here. "Sleep has been evasive," she says, answering my unspoken question, and I wonder again if she can read my thoughts. Specks of starlight brighten her gaze and a half-smile dimples one cheek. "I see the future. I see the myriad of questions you're about to ask, but I can't read minds. Can you imagine if the Warden had that power at his disposal?"

I don't want to imagine it.

"Neither do I," Alice murmurs, and we fall quiet, listening to the rhythmic clack of the shuttle as it spins a new image I refuse to look at. Where she is caught in what will be, I am tangled in the past, clinging to memories of green grass and cool forests and the mist of a waterfall on my skin. Fading memories, clouded with smoke and ruin and bloodshed, brutalised with gold.

No good comes from longing for what once was, but knowing the future—seeing the end before we've begun—leaves no room for hope. I don't know how the Spinner has any peace with such knowledge at her fingertips.

"My name is Alice," she chides gently.

"Alice," I whisper, tasting her name, watching the slight dilation of her pupils, the way her lips part with her sigh.

She shivers at the sound; I shiver at the intensity of her starlit eyes as they meet mine. Her fingers still their weaving. The loom stops. Silence clads the incense, thickens it. My breathing slows to match hers inhale for exhale. There's more than certainty in her eyes. There's a spark of fear. Of not knowing and longing and something else I can't quite put into words.

"Penny," she replies, and my heart skips as her fingers shake. She's fighting the compulsion of the loom. I want to cover her hand with mine and lend her my strength, but I don't quite dare. With a twitch of a frown, Alice gives up, and the loom whirs into action. I tear my gaze away from her as the first picture slithers across the silk: a wooden mallet and a gavel, flags in shades of grey hung above twelve decrepit council members. The High Warden resides over them in his skull mask, seated on a golden throne of broken faces. Words wind in cursive across the top of the picture: *Twelve for, none against. Motion passed.*

Alice says softly, "I saw a contract. Did you sign it?"

I'm wearing a grey sweater of Ella's today, long sleeves covering half my hands. I push one up and flip my wrist so Alice can see the black rosebud marked there.

"I'm sorry." She shifts her attention to the drawn curtains, away from me. "This won't end well."

"We're in Halstett. Nothing ends well."

"But Death does not belong to Halstett."

"It belongs to the High Warden."

Her fingers stutter, tripping over an invisible thread, and the shuttle shivers, catching a tiny knot into the silk. "Death belongs to no one. No one belongs to Death."

She obviously hasn't seen Lord Malin in her visions. If anyone belongs to Death, he does. Alice doesn't answer, and I realise I had no intention of telling her about Malin today. I wonder how far into the future Alice weaves, how much she really knows.

"Was that all?" I ask quietly, reluctant to leave her, desperate to go. I need to escape the cloying dimness and her ever-watching loom. But I want to sit by her window too, tell her about my sisters, how Ella is changing—hardening and keeping secrets—and how fragile she seemed when I found her in Death. That Mila is struggling with her responsibilities as thorn princess, and I'm stuck in the middle between my sisters more and more. How Grandmother spoke of the Sorcerer's knife, that there's a Resistance trying to reforge it. But that would lead into explaining about Malin and the deal I made. I'm not ready to put that into words.

I wonder what Alice knows of the past and what is true and what is not. I wonder if she's as lonely as me.

Alice stares, unblinking, as if reading the conflict of my thoughts. "I won't summon you again."

Disappointment wells in the space below my diaphragm.

She slices it away. "I won't have to."

I glance at her wrists, at the Warden's golden cuffs sparkling as she spins a never-ending song into silk—a boy younger than the one I helped gild is spread-eagled on a table, a half-mask about to be applied to his face. I turn away from her weavings of the future, glancing at the door. I don't want to know what she sees.

She tells me anyway.

"The council will pass a motion this afternoon to lower the age of gilding to sixteen." Alice closes her eyes, signalling the end of my audience.

As the guard escorts me back to the Thorn Coven's wing, I wonder why she summoned me at all.

Mila walks tonight. She burned an hour ago. Heat from her crossing still warms my skin.

The Gilded pronounced Death safe after their patrol, and with Grandmother and Mother too drained to walk, Mila was sent instead. They rescheduled my first walk, altering my place in the rotation so I'll step into Death with the Thorn Coven's aid in five days. Which means five nights of crossing alone with no help, no one to share the pain, and no easy way to burn.

I can't use the chamber. Mother holds vigil there tonight, anxiously awaiting Mila's return. I have one path into Death. And I don't like it. At all.

Ten chimes of the bell signal the beginning of curfew as I slip out the doors. Lamplight pools on rain-slick paths, shadows gathering between them. I tug the hood of my cloak to cover my face better. I'm a darker shade of shadow, a whisper in the rain. The black walls of the Gilded Barracks meld into the night. While it's not the first time I've been out after the night bell has rung, it is the first time I've run *to* the Gilded instead of from them. *Cast your net wider*, Alice told me—I don't know that I could cast it wider than this.

Voices murmur from the courtyard below Alice's window, footsteps splash through the puddles, and I duck behind a low stone wall as the fine-misted rain heavies into marble-size drops. A storm is headed in off the Penrith Strait. The Warden must have ordered the Storm Coven to steer it toward us. He controls the weather, like he controls everything else.

Two palace guards march past, silver breastplates streaming with rain, their sodden cloaks clinging to their steps. They're deep in muttered conversation, brows furrowed, attention on each other. I watch them pass, barely daring to breathe, cursing the loudness of my heart as they march out of sight.

The doorway to the Gilded's barracks stands open, light reflecting in a distorted, flickering rectangle across the slowly flooding courtyard. At this hour, it is unguarded, the halls beyond silent. The Gilded also burn, a ceremonial occasion rather than a regular schedule, and their stake is not locked away. It stands in the centre of the amphitheatre above the pit of blue fire that never goes out. I don't know what Gilded do with their spare time, but I'm reasonably sure milling around the amphitheatre isn't part of their off-duty plans. It should be empty. Still, I cling to the wall and its safety, steeling myself against failure while praying for success.

Holy Dark Mother protect me. There has to be a path into Death better than this! But I can't access ember magic to set myself aflame with a match and no pyre. Maybe I should have risked Ella's wrath and joined the Resistance, made friends with the other covens' witches and asked for their help. Or asked Miss Elsweather for more poison. I groan inwardly at the five nights of easy passing I wasted in one dose the night before last. A number of doses suspiciously matching the number of nights I need to burn alone.

Miss Elsweather knows too much already, and Ella...well, Els picked up the overprotective sister mantle when Mila let it go, but she's always leaned toward the hypocritical. One rule for her, another for me.

I'm procrastinating. But I have no desire to relinquish my soul to Malin's care quite so easily. Not this evening. Not when there's a stake right there, fires unguarded, a single unbolted door between me and keeping my end of our bargain.

I check both ways one last time, but there's only me and the storm.

No excuses. I let go of the safety of the wall and run. Rain soaks my skirts, sticking the fabric to my legs as I speed across the cobbles, up the steps, and into their black granite hall.

Across from the main entrance stand huge double doors. Beyond them are the eternal fires.

I slam to a halt in the shadows of the threshold, frozen and unable to take another step. The grated door to underground groans with the rising wind sweeping in from outside, driving rain against my back. Behind its bars the scent of fear gathers, seeping into the hallway and creeping across the floor. In the cells and chambers of the Gilded dungeons, no one screams, no one makes a sound.

The Gilded might cross the veil clumsily, but they use their command over Death for a different and more delicate purpose. Living execution: a punishment more painful than burning, a future more devastating than having none.

We've all seen the victims. They never recover, never truly escape what happens beyond that door. I swallow hard, trying to squash the lump of dread in my throat. I should have told Ella; she'd have helped me. She'd have berated me, but she'd have helped me—and hurt herself into the bargain. I can't go back. I can't involve her too.

A shout rings across the courtyard behind me, cutting off my escape. "Halt! Who goes there?"

Oh, Holy Dark Mother, no! I refuse to be caught, but there's nowhere to hide. I run, wet footprints marking my flight. Drips off my sodden skirts leave a trail across the floor. My heart screams against my ribs, and there's no time for hesitation. I slam shut the door to the amphitheatre behind me. The noise echoes, bouncing off stone-carved seats raked sharply to the ceiling. It can hold five thousand for entertainment or a warning, depending on who they invite.

I chant between gasping breaths as I sprint for the pit and the stake. I reach for the veil. Find it.

The stake is broader than ours. Manacles hang from a sharpened hook and there is no platform to stand on—no circle of twelve coven sisters to help me either.

I skid to a halt at the edge of the pit, the steel grating burning my toes, and glance down, my courage faltering. Blue flames spiral and swirl. Heat ripples the air—the kind of heat that scorches flesh from bones in seconds. At least it will be quick.

I close my eyes and jump, slipping through the veil as my blood evaporates from my veins.

By the time the Gilded reach the amphitheatre, hunting the one who broke into their hallowed halls, my bones are ash and my foot-prints have evaporated from the steel grate.

I step into the cool dark of Death, and this time, I will not walk alone.

Chapter Fourteen

There's no time to adjust to the slicing away of my heartbeat or the absence of air in my lungs. I hit the sand running, forcing my fear aside. Fog-wraiths are a complication I cannot afford with the Gilded after me.

Ignoring the slow parade of souls across the desert, I listen as I run, feeling for Mila's lifeline. She's another complication I can't afford. Grandmother will kill me, literally, if she discovers what I've done. Oh, Holy Dark Mother, what *have* I done?

The mists roar, and I wheel away from the veil toward the dark smudge where Lord Malin's manor awaits. And I'm not sure that's any better than the Gilded catching me. I'm keeping half my bargain by returning, but the other half, spying on the Warden—I have no idea how I'm going to fulfil that.

I hear someone cross with a rip of churning water. Another and another, and I itch to look back.

Don't look back!

The manor forms quicker than last time I was here. Maybe it's closer? I don't know how impossible buildings in Death work. I should have told Ella about my bargain with Malin; at least she'd know where I am if I don't come back. But hindsight is an exact science. It's easy to regret when consequences hit us in the face. And I'm pretty sure if I'd told Ella, I'd be regretting that right now instead.

The desert shifts and sighs. A dune erupts at my feet, throwing me off balance and sending me reeling backward. It rises, higher and higher until the manor vanishes. Armour clanks behind me, running boots shudder through the sand, and a spell murmurs on the absent air. I feel magic clutch at my skirts. Shit. The Gilded are manipulating Death itself to slow me.

Scrambling up a sand dune is difficult. Trying to climb one whose motives clash against mine is futile. As fast as I run, I slide back. Panic rocks my bones and I hear my mother whisper, *Smell a rose, Penny. Blow it away..*

Inhale.

Exhale.

There's no air, but it helps. With one final push, I scrabble to the top. The manor stretches out below, its grounds like a painter's palette abandoned on a dusty floor. Walls enclose a forest that seemingly has no end, and the portcullis is already open. A dark figure stands inside the entrance, arms folded, feet apart. Eyes pinned on me. Anger oozes from Lord Malin's stance, and I nearly crumble right there, but the ground lurches, tipping me off my feet and sending me sliding down the dune on my backside.

Sand grabs at me with fingers of Gilded magic, and I manage to slither to my feet without stopping, and then I'm there, tripping over Lord Malin's doorstep and landing on my knees on the grass at his feet. I'm making a habit of this. If he expects me on my knees every time I arrive, he's going to be sadly disappointed.

The portcullis slams down.

"Interesting arrival, Penelope," Lord Malin says in a velvet tone that amplifies the sandy mess that is me. "I strongly advise staying there and closing your eyes."

I have no intention of closing my eyes. Or staying here, kneeling at his feet. I try to stand, but the world spins. Rosebushes bordering the path lean closer and fold in on themselves. I squeeze my eyes shut and cling to the grass, my stomach lurching. The sound of crumpled paper fills my ears and the smell of spilled ink spirals up my nose.

My bones fold painlessly, my skin crinkles, and my hair twists close to my scalp.

Silence slices away the crumpled paper noise.

The world stills.

Lord Malin's voice drips with sarcasm. "Are all your arrivals going to be so dramatic, Penelope? If they are, it's going to make for an extremely long thirty nights."

"Twenty-nine," I reply, surprised my voice sounds so normal, that it doesn't hurt to talk, and I unpeel my eyelids, which seem to have been glued together in the maelstrom of...whatever the heck that was.

"Three Gilded were after you." He offers a hand, and I ignore it, clambering to my feet and stumbling backward, nearly trampling a recently unfolded rosebush. His lips twitch as I right myself. "I had to relocate, and relocation is inconvenient at best and downright annoying at worst."

"Is that what that was?" If he's moved us, how am I going to find my way back to the veil?

He inclines his head. "Indeed."

"Did they see me?"

"The Gilded? Who knows what those soulless creations of your High Warden see. They saw someone vanish in plain sight. I suspect they knew the someone was female. I couldn't tell you if they knew the someone was Penelope Albright, granddaughter of the infamous Thorn Queen. But they won't have seen my manor. And now I've relocated it, they won't have any idea it was ever there—if they're capable of ideas?"

He's asking me a question, and I have no idea how to answer. Silently, I shake my head.

"They aren't?"

"I'm not sure."

"Your sister was adamant they were."

"Ella?"

"How many sisters do you imagine I've had the pleasure of meeting? I'm not running a sanctuary for thorn witch failures—though I see how it might look that way." He raises one perfect, infuriatingly mocking eyebrow, and turns on his heel. "You're late, and our contract involved a report."

A path lined with roses meanders toward the front door, peach and pink and yellow blooms nodding their heads in an absent breeze. I swear they were red last time. Birdsong serenades our walk. Chirrups form a melody that sounds oddly familiar, sparking an uncanny sensation that I've experienced this before: this walk, the conversation we just had, the way the door opens before Lord Malin reaches the top of the white marble steps.

I halt at the bottom, unwilling to step inside his enchanted manor and risk falling under his spell like a princess in a fairy tale. I have to get back. If I vanished into nothingness like Lord Malin said, the Gilded will return to Life and report the violation—that they lost their target. They'll require the Thorn Coven to heal the veil. Grandmother will be involved. If they check my room and I'm not there, I'm ruined. The realisation slams into me so hard, I lean against the wall to catch my breath.

Lord Malin stares down from the doorway. "Are you coming inside?"

"Does our contract say I have to?"

"If you'd read it, you'd know it does not. You're stalling. Clumsily. You do have a report?"

I raise my chin and counter, "How far from the veil are we?"

"Answer my question, and I'll answer yours."

"Of course I have a report." I don't have a report.

"Then, we are precisely the same distance from the veil as I always am." He prowls down the steps, and I push away from the wall. "Exactly how did you pass into Death tonight?"

"You can have a report on the Warden or my methods of crossing the veil. Not both." I hold my ground as he reaches for my ghosted crystal hung on its chain. He pauses without touching it, so close the ice of his fingertips chills my skin. For one skip of my now disobediently beating heart, I want to lean into him.

Black eyes sparkle with a whisper of mirth. "Very well," he says so softly the fine hairs on the nape of my neck prickle with warning. "What information do you have on the High Warden?"

I try to repeat what I learned about the Resistance existing—surely an underground society aligned to remove the Warden from power would fulfil our deal for tonight. But it seems blood vows made in Life hold in Death. When I open my mouth, the words die in my throat. The dot in the crook of my elbow prickles, and my mind goes blank. Completely and utterly blank.

Lord Malin smiles. "Ticktock, Penelope. I thought you were in a hurry."

I am. I snatch at my conversation with Mila in the workrooms. "The veil is weakening," I reply, hating how quiet my voice is, how small I sound.

"Anyone with eyes can see that."

"The Warden is getting desperate. My grandmother too." I'm clutching at straws.

He catches my wrist and gently pushes the sleeve of Ella's sweater up, exposing the black rosebud mark. "This is not *information*. Do I need to provide a dictionary so you can look up the word?"

I silently run through everything I know about the Warden. There has to be something worth Lord Malin's time. Something that will stop his thumb tracing the inside of my wrist, so devastatingly gently it makes me want to admit defeat and beg to stay.

The memory of Alice's silk gives me the answer, and I wish I could hug her for her cleverness. She gave me exactly what I needed and I didn't see it. "He passed a new law this afternoon."

Malin's thumb freezes, hiding the mark. "Better. What law?"

"The council voted to lower the age of the gilding to sixteen."

He drops my wrist. "Tomorrow, I'd appreciate a less dramatic entrance, preferably without the Gilded in tow. Get closer to the Warden, Penelope. I need more than scraps from his table. I want the knife from his plate."

My temper spikes. "Our bargain was information. There was no clause about the quality. I could tell you he wore blue shoes this afternoon and still keep my end of it."

"Did you read the contract?"

I...didn't. And he knows it.

He snaps his fingers, and the portcullis rattles upward. "Don't you have somewhere more important to be?"

I do. But I'm too angry to back down. Angry at him for being so intolerably smug, at myself for not reading the contract and examining every clause. I have to do better than this. Malin folds his arms and stares at me with half a smile, mocking my indecision.

I turn and flee, out of his walls, across eerily silent desert sands, following my lifeline back to the veil. I chant the words to part the mists, glancing left and right to check Mila isn't close by, that no Gilded linger in Death. Crossing is softer tonight, easier—maybe I'm getting better at this. I imagine my bed, the grey blanket, the book on my bedside table, and my grey cotton nightdress.

I open my eyes as the door swings open and pretend to rub sleep from my eyes.

Carlotta stares at me and I can't read her expression. Before I can speak, she says, "There's been an incident. The veil tore—fog-wraiths swarmed the barracks. Mila's back; she's being questioned. Ella's with Grandmother."

My heart drops as I gape at her. This is my fault. The Gilded chasing me tore the veil. All my worrying about myself—*my* soul and Lord Malin, *my* facing the Gilded if I was caught—I never stopped to consider my sister on patrol in Death. "Mila's not hurt?" I croak.

"She's fine."

"How many wraiths?"

"Five. They've been dealt with. But..." She pauses, unhooking my nightrobe from the back of the door. "Someone used the eternal fires to cross. Everyone's been ordered to report to the barracks for roll call—the Gilded too."

"And we don't have time to get dressed?"

She lowers her voice to a whisper as she helps me into my nightrobe. "Anyone not there in the next five minutes will be under suspicion—I'd hate you to get found out." She knows. Of all the people to have caught me, it had to be Carlotta. When I fumble with my belt, my fingers numb from crossing, she ties it for me just a bit too tight and nudges me into the corridor. "You found Ella. Any fool could work that out. What I don't understand is why you crossed again. And why Grandmother can't see it. Where did you go, Penny?"

"I have no idea what you're talking about."

"Oh, I think you do." Thankfully, she drops it, but her eyes narrow as we step out of the corridor into the night.

It's still raining as we cross the courtyard beneath Alice's window. Her light is lit, a rectangle of warmth in the grimmest of nights. Her curtain twitches and a slice of brightness outlines her, fingers pressed against the glass, blonde hair shining. Our eyes meet through the rain, relief in hers, worry in mine, and she waves a tiny wave, her cuff glinting like a lighthouse beacon warning of rocks in a storm before she lets the curtain fall back.

The barracks grins in the dark, a skull's grin of missing teeth and hungry eyes. Carlotta leans closer as we walk inside and head toward the amphitheatre doors; rain drips off her hair onto my shoulder and our nighties are sodden. Where there were just my wet footsteps earlier, now dozens are marked by bare-footed thorn witches dragged from their beds and hundreds of Gilded boot prints melding into one slick of slippery floor.

Carlotta pats me on the shoulder, the picture of a reassuring cousin. "We can go back to bed soon."

If I was recognised as I fled across Death, I'll never go back to my own bed again.

A Gilded holds open the door and we step inside the amphitheatre. Seats that were empty before are filled with row upon row of half-masked faces. By the eternal fires, a Gilded with a whorl on his mask barks numbers from a roll of parchment that spills from his hands and curls around his steel-toed boots. Each number is answered by a rasp of metal and a raised gold-gauntleted hand.

One side of the arena is cluttered with exhibition apparatus; ten-foot-tall box frames with wheels attached and chains fixed to the spokes, a whipping post that can be bolted to the floor, and an assortment of coloured flags. Beside them stands the platform where the Warden sits on the rare occasion he makes a public appearance. His throne is empty tonight, but at the platform's base the Thorn Coven stand in bedraggled lines, grey nightrobes drenched black by the rain. We hurry to join them as the huge Gilded reads the number 237.

Silence answers.

He reads the number again. A thousand blank faces stare back. My skin crawls.

Eerie blue light shimmers on a Gilded's mask as he replies, "Unit two-three-seven is with the High Warden, as are the rest of his personal guard."

He makes a note on his parchment and continues barking out numbers. The Gilded who held open the door lets it swing shut and seals it with a huge metal beam that slots into place, barring our exit—no thorn witch could lift that beam to release us.

I swallow, and it tastes of fear. Using the eternal fires was a mistake. A huge one.

Carlotta laces her fingers through mine as the Gilded with the whorl on his mask marches toward us. Panic slips down my throat, wraps my ribs, and clenches tight.

Slowly, he paces our line. He asks for our names, one by one.

"Penelope Albright," I whisper when he reaches me.

"Have you left your quarters tonight, Penelope Albright?"

I shake my head and fix my eyes on the toes of his boots. They're polished so bright, the blue fires flicker in the sheen. A metal finger hooks under my chin and forces me to look at him. His eyes are silver but they are not dead. Not soulless. They narrow with distaste. I swallow and hold his gaze, forcing my heart to steady. I know him.

This Gilded, the monster with the whorl on his mask, is my father.

Logically, I know my father died the day they took half of his face, but seeing him hurts. Bitterly. He knows it, smiles a cold hard smile as he tilts my face to the left and then to the right. My breath catches somewhere below my throat. My imagination is tricking me, making me believe in the impossible because it's my father. Gilded don't smile.

His grip tightens on my chin. "Where were you when the curfew bell rang?"

"In bed." I swallow again, trying desperately not to tremble.

"Good girl," he says so softly, if I closed my eyes, I could imagine I'm a child again with my father lifting me to reach the cookie jar.

But I can't close my eyes. And this isn't my father anymore, it's a monster wearing his skin and talking in his voice. He releases me, and I want to crumple with relief. Carlotta gets the same treatment, her hand clamping tighter and tighter on mine as she answers his questions.

Seemingly satisfied, he leaves, giving me one last piercing stare before marching back to the Gilded gathered by the eternal fires and barking his final order. "See them back to their quarters and lock the doors. Release them in the morning."

Chapter Fifteen

Ella and I are on library duty this morning. We walk there in silence, heads bowed. I wonder if she knows I violated the Warden's eternal fires. She's thrown me more than one raised eyebrow since breakfast. She inhales as if she's about to ask a question, when a tap on my shoulder spins me around. "Shit," Ella hisses, the third time I've heard her swear in my life.

Beatrice grins, so uncomfortably close her elbow brushes mine. The scent of molten metal clings to leather breeches and a black shift tied with a yellow sash. She has a book clasped in one copper-nailed hand. I stare at her in astonishment—ore witches are not famous for their love of literature. "Found the Grimoire yet, little thorn witch?"

I shake my head and glance again at the book: *A Complete Illustrated Collection of Fables and Myths*. "You read?"

Beatrice's grin sharpens with offence. "You think we can't? The *exalted thorns* flounce around acting superior; at least our coven queen didn't jump into bed with the Warden the first chance she saw." Her words sting: That's not what I thought at all. I was just surprised to see a full-grown witch with a storybook. Beatrice throws an exasperated glance at Ella. "Sort your sister out. She'll get short shrift from the others with an attitude like that."

"I just wondered what you were reading...I don't think...I didn't..." I falter under Beatrice's copper-eyed stare.

"Thorn witches never think," she says mockingly, and stalks off down the corridor without looking back.

I turn to Ella and find her exactly as exasperated. "That's not how to make friends."

"I didn't mean...None of the thorn witches read. It was a surprise, that's all."

"As was her reading material." Ella frowns and tugs me toward the library. "Beatrice is worried; we all are. Grandmother's decisions are vile and they taint us all."

Ella's not being entirely fair. Grandmother has done some questionably awful things, but she made hard choices so that we didn't have to. "She protected us!"

"She protected herself and her crown, Penny. If you can't see that—"

"Of course I can see that, everyone can see that, but it was for the coven too." As far as I'm concerned, they're the same thing, the crown, the throne, the coven. Aren't they? I grasp at anything to say in her defence. "She's helping witches hide down in the city, did Mila tell you?"

Ella scoffs. "Grandmother's been doing that for years. It's nothing new. All the covens are in on it. Gives us access to the black market. You can be so naive. Where else do you think our gingerweed supply comes from?"

I bite back a retort at being called naive. I'm trying to build bridges, not burn them. "She's our grandmother. Father said to respect her. He made us promise, Els. Before he—"

"Before what? Before we lost him? Before he gave up on us and escaped into oblivion?" There's anger simmering in her voice. "Whatever promise we made Father back then is beside the point. There's nothing of Grandmother left to respect. Unless we stand against her, we're as bad as she is."

"I did stand against her! And you stopped me joining the Resistance!"

She pulls me into step beside her, hurrying toward the library before we're marked as late. "I was trying to help you, but last night you made it damned impossible."

My anger is rising to match hers, tired of her nonanswers. "Why don't you tell me what the heck you want me to do then, Ella?"

"It's so far past what anyone wants, Pen." She squeezes my elbow lightly. "The Warden's put the Gilded on patrol in Death. Once a week."

I freeze, and she jerks to a stop next to me. "But... that risks the veil."

Ella sighs. "Which is why Beatrice is on edge. All the covens are concerned. The thorns aren't the only ones worried about the veil, though to hear Grandmother, you'd be forgiven for thinking so." She watches me carefully, considering. "By rights, I should tell the Resistance."

"Tell them what?"

She taps me on the elbow, right where the little black freckle marks my oath of silence. "About where I think the Grimoire is. About the colour of your crystal. They'd love to know about that."

I stare at her as she propels us forward again. She can't trust them that much, can she? Ella wouldn't tell them about me.

She shakes her head in frustration and drops her voice as we reach the connecting corridor between the spokes of the wings. "Of course I wouldn't actually tell them. There's a word in the spell they're using, the one that got Haylea caught in the veil last year, that they think is about a black crystal. Which is why I was trying to find the original spell, in the original Grimoire, *before* I involved you in any of this."

I wince at Ella's casual mention of our cousin's death, biting my lip to stop myself snapping. I know she misses Haylea as much as I do. Then, the pieces click into place, and my eyes widen. "You believe the Grimoire is on the Ninth." Ella spins on her heels and stalks away without answering. I follow. "Ella..."

She cuts me off. "Stop."

"Tell me I'm wrong?"

She shakes her head. "Penny, leave it."

But I can't leave it. "It's on the Ninth."

"It might be." Ella pulls me closer to the wall and ducks behind a tapestry depicting the fall of the Sorcerer from the Dark Mother's grace. "Whatever happened to the Sorcerer of Halstett, our library was his. People forget that. He built it book by book and wove magic into the stones deep under the Colligerate. I think he hid his magic books on the Ninth and spelled an impressive ward to keep people out, complete with little shadowy sentinels with luminous green eyes to scare us away."

I hide a shiver, remembering the green lights that knew my name, that occupied the elevator and winked between the shelves. "You've seen them too?"

Ella nods and her cheeks flush pink. "They started appearing after I first walked. Mostly at night, darting between the shelves, lurking behind books. One won't stop moving the bookmark in the spell book I'm trying to read. I think it's book sprites."

I narrow my eyes. "You believe in book sprites?"

"Legends live in libraries. They were here long before Halstett was the only spark of life in the ashes of a continent." She frowns. "That's what Miss Elsweather said."

"But Miss Elsweather knows the library inside out; if the Grimoire was here, she'd know about it."

"She doesn't know the Ninth, Pen. No one does."

I ponder Ella's words. Wherever the Sorcerer of Halstett is, however the Grimoire and the spell to forge the knife came to be lost, she's right that the ninth floor of the library is the most likely place we'll find anything to help us.

And I think I know how to get there. With the Gilded now on night patrol in the Colligerate, we can't risk breaking curfew, but I have another way. A ridiculous one. It's a horrible idea. But, I think it will work. I'm just not sure I'm brave enough to do it alone. "We need to try again, to get to the Ninth."

Ella looks like she wants to argue, but she doesn't. "Together?" she offers.

"Together," I reply.

Until recently, life was simple even if it wasn't what I dreamed it would be. I long for sunshine and moonlight and a weather system not controlled by a tyrant, a future not contained within Halstett's walls. But those aren't choices I can make.

Since the grey wastes reached the edge of our village and the Gilded shattered our wards, dragging us to the *safety* of Halstett, I've done everything I was ordered. I've collected blood to register witches, built pyres and helped my coven burn, studied hard at my lessons and tended Mother's glass-enclosed poison garden, worked in the library and kept my head down and my mouth mostly shut. I might not have agreed with it, I might have questioned when I shouldn't, but I followed the rules. I faced my fate and prepared to walk in Death the day I turned twenty-one.

Now—now, I've signed a contract with my soul as collateral for my sister's life and I'm entangled with a Resistance I didn't believe existed until two nights ago. Suddenly, I wish I could knock on Alice's painted door and ask her for the answers I can't find the right questions to.

I sigh and dust wafts from the mythology book lying open in Ella's lap. We're supposed to be shelving returned books on the second floor, but fairy tales full of twisted magic, book sprites, and princesses fighting for their lives don't make great company today. To add an extra layer of discomfort, Miss Elsweather simply watched us for the first part of our shift, choosing a worn leather chair beside a glass lamp and opening a book on the table next to her without looking at it once.

As soon as Miss Elsweather's attention turned elsewhere, Ella vanished to the reference section, a row of shelves that takes the magic of fairy stories and drains it, each book as bone-dry as the skulls in the catacombs below the Colligerate. She returned with a faded tome, at least a year's worth of dust on the cover. In a magical library, it takes a lot of effort to find a book as unloved as this one.

Ella smooths a hand gently across the page and settles back on her knees beside me. Her fingertips trace the colour plate, rainbowed stained-glass roses painted across the thicker inserted paper. "How much do you remember?"

Her question could mean so many things so I stay quiet and wait, not wanting to disturb the softness of her eyes. A dreamlike mist of memories stills Ella's finger on the point of a thorny-stemmed rose in the picture. "I thought they were made up. The Gilded. I thought they were monsters that Grandmother hid under the bed to stop us going out at night, like the mud beast Father told us stories of to keep us away from the estuary flats. Do you remember the morning the monsters became real?"

"I remember, Els," I reply. "The fog and the blood and the screams. The silence."

Ella nods, relief in her eyes, and slowly, tentatively, she turns the page of the book in her lap. Tucked between the pages is a sheet of notepaper, faded pink and with the lines of an erased flora diagram indented into it, belladonna maybe before she rubbed it out. Ella's handwriting criss-crosses the paper. She passes it to me and quietly waits for me to read.

At the top is the date, the day before Ella's twenty-first birthday two years ago. Before her first walk in Death. Beneath it, she's written: *I refuse to forget.* Then comes her tale, in such pretty handwriting, delicate with a precise slant that jars against the brutality of her words.

> *They came with the morning mist.*

I don't want to read this. I don't want to see the fog stained red with fire. Our estuary filled with gold-edged steel in the rising winter sun.

But I also don't want to forget any more than Ella did when she wrote it.

> *The first scream was muffled. It came from the edge of the village. It was damp, that scream, damp and broken and over before it began. He was lucky, Aunt Shara said afterward. He died in his own bed in a cottage his grandfather had built from solid oak boards smoothed with a plane. His husband died beside him, murdered by the same knife. The hand that held the knife was gold. Aunt Shara told me that too. She refused to tell me his name.*
>
> *The second and third screams came together. They cut off together too, and the silence after was worse. We watched, me and Mila, as fire cracked in straw thatching and licked witch-warded clay walls on the edge of the woods. Penny hid her face in Mila's shoulder. She was only eight. No one should see their*

family and friends burned slowly, alive. Not at eight. Not at ten either. Or twelve, like Mila was.

I can't forget like Mila has either. How did she forget?

Remember, Ella. Remember how the silence broke with the rising chant of our spell. Voices joined from inside huts and doors swung wide, the coven greeting the threat of attack. The sentries died quickly, caught off guard. Their souls stepped neatly from the flames as their bodies charred into ash and dust. They didn't come back. I knew they couldn't even as I watched them die. No one breaks the first rule of Death and survives it.

Remember the crack when the Gilded shattered the wards. The ground trembled and shook as if the mountains beyond the forest split clean in two. An oak tree snapped. Remember the inferno the Gilded unleashed upon us, familiar ember magic twisted into something vile, the choking bitter sweetness of the smoke. Remember those who died so we might survive.

I heard the veil that morning, from the doorway of our cottage. Death came so close to Life, its roar was deafening. I didn't hear it again until the burning tonight. I wonder if Pen heard it too? Did Mila? Or Haylea and Carlotta? They say they didn't. So why did I?

I press a nail into the page there so hard Ella's fingers twitch to protect the memories she committed to the safekeeping of paper and ink two years ago.

"You heard the veil?" I whisper.

Her bottom lip sucks in between her teeth, her eyes harden from mercury to steel. "You didn't?"

"I...I don't know."

"You should write it down. Everything you want to keep safe. Before you walk." I look at her and she adds, "Again."

"Does Mila ever talk about it?" I ask quietly.

"Does anyone?" Ella shoots back. And she's right. No one talks about that morning. Ever. It's a topic as off-limits as Father being Gilded. "Read the rest. I need someone else to see it, just in case...if anything happens to me."

Nothing can happen to her. I won't let it.

"Read it, Pen." Ella grabs a book to shelve from the trolley beside her. "Please."

Ella's writing is visceral—it forces me to taste the smoke, feel the heat, relive the destruction. I need to breathe, steady myself before I read any more, solidify my own memories in the face of hers.

Before it was razed to the ground, my village protected its children, preserving our naivety as best they could, for as long as they dared, but I remember the day they stopped shielding us. I was seven.

Grandmother returned from the Witch Queens' Council and summoned us to assemble before the Thorn Shrine. Danger was creeping closer, she said. Unstoppable. An army made of gold.

I listened from my aunt's knee while my parents sat with Grandmother and the senior coven members on a platform at the entrance to the shrine. The closest ember coven was retreating behind wards on their walls, she told us, the ore witches descending deep into magic-sealed caves. All the covens were locking themselves away. We'd never welcomed strangers, but now we were suddenly forbidden to leave.

Dust storms raged out of the forests as covens inland fell to Gilded control. Ember and ore magic burned green land and transformed fertile soil to grey desert sand. Tide and storm magic drained the water from the rivers and withheld the rains at the Warden's command. The thorns handed him the greatest gift of all: an army that would not die.

We knew none of that, not then. All we knew was what Grandmother told us: The danger would pass. This was not our war. We were safe inside the village. But the wind carried a heat that was a sign of what was yet to come.

My father wove the wards. We watched, my sisters and cousins and me, clutching our crystals, open-mouthed as silver-thorned magic threaded across the clay bricks of our walls. From that day forward, none left our village. And none stepped inside its gates alive.

Until the Gilded came.

I swallow and face Ella's writing again.

Death was supposed to be a desert. It was meant to be an end. For us, it came on a tide of sharp steel under a banner of silver and gold. The Thorn Queen watched it approach, she saw her wards fall, and she stood on the steps of her shrine and let us all burn. Mutilated witches with half-golden faces tore my father from Mother's arms. Grandmother pulled out a matchbox as her eldest son died, drew out a match as Father fell to a gold-plated fist, and shut the box as my mother and aunts were dragged away, my cousins shoved into carriages borne by terrifyingly huge birds with golden cuffs around their legs. Silently, my family accepted their fate.

Mila fought it. She tried to get us out. She denies it now, and I have no idea why. Last time I mentioned it, she refused to speak to me for a week. But I remember. I think Father hid the boat. It was buried beneath dead branches and protected by a ward Penny's crystal unlocked. It took all three of us together to get it into the water. Only Penny made it inside.

The Gilded who caught me was an ember witch once, eyes void of emotion behind her half-mask of gold. She set the boat on fire as Mila tried desperately to set it free. The Gilded who caught Mila was a tide witch; he brought the boat crashing into the bank. I didn't see who captured Penny, but I heard my mother scream when they did.

Grandmother watched it all, surrounded by ten brutes like statues of solid gold. She closed her eyes for a moment, just a moment, breathed in the stench of her burning world, and set herself aflame.

She crossed as we were taken away. I watched her go. I watched the Gilded go after her. And then I don't remember any more.

Grandmother chose Death over her coven, Father chose gilding over me, Mila chose the coven over us. Tomorrow, I face Death, and I will not leave Penny alone.

We can choose each other over the Warden's regime. But if I take that path, there's something I must do. I can't trust anyone else: Grandmother is in the Warden's pocket, Mila lives in Grandmother's shadow, Mother will never stand against either. There's only one direction I can turn. Summon the dark. Surrender the light.

Ella signed it with a flourish of an *E* and a tiny picture of a rose on a stem made of thorns.

I blink back tears as I look at my sister. "You joined the Resistance for me?"

She won't look at me, her bottom lip is still between her teeth, and she slides the notepaper back between the pages, closes the book. The title stares at both of us, accusing us with its irony. *An Examination of Thematic Communication in Mythology.* "The most boring book I could find," Ella says with a wobbly smile. "No one missed it. I hid it between the shelves. I was never going to show anyone."

She stands and hurries away, leaving me alone on my knees in a library full of book sprites. My heart thuds out of time as I glance around. But no eyes peer from the bookcases, no shadowy figures hide beneath the desks or whisper on the stairs. I sigh with relief, feeling childish for allowing myself to be so easily scared.

When I turn back to the trolley of books we were supposed to be shelving, there's only one there. And it's wide open. I didn't leave it like that. I stiffen and look around again, but I'm still alone; there's no one nearby who might have moved it. Gingerly, I pick it up, mark the page with one finger, and check the cover: *An Alphabetical Guide to Magical Mythos.* So many fairy tales seem to be coming true, the pages of a mythology book seems as likely a place as any to find answers. I flick back to the colour plate, a picture of a bookcase covered in shadowy forms with little green eyes peeping mischievously from between the tomes.

A book falls over on the shelf beside me. I jump half out my skin, but there's nothing there. I swallow hard and quickly read the entry on book sprites. Tiny sentinels of ancient libraries. *A rainbow of sparkling colour if you know how to see*, the myth says, *if your eyes are open wide.*

I saw the manor in Death clearly enough. Malin confirmed the Gilded can't. And no thorn witch has come across it on patrol except Ella.

I wonder how my eyes were opened—how Ella's were.

The first night I walked and woke on the eighth floor there were little lights too. The light that swarmed down the elevator and broke Miss Elsweather's door the other night might have been book sprites protecting their territory?

Still holding the book, I rest my arms on my knees and my head in my arms, taking a moment of peace where I can. It feels like I haven't stopped thinking in days, and only the Dark Mother knows where I might find another chance to pause. Book sprites might inhabit the library, but this is my place too. Maybe I'll hear them again if I'm quiet.

Dark Mother Creation Story

At first, she was just a thought floating in a nothing that was made of everything that came before and all that once might be. She rested in the silence, a moment of wonder in an absence of time, and in the quiet, her thoughts grew deep. In a void of black nothing she imagined light. Stars prickled the darkness, pinpricks of something that lit a land beneath her feet. She pictured sunshine and clouds, forests and streams, and the land moulded to her will. Oaks erupted from fertile soil, mountains rose into the blue-painted sky, and flowers opened petals to the sun. Her laugh was the morning, her sigh grew into autumn on a wind she created with a wave of her hand. She wore rainbows in her hair and moonlight in her eyes and skirts spun from fog off the sea. But she was lonely. And so, she created him, and together they populated the world with the magic of their dreams.

The Mother of Creation: Fairy Tales for Young Readers. *Retrieved from the library of the Thorn Shrine in the fifteenth year after the fall. Author: Unknown.*

Chapter Sixteen

My eyes fly open as boots turn onto the second-floor landing and stop by my side. Palace guard boots. I stare at them a moment, not moving while I collect myself. Alice said she wouldn't summon me today, but maybe she changed her mind. I glance up at the palace guard, her grey tunic trimmed with silver, a dagger belted at her hip.

I silently shelve the book before pushing to my feet. "The Spinner?"

She doesn't answer, just turns away, and I abandon our trolley to hurry after her, out of the library and into morning-quiet corridors.

We're still in the corridor to the Warden's palace when she suddenly shoves me through a doorway and steps forward to bar my escape. It's a classroom, unused, windows still shuttered after the storm last night. Desks with hinged lids and little individual ink-wells are shoved into a shadowed corner, chairs haphazardly piled around them.

A flame flickers to life in an inkwell. And another and another. Ink burns like little candles, brightening the gloom and illuminating two figures lurking there.

The door locks with an ominous click, and I backstep into the palace guard's metal-clad chest. She steadies me with a hand on my arm, and I forget who she is. Forget what she can do if I defy her. "You said I was going to see Alice!"

"No, Penny. You said that, not me." She gives me half a smile. "Alice told you her name. I wondered if she would."

I'd step away from her, but our daily walks to Alice's rooms have earned her a shred of trust. Trust that's in danger of tearing apart right now, but she's safer than whoever is waiting in the shadows.

She sticks out a hand and I flinch. "My name's Clair."

"I don't care. Let me go."

"You should care. The Warden takes names. Strips us of them. Hold on to yours." She takes my hand, shakes it gently, and I'm so aware of the figures lingering in the shadows, I cling tighter than I should to her fingers.

It makes her real. Clair. A person, not a number stamped on a silver breastplate. She's the girl in the closet the night I stole the matches, smelling of jasmine and laundry soap, hiding her secrets as I try so hard to hide mine. I'm not sure I like it. "Now you've told me your name—which I can never use—will you let me go?"

Clair shakes her head. "I can't do that."

Footsteps shuffle behind me. I spin around, snatching my hand from Clair's.

Evelyn, the unblinking ember witch, swings a chair out of the corner and thuds it into the floor. "We need to talk."

Beatrice smiles, sharp as a knife. "Without your sister interfering."

Evelyn pulls three more chairs out and sets them in a cosy circle. "As much as I love Ella, when it comes to you, Penny, she's a pain in the arse."

This is not a conversation I want to have. I shift my weight backward, considering the door key curled in Clair's fingers. If I time it right, I could snatch it and run. Then, Clair says the one thing I do not want to hear. "The Gilded know you broke into the barracks last night."

"Shit." My heart stalls. I need to get out of here. I need to warn Ella before they come for me. I stare at Clair, at Beatrice slipping to her side as if it might take two of them to stop me escaping. "How?"

"They saw you," Evelyn says. "You left drips all over their floor. Did you truly think they wouldn't find out who it was?"

"Well..." I stutter to a halt as Evelyn raises an eyebrow. Her eyes are scathing, her irises bright with fire, and the challenge in her glare wakes my temper. "The fact I'm not in the Gilded dungeons rather implies that they had not."

Evelyn's glare burns brighter, Beatrice chokes on a laugh, and Clair says quietly, "Sit down, Penny."

I take a chair opposite the one smouldering beneath Evelyn's grip. "If they know it was me, why haven't they arrested me?"

Clair sits down between me and the door. "Toby intervened. You're lucky he's the one who received the report. He delayed it, bought you as much time as he can, but it's about to run out."

"Who the hell is Toby?" I shake my head. "Actually, don't answer that. I don't need to know. Just say what you brought me here to say so I can—"

Evelyn cuts me off. "So you can what? Skip off into Death? Carlotta told us all about your night-time excursions across the veil. What are you doing there?"

Beatrice kicks the leg of Evelyn's chair. "We're supposed to be convincing her, not interrogating her!" She exchanges an odd glance with Clair and picks at an emerald decorating the back of her hand with a copper nail as she turns to me. "Look, your grandmother is an insufferable—"

Clair catches Beatrice's wrist and yanks her down to sit. "Insulting her grandmother won't convince her either."

Beatrice grins, her eyes sparkling. "I'm not saying anything she doesn't know! Ella's brilliant, but the Thorn Queen is—ow, stop squeezing my arm!" She twists free and throws a gentle punch at Clair's shoulder.

"I get it," I say, snaring their attention again. "My grandmother is insufferable and terrifying. Ella's overprotective, and Mila's a—"

"Bitch?" Evelyn grins.

I narrow my eyes. "Watch it, she's still my sister."

Beatrice coughs. "Clare's right, we're not here to insult Penny's family." She turns the full force of her copper gaze on me and asks quietly, "Why are you crossing the veil?"

I was hoping she'd clarify the purpose of their ambush. "I... well, the Warden's lifeline fuels it," I stammer. "And the Warden's sickening, so my coven..." I trail off.

Obviously dissatisfied with my answer, Beatrice shakes her head. "Where do you go when you cross?"

I shrug. "Death! It's right on the other side of the veil. You want me to recite the creation myths? How the veil separates Life and Death? If I'd known that, I'd have grabbed the book for you on my way out of the library."

Evelyn rolls her eyes. "I suppose your version says the Dark Mother favoured the thorns and blessed your coven above all others with magic crystals and the power to cross the veil."

That is, in fact, what I'd been told. But I'm not giving her the satisfaction of confirming it.

Unfortunately, my confusion must show on my face, because Evelyn dissolves into the kind of unrestrained laughter she doesn't look capable of. "Gosh, what a pile of bollocks," she manages.

Irritation clenches my fingers tight together in my lap. Clair tricked me into coming here and told me the Gilded know I trespassed in their halls, and now, Evelyn's mocking me. Anger bubbles under my ribs, chilling when Clair fiddles uncomfortably with one end of the key, reminding me I cannot leave. "While I'm thrilled I could entertain you, whatever this bullshit is, will you spit it out and let me leave? I'm done here," I say coldly.

Beatrice's gaze hardens, her irises shining coppery bright.

Evelyn doubles over laughing, and the inky candle flames jump from the inkwells, scattering across the desk. Beatrice kicks Evelyn's leg this time. "Honestly, Ev! Stop." Beatrice shakes her head as the flames skip back to their inkwells, then looks at me kindly. "Ignore her. We're all taught some version of the same: Our coven is different, better than the others, chosen in some way."

I stare at her. "Why?"

"Why what?" Beatrice asks, confused.

"Why are you giving me a history lesson instead of explaining why I'm here?"

Beatrice opens her hand and a poison vial lies in her palm. "Keep your secrets, I don't blame you. But you wouldn't be going to so much trouble if you didn't have a very good reason. Miss Elsweather might be too nice to blackmail you, but I'm not. You want an easy crossing, join the Resistance. The Grimoire is in Death and we need you to find it."

That's not what Ella believes. "What do you actually know about Death?" I ask.

Beatrice opens her mouth and closes it. Clair's brow creases. Evelyn blinks slowly.

"Death is a desert. The only place to hide a book would be to bury it beneath the sand, and if someone did that, there's zero chance we'll find it again. There's nothing there."

"If there's nothing there, what's worth risking the eternal fires and the Gilded to get to, Penny? That's the real question," Evelyn says, not laughing now. "The first time was for Ella. But what about after that?"

I continue on as if I hadn't heard her. "If the Grimoire exists, surely it's hidden in the library with the rest of the spell books?"

"Miss Elsweather's catalogued the entire contents of the library. Twice," Clair answers. "Once for the Warden and once for the Resistance. If it was in the library, she'd have found it—unless it's on the Ninth and then we're shit out of luck. We'll never get it."

But I only meant to distract them. The minute Beatrice offered the poison, I was always going to agree—I just didn't want them to know quite how desperately I need it. "Ella will kill me," I whisper.

Beatrice says nothing, just holds out the vial.

Evelyn seals the deal. "Ella doesn't have to know."

I pretend to ponder it for a moment, before offering a jerky nod. "Where do I sign?"

A sly smile creeps across Evelyn's lips. "You don't have to sign, thorn witch, just drinking the poison tonight will do. You accept our offering and our terms, and you're bound to the Resistance as tight as the rest of us. And once it's done, there's nothing Ella can do about it."

There's plenty Ella can do. They clearly don't know her as well as they think. I force a smile and hold out my hand for the vial. Beatrice passes it over, and a wave of relief hits me. I can burn tonight.

But then I remember I might not even see tonight. The Gilded know I broke into their barracks; I won't be safe in Halstett for long.

Clair holds me back as Beatrice and Evelyn leave. They're less scathing with their goodbyes than they were with their hellos. "I tried to tell you," Clair says when they've gone.

"Tell me what?"

"In the cupboard, the other night. I tried to tell you I was with the Resistance. I've felt awful ever since, that I didn't make it clearer." She pushes a folded square of silk into my hand. "From Alice. She said it would help. Summon the dark, Penny."

Chapter Seventeen

Night has fallen and I'm back in my room after the coven's nightly burning. I unfold Alice's silk square for the hundredth time since Clair handed it to me. She's given me information to pass to Malin, a picture of a Gilded with a whorl on his mask and the words *The mark gives them more power* embroidered across the top. That's a concern in and of itself, but it's not what makes me reluctant to cross into Death tonight. It's what's written on the piece of parchment Alice tacked to the square with a single gold-threaded stitch.

The path you've set your feet on has one end—mine. Be careful, Penny. Always. Alice.

What does she mean, her end? Does she mean she'll die? Or that I'll end up in the same position as her? If only she wasn't so cryptic. If only I could ask.

If only... those two words are plaguing my life.

The curfew bell rings and I'm out of time.

Quietly, I tuck the silk in my pocket and roll back the grey rag rug covering my bedroom floor, trying not to think about cleaning my ashes off the stone later. Maybe I can just cover them. I uncap the vial, take a tiny sip, and roll it under the bed. I hold tight to Alice's silk as I cross, hoping I get it right, that I can take it across the veil and make it reform as I do.

Fire races through my veins, scorches me from the inside out. I burn, again, but this time, I step into Death's waiting silence with gratitude and Alice's silk in my pocket. I'm safer here than I am in Halstett. As I approach the manor gates, I feel closer to home than I have in years.

To my utter horror, tears prickle my eyes.

Lord Malin waits, a silhouette against the light of his gardens, arms folded, feet apart. He's wearing a suit, charcoal brocade patterned with a deeper shade of dark. His jacket is open, revealing a black shirt with the top buttons undone, and a gold-hilted dagger hangs at one hip. "Not brought your friends along? That's quite an improvement."

My tears dry.

The portcullis clattering shut hides my sniff, and when Malin stalks off down the path, I make a rude gesture at his back. I think he chuckles, though I have no idea how he can see what I did.

The gardens are a riot of colour around us; velvet-purple roses nod in a gentle summer breeze, pink gladioli stand proud beside red-hot pokers, flowers as scarlet as their name suggests.

Malin pauses at the bottom of the steps, one eyebrow infuriatingly raised. "Are you coming inside, Penelope?"

"My name is Penny."

"That isn't an answer."

I want to tell him that he can stick his question where the sun doesn't shine, but there's no real sunshine in Death, just a light as mysterious as he is. So, I nod, and he smiles as if he won a game I didn't realise we were playing. In the entry hall, he waits for me to remove my cloak without speaking, merely watching as I hang it on a hook. Then, he clicks his fingers, the door shuts with a snick of a lock, and when he speaks again, his voice is as velvet soft as the roses in his garden. "You came back."

I had no choice, yet he sounds as relieved as I felt when I stepped into Death.

Before I can respond, he vanishes through the same door as the first night—now with a different room behind it. "Sit down."

I ignore the sharpness of his order, chalk it up to Malin being an arrogant arsehole, and pick a squishy red armchair by the window, taking my time to tuck my feet up and drink in the colour. Pale lemon flowers drift along the wallpaper above cherrywood panelling. The fireplace is rose marble, images of legends in bas-relief carved up each side; the Sorcerer and the farm boy, the rose and the princess murdered with a single thorn, book sprites guarding a spire—and tiny crystals are etched into stone around the edges, glittering red and yellow, purple and green and blue.

On the mantelpiece, six flamingos in the most vivid pink I've ever seen stand on one leg all attached to the same plinth. A gold-framed mirror hangs above, reflecting sunshine streaming through airy voile curtains and bouncing light around the room.

Malin doesn't move as I take in his décor, and when I glance at him, I realise I'm smiling. But he's all business, and my smile falters as he meets my eyes. His gaze burns hotter than the flames of any pyre. My cheeks heat in response.

"I assume you have information on the Warden?" Malin's voice is steady and calm, no trace of the confusion he's sparking in me; my blood doesn't know whether to run hot or cold.

"Better," I reply, making my smile bright and my tone brighter. "I brought you a picture." I hold out Alice's silk square. I left her note tucked under my mattress.

He stiffens and snatches the silk from my hand. But he's gentle as he unfolds it, almost reverent. I try not to notice the elegance of his fingers.

He examines it in taut silence. "You've done well," he finally says.

"Is that a compliment?"

"An observation."

"I'm taking it as a compliment."

"Take it as you will." He folds neatly into the armchair by the fireplace, leather squeaking in protest as he settles, and spreads Alice's silk over one knee. "Where did you get this?"

I'm not telling him about Alice. "A palace guard."

He tilts his head. "You stole from a guard?"

I think of how Clair fooled me this morning and use her method, shrugging as if it's nothing. Not lying. Not telling the truth. "Have I met the dictionary definition of information this time?"

"Indeed." He stares at me, and I want to shrink back, make myself smaller somehow. "You're really quite intriguing, Penelope."

"Penny," I say, trying to make the set of my shoulders match his. "My name is Penny, not Penelope."

He ignores me and runs a fingertip over the words on Alice's silk. "Do you know what this means?"

I have no damned idea. I'm sure he's aware of that too. "I assume it means what it says. The Warden is making stronger Gilded, which we could do without. They're awful already."

"It means your Warden is using magic he shouldn't be."

"He's not *my* Warden. Will you stop calling him that?"

"The implications..." Malin's muttering now, forgetting I'm here. I wonder if he's losing his mind with loneliness. "...the risks. Waking the Sorcerer's power—using it—" His attention snaps to me, and I bite back a gasp. His eyes seem even darker now, fathomless. "Has he stepped inside the library?"

"I...no. Not for years," I manage.

"His Gilded?"

I shake my head and glance at the window, wishing I could escape through it.

His gaze slips to my crystal. "If your Warden—" He pauses. "If *the*

Warden happens to take an unusual interest in the library, I should very much like to know about it."

I preferred him as an arsehole. At least then I knew where I stood. "Will that count as information?"

"It will. Now, would you like a cup of tea before you go, or are you in a hurry to return?" I'm not sure it's as simple an offer as he makes it sound. Nothing about him is simple.

The truth is, I want a cup of tea. I want to wander through his gardens, lie in the grass, let the scent of the flowers wash over me. Perhaps read a book. But his gaze trails along my collarbone and my skin tingles in silent reply. I bite my lip, trying to hide the hitch of my inhale. I can't spend another moment with the confusion of him—not without saying something I'll regret. "I should go."

"As you will." He stands and offers a hand to help me to my feet. I ignore it. A suggestion of a laugh flares his nostrils, and he gently grabs my elbow as I go to leave. I freeze like a startled rabbit. "If this is true—" He hands me Alice's silk. "This will end rather horribly if you venture onto the Ninth, Penelope. The Sorcerer's magic should not be disturbed. Promise me...promise you will not go near the ninth floor." He sounds like he's worried. About me.

I answer in a voice I mean to be strong, but his thumb runs softly down the inside of my elbow and it comes out shaky. "Is that in our contract?"

He laughs and folds my fingers around Alice's silk. "Remind me next time you're here and I'll let you read it." And he's back to the smooth, arrogant Lord of the Manor. His eyes meet mine, and this time I do gasp. Silver flecks his irises, a starry ring of magic circles the midnight of his gaze. Death-walking magic. A sea of bright constellations, not a void of endless night. I shut my eyes, unsure of what I'm seeing.

"Penelope," he says too softly, too carefully.

When I open my eyes, he's standing so close his exhale lifts a hair on my cheek. Ice slithers down my spine and I see his shoulders stiffen.

I step back, but his hand clamps around my wrist. I'm a moth with its wings stretched wide and a taxidermy pin poised over its heart.

Malin is lethally still, his grip on me unbreakable, but there's a softness to the hard line of his lips and a tic to his stubble-dark jaw. The birds stop singing. The flowers deepen their petals and turn their faces away from the glowering sky.

Fear binds my ribs, attempting to silence me. "Who are you?" It comes out a whisper.

He cocks his head to the side just a little, an inhuman awareness sharpening his silver-shifting eyes. "How, Penelope, has it taken you so long to revisit such a vital question?"

I open my mouth, close it again, and clamp my teeth together to stop my bottom lip from wobbling.

"More to the point," he continues, his tone low and hypnotic, "what, I wonder, makes you ask again tonight?"

He pulls my arm toward him, turns my wrist over, and rolls the little braided bracelet Ella gave me away from the black rosebud marked on my skin. Delicately, he traces the petals, the stem and each thorn, his touch so light I barely feel it at all and yet, it's all I can feel. He fills my awareness so completely there is no room for anything but him and his caress, his breath on my skin, his fingers on my arm. I inhale and the scent of him is overwhelming, midnight rain tangled around dark chocolate and bitter almonds. Where before was only fear, now there is longing—intoxicating and sweet and…

"Stop," I whisper. And it takes everything in me to close my eyes and break the hold he has over me. "Malin." Louder this time. "Stop."

His fingers still and he steps back, holding me at arm's length like a curious fish he hooked from a stream. "Who do you think I am?"

I focus on the hollow at the base of his throat, a scar marked there in the shape of a crescent moon. "I have no idea..." I falter. So much has happened since the night I signed our contract, I've not thought much beyond his reassurance that he's not the Sorcerer.

He's watching me as if I might run. As if he'll never see me again if I do.

I feel so young and stupid and abominably tired. "Were you telling the truth before? You aren't the Sorcerer?"

Malin's expression is unreadable. "Go home, Penelope."

"Who are you, Malin?"

His voice roughens at the edges. "I'm not a sorcerer of any kind. You don't need to be frightened of that."

"I'm not frightened!" I snap.

"No," he replies. "I suppose you aren't." He pauses, shakes his head as if clearing his thoughts. "Go home. Stay away from the Ninth. And tomorrow, don't be late."

Malin releases my arm. I don't care anymore who he is or what he thinks of me; I turn and flee, clutching Alice's silk tight in one fist. His laughter follows me all the way to his portcullis and out across the deserts to the veil.

I take an enormous amount of satisfaction in holding the staircase to the Ninth in my mind as I cross. I'm fed up of not being in control.

I'm going to the Ninth to find the Sorcerer's Grimoire for myself.

Chapter Eighteen

I wake in a crumpled ball on the eighth floor as the bell in the Colligerate clock tower sounds some unholy hour. The stairs to the Ninth yawn into darkness above.

Steeling myself, I clamber to my feet and peer down the stairs toward the Seventh, listening to the quiet of books sleeping on their shelves in the thin moonlight, the absence of page-muffled sound. On the Eighth, darkness thickens, grim and foreboding. Shadows flicker, though no one moves.

Glittering eyes peep from the back of bookcases.

Book sprites. I'm sure of it, now.

Shadows weave around my skirts and green eyes sparkle everywhere, lighting up the dark. They whisper my name and tell me to hide.

"Why?" I ask softly, so as not to disturb the quiet that surrounds us.

A hand clamps over my mouth and drags me between the shelves.

I fight to unpeel it, struggling when it clamps tighter. Twisting, I ram an elbow backward and hit ribs. Air whooshes past my ear with a forced exhale, but an arm wraps me like a vice and pins me still. I smell cinnamon and metal polish—and, Holy Dark Mother, they're strong. I try to wriggle free, working a space to slide one arm loose. A male voice hisses against my temple, "Summon the dark."

I freeze.

Emerald-jewelled eyes blink at me from beside the spine of a book by my head, and a small shadowed hand reaches to tug the ribbon in my hair.

My assailant murmurs close to my ear, "Try not to be an idiot. There's someone on the stairs."

Footsteps cut through the quiet, and he tenses against my back. The smell of him hits me again, clove oil and the barracks and something deeper, older.

The book sprites' eyes wink out. The shadows close around us, hiding us.

A figure slinks along the landing. A man, black-cloaked and light-footed, pauses at the bottom of the stairs to the Ninth. The shape of him is silhouetted against the moonlight leaking through the windows on the floor below. He turns his head, staring right at us from beneath his hood.

The man behind me goes lethally still. He doesn't breathe, and neither do I. The next minute lasts an eternity. A silent standoff. The figure on the stairs is aware something is wrong—but not that we are here, not yet.

A book sprite lights up at my feet, its eyes gleaming the deepest of amethyst hues. Before, they've always been green. It scuttles away, wrapping inky shadows around the stranger's robes and tugging him back toward the stairs down to the Seventh.

He shoves it away with his boot.

Its eyes blaze scarlet.

The man behind me relaxes his hold, unpeels his fingers from my mouth. "Fool," he says quietly. "Now he's done it."

One by one, a hundred book sprite eyes light with a blood-red glow that drips down the staircase from the Ninth. The intruder recoils, takes one unsteady step backward, and then they're on him.

Darkness clings to him like smoke, seeping around his feet like ink on blotting paper. Shadows crawl up his legs, wrap his waist, and claw at his shoulders. They snatch his hood back, revealing dark hair tied in a low ponytail, a man's jaw, stubbled and rough—a gold mask covering half his face.

A Gilded in the library.

Scarlet eyes blaze bright. Horror spills into my lungs as the first tendril of shadow creeps toward his left ear.

The man screams.

I flinch into my captor's chest, and tension uncoils from his muscles as he wraps both arms around me. "Watch, Penny. You're all right." I'm caught between confusion that this man knows my name—that he seems to be with the Resistance and knew I'd be here—and terror at what's happening on the landing.

Ink dribbles down the man's neck and his knees buckle. He doesn't fall. The book sprites hold him upright, tearing with a thousand tiny hands, consuming him piece by tiny piece.

Ink spills from their fingers, a web of black that wraps him and tightens, slowly shredding him. But he does not bleed.

I'm not sure what's worse, the screams echoing around the library atrium, or the silence when they stop. Shadows smother him, blanketing him in soundless death.

I sense his lifeline droop from his chest. It coils on the floor, and the book sprites pounce on it. In three beats of my heart, it is gone.

All the while, the lights of the book sprites' eyes shine brighter and brighter and brighter.

I count each breath to stop myself tipping into blind panic. I have seen death. But I have never seen anything like this. Unstoppable, irreversible. Even the Gilded, experts in withholding prisoners from Death, couldn't have kept him alive.

Silence fills the library. Words whisper around us, and I watch the crimson tide retreat back up the stairs. An unnatural waterfall of death flowing uphill to the ninth floor.

"That is why you should never kick a book sprite."

I blink, eyes fixed on the space where the intruder was. No blood stains the floor, no entrails scatter the stone stairs. Not even his half-mask remains. "The Gilded don't come into the library. Was he looking for us?"

"You aren't the only one trying to access the Ninth."

He gives me a moment to gather my courage, to piece it back together breath by measured breath, then releases me.

I turn to see who helped me and nearly scream.

Half his face smiles. The other half is coated in gold.

I fly backward in alarm and slam into the banisters. A *Gilded* just protected me. A Gilded knew the Resistance words, and what's worse, he knew I'd be here!

"Penny," he says carefully. "I'm on your side. I'm with the Resistance and I know Ella." He pauses, maybe hoping I'll speak. I don't. "My name is Tobias," he offers.

Gilded don't have names.

Silver eyes meet mine. He's a death-walker too—I wonder which thorn coven he came from. Half his face is unreadable, gold clinging with an expressionless sheen to the hard lines of his jaw and strong cheekbones. The other half frowns, a human expression—almost.

I'm trembling so hard I can't stop myself. I must look pathetic. But I'm so tired. Four death-walks in five days have drained me.

My vision wavers and a fat tear rolls free. I don't bother to wipe it away. I read the number stamped on his breastplate in denial of his name. "Unit two-three-seven."

"Tobias," he repeats. "Burning in the barracks was the most stupidly magnificent thing I've ever seen anyone do. Tonight, however, was just plain stupid."

I don't react. I don't dare. I force myself to breathe. Make my words steady though my heart hammers so hard against my ribs half the Colligerate must be able to hear it. "I was in bed that night—it wasn't me."

"Penny." He says my name so softly, I look at him, properly this time. I'm terrified, and I pity him. But Tobias's eyes hold a glitter of warmth, even the gold-lidded one shimmers with life.

It's an illusion. There is no escaping the gilding's severing of your soul. I've watched it happen. Helped it happen. "Please, it wasn't me."

"I was there. I saw you."

I'm trapped like an insect in a web. Fear siphons the strength from my knees and I lean hard into the banister.

He lowers his voice. "Unfortunately, I wasn't the only one. I've held their reports so far, but with escapades like this—" He gestures to the space where the intruder was, where his blood should be. "You're not making it easy to help you."

Tobias. The name catches on a memory. Maybe he's telling the truth. There was something more behind my father's eyes too. "Toby?" I whisper. Clair mentioned a Toby.

He smiles and it's a warm smile, friendly and relieved. "You spoke to Clair?" His lips twist down at one corner.

I nod. I have a thousand questions. "How did you know I'd be here?"

"I didn't," he answers, and there's more he's not saying. I'm sure of it. "When that Gilded doesn't return, more will swarm the library, and us being here when they do is probably not for the best."

I believe he's telling the truth. That he's aligned with the Resistance, not the paper chain of military command and the Warden's orders. What I don't understand is how he evaded the gilding's excavation of his soul. And if he evaded it, is there a chance my father has too? Tobias reaches for me, and I skip back. "I'll go."

"Let me walk you. There's worse than Gilded and book sprites in the Colligerate hallways at night."

I glance at the floor where the Gilded died, and I really, desperately, do not want to believe him. "Nothing could be worse than what the book sprites just did?"

"You've never visited the barracks' cells then. Or had the misfortune of being in the Warden's throne room when he brings a prisoner out to *play*." Tobias winces slightly, and somehow, that expression makes him seem more human. When I shudder, he nods toward the stairs, and I fall into step beside him.

He talks quietly as we walk back to the Thorn Coven's quarters. He explains what happens in the Warden's throne room of an evening, the wine and the excess. He describes the throne forged by ore magic and crafted from the half-masks taken from fallen Gilded's faces, how it is raised on a dais above the court, the dead watching through obsidian gemstone eyes, and how the Spinner is made to kneel at the Warden's feet night after night, and Tobias is made to guard her.

I'm grateful for it, the protection and the distraction. He doesn't question what I was doing near the Ninth either, and I'm grateful for that too. But I don't like that he's telling me at all. Almost as if he's giving me information I might need later while he has the chance.

"Good night, Penny. I'm glad we finally met," he says at the doors to our wing. "Thank you."

"Thank you?"

"For seeing behind the mask." His crooked smile twists guilt around my ribs. I'm not sure I did see behind it. I'm so confused. It's odd feeling some sense of safety in a Gilded's presence.

"Tobias," I say carefully. "If you really know my sister, please, don't tell her I was on the Eighth tonight."

He laughs under his breath. "I do know Ella, extremely well. Stop appearing in places you shouldn't be, and you have a deal."

Chapter Nineteen

Ella has been glaring at me since breakfast. My yawn makes her glare harder. Mila, on the other hand, grins and hands me a brush and a long-handled pan. "Get sweeping, Pen."

I hate chamber duty. It's not as bad as cleaning up my own ash off my bedroom floor last night though.

I'm making half-hearted sweeping motions when Mila quietly locks the door and rounds on Ella. "You joined the Resistance."

Oh! I try to keep the rhythm of my brush even, but Mila notices my falter and sighs. "I knew it."

Ella rolls her eyes and carries on sorting twigs on the table. "The Resistance doesn't exist. Who've you been talking to, Mila? Not like you to believe rumours or hang around with the kinds of people who spread them."

"I've been hanging around with no one. But I still hear things. I'm the heir to the Thorn Coven, in case you've forgotten."

"Maybe if you gave us a chance to forget, you'd have someone to hang around with." Ella snaps a twig in two.

Mila leans against the door and twirls the key between her fingers. "What happened in Death?"

"I have no idea what you mean." Ella is still as frozen water.

I give up any pretence at sweeping as Mila sparks with anger. "You vanished and then miraculously reappeared. And as if that didn't scare me enough, Penny starts walking in Death on her own. Something happened. And neither of you will tell me what!"

Ella shrugs. "You're imagining things."

I think Mila's going to either explode or cry and I want to hug her, but she might slap me for trying. Instead, I speak quietly into the pause of their standoff. "You were scared?"

"Of course I was scared, you idiot! I love you!" Tears brighten Mila's eyes; frustration tightens her fingers on the key. "And you keep shutting me out."

Ella snaps, "If you weren't such a perfect little witch queen heir, so far up Grandmother's backside you've lost sight of what matters, maybe we wouldn't have to."

Mila opens her mouth, closes it, and her lips form a tight line. I can see that Ella's words have cut her deeply. "Fine. Don't expect me to help when everything falls apart."

"Mila..." I drop my dustpan and move toward her as she unlocks the door, but she slips out and slams it in my face.

I turn on Ella and brandish my brush. "Mila has a point. It's not her fault she has to behave a certain way. She's still our sister."

"She's not part of the Resistance. You try talking to her; see how much that oath will let you say. And stop shaking Aunt Shara's ashes all over me!"

"You didn't have to be so cruel about it." I lower my brush and meet her glare. "What happened to you in Death?"

I expect her to snap again, but the fierceness slumps from her shoulders. After a moment, she hitches herself up onto the table. Legs crossed, she pats the space beside her, but I'm pissed at the way she spoke to Mila, so I perch on the platform at the base of the stake instead.

Ella sighs. "It's a long story."

"We have time."

"Fine." She picks at a loose thread on her sash, worrying the fabric at one end. She's never been able to think without fiddling with something. "After I tried to get to the Ninth and failed again—"

"Again!"

She scowls and drops her sash in her lap. "Do you want the story or not?"

"How many times, Els?"

"Does it matter?"

I scowl back. I'm sick of being stuck between my sisters' arguments. "It does matter, because we used to tell each other everything!"

Ella's fingers stiffen against the tabletop. "And you have no secrets from me?"

"I—"

"What are you doing in Death every night?" She pauses, her fingers drifting back to her lap to reclaim her sash.

"Els—"

"You're going back to him, aren't you?"

I wish I had gone after Mila instead of starting this conversation. The expression on Ella's face tells me I'm not getting out of it, though. "Ella," I say carefully, and her eyes narrow a little. "Why were you in Malin's manor, really?"

Ella blinks. "I was looking for the Grimoire."

I watch her, how she swallows, the slight crease at the corner of her eyes when she meets my gaze. I know she's lying. She knows I know.

She blinks again and rubs the side of her neck. "I saw the manor last spring—"

"Last spring!" It's the last thing I expected her to say. "Who else saw it? Does Grandmother know?"

Ella's lips twist. "No one else has seen it. Only a few of the Resistance witches know it's there. It vanished as spring turned into summer and I didn't see it again until the frost arrived on the morning air. Miss Elsweather knew I intended to knock on the gate the other night—she insisted whoever answered wouldn't be the Sorcerer." She rolls her little braided bracelet up and down her wrist. I reach for mine and rub my thumb against it.

"So, you just marched up and knocked on the door?"

"You don't understand." There's no blinking now, just my sister twisting her belt in her lap so viciously, so clearly hurting, I shove away my own upset and sit on the table beside her.

I place my hand on hers, stilling her fingers, and say simply, "Tell me."

Ella huffs a half-choked laugh and leans her shoulder into mine. "I'm trying. You keep interrupting."

"I'll stop."

She nods, takes a deep breath, and begins. "Lord Malin was so polite, so welcoming when he opened the gate. He offered me tea in the prettiest parlour and showed me his gardens. We got so involved talking about his plants and the difficulty Mother's having with her corpse flowers, when he offered to show me a botanical reference book, I agreed. In hindsight, it was too easy: I was looking for a book and there he was, inviting me to his library. Then, his gaze slid down to where my crystal was, and his smile, Pen—it turned my blood to ice. That's when I realised something was off. My heart was beating."

"You should have run." I've seen that smile of Lord Malin's, the knowing curve of it, the anticipation shining in his eyes.

"I needed the Grimoire."

"The Resistance came before your safety?"

"*You* came before my safety." Ella pushes away from me, slipping off the table and returning to work. Gathering a bundle of twigs, she stabs them in my direction. "I want to reforge the knife as much as any of the others, but people keep dying. Last time we tried, Bea's sister was incinerated by her own magic right in front of us, and Haylea—" Ella wraps her arms around herself. "Haylea's crystal shattered."

"Oh, Ella!" My throat chokes shut and my fingers press into my sternum. Our crystals anchor us in Life. Without one, our minds slowly fracture and our magic drains away.

Ella's breath catches, and I want to hug her but the tension in her shoulders suggests she doesn't want to be touched. "The spell spiralled out of control. It caught Haylea and dragged her halfway through the veil and her lifeline tangled in it. We couldn't do anything to help her, I couldn't even cross and hold her hand. Dawn broke..." She squeezes her eyes shut, and I reach for her hand. I've been in Death as the sun begins to rise over Halstett, felt that tug in my lifeline. So has Ella. It must have been excruciating. "It was horrible, Penny. She couldn't go toward the Horizon, couldn't come back. No one in the coven was allowed to cross into Death to help. Even then they wouldn't let us break the rules. The Gilded cut her free in the end. Grandmother said we could never speak of it. She said Haylea was a fool who was outsmarted by a fog-wraith and refused to walk into the Horizon as she should have.

"The Resistance witches believe we need a darker crystal if we're to have a chance at successfully forging the knife. If they discover yours is black, they won't stop until you agree to help. And I won't watch you die. I can't." She shakes me off and begins to lay the pyre. "So you see why finding the original spell was important. Why I went to the manor and knocked on the door."

I slide down and move beside her to finish the sweeping. "What was in the library?"

"I have no idea," Ella says softly. She builds the pyre higher and higher until it touches the platform. She sounds reluctant now.

Hesitant. "I think I fainted. The last thing I remember is walking into the woods and Lord Malin swearing, loudly, and saying he was close, after all this time, so damned close." She swallows and stares at me. "He shook me and asked if I had a sister. The next thing I knew, I was waking up by the veil and Lord Malin was staring at you with that wolf-smile on his lips like he wanted to eat you alive."

A door slams in the corridor above, and Ella quickly changes the subject, dropping her voice. "What do we do about Mila? She's asking all the wrong questions."

"We could try trusting her?" I whisper back. Even after her confession, Ella talking about Mila as if she's the enemy stings. I love them both. "She's our sister." I quickly replace the dustpan in the cupboard, hang the brush on its hook.

"And the Thorn Queen is our grandmother. You want to try trusting her? What about our Gilded father, shall we trust him too?"

"It's not the same."

"Grandmother will tie you up with a bow and hand you to the Warden if she finds out you're running around with the Resistance." Ella sounds exactly as tired as I feel. "Only Father might have defied her. Shame he chose to be gilded."

"Father didn't choose to be gilded!" I frown, and Ella sharpens.

"Grow up, Penny. Father took the easy way out and left us to live with the mess."

"How could he have resisted?"

"You met Tobias." Ella stares at me as if hoping I'll deny it.

I wish I could. "He wasn't supposed to tell you that."

"He didn't," she says a bit sadly. "But that's beside the point. Tobias resisted. If he survived with *himself* intact, why didn't Father?"

But I saw Father and his eyes weren't completely blank. Maybe he isn't as lost as we think. The idea of it even being a possibility is overwhelming.

She looks away. "Father was the strongest person I ever knew. If it's possible to resist, he could have. Instead he chose to feel nothing."

"You think maybe—"

"I've seen Father. There's nothing left. Don't start chasing rainbows." There are tears limning her eyes.

"What if there's a way to undo it? The gilding. The Resistance might help?"

"If there was a way, they'd have found it by now. You're not the first to ask that question." Footsteps sound at the top of the stairs, and Ella snatches up a bundle of kindling off the table. "Don't join the Resistance, Pen. Not yet. Promise."

I wince and confess, "I already did."

The door handle turns and I don't think I've ever been so relieved to see Grandmother.

She inspects the pyre, the clean-swept stone floor around it, and stares first at me, then at Ella. But if she suspects the conversation we were just having, she gives no sign of it. Her voice is cheerful, her eyes bright. "We have a few changes to the patrol schedule to go over. You're walking, Penny. Tonight."

CHAPTER TWENTY

Burning with the coven is a relief. Sure, my return will be watched for, Grandmother will require a report, and upholding my bargain with Malin will be trickier. But for the first time, I don't burn alone or fear being noticed as I walk.

My coven sisters chant as the pyre Ella and I set earlier blazes into life. I don't need to force myself to die. I just... do. The veil is an open pathway, the flames barely touch my bones. I slip into Death, and it welcomes me as if aware I need a rest.

Coven duty first, I turn left and walk, following Grandmother's instructions to the letter. The mist-threaded veil shimmers in the grey light of Death. It is whole and shining: no dull spots, no frayed threads. The dead walk into the Horizon exactly as they're supposed to: None stray from their path into the light. None look back.

There are more tonight than any other night I've crossed. Men with hunched backs and burnt clothes, blistered hands and faces healing with each step. Children in nightgowns and women in soot-stained skirts. A fire in the docks? Blazes in the tinder-dry warehouses aren't unusual. Their lifelines string into the Horizon, guiding them home, humming peacefully against my senses as they walk.

Except one.

A soul staggers sideways, breaking off from the rest. He falters, zigzags a little, and I sense his lifeline: charred and frayed. Snapped.

Ice tiptoes down my spine.

He stops, feet planted apart, one hand twitching.

I drop to a crouch. "Don't look back," I whisper and sketch a knife in the sand. Magic floods from my fingertips and cool metal forms beneath my palm, a long, curved blade, lethally sharp.

Slowly, his head turns.

He looks back.

Shit.

There's a hole in his cheek and his face is carved with whorl after whorl. Anger shines in his eyes. No regret. No fear. Just pure fury.

Tendrils of darkness wind up from the sand and wrap his ankles, eating away at the solidity of his form. His legs elongate; if souls had bones, his would be breaking.

He meets my gaze and smiles as the fog takes him.

Firming my grip on the hilt of my weapon, I run toward the fog that once was a soul. Fire races down my blade as a mist gathers into a humanoid form, a distorted memory of what a person should be. His face is round, his eyes are white, and his mouth filled with too many teeth.

I stop in a skidding shower of sand. I can't let him scream. One sound and others will wake and swarm across Death to his aid. A lone new-made wraith I can handle—a horde and I won't survive.

Too-long fingers snatch my arm as I swing. Poison-tipped nails tear my sleeve. Water drips down my skirts; his hand twitches by my feet.

Two more swings hold him off, and I grasp his lifeline with my free hand. It's sticky against my palm, hot like fresh-spilled blood. He opens his mouth wide. I tug on his lifeline before he screeches. "Walk," I say.

He stares at me. I try again, attempting to sound in command as his lifeline squirms in my hand. "Walk!"

He jerks like a broken puppet. I release his lifeline and infuse my voice with magic. "Walk," I order. He takes one reluctant step and another. I watch him go, whispering a silent prayer of thanks as he fades into the Horizon's light. Once he crosses, he won't return. I add a second prayer that his soul finds peace in the afterlife beyond the Horizon.

At least I'll have something to report to Grandmother.

Now, I just need something to report to Malin. I think as I walk, racking my mind for any scrap of information. But my mind is frustratingly blank when the portcullis rattles open.

Malin is waiting. He takes me in, a slow assessment from head to toe that snags on the water of the fog-wraith's banishing dampening my skirts, the curved blade in my hand, the tear in my sleeve. He scowls, and my heart skips out of time. "Careless, Penelope," he says by way of greeting, and stalks up the path and into the manor. I hurry after him, fighting a need to apologise or snap at him—I'm not sure which. Maybe both.

His parlour is green tonight. Apple blossoms drift across the walls and the sofas are velvet shades of spring meadow hues. He rounds on me as I step inside, takes my wrist gently, and carefully rolls up my sleeve. His fingers are cool against my skin. "Fog-wraith poison is a most unpleasant way to die. You're lucky. It didn't break the skin." He smiles, chilled and knife-sharp. "I assume you banished it?"

"Of course."

His grip tightens. "You watched it all the way into the Horizon?"

I raise my chin, fighting the itch to break free of his hold, longing to lean into it. "I'm a thorn witch. What do you think they've been teaching me for the last ten years? How to make cakes?"

His left eye twitches, and I think I just won a round of this mysterious game we seem to play.

I grin and make my report before he has time to demand it, telling him everything that happened in the library last night: the Gilded, the book sprites. I'm so carried away I don't notice when he releases me or the way his fingernails dig into the back of the velvet chair until he cuts me off.

"You went to the Ninth."

Shit. "The Eighth," I correct. I glance at the carriage clock on the mantelpiece, a pretence of checking the time, which won't match the hour in Life. "I should leave."

I move for the door, but he's there before I can reach the edge of the rug, blocking my exit. "Why were you on the eighth floor, Penelope?" he asks with exaggerated patience.

"My name is Penny." I roll my eyes, hiding the flutter of fear in my chest, and give him half a smile as if I don't care what he does next. I care desperately what he does next. I really need to read that contract—I have no idea what he might do, what he *can* do under the terms of our deal if I disobey him.

"Why were you on the Eighth?" Less patience now. The light inside dims from springtime sun to storm grey, darkening the shadows under his cheekbones, deepening the haze of stubble on his jaw.

I want to step back, but I hold my ground. I'm not giving him an inch. "Trying to get to the Ninth."

His eyes flash. He's angry. But...worry lurks behind his rage. What in the name of the Dark Mother has *he* got to worry about, safe in his manor, free from Halstett's constraints, with such beautiful gardens to stroll in and a forest full of green and growing things and pollen dancing on the breeze. I almost resent him for his freedom, his unfettered access to colour and light! Almost.

His fingers twitch, thumb curling into the centre of his palm. Muscles tighten in his forearms, setting the silver bands on his wrists sparkling in the fast-fading light. "Did you listen to nothing I said last night?"

"I listened. You refused to tell me who you really are, and said that where I do or do not go in Halstett isn't covered by our contract." Inside, I tremble, and I fold my arms to hide it.

Malin's hand flexes, fingers twitching as if summoning a spell, and he stares at me. Silence stretches between us, tightening until I think he's going to explode. Then he storms out the parlour, locking the door behind him—locking me in.

I'm fairly sure that isn't in our contract either: locking me here, preventing me from leaving. I glance around, unsure what to do. He's never left me alone before. The room seems bigger without him in it. His presence takes up so much space it's difficult to see anything but him when he's near. The wallpaper fades, apple blossom petals softly drifting down to the floor, and I brush a finger along the mantelpiece as the shine dulls and a brass peacock with jewel-bright enamelled feathers folds up its tail. The air turns stale.

I snatch my fingers back and hurry to the window, relieved when I find it unlatched; the window slides up with a single shove. A breeze dances in and I lean out, breathing the clean air. Outside, the lawns are still green and little puffy clouds scud across a water-blue sky. Whatever upset the parlour has not affected the gardens or the woods beyond. I could slip out, run to the woods and see what I can find; Ella mentioned being near the woods when Malin offered to take her to the library...

I hear the sound of a door slamming in the corridor. My heartbeat pounds in my throat as I slowly hoist myself onto the sill. I hear another door open and shut. I have one leg out the window when a hand clamps on the top of my arm and hauls me back inside. My heart sinks. I didn't even hear him open the door.

He tosses a sheaf of papers onto the coffee table without letting me go. "Out of interest, how far did you think you'd get?"

I glance at the window, at the woods lying dark and mysterious beyond the lawn, hiding secrets in their mossy depths. A muscle tics in Malin's cheek and he snaps his fingers. Thorns erupt from the lawn's edge, snaking and weaving into a knotted wall that shutters the woods from view. It's the ugliest thing I've seen—and I've spent thirteen years in Halstett. "You ruined your view," I say through gritted teeth.

Malin's eyebrow rises and he clicks his fingers again. Roses bloom across the thorns, and he gives me a grim smile. "Better?"

"Much."

"Good," he says. "Now read."

I realise the papers on the table are our contract. There must be some fifty pages there. "I only signed one piece of paper."

"May I suggest, next time you sign something, you read the fine print. That"—he jabs a finger at the table, and I sink into the sofa with a huff—"is the fine print. Read."

"I have to cross back."

"Read fast."

"If I'm late, my mother will worry. After what you did to Ella—"

"I did nothing to Ella. Ella looked back."

A lie. One he's sticking to. I don't correct him.

He sits with feline liquidity in his favoured armchair. He always sits close to the fireplace even with it unlit. His fingers steeple against his knee, and he asks, "What did you want in the woods? Are you looking for something, Penelope?"

I think he knows precisely what I'm looking for. The narrowing of his eyes suggests I'm right. Damn him. Maybe I should ask him outright what he hides in his woods. But his wall of thorns suggests he won't be very accommodating if I do. I pick up the contract and skim through the first page, shivering at my blood-marked *P* caged by his *M*.

"Penelope, I asked you a question."

"Shhh," I say. "I'm reading."

I wade through long-winded clauses on failure and paragraphs on the quality of my information, all written in curlicues of ink. I have to fight the twitch of my eyebrow at the ridiculousness of some sections: *Penelope will not allow any pets to accompany her into Death, nor bring any items of significant personal value.* As if I'd bring Miss Elsweather's cat or Mother's wedding ring! What kind of person would do that? I skim by a subparagraph about a goldfish. One section in particular tips me over the edge and I choke on a giggle: *Penelope agrees to never wear gumboots under any circumstances in Lord Malin's presence. Failure to comply will result in her immediate expulsion from the premises no matter whether it impacts her ability to fulfil the terms of the contract.* Malin shifts against the leather chair, and I swallow my laughter.

"I just hate them," he says, and snaps his fingers, conjuring up a pot of tea and two cups. "Awful things."

"I've never owned any."

He glances at my bare feet tucked up on my chair and hands me a cup and saucer. "Do you own shoes at all?"

"Do you want me to read this, or would you rather discuss my footwear preferences?"

"Read," he says, smooth as silk, and I hide my grin behind the teacup with a sip of blissful, perfectly brewed bergamot.

There's a section on what happens should I choose to stay. I raise an eyebrow and glance at him. He meets my eyes and smiles and I have a horrible feeling he's aware of precisely how confused he makes me. Why would I stay? I should be horrified at the thought of it. Instead, I've stood on the threshold to the manor, wishing I didn't have to go. Even now, I'm dreading the idea of it: returning to the Warden's cold regime when Malin's manor is a tiny oasis of colour and freedom I could choose for myself.

That point is made clear in section 42, subclause b: *If, before midnight on the completion date of the contract, Penelope Elizabeth Albright decides to remain in Death beyond the rise of Halstett's dawn, she will relinquish her ability to cross the veil, renounce her mortal form, and retain all rights to her soul for as long as she resides within the manor walls.*

It's repeated other places too, a constant reminder of the temptation of choice. I could choose this, here. Even with Malin as my only company, staying here would be an improvement on Halstett. The manor shouldn't exist, but there's a curious peace within its walls. I feel safe here.

I'd be free. Free of the Warden who controls my coven, the Resistance who want to use me, and from Death's deserts too.

But my sisters and mother would not. Nor would my aunts and cousins, Alice and Tobias and Clair, Beatrice and the other witches or Miss Elsweather. And I cannot give up on them.

I shake my head to clear it and continue reading. Where I am and am not allowed to go is detailed clearly, and rather validates Malin's new rose wall: *Penelope will not leave the gardens in the immediate vicinity of the manor without Lord Malin's express permission, nor will she venture into any rooms she is not invited into.*

I wonder which rooms he doesn't want me seeing. I frown and carry on, my eyes itching at the strain of reading so many words in such looped and decorative handwriting. Malin's elegant penmanship puts mine to shame.

He watches me quietly the entire time. I reach the last sentence and swallow hard. *In return, Lord Malin agrees to give up any and all claim on Penelope's soul at midnight on Samhain Eve, and, if she should fail to meet her contractual obligations, confirms he will take excellent care of her soul once it is in his possession.* And that is the crux of it, the collateral I gave him in exchange for my sister. I don't regret it. I'd sign it all over again given the same choice, but seeing it written down in black and white... reality bites deep and its teeth are sharp.

I glance up at Malin, and for a flicker of a heartbeat, I catch him unawares; softer and wistful, not sharp with calculation or challenge. Sadness tugs down the corners of his mouth. He's far away, lost in thought, and his thumb rests on his wrist at precisely the spot where he marked me.

His eyes are regretful when they meet mine, and he smiles—a real smile, not one with an ulterior motive hiding in its curve. His lips part, just a little. And then his cold front snaps into place. "Are you done?"

I restack the papers on the table. "All memorised."

He chuckles. "I doubt that."

"You underestimate me."

"I suspect, Penelope Albright, granddaughter of the Thorn Queen, that is not an uncommon problem when it comes to you."

I'm still wondering what the heck he means, whether it was a compliment or an insult, when he unlocks the door. We walk through the gardens in silence, but when he raises the gate, I ask him, "Why did you make it so complicated?"

"The contract?" When I nod, he replies, "I wanted you to stay."

It's not really an answer. I open my mouth to demand an explanation, but he bends closer and his fingers brush my cheekbone, silencing me with a frisson of warmth right behind my navel. Slowly, he tucks a loose strand of hair behind my ear. "Go home, Penelope."

"My name is Penny."

His thumb runs along my jaw, and he straightens to stand back, gesturing to the grey expanse of desert on his doorstep. "Go home before it's too late."

I want to tell him I don't have a home, but my heart's pounding too hard and my lifeline isn't strung tight. I have time? I look up into his eyes and they're filled with a hunger that curls my toes in the sand. A longing I can't allow myself to match—not after reading the contract.

When the portcullis rattles down behind me, I make my way quietly across the desert dunes to the veil, returning to Life, leaving Malin behind. I feel him watching me as I go.

I'm so confused. I've never felt like this about a man before. Clair was a safer attraction, but when I met her in a Colligerate cupboard, it could never have been anything. Now, Malin's in my head, the ghost of his fingers still tracing my cheek; there's no room for anyone else.

I wish I could talk to Ella or Mila about it. I think of Alice, and a thought pops into my head, that maybe I could talk to her. She'd keep my secrets. She has plenty of her own. Something about the way she listens when I talk, the way she says my name, invites confidences. I'm still distracted as I whisper the words to part the veil and step into the gap, imagining the Chamber of Flame and Smoke as Mother told me to.

But the veil is sticky tonight. It clings to my skin in flypaper strands and wraps my wrists.

I fight free of the cool clutch of Death—and wake in Life to a gold-gauntleted hand dragging me to my feet.

Chapter Twenty-One

I'm in the Chamber of Flame and Smoke, but Mother is not here. Grandmother is.

So are no less than five Gilded.

"Penelope Albright?" My name is barked in my face, and I shy back, my blood curdling.

"That's her," Grandmother says in a flat voice.

"Excellent." The Gilded holding me has a whorl marked on his gold-plated cheek and his eyes aren't soulless and dead, but whatever is behind them despises me.

Shouldn't he be blank and broken like the other Gilded? Hope flutters, deep in my chest. I stare at him, trying to see behind his mask, but there's hatred in his glare, top lip curling in disgust. Hope shatters with my father's smile. It isn't warm. "The little witch who broke into my barracks and defiled my eternal fires."

I shake my head in denial. Fear sticks my tongue to the roof of my mouth.

"I have four reports stating otherwise." He pulls me closer and hisses so low Grandmother won't hear, "You'll pay for every footstep you marked across my entry hall, every drip on the sand of the amphitheatre. You will regret the day you trespassed in my halls. I'm going to take my time with you."

The threat hits my cheek, spittle-flecked and awful.

I will not fear him. I will not.

I do.

"Your halls?" I whisper.

"Mine," he confirms, and his smile stretches so wide I think his mask might split.

He straightens and holds out a hand to Grandmother. She doesn't look at me as she passes him a small velvet pouch. Her lips are a thin line of contempt, her eyes bright with rage. I'm not sure if it's aimed at me or the Gilded's invasion of her territory. Neither would surprise me. It's probably both.

The pouch disappears into my father's fist. Fear tangles my thoughts. What has she given him? What was in that pouch? If she's handed my crystal over, my real crystal, I'm done for. The Warden will destroy me. In Life, I will have lost. But I was never going to win and there's a grim sort of satisfaction in knowing that when I fail to show up in Death tonight, this will end. I'll be useless to the Warden with my soul in Malin's possession. There'll be nothing left of me for my Gilded father to take his time with. All my choices will vanish and I can stay in the manor.

My only regret will be Ella and Mila. And Mother. Though maybe I'd be able to see them when they walked?

But then there's the Resistance I could have helped. I'd have preferred my end to mean something—to bring the Warden to his knees.

I wish I'd found the Grimoire and the spell and attempted to reforge the knife.

I wish I'd helped Alice, locked in her room, alone and lonely just as Malin is.

I manage not to stumble as I'm marched up the stairs and into the coven hallways, which are quiet with the chill of dawn. A Gilded stands guard at each bedroom door and two bar the exit. My father's hand—the hand that used to offer safety, helping me balance as I skipped from rock to rock across the stream—clamps so tight on my arm I'll have a patchwork of bruises there tomorrow. I was a fool for hoping before. For imagining some part of my father remained.

A door flies open and my mother's voice slams my father to a halt. "You *bastard*. That's our daughter."

Slowly, he turns me to face her. "*Your* daughter, Agatha." Somehow, him using her name makes this more real. My father, the man who told me stories and tucked me into bed, is handing me over to the Warden. Any hope I had when Ella said Tobias resisted the gilding dies with the chill of my father's words. The space it leaves behind is cold and takes up too much space. I can't breathe. I can't cry either.

Mother's eyes blaze with anger. "Traitor."

Father ignores her and turns to Grandmother. "The Warden appreciates your assistance, Mother, but might I suggest keeping the rest of your coven in line."

Grandmother nods, but I see regret lurking in the steel of her eyes. She always loved Father best.

Mother tries to step past the Gilded barring her door. I see her struggling against his hold as my father marches me away. I hear her low threat to Grandmother as we reach the doors, "Bitch. I'll kill you for this."

Hear Ella's soft reply under the stamp of Gilded boots, "Mother, stop."

The Gilded fall into step behind us as we leave. The corridors of the Colligerate echo with their footsteps; the wide and luxurious halls of the Warden's wing muffle them with drapes and padded rugs.

I hang my head and pray to the Dark Mother that the pouch in my father's pocket does not contain my crystal. After everything Grandmother's done to conceal me, it's unlikely—after everything I've done to expose myself, there's nothing else it could be.

They march me up a flight of stairs, and I glimpse Alice's door, all brightly painted with flowers and trees, before I'm shoved through the door beside it.

It's dark inside, the curtains drawn against the rising day, and dust heavies the air. Not the kind of dust that whispers of forgotten stories and worlds beyond ours in the library, but the kind of dust that suggests secrets buried so deep they'll never be found. It smells of bones and decay and the catacombs beneath the Colligerate.

My father releases me. "Ensure the witch is appropriately restrained," he barks. "The Warden will summon her when he's ready."

The door slams, a match catches and touches to the wick of a lamp, and I press into the wall, into the shadows, out of the light. Carefully, I raise my eyes and sag with relief.

Tobias shakes his head. "I tried to stop this."

I'm not sure how to answer.

He glances at the door and speaks quietly. "A prisoner gave you up—your crystal. Everything. There was nothing I could do."

My heart plummets. "No one outside the Thorn Coven knows about my crystal." *Tobias* shouldn't know about my crystal.

"The prisoner was a thorn witch."

"Was?" My mind races. Who in my coven would have anything to gain by giving me up to the Warden?

"She's dead—or soon will be. Paid for an end to her torment with information." He takes a step toward me, and I lean harder into the wall, wishing I could vanish through it. If I was an ore witch, I could make it swallow me whole.

"Your grandmother handed you over this morning. Your crystal too."

If my grandmother has cast me adrift, I'll be worse than dead. At least the dead are mourned. I'll be forgotten. Erased from existence. A shiver dances down my spine.

Tobias pulls a pair of cuffs out of his pocket. I dart sideways, tipping over a low card table and snatching at the curtains to steady myself. Dust showers down and stings my eyes. I won't become the Warden's plaything like Alice. I won't. The Warden has locked Alice in a room and forces her to weave the future, ceaselessly. What will he force me to do?

"Tobias, please." My words catch on a sob. Panic forms a lump in my throat. "You helped me last night. Please. Please, don't do this."

He pauses, and for one foolish second, I think he might help me again now. "We can get you out," he says, but there's an edge to his offer.

"There's nowhere to go," I reply.

"There's a safe house."

My heart stills, squeezing tight against hope. "Where?"

"I can't tell you that."

"Is it inside the walls?"

Tobias sighs. "I can't tell you that either."

I swallow hard. "How safe?"

The line of Tobias's shoulders softens and he takes a step closer with a sad sort of smile. "If it was anyone else, Penny, I'd tell them it was safe enough—it would be safe enough—but for you... they'll hunt you down, won't stop until they retrieve you. I don't know how long it'll stay safe." He holds out the cuffs, his lip curling with disgust as they clink together. "Or you can let this happen. And we'll help."

"We?"

"The Resistance. Your grandmother made the cuffs. It's the same magic that controls the Gilded. Bea realised what they were doing and why, and swapped the spelled gold. You just have to pretend to be under his control."

I bite my lip so hard the metallic taste of blood slides across my tongue. He's offering me a choice, a say in my fate. As the Warden's curious thing, I'll be paraded before his court each night like Tobias told me Alice is. If I can find a way to cross the veil, I'll hear things I can report back to Lord Malin. If I run, the chance of escape is less than none.

There is no choice, not really. Silently, I nod.

"You're sure?"

No.

I nod again. "Get on with it."

He snaps the cuffs open one by one. He's careful as he fits the first and seals it tight.

I want to snatch my hand away.

He catches my other wrist and pauses, waiting for my final reluctant nod before he rolls up my sleeve. The black rosebud winks at us, shimmering in the dust-moted light. But he says nothing as he slides out his knife and cuts off the braided bracelet Ella made. It hurts, losing that piece of me.

"I'll give it to Ella. She'll keep it safe." He tucks it in his pocket and fits the second cuff where my bracelet used to be.

It snaps shut and I'm now property of the High Warden, Protector of Halstett.

My lips wobble at one corner. At least the cuff covers Lord Malin's mark, and I'll have information that won't involve the colour of the Warden's shoes or snippets from Alice. Two problems solved; more heavy on my shoulders. How am I going to cross into Death undetected if my crystal is in the Warden's possession? How will I burn?

The pity I used to feel for Alice is reflected in Tobias's eyes. I hate it. I hate him and the Resistance. And I hate the Warden most of all.

"Come on," he says softly. Carefully. "You can wait with the Spinner. I'll order your rooms cleaned to give you some time."

Alice is silent when I enter. She knows before I'm shoved through her door what they have done. She tried to warn me with her note. Without speaking, she drifts to the curtains and throws them wide. She unlatches the window and throws up the sash. And gently, so gently, she pushes me into the window seat.

"Breathe, Penny." Two words. Quiet ones. I obey.

She huddles in the corner of an oversize chair beside me and curls her feet under her, black skirts tucked around her knees. Not a serpent or a scorpion today; today she's a girl with understanding in her eyes. Today, she's just like me.

Her fingers weave through the air, and the loom works her magic. Images spun in silk pile on the floor: a girl with red hair on her knees, a forest flickering with flames behind her. Gold binds her wrists and darkness crawls across her skin, uncoiling from her fingers to reach for the skull-faced tyrant towering over her.

The Warden reads her spinnings; he'll see what she predicts.

"He sees what I want him to see," Alice says softly. "He won't see that."

I curl into silence, staring out her window.

"They say it gets easier." She inspects her cuffs, running a finger between skin and metal. "It doesn't. Alice. My name is Alice, I told you that. Don't forget your name, Penny. He's going to take it."

"You brought his attention to my door." Even as I snap at her, I know I'm not being fair. This is my fault. The decisions I made brought me here.

"You snuck into the Gilded's barracks and burned in their fire-pit. They saw you. Did you think there would be no consequences?

This is clemency compared to the Gilded's demands and your grandmother's proposal."

"What did they demand?" I make myself ask even though I'm afraid of the answer.

"The Gilded want your unending torment." Alice tenses, her lips twisting a little at one side. "The Thorn Queen offered to shatter your crystal herself and set you adrift in Death. The Warden denied them both. We'll be like bookends, you and I, kneeling beside his throne; his death-walker and his life-spinner." Bitterness drips from her words and the black depths of her eyes catch fire. "But you hear things, Penny. Things not meant for our ears. He forgets we exist. We're ornaments—useful, but ornaments all the same."

I run my finger under the gold cuff. "He has my crystal and I need to walk in Death, Alice."

Something within her seems to unfurl when I use her name. Hope burns in her eyes, and I wonder how long she's been here, locked in this room alone.

"I was five," she says, answering my unspoken question. "Sixteen years. I won't be here another. Nor will you. Help me live, Penny, and I'll help you die. Together we might survive him—I can't see further than that."

There's strength in Alice. Beyond these walls, I know she is seen as weak, something to be pitied. But she is someone, not something, and at the moment, she's more than me.

Her loom slows as her fingers wander through the air. They don't dance now; they caress and coax. A storyteller's rhythm, not a recorder of nightmares. She's looking back, not forward, and the past has more capacity for pain than the future. It is human nature to hope; no matter how dire the circumstances, we cling to it. We tell ourselves we can change the future, while the past is set and rigid.

"It was the week after my fifth birthday. Time should soften it. It doesn't. They came after midnight. Tore mother from child and husband from wife. I saw it happen, Penny, a week before it did. But no one listens to a five-year-old girl speaking in riddles about gold-faced men. I begged my mother to hide, my father to pack up our things and leave. At first, he laughed, dismissing my ramblings as a childish fancy. Then, he got angry when I wouldn't stop. He stormed out and didn't come back.

"It was dark when the Gilded broke down our door. My brother dragged me out of bed, and we ran as fast as my five-year-old legs would carry me. I didn't know it was me they hunted.

"We hid behind a half-rotten log and watched as they decimated our village. The forest filled with Gilded. My brother tried to protect me, but he couldn't shield me from the ugliness of men. For a long time, I hated him for that. In my brother's arms, I watched my parents murdered. I see their blood at night, all over my hands."

She falls quiet, her fingers whispering sorrow, and upon her tapestry, a small girl with silver-blonde hair cowers behind a log with a boy a few years older.

Alice sighs. "Night bled into scarlet-skied dawn, the smoke from our razed village curled through the trees, and finally, they found us. My brother gave me the gift of anger that night. I never saw him again. They tied me to the loom and locked me here. And here I've stayed ever since, except at night when I'm paraded before the Warden's court."

"I'm sorry." The hollowness of my tone matches the sadness in my heart.

Alice cocks her head to one side; her fingers pause with the tips pressed together. "Why are you sorry, Penny?" The loom stops, and she reaches for me, resting her cool palm on the back of my hand. I cover it with my own and her pulse flutters beneath my fingers. "You did not burn my village. You did not lock me away." Her grief hardens; fury blazes in her eyes.

She doesn't deserve my pity; she deserves respect. "For not seeing you."

Her fingers snap away, and she's weaving again. "Soon, they won't see you either." She flashes me a poison-sugar smile, sweet and deadly. "And when you become invisible, that's when they hand you the knife to slice open their gut."

The room is quiet as I consider her words. Her face grows still, her eyes glaze, and a smile tugs at the corners of her lips. At her feet, the loom has spilled her weavings into a silken pile. I watch her work, the way her elbows rest. She kneels to cut a section free with a golden knife, her movements fluid. She folds it carefully, slides it under the loom, and tucks her hair behind her ear. There's a wicked light in her midnight eyes as her fingers begin to dance again. The shuttle clicks and clacks, and blank silk tumbles from the loom. A rainbow of colour with no image to read.

When they come for me, slamming open the door without knocking to announce their arrival, Alice looks at me intently. "I'm sorry too, Penny."

"See you on the other side," I whisper.

"Together," she replies. "Together, we'll survive."

Chapter Twenty-Two

There are six gold-clad brutes gathered on the landing alongside Tobias when he orders me out of Alice's rooms.

I don't know what the Warden expects of me, but I assume he's about to be disappointed. I am no more or less than any thorn witch. If anything, I am the least of us all.

What the Warden might do when he discovers that terrifies me.

Three Gilded fall in ahead, three behind, and Tobias pulls me into step between them as I'm marched down the stairs. His eyes are hard now, cold. There's no trace of the man I glimpsed behind his mask.

Servants clear our path, scuttling against the walls and glancing at Tobias and me with fear-filled eyes. The other Gilded step smartly out of our way, but their eyes are blank: I am a prisoner, nothing more. The palace guards' eyes are not. Some are disgusted, others soften with pity.

Yesterday, I was the Thorn Queen's granddaughter, third in line to inherit her crown. Not that I want it—I can't imagine anything worse.

My name is Penny and he cannot take that away. I won't let him.

The corridors empty as we reach the huge black-and-grey throne room doors. My father joins us as we wait for admittance. Tobias tightens his hold as the doors open and snaps, "Eyes down." Obediently, I fix my eyes on the floor and he shoves me forward.

The silence inside is so thick I could touch it. The court watches my entrance. The nonmagical nobles on the Warden's council wear silver chains of office over grey silk robes. They all look up as I walk, taking in this new creature the Warden has acquired.

As I walk, I hear the beat of hearts and smell sweat beading on brows.

I smell the Warden. Tarnished metal and the spilled blood of thousands—and the rot-festering wound that refuses to heal.

Grey marble tiles chill my bare feet as Tobias escorts me past lines of spit-polished boots and pale grey skirts brushing the floor. I want to tear free and run, hammer on the door until someone lets me out. Then, we reach the first step leading to the dais and the Warden's throne of faces, and Tobias pushes me to my knees, holds me there with a grip on one shoulder—and, so quick I might have imagined it, a tiny reassuring squeeze.

I hear the Warden stand. His steps crack like a bullwhip as he approaches. None may look upon the faceless monstrosity who styles himself as royalty without his explicit permission, and even then, he is hidden behind a mask. The closest I've come to seeing his face is the statue in the Colligerate hallway.

The toes of his black satin shoes are decorated with scrolls of gold, and bile rises in my throat at the stench of his wound. Decay clings to the Warden. It crawls across his skin and delves into his bones.

I hear a low rasping whisper, but I can't make out the words.

Tobias barks, "Clear the throne room. By order of our Great Protector, the Holy High Warden of Halstett."

Holy? I want to laugh. The Warden destroyed anything that might have been holy in Halstett centuries ago.

The throne room empties with shocking speed. The room echoes with the final slam of the door, and Tobias's grip on my shoulder tightens as he pulls me to my feet. His breath catches.

A chill sneaks across the floor. I feel them enter the room. Three lifelines stretch out over our heads. One is barbed and gilded. Two are broken. Nausea wells in my throat, bitter bile I can't swallow away. I try to look up, but Tobias snaps, "Eyes down," in his Gilded voice. His fingers dig in, half reassurance, half warning, and I wonder if he senses the lifelines too. I've never felt anything like this. They beat with a flickering pulse I sense so acutely it itches at my skin.

They are unanchored.

Unnatural.

They snake closer. Shuffling feet accompany them, and two prisoners are slammed to their knees at my feet. Everyone has a lifeline, and all lifelines lead into the Horizon—except for the Warden with his lifeline anchored to the veil in Death.

But these lifelines are severed, destroyed by torture and brutal magic. This is the work of the Gilded.

If a lifeline was a knotted thread, thorn witches smooth their snarls. That's what Mother and Grandmother do when they treat the Warden's wound. The Gilded don't smooth lifelines, they yank them. Their preferred method of torture is the refusal to allow their victims the release of death at the end. In their hands, there is no end. They allow them a glimpse, a sight of the desert and the cool sands, and jerk them back into Life. And dragging a soul back from Death again and again inevitably snaps them.

The Warden hisses something at Tobias, and the prisoners droop like broken wheat stalks. Tobias clears his throat. "Kill one," he orders.

I blink in confusion. A muscle twitches in Tobias's jaw: He wasn't expecting this either. He offers a knife, hilt first. "Kill one," he says again. No emotion in his tone.

It's a simple instruction, and I've been taught to wield a blade in defence of the veil. But ending a life is different from ensuring the dead stay in Death where they belong. My stomach twists. I am not going to become an instrument to execute prisoners. I will not.

My father scoffs. "Do you need motivation, thorn witch?" He turns to the guard at the door. "She has two sisters. The oldest was included in the Thorn Queen's bargain." He says *bargain* as if it's a joke. A private one. And I hate him for that. This isn't my father. Ella was right. It's a Gilded wearing his face.

The Warden laughs, a thin wheezing huff of mirth. My hands clench at my sides as my father continues, enjoyment of my situation dripping from every word. "The younger sister has no such protection. Fetch her."

It takes me a moment to realise he means Ella, and my heart stops. Fear spikes, hot and burning beneath my ribs. "No!"

Tobias's fingers dig into my shoulder so hard my collarbone creaks.

My father smiles. "No?"

"I'll... I'll do it." My hand trembles as I force myself to take the blade.

I finally look at the prisoners, and when I do, it takes all of my willpower not to vomit. Now, I cling to the knife. Their lips are sewn shut with thick silver thread. Rags that might have once been clothes hang from their thin bodies. They are broken beyond repair. I smell their defeat beneath the layers of grime and blood. They breathe, their hearts pump blood through their veins, but Death owns them. Their lifelines are already destroyed.

The bigger one braces himself against the floor, his breath gasping and damp. The smaller is a woman. Her hand creeps across the stone until her littlest finger brushes his hand. He goes rigid. His finger wraps hers like a pinkie promise, and his breathing slows, his shoulders relax.

My heart breaks. It takes everything I have in me to keep the tears back, but I cannot cry in front of the Warden.

The Dark Mother knows how many times these two have died and been dragged back. The blade in my hand will set them free.

That's how I try to justify it, anyway.

For Ella, I can do this. I can't watch her hurt. I can't watch this happen to her, her lifeline manipulated, her skin scarred. I can't undo what's been done to the Gilded's prisoners, but I can stop it. I can make it end. Refusing to do this gets me nowhere and hurts everyone else more. Still, tears ache in my throat and just for a moment I consider turning the blade on myself.

Two pairs of eyes raise to mine. One set is silver-bright. The blade trembles in my fingers. She's a thorn witch—I know all the non-Gilded thorn witches in Halstett because they all reside in the Colligerate with me.

But then I remember the trip to the city, the illegal tide witch hiding above a hat shop. Maybe there are other death-walkers hiding too. The witch in front of me is unrecognisable beneath the scarring on her face. Whorls and geometric shapes cover her cheeks and jaw. Some gape open and some are gnarled white lines. Blood crusts around the silver thread binding her lips.

The man's right ear is missing, but the worst of his pain lies in his eyes. He tightens his hold on the woman, and raises his chin, silently asking me to end him.

I swallow hard and whisper, "I'm sorry."

My hand steadies as I position the point of the dagger where the pulse beats in his throat. My fingers clench around the hilt. I don't have to push hard. It's horribly easy. The blade slides like a hot wire through butter, blood spills bright and shining over my hands, and it's over in seconds. Tears sting my eyes. His body slumps to the marble with a wet thud.

And then, at the precise moment before his lifeline vanishes, it shimmers scarlet and blue. I blink and the other lifelines in the room wink into existence. They sprout from each chest and rise into the air, dancing like kite strings in the breeze. The Gilded's pulse silver. The remaining prisoner's is bruised shades of silver and purple, a silken cord reaching from her chest to the blackened frayed end clamped in my father's fist.

My eyes widen—and I realise too late that is exactly what they were waiting for.

My reaction.

He snatches away the knife. Evil shines behind his golden mask. "Now, kill her."

"How?" I ask. I want to spit in his face.

"Uproot her lifeline. Bind her to Death."

I watch the man's blood trickle across the floor. I slow my breathing, and make myself look at the woman.

She tries to smile, silver stitches straining, and a wound in her chin turns it into a twisted grimace.

Slowly, almost beyond my control, I reach for her charred lifeline. It twitches as if caught in a phantom wind. What awaits her in Life is worse than Death could ever be.

Her lifeline wraps my fingers, fragile like a dusty cobweb. My throat twitches with revulsion at what I'm about to do. No one should have this power—life or death at my fingertips.

I pause and the lifeline clasped between my finger and thumb trembles.

No one in the throne room breathes.

Silver limns the woman's eyes. A tear tracks through the dirt on her deformed cheek.

She nods, permission to end her life. A plea for release.

My vision blurs. I hear her sigh. Magic churns in my veins and flows from my fingers as I pull gently on her lifeline. Her scars close into pale new skin. Her lifeline smooths, crisp like an apple fresh from a branch, silver shot through with green. The silver stitches fall from her lips like grave-worms sliding from a corpse. The prisoner on her knees is whole and perfect. I healed her. Her lifeline glittering in my hand pulses with life—and her eyes are wide with horror.

I know her.

It's my cousin Haylea. Carlotta's sister. Ella told me how her lifeline got snarled in the veil attempting to reforge the Sorcerer's knife, that the Gilded banished her beyond the Horizon!

We stare at each other, and I can't keep the emotions from my face. I can't breathe. How long has she been kept at the Gilded's mercy? How many times have they hurt her? Killed her? Dragged her back to Life? I try to talk and all that comes out is a strangled gasp.

The Warden inhales slowly. A satisfied hiss of a breath. And I hear him speak for the first time. "Excellent."

Magic drains from my blood. I feel hollow with it gone. I try to reach for Haylea, but Tobias covers my hands with his so I can't let go of her lifeline. It twists against my palms and my knees weaken. Tobias keeps me standing. I want to fight him, but I feel the Warden watching, savouring every moment of my pain. I want to sit on the floor and gather my cousin into my arms. I want to protect her. "Haylea, I'm sorry. I'm so sorry! I've made everything worse and I've missed you so much. Grandmother said—"

"Silence," my father says. "Touching as the family reunion is, it's over."

"It wasn't me," Haylea whispers, her voice a scrape of chalk on a blackboard. "I didn't tell them. It wasn't me." She sounds desperate—she's warning me. Someone else turned me in.

"Finish it," my father snaps.

"I love you," she whispers.

I shake my head in denial. My whole body is trembling as I try to pull away.

Tobias's grip is steel. I can't fight him. I can't stop him when he jerks my hands away from Haylea so fast I can't let go. Her lifeline uproots. It dissolves in my fingers, corded silk disintegrating as her soul passes the veil. I want to follow her, guide her to the Horizon. She'll need her lifeline to show her the way and she doesn't have one. I tore it away.

I look at Tobias blankly. Then I look back to Haylea.

My cousin stares at me from the floor, her eyes empty. Her life-line gone. One curl of her hair darkens with the blood of the man I killed.

"Death-Weaver." The Warden's voice shatters my thoughts; his next words crumble my resistance. "That shall be your name. You are mine, Death-Weaver. Say it."

I am numb, too numb to do anything but answer. "I am." It's a scratch of a whisper.

He laughs. A grating, awful laugh. His lifeline snakes around his feet, oozing pus onto the marble, pooling slick on the stone. And the Gilded lifelines—the barbs and thorns fraying the threads—it looks agonising. My mind flashes to Aaron, the gilding I helped Grand-mother with.

In that moment, I thought Grandmother's magic was awful, and that she used it to gild at the Warden's orders despicable. But I just killed my cousin without a weapon. Yanked her lifeline right out of her chest. I still feel it on my hands, a faint stickiness I don't think I'll ever wash away. I didn't think it was possible to uproot lifelines. No one *should* be able to.

The room spins and I think I'm going to be sick.

With a snap of his fingers, the Warden dismisses me. I don't react when Tobias catches me under the arm and leads me away.

Chapter Twenty-Three

Tobias stands by the bedroom door, watching me as I sit on the edge of the bed, giving me the space I desperately need.

I want to put my head in my hands and scream. I just killed my cousin. I gave up my name. I submitted to the Warden's demands. I should have chosen the safe house. Then they'd have just hurt me, not Haylea and the boy too. Maybe I should have turned the knife on myself and rid the world of a monster. No one should have the power to kill like that.

A gasp sticks in my throat. A sob chokes me. Panic rises and I want to run. But I can't run far enough or fast enough to ever escape myself. For the first time in my life, I wholeheartedly long to cross the veil.

"Don't, Penny. You had no choice," Tobias says gently.

"I killed them." My voice doesn't sound like me.

"You set them free." Tobias doesn't move from the doorway, but he doesn't leave either, and I wish I could find the words to thank him for it. There's a lump in my throat and if I try to force words past it, the dam holding back my tears will break and there'll be no stopping the flood it'll unleash.

Tobias speaks quietly, softening a silence I can't bear to hear. Even the horror hanging in his words is better than the quiet, than being alone. "Haylea would thank you for it. What was done to her..." He fades off, and I'm not sure if his next words are meant for me or if he's reassuring himself. "I had no idea. I'd have tried to help her. And Charlie too. I should have known." He swears under his breath and presses a hand into the wall. The joints in his gold gauntlets creak a protest at the pressure. "He was an ore witch, Charlie. He'd have done anything for Haylea, worshipped the ground she walked on. They met in the Resistance, didn't so much stamp on the boundaries between covens as shatter them... Fuck!" His lips clench, and I think he's trying not to cry.

"Can they... can they cross?" I ask weakly. Tobias looks at me, confused, silver eyes limned with unshed tears, and I want to hug him. I don't dare. "The Horizon. I took their lifelines."

Tobias nods, and some of the horror eases just a little. "They'll find their way."

"Promise?"

He nods. "Els is walking tonight. I'll tell her what happened. She'll find them."

I swallow hard and a tear slips free, blazing down my cheek. "Toby, I'm sorry."

"Don't be. I should have warned you this was likely. They caught a suspected black-crystalled witch in a village a few years ago and did the same. But it failed. Because he wasn't really black-crystalled. And when he failed, they gilded him. He wasn't much more than a child." Tobias winces. "I just didn't think they'd do this so soon." He shakes his head and his eyes seem heavier, more worried than before, but I'm too numb to care or say another word. "Try to sleep. I know it sounds impossible, but you look awful. I can't stay... if I could..."

"I'm fine," I mutter. There's nothing else I can say.

He gives me a long hard look, and a grim sort of smile. "You're not. And I'm damned glad you aren't. Anyone fine after what you've just been through would be as much a monster as the Warden."

I whisper my next question, my throat thick around my words. "You don't think I'm a monster?"

"No, Penny. You're not a monster." Sympathy softens Tobias; not pity, genuine sympathy that makes me want to sob. "I have to go. I'm sorry. Try to sleep. Don't do anything stupid until I come back." Then he leaves and locks the door, and I make myself look around.

Someone has cleaned and the rooms smell faintly of polish. They're grander and more ornate than my bedroom in the thorn witches' quarters; the bed is softer, the sheets are fresh dove-grey silk, the eiderdown embroidered with white lilies. But it's a glorified prison cell. I cannot leave. And I can't sleep either.

Murderer: The word beats against my heart. An accusation and a reminder of the power and magic. If I close my eyes I see Haylea.

I killed my cousin. And worse, I healed her first.

I have nothing to distract myself from what I've done, from remembering how my cousin's lifeline disintegrated in my hand, how her eyes glazed as she died. I slip out of bed and tiptoe to the window in the sitting room. With my arms around my knees, I hide in the window seat as afternoon fades toward evening outside.

Dinner is set on my table by a granite-eyed Gilded, but I can't eat. I feel sick and it's too quiet. In the coven's dining hall, my family will be seated around the table. Tonight, they will burn and I won't be there to share it. I wonder if my place will be filled as quickly as Haylea's was. If I'll be dismissed as an irritating mistake, called a fool like Grandmother called her.

What lies will they tell about me?

My entire life, I've been a thorn witch. Now I don't know who I am, what I am—or how the hell I'm going to survive what the Warden wants from me next.

Night has fallen when a click beside the fireplace in the sitting room snares my attention. The top half of the walls are papered with black flowers on white, ghostly shapes that form faces and condemning eyes in the dark. The bottom half is panelled wood, as black as the night outside my window.

One panel snicks open, swinging wide to reveal pale hair and huge eyes.

Alice.

My heart skips as I see her, frozen on the threshold of my rooms.

Her whisper drifts across the floor. "I know."

Of course she knows, Alice sees all. I hang my head, shame coursing through me.

"No," she whispers, silently clicking shut the panel in the wall. "You did what you had to, Penny." She perches beside me, wraithlike in the dark, dressed in black, bound in gold, as am I.

I need to tell her, speak my crimes out loud. "I—"

"Hush," she says, fingers tracing my wrist below the Warden's cuff, lingering on the veins beneath my skin. "They made me kill so I could see them too. No one else can. Even those who kill so many cannot see."

"You can see lifelines too?" I should be upset she didn't tell me before, but all I feel is relief. Whatever is wrong with me, Alice knows and she's still here. Staring at me in the dark with understanding in her eyes.

"I don't see yours," she says softly.

I don't see hers either.

I lean into her a little, and she rests her cheek against my hair. "I see the paths they take. I watch them in my dreams. They never leave me, Penny. I have to weave them. Sometimes, I think I'm losing my mind." She lowers her voice to the barest of whispers. "My name is Alice."

"Alice," I murmur, and her breath catches, a stutter to her inhale.

Her pinkie finger dances soft patterns against my wrist. I wonder if she's painting my future there. "Are you all right?"

I open my mouth to say yes. I should be strong enough to be fine. But I'm not. And here, now, it seems silly to pretend. With Alice, I feel safe enough to let down my guard, to admit my weakness, and when my eyes prickle with traitorous tears, I'm not even ashamed. "No," I reply. A tiny, sad little answer.

"Tell me," Alice says softly. "Tell me everything. It might help."

I try to laugh, but it comes out a sob. "You'll have seen it all already."

"Not with you, Penny." The way she says my name sends a shiver down my spine, and I want her to say it again, just like that, with exactly the same inflection. "Tell me," she says.

And I do. I tell her everything, starting small; about Ella and Mila and the way they've been arguing, about Tobias and Clair and how they've helped me, the Resistance and Miss Elsweather and the ninth floor of the library. I tell her about my father and how I'd hoped we might be able to heal him and the other Gilded. How it hurt when that hope shattered. How my own father handed me to the Warden.

With each fresh confession, some of the fear twisted in my chest unfurls, and each breath is lighter. Tears are streaming down my cheeks and my eyes are sore by the time I tell her about Death and how it feels to burn night after night without a break. I think Alice is crying too when, finally, I tell her about the man behind the manor walls and the deal I made—but I cannot bring myself to use his name.

"Oh, Penny," she whispers. "They tangled you up tighter than they did me."

I pull away from her and rub the backs of my hands across my eyes. "Who did?"

Alice's fingers trail up my forearm, press lightly against the black freckle Evelyn made, and then drift to her lap to dance the song of her loom against her skirts. "The Resistance."

I blink through the stuffy aftermath of tears and sniff as I run through the conversation we just had, all the things I said.

Alice watches me steadily and tucks her hair behind her ear. She misses a strand and I want to smooth it for her but don't quite dare.

My heart skips a little when her eyes meet mine. "I shouldn't have been able to talk to you about the Resistance. I made an oath that would stop me. Unless..." I trail off and stare at Alice.

"I joined," Alice says simply. "The Resistance asked a favour, and I liked their terms. I was only sixteen. I'm not sure it was a mistake." She shrugs and her shoulder brushes against mine with the movement. "It's odd, not being sure. It only happens with you, Penny, and it's terrifying." She smiles, her eyes round and wide. "I think I like it."

Her knee presses against my thigh as she shifts a little, and I'm suddenly aware of the thin layers of silk between us, the warmth of her, the scent of primroses on her hair. "Alice?" She shivers, and I blink, utterly unsure and off-balance. "What are we supposed to do?"

"Survive," she replies. She closes her eyes, dark eyelashes resting against her cheeks. "Or," she says softly, a wicked curve to the corner of her smile, "we could fight." When she opens her eyes, they are as black as the space between stars.

"But who? Who do we fight? And what are we fighting for?" I lean away a little to look at her better, this captive witch no one realises is here. They see the Spinner, a spider-like weaver of the Warden's dreams and desires. But there's so much more to her than that.

Her reply confirms it. "You are the Death-Weaver, a thorn witch, a librarian, a sister and daughter and cousin. Third in line to the

Thorn Queen's crown. You're all those things. But most of all, you are *Penny*, and I'm on your side."

"I'm on yours." And that feels like a more unbreakable deal than the one I made with Malin—more binding than fifty pages signed in blood. This feels like friendship.

"I'll help you cross tonight. We'll survive him." She straightens and cocks her head to one side. "I have to go." And just that simply she's gone in a flutter of black skirts and silk-soft hair and a click of a panel slotting back into place.

The scent of primroses and spring sunshine clings to my skin and I don't feel as alone as I did before.

Quietly, I draw the curtains against the dark, curl into the window seat, and listen to the boots coming toward my door.

Tobias doesn't knock before he marches into my room and throws a black dress on the chair. "The Warden's ordered a celebration. You're the guest of honour."

I inch back into the cocoon of the curtains. The man who walked me safely to the Thorn Wing the other night is the same man who watched me kill. Haylea is dead because of me. Tobias helped me become a murderer.

He frowns. "I'm on your side."

"You're Gilded."

"We've been through this." He wears the High Warden's colours, black tunic trimmed with gold, and a number one is stamped on his breastplate. I can't see his lifeline. "I've been assigned as your minder," he says.

I stare at him warily. "How?"

"I pulled some strings." Tobias takes a step closer. I flinch back and he freezes. "Look, I should have tried to explain before, I'm part of the High Warden's personal Gilded guard. Highest rank—"

"You can't be much older than me! How did you get that position so young?" Anger flashes in Tobias's eyes at my question, but I can't take it back.

"I'm twenty-four." He sighs and the anger dissipates as if it was never there. Maybe it never was; I'm not sure I'm a very good judge of character anymore. "And you're right, I did some horrible things to earn the honour. But it's saved so many lives. Protected people. I really am trying to help you." Tobias shakes his head, exasperated. "I thought you saw me, not the damned mask. Do us both a favour and when we leave, look defeated. I was ordered to ensure you were thoroughly broken. Act it or we're both screwed." He nods at the dress he threw on the armchair. A gold tassel peeps from beneath black cloth. "Get changed. I won't look."

I silently slip into a black silk dress and tie the gold belt about my waist, and he keeps his promise, facing the door.

The corridors are empty tonight. None loiter in the hallways the night of a celebration. The Warden likes his entertainment, and it's not unheard of for him to order the nearest person in the halls fetched just to punish them for existing.

Tobias doesn't speak as we walk, the bare side of his face as smooth and empty as the gold-masked half. His silver eyes are ringed with black kohl, lining his lids and heavying his lashes.

He draws me to a halt and, as I face the doors, my heart lurches. It twists as footsteps draw closer and Clair brings Alice to stand at my side. Clair too looks different. Gone is the girl who passed me a message from Alice in the abandoned schoolroom. Her face is as emotionless as Tobias's. Her silver breastplate gleams; the hilt of her dagger gleams brighter.

This is Palace Guard Clair: as hard as Gilded Tobias.

I lower my gaze and remember Alice's words. *They say it gets easier. It doesn't.* I don't want it to. I don't ever want to accept this as normal. I won't let this be real.

Alice chuckles. She's wearing white, gold at her waist and glittering at her wrists.

Together, we are light and dark. Life and Death.

And together, we might survive him.

"We will," Alice whispers.

Palace Guard Clair hisses, "Silence. Eyes down, both of you."

The doors swing open to the gathered court. A string quartet plays in one corner, a lilting melody that wraps sorrow around my heart. We're led past drunken nobles adorned in grey council robes, merchants wearing satin shirts in shades of grey sipping at gold goblets of wine. Lifelines drift above all of them, a rainbow of silken threads I wish I couldn't see.

We climb the dais and drop silently to our knees, Alice and I: her on one side of the Warden's throne; me, the other.

This close, the stench of his wound is a solid thing. It knees me in the gut. I swallow and refuse to let it show. Clair moves to stand beside the consort's vacant throne, and Tobias joins the Gilded grouped behind the Warden.

I turn my eyes to the floor and listen to the slight wheeze of the Warden's breath, see his gloved fingers tightening on the arm of his throne in my periphery. Beneath the stench of his wound, I smell his fear and pain.

Advisors come and go, grey robes scuffing the floor, but nothing of importance is uttered. The court is full to bursting and there are too many listening ears other than mine.

Then, the throne room falls silent. Soft footsteps approach. Pink skirts flutter to a halt before my knees, the colour a shock to the senses.

The Warden greets her through clenched teeth. "How nice of you to join us, my dear."

The pink swirls closer, chiffon spangled with silver triangles brushing against my black silk. The high consort's voice drips contempt across the silent throne room. "You have a new pet, Reginald. It would have been rude not to welcome her to the fold." She bends closer and her nail scrapes lightly up my cheek to my temple, making me lift my gaze.

Dark curls are swept up with diamond combs and tumble over her shoulders. Her face is hidden behind a masquerade mask, a web of snakes with glittering gemstones for eyes. Like the Gilded, it gives her an emotionless facade; unlike the Gilded, hers is removable, held in place with gold ribbons wound into her hair.

Her lifeline is grey and dark, almost colourless in contrast to her dress. It looks dead and cold. Her gold eyes might have been warm once, but something in this consort is cracked deep inside. "Pretty too. How long before you ruin this one?" Her fingers trickle down my neck and she exhales as she releases me. I hear a soft rustle of cushions as she settles into her throne. "A matching set, Reggie. One spins you the future, but the new one? You want to command Death? I thought that's what your legions of half-masked, mutilated brutes were for."

"She's the Thorn Queen's granddaughter."

"The noose to hang the witch?"

"Not quite. But she'll be entertaining to play with." Mortification burns my cheeks, to be reduced this way. Guilt tightens around my ribs; this is how we talked about the Spinner before I met her. Before I knew her name was Alice.

Since I was eight, all I've wanted was to go home—back to our village with its cherry blossom tree by the banks of the stream. I wanted everything the way it was before.

Now, I have a new desire. I want to kill the Warden.

His lifeline coils around my knees, emerald-hard and wetly glistening. I don't think it would uproot like Haylea's did. I swallow hard at the memory.

I need to help the Resistance reforge the Sorcerer's knife. I need to find the Grimoire. I need to trust Alice when she says we'll both survive.

Alice shifts, and I try to see her without being noticed.

I fail.

The Warden's hand tangles in my hair and forces me to look up. A mask covers his entire face, a gold skull stripped bare of flesh. Removable like the consort's, it moulds to his expression, forming furrows between his brows with his frown and covering his eyelids so even his lashes are fringed with gold. Dark hair curls around it, hiding the ribbons holding it in place—if I didn't know better, I'd believe this was his skin. I see why people fear him as a god.

The Warden's black glare pins me. I want to close my eyes against it.

His growl of anger cuts the music short. Chatter stops. Laughter dies. "Were the rules not explained, Death-Weaver?"

I bite my lip and stay silent, staring past him to his throne. It stares back at me, formed from the masks of Gilded who died in his service, peeled from corpses and twisted into this gruesome creation by the Ore Coven. Obsidian glass sparkles in the eye holes.

My heart hollows at Alice's sharp inhale.

The Warden clicks his fingers, his gold-skulled face completely blank. "Stand them up."

Alice chuckles in defiance as a Gilded steps forward and yanks her to her feet. Tobias pulls me to mine.

The Warden looks twenty with his ageless mask and sharp-angled jaw. But he is older. So much older. Pain sharpens his eyes at the edges. And no matter what skills I possess, I will not heal it. Grandmother can keep him existing in pain.

I smile. I shouldn't, but I do.

His jaw tightens and he waves a hand at Tobias. "Teach them."

Tobias shifts his weight.

The Warden leans back in his velvet-padded throne. His consort shakes her head in distaste, but she does nothing.

Alice's lips move without sound, but I catch her words. "I said I'd help."

Tobias pulls two silver vials from his pocket. There's an apology in his eyes when he looks at me, and I decide, in that moment—with that expression he shouldn't risk here—that I can trust him. He unscrews the vial, presses it to my lips and tells me to swallow—and I do.

It tastes of ginger and lemon, not the charred pepper of the Resistance's poison vials. Ice slides down my throat.

I blink, confused.

Fire ignites in my blood, starting deep behind my navel and spreading with each beat of my heart.

Alice chokes and her blistering scream stokes the fire in my veins.

Clever Alice. Clever, manipulative, wonderful Alice.

Barbed Gilded magic hooks into my lifeline, keeping me from escaping to Death as fire consumes me from the inside out. We are not permitted that release.

I should be screaming. I should be writhing in Tobias's grip. But I've been trained not to react to pain. I've burned before.

And I won't give the Warden the satisfaction.

Tobias jerks his knee into the back of mine, taking my legs from under me. I crumple silently, and he stops me hitting the floor.

The Warden watches with amused curiosity. I am his curious thing and I have not disappointed.

He clicks his fingers, and Tobias loosens his hold on my consciousness. Darkness sucks at my mind. I fight, and he tugs me toward the dark with a hiss in my ear, "Go under!"

I close my eyes and sag in his grip. But I cling to consciousness with nails and teeth and desperation. If I let myself slip under, I won't be able to open the veil or set my soul free. I cannot go under. I can't.

The Warden sighs, satisfied. "Get them out of my sight."

I'm lifted in Tobias's arms and carried from the throne room.

Mutters and whispers follow us as we leave. Clair's boots ring sharp and staccato along the corridors and up the stairs, the Gilded carrying Alice marching at our side.

The door to my room thuds shut, and Tobias lays me on the table. I'm surprised he can bear to touch me. My skin begins to smoke, my lungs blister, and burning blood scorches my bones.

"Alice?" I murmur.

"She'll be fine." Cold metal presses against my lips, and I turn away. "Penny, it's the antidote."

I shake my head. "I need to cross."

"You want to cross into Death?" There's an accusation in Tobias's question.

I crack open my eyes, and it feels like I splinter as I do. "Please."

"If I'm caught...what another will do to you in my place. They'll destroy you."

"I made a deal." I sound weak. I can't afford to be weak. Alice put herself through this to help me cross. "I have to honour it."

Tobias must have a hundred more questions, but all he asks is, "How long?"

"Until dawn."

I wonder if Ella told him about the manor and the gardens in Death, about Lord Malin with his dangerous eyes and charming smile.

Smoke rises from the table beneath my fingers; smouldering wood taints the air.

Tobias nods. "Don't tell Ella. Be careful, Penny. Bea did what she could with the cuffs, but I don't know how they'll affect you in Death."

I try to smile a reassurance, close my eyes, and whisper the words to part the veil. Tobias whispers them too, his hand wraps my wrist, and he shares my pain.

With a sigh, I step out of my burning body and into the chill of Death.

When the World Divided

In the aftermath of Death's creation, the world grew dark. The Dark Mother sat atop the tallest peak of the west Wayvern Spine and watched the Sorcerer in his cave, far away by the eastern seas. She watched the little people she'd nurtured grow weak. Crystals of power clenched in failing hands. And ice filled her immortal heart.

Her sorrow rained from the skies, her anger crashed in the heavens, until she was spent. Finally, she looked at her people wandering lost and alone, directionless, and saw past their indiscretions. They were human, after all. Weak in the face of the Sorcerer's temptation. But she could not undo what was done. So, she sat down and began to weave the first lifeline from threads of rainbows and strands of fresh clouds. She spun another and another until her skirts were full, and then she stood on her mountain top and made the sun shine.

With a great breath, she blew her magic across the skies and her rainbow threads, invisible to mortal eyes, fell from the heavens. Each thread found a person and burrowed silently, painlessly into their hearts. A lifeline to guide them through life, giving them direction. And though all directions still led eventually to Death, her people found happiness again. The Sorcerer's magic crystals dissolved into their skin, power twisting into their blood, and so witches were made.

No mortal should have seen what the Dark Mother had done. But one witch watched it all. She saw the wind blow and the lifelines fall. She felt it take root in her heart, a rainbowed thread of colour and light. She watched from the shadow of the trees that grew in the foothills of the Wayvern Spine and reported to the Sorcerer, who had enlisted her help. The Sorcerer smiled. He showed her a thorn, how to prick her finger and take the drop of blood into Death's cold deserts and grow a magic crystal from the sand. And then he showed her how to return.

Coven Classics: Fables from the Wayvern Spine. *Found in the Thorn Shrine in the tenth year after the fall.*

Chapter Twenty-Four

The borders between Life and Death blur as I cross. Walking in Death is like wading through iced water. Fire quenches in my veins but my muscles are weak like damp string, and feverish pain is smeared across my skin, unable to decide if it is hot or cold. My wrists are heavy as if they're still banded with the Warden's gold. Thankfully, the cuffs stayed behind.

In the stillness, I feel the subtle shift of the sands—and a thorn witch's lifeline at the edge of my senses. Crisp and clear like a green apple fresh from the tree. Carlotta's.

The desert stretches into the Horizon, and souls amble gently toward it. I make myself walk away from the veil and my temperature plummets. My fingers turn numb where I've tucked them under my arms, and I can't summon enough magic to change my clothes.

I've walked a hundred shaking steps when the dark splotch that precedes the manor's appearance blackens the grey desert. A hundred more and my thighs burn as if I've just completed three hours of weapons training. My feet sink into the damp sand, grey silt squelching between my toes.

Exhaustion shields me from the dead who refuse to fully die. I'm too tired to be frightened. My lack of emotions blends me into the landscape, and no fog-wraiths notice me pass.

Twenty paces from the gate, my knees give way, dumping me to the sand. The chill creeps into my bones, and a giggle sticks in my throat at the irony: I burned in Life, now I freeze in Death. Colour shimmers beyond the portcullis, pink and purple flowerbeds blooming as if in the first throes of summer. The light is warmer there.

I'm too close to give up. I grit my teeth and force myself to my feet just as the gate rattles upward.

Lord Malin watches me struggle toward his threshold. Black hair curls across his brow and twirls under his ears. He catches me as I stumble. His arms fold me into his chest, solid and oddly warm, and relief prickles behind my eyes. Malin might have designs on my soul, but he's safe. Forgetting our contract, the imbalance of power, and that I have no idea who he really is, I lean into him, and he holds me closer. Normally, I hate being protected, but now I welcome it.

He's silent as he helps me down the path and up the steps, one arm around my back, and with his hand pressed against my waist, I don't have to be strong anymore. He ushers me into the parlour, which is decorated tonight in shades of grey and mauve that match my mood, and I don't resist as he settles me in one corner of a plush sofa. He sits carefully on the sofa beside me and his gaze pins me still. There is something gentler about him tonight.

And infinitely more dangerous.

"What did you do, Penelope?" The carefulness of his tone clashes with the hardness of his jaw, shattering the safety he offered before.

"Attracted the wrong kind of attention." I have nothing to tell him. No news of the Warden. I am failing as a person and a spy. I want to run but I don't have the energy. I want to hide my head in my hands and weep—but I don't quite dare. More than anything, I want to sleep.

His eyes darken. "How bad is it?"

I shrug, unwilling to admit how my death burns my skin, even here, and my wrists are sensitive and raw where the Warden's cuffs bind me in Life.

Weakness is defeat; weakness is failure.

"May I?" He gestures at my hand, and I nod my consent. Calluses on his fingers brush my wrist as he takes it—he's not unfamiliar with a weapon in his hand. "He could have done worse," Malin says under his breath, almost to himself. He shifts a little closer and his thigh presses against my knee, and I'm so distracted I nearly miss his next words. "A few days and your magic will adjust to compensate. You're lucky."

Malin's definition of luck is clearly different to mine. If I wasn't so drained, I'd bite back at his comment. Instead, I bite my lip and keep my thoughts to myself as he continues his examination. His fingers run softly along the curve of my wrist, and a shiver runs down my spine and hooks behind my navel. He doesn't care about me, I remind myself. He cares what I am: a witch in his service who's awful at espionage.

But Malin looks like he wants to hunt down whoever hurt me. Concern darkens his eyes, anger hardens his jaw. Slowly, his inspection of my wrists extends up my arms, his fingers gently tracing my forearms to the inside of my elbows. My heart clenches when he brushes the rough pad of one finger across the black freckle marked by the Resistance, but he doesn't react, no pause, no flicker of a feature to show he suspects anything.

For a long time, the only sound is his soft inhale, my breath hitching beside his, and the tick of the clock above the fire.

This is the man who bargained my soul for my sister, I tell myself as his palm cools my skin—the man who will own it, and therefore me, if I fail.

"You killed." It's not a question and there's no judgement in his words. No accusation.

I incline my head, watching his thumb move to my palm and follow the lines there as if he's reading a story. I have an uncomfortable feeling that's exactly what he's doing. "My cousin."

"It opened your eyes?"

I should pull my hand away, but he circles my wrist with his finger and thumb and I'm a mouse caught in a trap—not an entirely unwilling one.

"Look at me, Penelope."

"My name is Penny."

He smiles, and it's not the oil-slick smile that normally curves his lips. There's no pity in it either. "What do you see?"

I don't know how to answer that. I don't know what he wants to hear. "A man," I say. "A dangerous one, with eyes like midnight and words like silk."

He chuckles under his breath. His thumb grows still on my palm. He leans closer. So close, his breath brushes against my skin. I should move away; I should push him back.

Danger, my brain screams, but my body doesn't listen. His eyes hold me as I tremble beneath his caress. I can't help myself. He's so steady, so safe.

He's not.

He's not.

I know he isn't, but I don't care. Right now, I just want to forget. I don't trust him, this man living in the desert of Death in a manor that shouldn't exist outside of a storybook. But I want his thumb to trace my wrist again. I want him to hold me in his arms.

He closes the space between us, so slowly my heart skips, speeding as it reclaims its beat. His pupils are dilated, his lips slightly parted, and I want to lean into him, see if he tastes as good as he smells. He pulls away and holds me by the shoulders, and the tiniest of noises slips free of my lips; half whimper or half sob.

"Not yet," Malin says to himself, not me. He releases me, and I'm so confused. Relieved and disappointed all at once. My heart sinks as he rests back into the opposite corner of the sofa and throws one arm languidly along the back of it. "You're tired, Penelope. You've had a difficult day."

I stare at him, incredulous. It's the understatement of the century.

"Rest," he says softly. "You must be exhausted. There's a while until dawn and you're safe here. I'll wake you with plenty of time."

Malin might be the most impossibly attractive man I've ever had the misfortune to meet, but it's his contract that's threatening to break me with lack of sleep. I should go back, but the idea of the room, the loneliness, and the Gilded standing guard outside, is soul-destroying. "How am I supposed to sleep with you right there?"

Malin stands and strides across the room. There's a piano in one corner I swear I've never seen before. Its rich black lacquer gleams in the gauze-filtered morning sunshine streaming through the window. I blink. I'm sure that wasn't there a moment ago. It definitely wasn't there when I sat down.

He opens the lid, sits quietly at the seat, and presses a single key. The note sounds true, and he begins to play. The tune dances with the breeze; at first it's a lullaby, soft and gentle, then it's a story, slow and sad. My eyes drift shut and my thoughts tangle around one another as I slip into the quiet before dreams.

I stiffen, jolting awake. It's dark here now. Death should not get dark, but flowers shouldn't grow in Death either, so I accept it without question. At some point in my sleep, Malin covered me with a blanket.

There's a clink of a saucer on a table and a lamp glows. "I made you tea," Malin says. "I was about to wake you."

"It's nearly dawn?"

"Not quite. You have time for tea." He sits opposite me, and I shuffle to sitting, rubbing the sleep from my eyes and wrapping the blanket around my shoulders like a shawl. "Then," he says quietly, "there's the matter of our contract, which has not been fulfilled this evening." Chilled wind sneaks in from outside, bringing with it the scent of roses and dew on the grass. "Do you have a report on the Warden?"

"I..." I have nothing bar the fact the man is an arsehole. I sip at the tea, bergamot and rosehip with a spoonful of honey. I've not tasted anything so delicious in years. "I'm sorry."

"Tomorrow, you can bring news of the High Warden and his court." He regards me thoughtfully, regretful almost, and I drink to hide the wobble of my composure. "Are you sure you want to play this game? Just say the word and you can remain here—with me. You're strong enough to survive it. I'd keep you safe." His lips smile. They don't match his eyes.

I try to laugh, but it's shaky. "I have to go back."

His smile hardens as his gaze slides down to the ghost of my crystal hanging around my neck. "It's been a long time since I saw a crystal like yours. Bring it tomorrow, Penelope."

"The Warden has it." Taking our crystals into Death is like throwing an anchor overboard with no rope attached. Even if the Warden didn't have it, I'd never bring it here. Especially not to show Malin.

"Then I strongly suggest reclaiming it," Malin says, as if it's as simple a task as buttering bread. "But do be careful, Penelope. I'd hate for you to miss a night. When you stay, I'd far rather it was by choice than by failure."

"I'll be here—and I won't be staying. And for the hundredth time, my name is Penny."

Reality slaps me hard. He's back to his old self, and I wasted an opportunity tonight. I should have taken advantage of his softer mood, convinced him to let me visit his woods, asked about the library he mentioned to Ella.

I feel the weight of my foolishness. But I've dealt with enough today. I can't deal with anything more.

Malin offers a hand to help me to my feet, and just for a moment, I think he's going to wrap me in his arms again and pull me into his chest. When he doesn't, just for a moment, I wish he had. "Tomorrow, I'll meet you as you cross. Walking in Death with the Warden's gold at your wrists is inviting trouble."

Being seen with him in Death will invite more than trouble. But, when Malin drapes his cloak around my shoulders and laces his fingers through mine, I cling tight all the same. I'm grateful when he walks me to the borders.

Sleep has revived me, my legs feel stronger than they have in days, and my mind is clear and sharp. I can do this. See this bargain through to the end, find the Grimoire, and help the Resistance reforge the Sorcerer's knife.

"Be careful, Penny," Malin says gently.

He called me Penny.

I want to look back. But the veil seals shut before I can.

Chapter Twenty-Five

I fall into a woolly sleep filled with fragments of conversation that don't fit together, watched by silver eyes glazed with death: Ella's and Mila's and my mother's. Haylea's. I can't stop her dying in my dreams any more than I could in reality.

It's still dark when I'm woken by a gentle hand on my forehead.

I smell her before I open my eyes, spring sunshine and primroses in full bloom.

Alice.

"I couldn't sleep," she whispers. "I couldn't see you."

"I'm fine." My tongue is thick around my words. Someone, Tobias maybe, has left a large glass of water by my bed. It eases my throat, and when I speak again my words are clear. "Are you all right? What you did—"

"It's not the first time I've burned; it won't be the last. Pain is different. Normal never changes. I like different."

"It could have killed you!"

"It did kill you." She giggles and the sound is too loud. I shush her and grab her hand to pull her closer. She whispers my name into my hair, shifting a little so we're nearly nose to nose. I let her hold me and tentatively, I wrap my arms around her. She feels slight in my arms, almost like nothing at all. When her forehead rests against mine, a warmth settles in my chest. A comfort I can't explain. And I don't want to. We stay like that for a while. Me sitting on my bed, her perched at my side, holding me as I hold her.

Her eyes sparkle. "Don't forget. No matter what happens, don't forget." She exhales slowly, gentle as a breath of wind, laced with anticipation like the silence before a spring storm breaks. "Promise me."

I nod and run my fingers down her arm, trying to reassure her. "I promise." I'm not sure what I'm promising, but she seems satisfied. Her hair gleams silver in the moonlight sneaking through a gap in the curtains. I pull away to look at her better, and her smile makes my heart flutter. My eyes fall to her lips, and suddenly I'm blushing.

I don't want to complicate everything. Alice's friendship is precious. I need her, and I think she needs me too. I've never felt like this—never wanted to kiss a friend. But I've never really had a friend outside the Thorn Coven before either.

"I need to sleep, Alice. Tomorrow, I have to get my crystal back and—"

She presses a silk bundle into my hand. Power jolts through me as she folds my fingers around it, and it vibrates softly against my palm, setting my lifeline humming like a bowstring strung too tight. My heart skips. Carefully, I unwrap the silk, and Alice watches my silent reaction.

My crystal. Obsidian-black, deep as a starless midnight sky.

I stare at it in shock. I haven't seen it since I was eight.

"Alice! How?"

"Clair helped me," she says quietly.

"But I thought… the Warden had it."

Alice chuckles. "The Gilded had it. I asked the loom how to get it back. Evelyn set fire to the workroom at the gilding this afternoon,

Beatrice created a gap in the wall while everyone was distracted, and Clair slipped in and found it."

I'm horrified by how reckless they have been with their own lives. "Alice, how could you? If you had been caught..." I shudder at the idea of it.

She glances away to the door. "We knew it would work. The loom wove it so. We didn't tell the rest of Resistance you have it back. Not yet. And the Gilded in charge of your crystal won't admit to the Warden they lost it, not until they have to."

"Still!" I bite my lip; so many people put themselves in danger to help me. They haven't asked for anything in return. "I owe all of you so much."

"Friends don't have debts." Her voice falters on the word *friend*. I wonder if she's had a friend before. "Just Clair," she says, reading my mind as always. "Now you. There was one before, a long time ago. He vanished in the night."

She shivers, and I hesitate before lifting the covers for her to slide in beside me. "This won't last if you're missing from your bed and found in mine."

"Don't worry, Penny," she says in a sing-song whisper. "The loom won't let me be away for long enough to get caught."

We curl together, her arms around my neck, mine around hers, our legs tangled beneath the sheets. There's such comfort in her presence. It soothes the ache of missing my sisters, soothes away the memory of Malin's fingers on my wrist. The beat of her heart against my ribs eases the feverish chill that followed me from Death, and I fall asleep to the gentle brush of her fingers dancing softly through my hair.

Dawn has broken when I wake again. Alice is gone, but the space beside me is still warm. A piece of silk peeps out from under my pillow, and when I ease it out, I smile. Embroidered in jewel-coloured thread, two figures stand hand in hand, a field of scarlet flowers at their feet. One is Alice, crowned in silver. The other is me, crowned in gold. Our skirts swirl together, sapphire blue and amethyst purple.

I slide the silk under my pillow, resolving to hide it under the floorboards later, and hurry out of bed. Sleep has strengthened me—or maybe it's having my crystal so close. Maybe it was Alice. My mind is clearer, and where my problems were fuzzy before, things I had to survive, now they leap into sharp focus.

Yesterday, the Warden made me kill. I owe him for that. And it's seeded anger where before there was only desperation and fear.

I'm glad I'm not Alice and that I cannot see the outcome. I'm glad my future is not hers to spin on her loom. I'll fight no matter the end—but I'd rather not see myself fail.

Today, I have two issues: I need a way to burn that doesn't involve Alice burning too, and I need better information on the Warden to take into Death. My heart quickens at the thought of Malin. Withers at the idea of failing—again. He's given me so many chances, it's almost like he wants me to win.

There's a frustratingly easy answer to the first problem: four nights' worth of poison are tucked inside my pillow in the Thorn Coven's wing, but I can't get back to my room to retrieve it. Ella would help me, but I have no way of contacting her that doesn't risk tightening a noose around her neck. The second problem I suspect will solve itself, so I set that aside and spend the better part of the morning trying to unlatch the panel Alice came through last night, hoping there might be a passage behind it linked to the catacombs. I could get close enough to sneak to the Thorn Coven's wing. But I find nothing. No secret notches, no concealed springs or catches.

By lunchtime, boredom creeps in. I have no books, no work, no way to escape. I've counted every black rose on the white wallpaper in the bedroom. I've counted every white one on black in the sitting room too. I've stared out of the window and written it off as an escape route; there are no handholds on the walls, no trellis or downpipe. Jumping will break my bones on the cobbled courtyard below.

I watch out the window as the day passes without me. It begins to rain, huge raindrops that match my mood. A tide witch crosses in front of the barracks, the rain parting to keep her hair dry. She spots a palace guard on the other side of the courtyard, smiles a tiny secret smile and twitches her finger, directing the rain to fall harder on them.

As the afternoon passes, I see one tiny act of rebellion after another. A storm witch sends a puff of wind to snatch away a pile of papers. An ember witch extinguishes a lantern outside the barracks. An ore witch gives a gargoyle on the roof of the barracks a stony grin. Small things. Little differences.

I watch Mila hurry up the steps into the barracks, her arms wrapped tight around herself, her lifeline dancing silver above her.

I frown. Mila should have no need to be in the barracks at this time of day. But she disappears inside and doesn't emerge. My worry rises again, and I sink down on the very centre of the rug in the sitting room. Its pattern of triangles forms a star mostly hidden by my black nightdress. I wish they'd left a change of clothes. I wish I could speak to Alice; she's so close I hear the click of her loom next door, a steady metronome counting off the minutes and hours. But I listen to the shift of armour and boots on the landing and count four Gilded between us.

Four Gilded guarding two girls seems like overkill. I wonder if someone else saw the possibility spun into Alice's tapestry. There are other, less accurate, methods of divination. Crystal balls glimmer in the ember witches' chambers, rune bones are scattered by the storm witches. Tyromancy, floriography, and scrying; each coven has ways of seeking the truth and the Warden controls them all. Any could have uncovered what Alice spun in her web of dreams—the red-headed girl on her knees reaching for the Warden.

Ice-cold fear grips me, and I shiver. I need to focus on what I can control, not what I cannot. And right now, I need to hide my crystal. It should have been the first thing I did.

I roll back the rug and check the floorboards. I search under the bed and behind the other furniture. Finally, behind a chest of drawers, I find a loose plank covered in tally marks as if someone was crossing off the days. With a sigh of relief, I unfold Alice's silk.

My crystal is so black it seems to absorb the light, and magic sparks deep inside. I brush it with one fingertip and cool stone meets my fingers with a jolt of power. Magic floods like pins and needles through my blood. The future doesn't seem as bleak as before. Possibilities shine where once there was a void.

I'm curled into the window seat, watching smoke drift out the barracks chimney, rising to meet the haze of low-lying cloud, when the door opens. My shoulders tense, my breath falters, but I don't look. Instead, I shift my focus to the reflection in the glass and the gold-plated Gilded closing the door behind him.

"Ella told me what you did for her," Tobias says quietly.

My chin jerks up, and I meet his silver gaze. "Is she being interrogated?"

A muscle twitches in his cheek. "I wouldn't let that happen."

"You could stop it?"

"Yes." His voice is low and there's a brown paper parcel tucked under one arm. His gauntlets are absent today, his breastplate replaced with black fatigues, short-sleeved and edged in gold. He's thrown his cloak over the back of the chair. He's off duty. "Don't worry about Ella."

"After she vanished and got herself tangled up with you while I wasn't looking, it's difficult not to."

"She's worried about you, Penny. She told me everything, how you found her in the manor in Death. She blames herself for you being here."

"It's not her fault."

"I told her the same. She asked me to give you this." He hands me the parcel, and I unwrap it, cautiously tearing off the paper. Inside is a nightrobe. The deepest of greys and the softest thing I've ever felt—and it has pockets. It smells of honeysuckle with a hint of cindered ash under the sweetness. It's Ella's. Holy Dark Mother, I miss her.

I slip down from the window, wrap myself in Ella's robe, and huddle into the armchair beside the fire. "When can I see her?"

"Not yet." Tobias presses a thumb into his temple, rubs it hard, and sits stiffly on the black velvet sofa. "We need to talk about what happened last night. Burning like that—"

I lower my voice. "I have to cross again."

He shakes his head as if he can't quite believe what he's hearing. "You're crazier than she is!"

"Which *she*? Ella?"

"The Spinner."

"Her name is Alice. And she isn't crazy."

He softens. "The stunt she pulled last night was. Why are you walking in Death?"

I keep my face carefully blank. "My sister was in trouble, and no one else would help her."

"Which only explains the first time you walked and begs the question: How did you get her out?" He's staring at my wrist. I go to tuck my hands in my pockets, but he's on his feet too fast. He catches my hand and holds it accusingly in front of my face, sliding my cuff up my arm just enough so the stem of Malin's rosebud mark peeps out. "Who did you bargain with?"

I pull my hand away and shove the cuff down. "Ella was dying."

"So you made a deal?" he prompts. I don't answer and Tobias looks like he wants to shake me. "What did he say his name was?"

I've not even told Ella about the deal I made in Death. I probably shouldn't tell Tobias either, but I need help. "Malin," I whisper.

Tobias goes pale. "What's he got you doing?"

"Spying on the Warden."

He sucks air through his teeth. "One mistake... Do you realise what the Warden will do if you mess up, Penny? If he finds out you're spying on him?"

I try for humour. "I'll get locked in a room and cuffed with gold?"

"He'll have you gilded." He slumps into the sofa, watching to see if his words have landed. They have. A gold half-mask would be infinitely worse than this. "What were the terms? How long's he got you for?"

"Thirty days." That seems like an impossible length of time spoken out loud.

"Collateral?"

"Me. Look, I read the contract before I signed it. I knew what I was getting myself into." I didn't but I have now, so I allow myself the lie. "I'm not the naive little girl Ella seems to think I am."

He raises an eyebrow, the one not masked in gold. "Debatable." He pauses, considering. "And you have to report every night?"

"Yes." I feel relieved that he knows. It's easier not to carry this alone.

"You should have asked me for the poison, not dragged Alice into it. I'll help you," he says, gruff and quiet. And then—"Thank you."

"For what?"

"Saving Ella. I asked her to marry me. A few weeks ago."

I stare at him in shock. "You're who she was meeting!"

"She said she'd told you about us." He picks at an imaginary bit of fluff on his knee, his normal confidence suddenly gone. Pink flushes his visible cheek. It's endearing, and I can suddenly see exactly why my sister fell for him.

"She told me she'd met someone. I didn't know it was you." I give him a little smile. "What did Ella say, when you asked her?"

"She's not given me an answer. There's been a lot going on." He shoots me a crooked grin. "You're not shocked a monster proposed to your sister?"

"You're clearly not a monster, Toby."

"I'm Gilded." His smile stiffens.

"You're different." I fiddle with the belt on Ella's robe, remembering the conversation we had about Father when she told me Tobias resisted the gilding. "How did you do it?"

"Stop them severing my connection to my soul?"

I wince at his directness and nod.

"You've seen a gilding?"

"Of course. Is there anyone in the Colligerate who hasn't?"

"They make sure you'll submit first, by threatening someone you love. They threatened my sister, but I couldn't leave her alone. Not here. I was all she had left. So I pretended to submit. Acted broken. It hurt like blazes to start with, it's indescribable. First, it's just your skin burning, then fire claws down, right into your chest, and I...I felt my soul unlatch..." He presses his lips together, lost in the past. His eyes catch mine and clear. "You know when you burn? The moment you force yourself to step and leave your body behind. It's like that, but in reverse. I just...focused. Held on. Didn't let go. Then it was over. And I was still there."

I can't imagine it, how it must have felt, how desperate he must have been. "Do you think there might be others? Other Gilded that did the same?"

"It's possible. But if you had any idea how hard it was...I don't know. I live with them, train with them. Never seen a sign of it. I'd say it's unlikely." He shakes his head as if he knows exactly why I'm asking.

I wonder if Ella had the same questions, the same hope about Father. Tobias shifts forward on the sofa, and I'm struck again by his lifeline. Before, I couldn't see it at all, but now it's hazy and not quite there. "Sorry, Penny. I have to go."

"Will you tell Ella about my contract with Malin?"

"No. But I think you should." Reclaiming his cloak, he pulls a book from the folds and slides it on the table. "Ella said you like to read. It was the best we could do. It might help make the time pass a little."

"Toby? My family..." The question sticks in my throat.

He pats me awkwardly on the shoulder. "Els was raging when I saw her. They won't let her see you. Mila's keeping her head down."

"Mother?" My voice breaks. "She stood against Grandmother and the Gilded the other night..."

"Your grandmother doubled her burning duties as punishment. She's fine." Tobias shakes his head. "A Gilded will collect you in an hour. The Warden requires your services in his chambers."

I jerk away. "His chambers? Why?" Appearing before the Warden in public was terrible enough. The thought of an audience in his private chambers turns my stomach.

"He wants you to heal him." He winces and drops his voice. "I think you know that, no matter what, you can't." Then he's gone, leaving me alone with a book and a heart filled with fear.

I stare at the book. It's the same one Beatrice had when we met her outside the library. *A Complete Illustrated Collection of Fables and Myths.*

I close my eyes and inhale the library smell: pages and leather and beeswax.

And curled in Ella's robe, cradled by the familiarity of her, I open the cover and escape this cage of a chamber.

I'm on top of a mountain in a blizzard with a young Ember Queen when a note flutters out from between the pages. Ella's handwriting loops prettily across the page and I have to blink away tears before I can read it.

You're an idiot. A brave, unbelievably stupid idiot. Do exactly as T says. He's a good man, even if he is... what he is. And I love him. I thought we had more time or I'd have told you all about him sooner. He had no choice in what was done to him. None of us do, really. But we're trying to find a way to undo it. I'll come when I can. When it's safe. When it won't make things worse for you. Please, please be careful. I know what you're doing, I just don't know why. That's another conversation we need to have in person. Don't be tempted to stay. Death cannot keep you, not yet. I won't let it. I love you. I love you so very much. E. xxxxx PS: Burn this.

Tears splash down my nose onto the page, blurring Ella's hastily scribbled note.

I knew the risk when I ran into the barracks and burned at the Gilded's stake. Even if I'd known the outcome, that I'd make a mistake and be discovered and locked away, I would still have gone after Ella.

For both my sisters, I'd do it again and more.

I reread the note, memorising every line and loop of her handwriting. Then, I tuck it away in my pocket, curl back in the chair, and pick up the book, resolving to share the stories with Alice when I see her next—and ask her if she sees where the Grimoire hides. I should have thought of that sooner. But in my defence, I've been preoccupied enough just trying to survive.

I look back at the page, finding the place I left off. *The Ember Queen held up her fiery crystal to light the dark of the mountain night...*

I frown and read the line again.

Why would an ember witch be written as having a crystal? Outside of the original creation myths, no other coven has crystals. Only thorn witches.

I flick to the colour plate on the next page, and it's right there in pen and ink, a bright red crystal with a fire burning inside. I flip a few pages until I find an image of a tide witch. And there it is, a green crystal on a chain clasped around her neck. The end plate is a storm witch with a blue crystal, lightning cracking the sky behind her, and on the inside of the front cover, there's a witch with a yellow crystal hanging from her hand.

My mind spins as I close the book and press my hand against the cover.

How much in this book is really myth, and how much is history lost to time and transformed into tale?

If the other witches can have crystals, what power do they hold?

If the other witches can have crystals, can the Gilded?

And more importantly...can we use them to anchor their souls?

Chapter Twenty-Six

Just like the throne room, the Warden's private chambers are black marble decorated with gold. The Gilded who escorted me here position me on the grey rug before the fireplace, one hand clamped about each of my wrists, and I stand like a compliant statue. It's almost impossible, keeping my shoulders relaxed, my eyes down. I want to run. I want to scream. How does Alice do it so convincingly and so often? How has she survived this for so long?

I examine the Gilded's lifelines as I wait, trying to keep my breathing even. They are silver like Haylea's was, but not flecked with colour. Stiff and cold like silk cord left out in the snow. Black barbs erupt along their length, the threads frayed where they break through. I wonder if I could heal them like I did Haylea's. I wonder if they'd still be Gilded if I did—or if they'd find their way back to their souls.

I wonder if I could heal my father. Heal the boy I helped gild. With a drop of the boy's blood, could I grow him a crystal? Use it to anchor his soul back to his body? Father though, he already has a crystal, and the Warden must hold it now...I shudder, and the Gilded tighten their grips on my wrists.

The crash of the door makes me flinch. The Warden stalks in, sinking onto the low sofa under the window. Black brocade groans and adjusts to his weight.

People should look smaller in nightclothes. The Warden takes up more space. He exudes confidence, fierce and powerful even dressed in a black satin robe, but his lifeline pulses erratically.

"At last," he says softly. "The answer to my eternal life."

I stare at the edge of the rug and swallow hard. His lifeline eels around his feet.

"Release her," he snaps at the Gilded restraining me. "She's my creature now, completely and thoroughly broken. Kneel for me, Death-Weaver."

I do as he commands, keeping my face carefully blank, not flinching as his lifeline coils around my ankle, slick and sinuous. A black-festering whorl cut into the back of his calf stretches from his ankle and vanishes beneath his robe at the knee. He hitches the fabric up, exposing thigh muscles cut from stone, and the full extent of his cursed wound.

It's deep, widening where it curls around his knee, and pitch-black veins snake from the torn edges. I'm not sure I could heal that even if I wanted to—which I do not. Will not.

His fingers are ice as he takes my chin and makes me look at him.

I fight to keep from reacting. He is unmasked. No one sees the Warden without his mask. No one sees his real face. My eyes should be blank, but they widen as I take him in. He looks so young. Five hundred years should mark a man, but his features are all hard lines of smooth white marble. Morning-hazed stubble darkens a sharp-angled jaw and his eyes swarm with pain. "Heal me."

My hands shake in my lap. "I don't know how." Tears blur my vision. One breaks free and slides down my cheek.

His fingers clamp tighter on my chin. "Tears are weak, Death-Weaver," he snarls. "Weakness will not heal me."

My throat twitches as I make my hand move. I rest it on top of his lifeline and my stomach lurches. Decay seeps into my skin. I feel the bitter darkness feeding on his soul and spitting excrement into his blood. I think I'm going to be sick. Magic recoils into my veins, burying itself so deep I'm not sure it'll ever come out again. "I can't," I whisper.

"Yet, you healed your cousin so beautifully." My stomach stops lurching and freezes as he smiles. "Maybe my Gilded can teach you a lesson? A few days with them, my little Thorn Princess, might motivate you. What use is my Death-Weaver if she cannot make me whole?"

"Please...please, I don't want to make the wound worse. I've never healed intentionally before." It's a feeble excuse. But it seems to be enough for the moment.

He releases my chin and leans back, twitching his gown shut. Black eyes hold mine so tight I can't look away. "Practice. An excellent suggestion." I made no such suggestion. My heart shudders in my chest. I don't want to practice. He ignores me and hisses his next orders at the Gilded who brought me here. "Take her to the barracks. Start her off with the condemned. When she is proficient, Lord Asphodel has an ingrown toenail he won't shut up about. I'll see her again in a week. Bring me the witch queen. Her efforts will tide me over until then."

He replaces his mask. It clings to his features like quicksilver and seems to stay in place through willpower alone.

I exhale the softest sigh of relief as he waves us to the door, dismissing us, and giving me a week to breathe. To plan. I hang my head, watch my bare feet pad softly between the Gilded's golden boots, and smile behind my hair.

But when the door to the barracks swings open and they march me down into dungeons filled with rotting bodies and festering lifelines, my smile fades.

When I'm handed to my father and the Warden's orders are

repeated, I swallow hard. I need to treat this as a means to an end. A learning curve not to heal but to kill the Warden.

But when the first cell door slams open and I see the prisoner behind it, I vomit, right on my father's boots.

By the time they return me to my rooms, sweat sticks my shift to my skin and I'm trembling all over. I healed five prisoners. Five. And they maimed each of them horribly when I was done. My magic aches, my jaw hurts from clenching, and I have blood drying into a crust across my feet. Dazed, I stand in the middle of my rooms, listening to silence. Alice's loom does not weave. The Spinner does not spin. It's late, night has eaten the day outside the window, the curtains have been drawn, and there's a silver dome on the table covering what must be my dinner.

Will I be taken again to the Warden's court tonight? The thought nearly drags me to the floor. I don't think I could bear it.

But the other option—that Alice is there facing them alone—is equally unbearable.

I inhale slowly to pull myself back together. I finally notice the scent of soap and steam coming from the bathing chamber attached to my room, and I want to cry with relief.

No matter what happens next, I need to wash the sweat and blood from my skin and the oily poison of the Warden's lifeline from my hands. If I'm called to court tonight, I can't go in this state.

The bath stands on gold-clawed feet on a white-tiled floor. Bubbles fluff on the surface and steam drifts lazily into the air. I unpeel my shift, discard it on the floor, and ease myself into the water. I soak until my fingers wrinkle and the bubbles have all popped. When I step out, I leave behind a murky slick of dungeon dirt.

I wrap myself in a huge fluffy towel and look away from the muck draining away. When the Colligerate clock tower begins to chime out the hour, I'm dressed in a clean shift someone left on the bed, but my hair is still wet. It's late. Later than I realised. Tobias comes with the second strike of midnight and the first tired click of Alice's loom. Exhaustion lines his eyes and frustration creases around his mouth.

He hands me a vial and ushers me into the bathroom. "Easier to hide the evidence," he says flatly.

He's not in a mood that invites asking questions, but I don't have anyone else. I stare at the vial Tobias gave me and say quietly, "Tonight... I need help getting back."

"I can't cross, Penny, they'll know." He steadies me as I step into the bath and kneel down.

"Back from the library—"

Tobias shakes his head and one dark curl comes untucked from behind his ear. He seems almost defeated. "The Grimoire?"

I nod. "If I use the veil to get to the Eighth..." My words die as anger flashes in his eyes. "I can't get back here without you."

"Fine." His teeth snap shut. "I'll meet you on the Eighth. Don't be late. After the dawn bell, I can't help you. You risk exposing everyone and everything if you screw this up."

"I won't. Promise."

"I'll hold you to that."

I force a smile and try to open the vial, but it's screwed too tight. He removes the lid, watches me sip the poison, and takes my hand. Squeezes it. Fire hits deep in my gut as I say the words to part the veil. His voice joins mine and he takes the pain. All of it. I want to thank him, but I can't. So I close my eyes, unpeel my soul as my body crumbles, and step through the gap in the veil, leaving Tobias behind to clean up the ash of my passing.

"You're late," Malin snaps as my body reforms around my soul.

"I was held up," I reply, not bothering to change my clothes and shrugging off his hand when he tries to take my arm. "Not everything revolves around you."

He turns in a flap of coattails and strides into the desert away from the veil. I have to half run to keep up. Aware of the time constraints, I try to make my report. "The Warden—"

"Not here." His shoulders stiffen, dark brocade creasing across his muscular back. "I was worried."

His admission takes the wind out of my indignation. I open my mouth, can't think of a thing to say. We walk in silence, me running every few steps to keep pace until the portcullis rattles shut behind us, locking out the cold expanse of Death.

He pauses on the path and asks, "Would you like to take a walk?"

"In the gardens?"

"In the gardens." He offers a hand and a stiff smile. I take both.

I'm going to regret this. Maybe not tonight, but something deep in my gut tells me this is the worst idea I've had since I snuck into the Gilded's firepit. And still, I take his hand.

His smile when I rest my fingers in his palm is worth any future regrets.

"I can't stay long."

"We'll make it a short walk."

Birds twitter in the forest beyond the wall of roses and twisted thorns, a heavy hum of insects fills the air, and I spill the horror of my audience with the Warden into the summer afternoon.

Malin listens in silence. He doesn't stare at my crystal, he doesn't try to touch me, or interrupt me while I speak. He is the epitome of respect and gentlemanly behaviour. I almost wish he wasn't. The memory of last night tangles around my thoughts. How gentle he was when I was exhausted and breaking. He's the same tonight—not cold and sarcastic—and I wonder which is the real Malin, which is the mask.

He listens so attentively that I find myself sharing more than maybe I should. I only meant to tell him that the Warden ordered me to heal him, that I refused, and I've been forced to practice. But I tell him how the Gilded hurt the prisoners straight after I healed them, I tell him how I hate the Warden and how he's divided my family. I tell him how I killed my own cousin, how it felt to hold her life in my hands and how I'm scared I'm a monster.

"You're not," Malin says quietly. The strength of his fingers wraps mine, reassuring and safe. "Did you want to kill her?"

I shake my head, horrified. "Of course not! I didn't want to kill anyone!"

"Then you're not a monster, Penny. The Warden is the monster in your story."

"For a while, I thought you were." I give him a sheepish smile, unsure of what his reaction might be, but he just looks mildly surprised.

"I made you sign away your soul, and you don't think I'm a monster?"

"Not anymore. And for the last time, you didn't *make* me do anything. You gave me a choice, I chose my sister. I'd choose her over and over again if she needed me to, in far worse circumstances than this turned out to be." I squeeze his hand, and he squeezes mine back. It's a relief to say all this out loud, and Malin seems to truly understand. "The Warden didn't give me a choice. He made me kill. And I intend to kill him." I bite my lip as I realise what I just said. Who I said it to.

We stop beside a rosebush laden with multihued buds, a promise of life in Death. Malin runs a hand through his dark, tousled hair, standing it up at odd angles as he stares at me. "You can't kill him."

"I can," I whisper. His fingers brush the air above the ghost of my crystal, and I freeze. He traces the line of my collarbone, the cool of his palm skimming over my shoulder. I can almost feel his fingers against my skin. Almost.

Our eyes lock, and I can't look away.

Let me stay. Keep me safe.

A soft noise grumbles deep in his chest. I'm too scared to speak in case I say something else I'll regret. My exhale hitches, and he snatches his hand away, resuming our walk as if nothing happened.

Nothing did.

But my heart is pounding, my pulse throbs across my skin, and when I look up at him, there's a hint of a smile dimpling one cheek.

His voice is quiet when he speaks, thoughtful, a softness to it that seems impossible for such an imposingly huge man. "You miss them? Your family?"

I try to shrug. Fail. And my voice catches when I reply. "I'm a witch; I'm lost without my coven. My mother and sisters, cousins and aunts. Even Grandmother, though I don't like what she's become."

"She should never have brought you to Halstett."

"No." I wonder how much he knows. "Maybe not, but our entire continent is grey sand and wasteland thanks to the Warden and his Gilded. It was Halstett or eternal death. I miss home."

"Tell me about it. Your home."

I'm still reeling from the way Malin touched me—nearly touched me—and the expression in his eyes as he looks at me. He's still looking at me. I talk too fast in my hurry to redirect his attention. And mine. I paint pictures with words, drawing our village by the banks of the stream and colouring the cherry tree delicate shades of pink. The blossom festival is safe ground; I can't step wrong and say too much. I finish as we loop back around to the gates.

"I—" He trails off, indecision in the slight twitch of his mouth. "Stay here, Penny. Let me keep you safe."

"If I stay here, you own my soul."

He exhales sharply. "I never meant for this to happen."

And I want to ask what he means: the deal we made, my current situation in Life, or maybe he means something more. Maybe he misses me when I'm gone.

Instead, I say quietly, "I have to go. Someone's waiting for me and they'll be in trouble if I'm late."

"You're going to the Ninth?" Worry brackets his mouth with lines where the dimple was when he smiled.

"How did you know?"

"You just told me you intend to kill the Warden. Where else would you find the means?"

I glance at the wall of thorns hiding his woods, and Malin stiffens. His eyes are steel. "Promise you'll be careful."

"I promise." What else can I say with him staring at me like this? As if he'd challenge the veil to stop me doing something I'll later regret.

He takes my hand and his thumb circles the curve of my wrist. "I wish we'd met somewhere else."

I wish the same but I don't voice it. I don't dare look at him; he'll see the effect the caress of his thumb is having. I stare at a curl of hair just touching the top of his collar and my traitorous, confusing mind imagines twirling it around my finger, brushing it off his neck.

I pull away, rubbing my wrist to erase the memory of his thumb, and shove my hands deep in my pockets.

"If you insist on going to the Ninth, the spell to forge the Sorcerer's knife is on page seventy-two. The ninth book on the ninth shelf of the ninth row."

I blink in shock. "How the hell do you know that?" Questions hit so fast I can't pick one and I just stare at him open-mouthed. What else does he know? Who is he? Where is he from?

"Because they used it on me," Malin says, flat and monotone. "And I remember the page."

"Who did?" I step toward him, but he steps back, maintaining the distance I put between us before. "Is that why you're here? In the manor? In Death?"

Devastation darkens his eyes. "I'll explain everything, Penny, I promise, but not tonight. Please."

"But... why help me now? Last time I mentioned the Ninth, you ordered me to stay away!"

"Did it stop you?"

I shake my head.

"Will it this time?"

I offer him half a smile.

"Then the only thing I can do, if I want you to come back, is help you." His voice catches, he looks away, and my heart breaks for him. I want to wrap my arms around him and hold him tight. I want to tell him everything will be fine and that I'll be back soon and we'll work it out together, but if I'm going to the Ninth, the reality is that I very well might not make it back here, and I've never been a fan of lying.

Malin presses a small metal pin into my hand, a rose with midnight-purple petals enamelled at one end. It shimmers in the half-light of Death. "You'll need that. Read the entire spell before you summon the dark. I'll see you tomorrow." He turns to the manor as the portcullis rattles up and walks away without looking back.

I face the veil and do the same.

I'm glad to escape the confusion of him. Penny in Life and Penny in Death are separating, and the divide between them will only deepen the longer this goes on. I am happy in Death, but if I lean into *this*, I'll lose the other part of me. Forever.

When I studied to walk with the coven, every book warned the same: each time a death-walker crosses the veil, a piece of their soul is left behind. I knew this would happen. It's every thorn witch's fate.

I just didn't know the pieces of my soul would be left in a rose garden belonging to a man I can't begin to understand.

I didn't know I'd want to stay there too.

Chapter Twenty-Seven

I come back to Life on the Eighth. Tobias has me on my feet before I'm fully awake, one hand hooked under my arm. "The quicker we get this done, the better."

I stumble, my legs not quite connected to my mind, and curl my fingers around the rose pin Malin gave me. It steadies me a little. "How long was I gone?" Even if Malin had a clock tower, the minutes and hours run differently in Death, never quite matching up with Life.

Tobias is tense, his answer clipped. "An hour. I came straight here after I cleaned up."

An hour? It felt like so much longer.

Steeling myself to face the Ninth, I shake free of his hold, and rest my hand on the banister at the bottom of the stairs.

"Toby." My whisper is muffled by books and a darkness so tangible I can taste it on my tongue. "Thank you."

"Don't thank me yet," he replies. "Thank me when we're out of here."

Book sprites flicker into existence, peeping from the back of bookcases, their tiny eyes lighting the space between shelves. Last time I was here, they killed a man.

But when they whisper my name, it's a welcome, not a warning.

A hush ripples along the shelves as we stand, staring at the darkness of the Ninth. My heart beats so hard, Tobias must hear it. "All right?" he asks quietly.

I swallow. "Not really."

He grins. "Me either. Come on."

We take the first step together. Then, there's a tug at my skirts and a wisp of shadow pulls me up the stairs, up and up. Rainbowed eyes light our way, little figures watching from on top of the banisters, from between them, hanging from them. Halfway up, the air chills, drenching us with ice like the wards by the Resistance tomb. I slip my hand into Tobias's. He's warm, so solid and reassuring. No wonder Ella fell for him.

My foot hits the Ninth. The rainbow of watchful eyes shutters from existence. The air heavies with magic. It sparks against my skin and prickles against my hair. We are alone. In the dark. I cling tighter to Tobias's hand in the quiet as our eyes adjust. Here, on the ninth floor of the library, it seems there is nothing but silence and shadows and dust.

Slowly, the chill softens. The darkness fades into the thin grey light of Death. I blink and see nine rows of shelves glowing softly in the dark. It's smaller here than the other levels. The shelves sparse. Crystals with no life to them sit beside elegant feathery pens and inkwells filled with glittering ink. There are brass scales with obsidian weights, and pestles and mortars made of glass. There's a picture too, in a brass frame. Then there are the books, standing in carefully curated lines. Tiny ones in a rainbow of colours that would fit in my palm, and huge ones bound in silver and gold that would take two Gilded to lift off the shelf.

I take a step.

A low snarl shivers through the spines. A magic that is not the wards floods the Ninth like brackish water in a mine. It reminds me of the fog-wraith when I cut off his hand.

I swallow hard, planting my feet to stop myself running.

Tobias firms his grip on my fingers.

The ninth row, Malin told me. The ninth book on the ninth shelf of the ninth row. So neat and tidy. Except it isn't.

The book spines shiver again, shifting on their shelves.

Shadows thicken and solidify into an ash-black mist. It reaches for us with tendrils of darkness, inspecting and examining. I want to back away, turn tail and flee down the stairs. Instead, I squeeze the pin Malin gave me so hard it digs into my palm.

Ribbons of black slither through the air, caressing my elbows and testing the golden cuffs at my wrists, then retreating. The mist splits into two, then four, and elongates into spindly humanoid figures that are everywhere and nowhere all at once.

Then, the whispers begin. They echo around the library and leave pricks of ice across my skin:

It is her.

We must be sure.

It cannot be.

Yet it is.

A pause that lasts forever and is over in seconds.

The four meld into one human form. A shadow hand runs down my cheek before stretching to Tobias. I feel his shudder against my side.

A masked one. One voice now. Deep and grating. *He should not wear it. He hides behind it.*

Arms and legs furl back into shadows, disintegrating as they shift.

Pass... The word hisses into silence.

It takes me a moment to remember why we are here. My knees tremble as I hurry to the ninth row and find the ninth shelf, tugging

Tobias behind me. The ninth book is an anticlimax. It's small and bound in nondescript black leather. Flat metal strips wrap it from top to bottom and side to side. Where they cross is a raised metal rose with a keyhole shaped like an eye dead in the centre.

The Grimoire.

I reach to slide it from the shelf, and magic snaps up my fingers, jolting into my elbow and shoulder. My heart squeezes. I snatch my hand back and the Grimoire thuds to the floor. It's so much heavier than a book that size should be. Power churns in my blood. My skin fizzes.

I've never felt so alive. The thorn magic that only wakes in Death swirls through my veins. If I drew a picture in my mind, I could call it into existence. I could create a monster to fight my battles. I'd never have to burn again. I could draw a door into Death and step through—I could fix my home. The stream and the cottages and the Thorn Shrine.

The Warden's cuffs turn to ice. Magic drains away, leaving me wanting. A tremor runs through the shelves and my name whispers through the books, and I reach for the Grimoire again.

Tobias steps in front of me. I want to shove him out of the way and press my hands against the cover. That Grimoire was meant for me. Not him.

"Easy, Penny," Tobias says quietly.

"Don't touch it," I snarl. "It's mine. I found it. Malin told *me* where it was, not you."

Tobias rests his hands on my shoulders, holding me at arm's length. "Look at me."

"Let go." I'm not looking at him, he'll only stop me from... I frown, suddenly confused. My thoughts are all jumbled. What will he stop me doing?

"Penny." Tobias's calm cuts through my confusion. "It's a ward on the Grimoire. It's not real. Whatever you thought was happening, it wasn't real." His face is troubled. "Thank the Dark Mother you touched it first. If I'd hurt you..." He shakes his head and pushes me behind him. "Ella would have gutted me like a fish! When I told her where I was meeting you tonight, she nearly set me on fire." He prods the Grimoire with a boot. It lies there innocently, unreactive, even when he picks it up with one hand as if it weighs nothing. Tobias takes my wrist and tugs me across the landing, down the stairs to the Eighth. He doesn't stop, hurrying down each flight. On the second floor, I lead him into Miss Elsweather's office and lock the door.

I snatch a piece of paper from the blotter on her desk and a pen from beside it, still clinging to Malin's pin so tight blood drips between my fingers. I reach to press the rose carving on the corner of the shelf. It's buried in leaves and twirling vines. The same rose as the one on the Grimoire—the same as the pin Malin gave me.

With a quiet creak, the entire bookcase swings outward and an abyss yawns beyond. I've had enough of the dark. Enough mystery and intrigue. Right now, I want nothing more than to go to bed and sleep for days and days. I want the book under Tobias's arm back in my hand. I want to feel magic like that again. We step together down the spiralling stairs that lead to the depths beneath the Colligerate.

Candles flare as we reach the bottom. It seems so long since I came here, desperate to reach my sister who'd vanished in Death. My problems seemed insurmountable then too, and they weren't. I saved Ella. I wince at the memory of drinking an entire vial of poison as we pass a Penny-shaped scorch mark darkening the foot of the stairs.

Tobias stares at it. "Do I want to know?"

"Probably not."

He shakes his head, and together we push open a door into a small chamber. Dust covers the table and coats the chairs. This place has been undisturbed for centuries. I stifle a sneeze and watch Tobias lay the Grimoire flat on the table. He traces an indented rose in the metal. "This needs a key."

I silently hold out my hand, displaying the rose pin red with blood. Tobias doesn't speak as he carefully unsticks it from my palm. Waves of magic roil from the Grimoire, seeping from the leather cover. In the wrong hands, it could be deadly. I've never been near a book this powerful.

"You know what you're looking for?"

"Malin told me," I whisper.

His eyes narrow, and I have the horrible feeling there's been some unpleasantness between Tobias and Malin in the past. I can't possibly put the pieces of that puzzle together tonight, so I save my questions and watch Tobias slot the pin into the lock. My blood shimmers and there's a tiny click. He doesn't say a word as he carefully pulls back the metal bindings and opens the Grimoire.

Magic hits me like a wall of iced water and I stumble into the table. Tobias's hands shake as he flips through the pages. I don't want to touch it again—and I desperately want to press my hands against it.

Tobias asks stiffly, "What page?"

"Seventy-two." I tremble all over. "Toby, I can't touch it."

"You don't have to. Here." He turns it to me so I can read it the right way up. Page seventy-two is marked down the side with a design of whorls similar to the one on my father's mask. There's a picture of a knife, five crystals embedded in the hilt—red and yellow, green and blue and purple—woven together with a thread of sparkling black. The spell to forge it is written in faded ink.

I copy it down, the picture and the spell, and catch on the last line. My heart stalls. All magic has a price. If I'm reading it right, this one is steep. I blink and hesitate, my pen nib trembling against the last wobbly word.

"Are you finished?" Tobias asks. He's backed away and is leaning against a cupboard, watching me carefully.

I am, but magic murmurs temptation in my ear. I have the spell to reforge the knife, but what else is hidden within the Grimoire's pages? There is power in words, and these are the most powerful of them all. There might be a spell to help Alice escape the loom or set Malin free—maybe I could help Tobias leave behind his mask. Return my father from his gilding. The possibilities in one grimoire are endless, and on the Ninth there were more.

Gingerly, I use the tip of the pen to turn a page. And another. I don't know when I set down the pen. No magic floods me. There's no jolt of power. My fingers caress the paper, running beneath the lines as I drink them in like I've stumbled across a desert and finally found water to quench my thirst. I pause on a spell to bind lifelines, scribble it down, and turn the next page, a plan forming as I write. Ella said she thought there was a way to heal the Gilded. Tobias is living proof it can be done. If this spell works, if all witches can have crystals, I think I know *how* it can be done.

"Enough, Penny." Gently, Tobias catches my wrist. Strain shows in the corded tendons in his neck as he shuts the Grimoire firmly. Dust puffs off the pages and magic whispers my name. He slides the rose pin from the cover, and the Grimoire seals itself. He stows it into the cupboard he was leaning against, locks it away, pockets the key, and hands me Malin's pin. "It's safer," he says. "Both having a key is safer." He's trying to convince himself as well as me.

Slowly, we climb the stairs, the Grimoire's seductive song trailing us as we go. It's not until we're in the main foyer of the library that we speak again, sitting on the bottom stair side by side to steady our shattered nerves.

"Are you all right?" Tobias asks.

"Yes. No. I don't know."

He nudges me in the ribs with his elbow. "You're doing well. Els is so proud of you. You stood up to the Warden and he doesn't even realise you've done it."

I shake my head. "I stalled. It's not quite the same thing."

Silence falls, the clock tick-tick-ticks on the wall, counting down the minutes until we must leave.

"Did you find it?"

I nod. The spell to reforge the knife is tucked in my pocket—but I don't want to use it.

"Can you work it?"

Silently, I hand him the spell. He reads it slowly. Twice. "Shit."

"I know."

He hands it back, and I fold the paper once, marking the crease sharply with my nail, then I do it again and again as if the folds can bury the words. As if making the paper smaller makes it less horrible.

The price of the magic to forge the Sorcerer's knife is a black-crystalled lifeline. My lifeline.

"Penny," Tobias says softly. "You can't do this."

"If I don't, who else can?"

"Don't tell Ella."

It's the last thing I expect him to say and I blurt out, "I'm glad she found you." I lean my shoulder against his, needing the reassurance of his warmth, lending mine to him.

He laughs, but it's sad and a bit defeated. "If word gets out, I'm going to spend the rest of my existence dancing the line between Life and Death, but Els is worth the risk." I feel his lifeline tremble slightly.

"She is," I reply, and frown. "Did you read the letter she wrote me?"

He shakes his head. "Of course not!"

This would be easier to ask if he had. "I think the gilding is reversible."

"It's so unlikely." Tobias shifts away a little to look at me properly.

"Did you see how many spells were in the Grimoire? There might be one in there..."

"There's something I haven't told you."

I give him a tight smile. "Does it have to do with why I can't see your lifeline properly? Everyone else's is clear and bright, but yours is hazy, and I can't see mine at all—or Alice's."

Tobias slips his hand in his pocket and holds out a small square of white silk. Unfolding it reveals my answer. A nugget of deep, dark, colourless grey, swirling with mists of smoke. Raw and unpolished—and not held by the Warden.

"Oh!" The word matches the shape my mouth makes. "It was you! You were the black-crystalled witch the Gilded thought they found before. The one the Warden tried to... Oh, Toby. I'm sorry."

"Don't be. It was long ago. Water under the bridge." But the hurt in his eyes belies his words. "It turned out for the best. Set me high up the Gilded chain of command. I've saved more lives than I've taken."

"They think you have more power than the rest of them?"

"Indeed," he says. "It's how I made it on to the Ninth too. The Sorcerer warded the floor so only black-crystalled can pass. Mine's close enough."

"Does Ella know?"

"Yes." Tobias's lips twist at one corner as he glances at the clock. "Copy the spell down and give it to me before the Resistance meeting tomorrow. I'll deal with it. Just let me talk to Ella first."

"But the Grimoire—"

"No." Tobias cuts me off. "Don't go near it again, Penny. I'll work the spell to forge the knife. Get rid of the Warden, then worry about setting the Gilded free."

"Toby, you can't! It says—"

"I know what it says. It's worth a shot. If it doesn't work—well, it's better than losing you." He springs to his feet, offers a hand to pull me to mine, and changes topics so fast my head spins. "Alice's is all rainbows and fractured light."

"Alice's what?"

Tobias grins. "She has a crystal too. The Warden used it to bind her to the loom, trapped her in Life so she can never die."

As he resumes his Gilded stance and takes hold of my arm, I wonder how he knows.

Tobias marches me through the night-dark corridors, a confidence in his step that suggests he's supposed to be here, at this hour—with me. But he's timed it perfectly and none cross our path. He knows the schedule of the nightguard; he made it. We slip into the tunnel behind the Warden's statue's boot without mishap and don't stop until we reach the secret entrance to my rooms. As he unlatches the mechanism, he says, "There's a notch here, but it's for emergencies only. We can't afford to compromise the tunnel network."

Then, he swings open the panel to my sitting room and Alice is waiting.

She's huddled in the corner, her fingers dancing through the air. Fear darkens her eyes.

Tobias gives her a brisk nod. "Don't get caught," he says and leaves us alone.

She rises to her feet as the panel clicks shut. "Penny?"

I hold out my hand, and she slips to my side. Black silk clings to her shoulders, a night robe belted with gold at her waist. "Alice, you shouldn't be here."

"I saw something," she whispers.

"Tell me." I pull her into my room, and we perch together on my bed.

"Penny, I saw you die."

Terror crawls spider-like down my spine. The spell in my pocket shivers. "Of course you did, Alice. I die every night."

Her black eyes widen, round and deep. "This time, you didn't come back. The threads are changing—even as I weave, they slip from my grasp. They break and catch and knot. I can't see you." Pale hair sticks to her brow, and I smooth it away with one finger, tucking it behind her ear. I go to speak, and her thumb brushes across my bottom lip. "Hush, Penny. Hush. I don't know where you go. I made a mistake..."

She's scaring me—the light in her eyes is distant and far away. "Alice, please. I went to the Ninth with Toby. I'm fine. I promise."

"You found it," she whispers. "The Grimoire and the spells." Her fingers trickle down my neck to my breastbone and pause so close to my lifeline I can feel the warmth of her brushing against it. A shiver of starlight catches at my soul. No one has touched my lifeline before. "But you haven't decided. That's why I can't see."

She pulls away, and I'm breathless and lost for words and so very, very confused.

The night sky hangs in her gaze, cloudless and filled with fading stars. "They're coming."

"Alice?"

"I have to go." And she untangles herself from me, hurrying through the panel in the walls, leaving me alone, unsettled and with my heart pounding. Wishing I could go after her.

No one comes. There's no knock at the door, no click of a key in the lock. No Gilded storm my rooms like I expected when Alice ran. I can't sleep. Exhaustion weighs my limbs and turns my blood to lead, but I cannot sleep.

I wish had the courage to try and unlatch the panel between our rooms. I wish Ella was here. I wish I could talk to Mila—I know she's had dalliances, though I never knew who with. It was safer not to talk about it. But I need advice, because I have no idea how to handle this.

I care about Alice. I don't want to break that. And I think our friendship is deepening into something more. I can't stop replaying the way her fingers paused right by my lifeline, nearly brushed against it. The delicious surprise of the sensation.

And then there's Malin—irresistible and deadly, a poison so exquisitely intoxicating it's hard to resist. I haven't kissed him, but we've come close, and Holy Dark Mother, sometimes I want him to. I want him to gather me into his arms and...I exhale shakily. If it was as shallow as a skipping pulse every time I see him, it would be simpler. What I thought was pure attraction deepens the more I know him.

I should look at the spells from the Grimoire, take my mind off the confusion of Alice and Malin and focus on finding a way to set them free instead—Alice from the loom, and Malin from Death—but I can't bring myself to read them again. So, I crack open the curtains and pick up the book Ella sent. The pages flick through my fingers, lines of stories blending into grey shadows in the sliver of moonlight.

Pictures blur, words wavering as I hunt for a picture that catches my attention. I find one: a forest guarded by a wall of roses and thorns that looks suspiciously like the one Malin conjured.

"The Dagger in the Dark." I know it as a cautionary tale for children, but now I read with different eyes.

Once upon a time, in a land where death did not exist, a farm boy lived at the edge of a deep, dark forest. Each morning, he rose with the sun and fed the pigs and watered the goats and fetched eggs from the chickens. When his chores were done, the boy played on the edge of the forest, imagining adventure—sticks were mighty swords, a fallen tree became a fearsome dragon. But he always heeded his mother's warning: Never go into the woods. Deep between the trees, she told him, there lived a sorcerer who feasted on small boys like him. Then, on Samhain Eve, the boy, nearly a man now, but not quite, wandered into the ancient woods.

I keep reading as the boy finds the sorcerer and is offered power if he fulfils a task—retrieve a magical dagger from a cave in the mountains.

I turn the next page and trace the coloured plate of the mountains. It reminds me of home; the same stream curves down between the foothills.

The cave was dark and echoed with whispers like the turn of a page in a book. Shadows danced around his feet and tiny eyes lit up the dark.

I blink and read it again, angling the book so the moonlight highlights the words. Book sprites?

"Come," they whispered. "Come. Faster. Hurry." The boy smiled; this was the adventure he'd dreamed of. The tunnel opened into a cave and the cave opened into a chamber so high he couldn't see the top for darkness. Shelves ran up the walls and vanished into the gloom, and row after row of glass jars lined them. The boy thought he saw eyes, black as midnight and wide with desperation, peering from the jars. He thought he heard nails on glass. But in the centre of the cave, the dagger shone with its own light, and it chanted

his name until the sound filled his ears and the yearning for power embedded deep in his heart.

He took up the dagger and the curve of the hilt fitted perfectly in his hand. Proudly, he presented it to the sorcerer. But the sorcerer was devious. He offered the boy more, more than power over lands and people; he offered power over Life and Death. Immortality in exchange for an oath marked upon his skin.

He promised the boy a throne.

The farm boy was tired of fetching water for goats and eggs from chicken houses and sleeping in a narrow cot beside the fire. He was tired of going to bed hungry and waking with chilblains itching his toes. He wanted a life, not an existence, and so, he agreed. With the tip of the dagger, the sorcerer marked the boy's calf. The skin closed, leaving an etching of black lines, and the boy went to claim his throne, unaware of the price he'd paid.

Chapter Twenty-Eight

Two days later, afternoon sunshine floods my room in Halstett, when the panelling at the bottom of the wall clicks open. Clair steps through, cobwebs clinging to her neatly made bun, her lifeline yellow and bright. She holds open the panel, and my hand flies to my mouth.

Ella.

My book slips to the floor. I'm on my feet and in her arms before I can breathe again. When I inhale, the familiar lilac and honey smell of her brings tears to my eyes. "Els, you came." My whisper hitches against a sob. Ella is here. She's real. Freckles and red hair and soft silver eyes. Her lifeline is silver and speckled with lilac sparkles. It suits her.

She smooths a strand of tangled hair off my brow as she looks at me. "I had to see you. I couldn't trust anyone else's reports."

Clair lets out a disgruntled huff. A smile curves Ella's mouth, and she shoots Clair a wink. I don't think I've seen Ella wink in my life.

Lips twitching at one corner, Clair ducks back into the space between the walls. "I'll be with Alice. Leave the panel open. One hint of someone coming, and you get out. Understand?" She waits for Ella's nod before she vanishes, leaving us alone, my sister and I.

As soon as she's gone, I push Ella against the wall and whisper, keeping my voice low enough that the soft click of Alice's loom hides my words, "When were you going to mention that Toby proposed?"

"It was a difficult conversation to start." Ella grins.

"You should have told me!" I pinch her arm lightly.

"He's Gilded. You'd have done everything you could to stop me. I'd have done the same for you or Mila before I met him. I love him, Pen." She pushes me away and says quietly, "I'm going to say yes."

I huff. She's not getting away with it that easily. "You should. He's probably the nicest person I've ever met."

Ella softens, her eyes sparkle. "You have no idea how much that means to me."

I think I do. "Does Mila know?"

"Mila..." Ella falters, and my heart sinks.

"What's she done this time? I wish you'd stop fighting her. She's doing her best."

Ella scowls, and I expect another tirade. "She's doing better than that."

"Better than her best?"

She nods. "After the night the Gilded came for you, everything changed...What Grandmother did...Mother's burning too often as punishment. We're all worried about her, Carlotta's in some kind of trouble too, and with you gone..."

"You and Mila made up?"

"More or less."

The weight of my worry lifts, just a little bit. "I've hated you two not getting along."

"She joined the Resistance you know," Ella says archly.

"Mila did *what*?"

Ella laughs. "Don't look so surprised. She *is* our sister." She shakes her head. "She thinks I should say yes to Toby as well."

"Did she eviscerate you for sneaking around and falling in love with a Gilded?"

"She did."

"As long as one of us did."

Ella smiles, and we curl together on the floor, leaning into each other, shoulder to shoulder. "Truce?"

"Truce. But you shouldn't be here, Els. It's too dangerous," I whisper. "I'm so glad you are."

"I'm on library duty; Miss Elsweather will cover for me. You're an idiot, not running when Toby gave you the option." It's an admonishment, a gentle one.

"It wouldn't have worked. They'd have found me, and it would have risked so many people." I pause and give her a weak smile. "Tell me everything. How did Mila join the Resistance? Why did Grandmother hand me to the Warden? What did you mean in your letter about undoing the gilding?"

"That's a lot of questions." She turns me away from her and runs her fingers through my hair like she used to back home in our village, curled before the fire on bath night, with Mila nibbling on one of the candied pears she had an endless supply of. A perk of being Grandmother's favourite—or maybe she just stashed them after the blossom festival and made them last. "When Mila found out the Resistance were helping you, I got permission to bring her to meet Miss Elsweather properly. I suspect Evelyn had something to do with her request to join being approved. They vanished giggling after the first meeting Mila attended, and I found them in a hidden alcove in the catacombs last night."

"Evelyn and Mila!" I can't remember the last time I heard Mila giggle.

Ella continues, separating my hair into strands as she speaks. "Mother's not involved, but knows we are. She misses you, Pen. Said to tell you she loves you and she's doing what she can with the coven. I really thought Mother was going to murder Grandmother the night they came for you. Aunt Shara had to step in, she spent the night in Mother's room, and Grandmother's healing the Warden so often, she's stopped burning completely."

"So you're two witches down? How are you holding up?"

Ella flicks me on the back of the head hard. "You're a fine one to talk. I'd imagine I'm holding up better than you, little miss I'm-walking-in-Death-every-night."

"Toby told you?"

"He told me." She throws her arms around my shoulders, gives me a squeeze, and goes back to her braiding. "*Thank you* doesn't cover it."

"I thought you'd kill me," I confess.

"I planned to. Lucky for you we called a truce." She tugs my hair a bit and carries on twisting my braid. It's soothing, the gentle pressure, the rhythm of her fingers, but she sounds reluctant when she speaks again. "The Resistance don't think it was Grandmother that gave you up to the Warden."

"And you believe them?"

"I don't know. Someone did. Toby insists it was a thorn witch."

Tobias still thinks it was Haylea. Holy Dark Mother, I hope Ella doesn't. For too many heartbeats she's silent, collecting her thoughts as she ties off one braid and begins on the other. "It can't have been a thorn witch. No one is missing and anyone who knows about your crystal was blood-sworn to secrecy. Toby said there was one in the dungeons, but wouldn't tell me who. He said to talk to you."

"It was Haylea."

Ella's fingers pause their braiding. "Haylea died last year."

"She didn't." Ella's grip on my half-finished plait keeps me from hanging my head. "Els...they made me kill her." Tears sting my eyes. "But she said it wasn't her that gave me up before she died."

"Fuck." Ella never uses that word.

I'm glad my back's to her so she can't see how much it hurts. What I did to Haylea isn't even the worst of it anymore. Our father made me heal five prisoners this morning. I can still see their injuries—the infected wounds made perfect, their lifelines shimmering and bright. I see their pain as he undid my healing. He promises worse if I do not obey, and each day, his smile grows crueller. I shudder, push the thoughts of Haylea and what came after away, and whisper, "I'm scared."

"So am I." Ella quietly finishes my plait. She lets it fall against my back and it hangs like a rope down to my waist beside the other. "I'm sorry, Pen. I've let you down."

"You haven't."

"You've been dealing with all this on your own. I should have been here."

We rest back against the wall. Ella will leave soon and our parting hangs between us, a slow-building tension that makes me want to cling to her hand and beg her not to go. Not to leave me again. Ella nudges me, leaning a bit harder against me, and asks quietly, "Toby said you found the Grimoire on the Ninth the other night?"

"We found it. I wrote the spell for the knife down." I try to smile and twist the conversation away from the spell to reforge the knife. She can't know the price of it. "And...I think I know how to save the Gilded too. If we could heal them, we'd steal the Warden's army."

"What?" Ella bolts upright. "Penny, that's...that would change everything. How?"

"I think all witches can have crystals," I reply, trying to sound excited. "The other covens just can't walk into Death to create them."

Ella frowns. "But why would they want them? It's hardly a benefit, is it, having our magic tied to an object? Crystals can be broken."

I never thought about crystals as a weakness before. It explains why Evelyn laughed so hard the afternoon they persuaded me to join the Resistance. It feels so long ago. I've gained a whole new identity as the Warden's Death-Weaver since then. "The gilding severs the Gilded's connection to their souls, right? So, if they had crystals, we might be able to use them like we do when we walk in Death and anchor their souls back in their bodies." I shake my head a little and pick at my skirt. "I found another spell in the Grimoire. One to bind lifelines. I haven't worked out all the details. It's still an idea."

"That... that makes a curious kind of sense." Ella's eyes shine with calculation. "Without the Gilded, the Resistance might finally have a real hope at destroying the Warden."

And maybe we could get Father back. "Els, I want to go home."

"Maybe we can. When this is over? We could go back and rebuild." A scuff of a boot outside the door freezes her hands on my shoulders. She scrambles up. "I have to go."

Ella hugs me tight and I hug her back just as fiercely. "I love you, Penny. I love you so much. There's a Resistance meeting tonight; Toby will bring you to it. Don't do anything stupid. Don't agree to anything. We need to know who handed you over first. If it was someone in the Resistance—"

"Tell Mother I love her. Ella—" I don't want her to go. I cling to her as she holds me. "I love you."

The key fits into the lock, and we fly apart. I barely have time to whisper goodbye, and she's gone with a click of the mechanism behind the panel falling into place. By the time the door opens, I'm back on the sofa, curled in a ball, smoothing out the pages of my book.

A Gilded fills my doorway, suspicion hardening his eyes as he sweeps the room. Not a thread of a cushion is out of place, not a chink in the panelling to show Ella was here. He pins me with a glare that slices through my composure. The nostril not constrained by his gold mask flares. I know what he smells: lilac and cindered honey. Ella.

I keep my face carefully blank.

He leaves and slams the door behind him. With the turn of the key in the lock, I curl tighter into the sofa, wrap my arms around my knees, and allow myself a single, silent sob of relief.

What the Resistance don't know has been killing them. It was foolish to attempt the spell to forge the Sorcerer's knife when they only had a copy. The missing pieces are hidden behind the dresser, under the floorboards beside my stockpile of poison, Malin's rose pin, and Alice's dreams spun in silk. They think they've been working together, but they haven't. The cost of the reforging won't just be mine to pay.

As the sun dips below the horizon, Tobias comes for me wearing his Gilded facade. Court is full tonight, anticipation tightens the air, and every lifeline is sharp and alert. Alice behaves impeccably. She kneels quietly beside the Warden's gold-scrolled shoes and folds her hands neatly in her lap, pale fingers twitching against white silk skirts. I do the same, resting my hands in my black silk and not moving an inch. Neither of us can afford the Warden's anger—not if we want to attend the Resistance meeting.

A gaggle of advisors sip on expensive whiskey and fine brandy, chains of office clinking as they wave their glasses. Cigars that smell of grave dirt drift ash across the marble tiles.

Cramps knot my thighs and my knees stiffen as the clock ticks slowly round to the night bell. I try to vanish into my imagination, pretend I am anywhere but here, and find myself lost in the tangle of Halstett's history.

If the Warden was put on the throne by magic, then why does he hate the witches who wield it? If the Sorcerer raised him to power, why did the Warden banish him? And where did he banish him to if not into Death?

I fight the tremble of my fingers as my thoughts swirl, and I'm distracted until the Warden raises a hand.

The court falls utterly silent. The chairman of the Warden's council, jowls wobbling with his own importance, raises his voice. "In honour of Our Holy Warden," he announces, "a ball will be held on Samhain night. Every witch over the age of eighteen who resides within Halstett's walls, every noble, every Gilded will be required to attend and give tribute to our most excellent of leaders."

Mutters ripple through court. It is unheard of for witches to mingle with nobles, for Gilded to attend social functions. Halstett does not have social functions! The Warden has never held a ball in the thirteen years we've been imprisoned here.

Samhain night. When the veil is at its thinnest and the risk of fog-wraiths breaking into Life its highest. The one night of the year the Gilded should be doubling their watch, they'll be attending a party—and so will I.

My heart sinks. So far, I've avoided my coven seeing me reduced to the Warden's Death-Weaver, but if attendance is mandatory, my shame will be displayed before every witch in all its despicable glory.

The Warden leans over the arm of his throne, gold mask emotionless and cold, dark eyes focused on me. He runs a finger gently along my face, tracing a line across my forehead and looping it across my cheekbones, and says quietly, so quietly no one else can hear, "And by Samhain, Death-Weaver, I will be healed and the veil will be mine—the scourge of the Sorcerer finally disposed of and his magic with him."

The effort it takes not to react, not to flinch away from his breath on my face, is almost too much. But I bury it. All of it. Hide myself behind my eyes so I cannot give myself away.

Laughter shakes the Warden's shoulders, silent and wicked. "Soon, Death-Weaver, I have a little game planned just for you."

He's still laughing as Tobias pulls me to my feet, and I feel the Warden's eyes burning right between my shoulder blades as I am escorted from the throne room.

This man on his golden throne has made me kill, made me hurt. He stole my home and my family and my freedom. He ruined my coven and corrupted my grandmother.

I won't let him destroy our magic.

Tobias stares out the window as I change from the silk dress I wore to the Warden's court into a more practical shift. "What was that all about, with the Warden?" he asks.

"Nothing."

"Penny? If you're hiding something—"

"We're both hiding things, Toby."

"We're not both about to face the whole Resistance for the first time. They'll want to know what he said. They have eyes everywhere."

"The Resistance want a lot of things: information here, deadly magic there—" The night bell rings from the Colligerate tower, cutting short my retort, but Tobias's shoulders stiffen. "You can turn around. I'm decent."

"Did you copy the spell?"

"No."

"Penny!"

"I don't want to talk about it." I gesture to the panelling. I know I'm being rude, but I can't bring myself to care. "Ella will worry if we're late."

He shakes his head. "Idiot. I'm trying to help you."

"No, Toby. You're trying to protect me. Those are two very different things. And I'm sick of it. Especially when—"

He whirls on me. "You think going to the Ninth the other night was me protecting you?"

"Well..."

"Or when I've helped you to burn and cleaned up the mess afterward? If I was trying to keep you safe, do you think I'd have trusted you to read that Grimoire on your own? I wouldn't have let you touch it! I'm not fucking protecting you! I am doing my job." He's whispering so loud it's a wonder the guards outside the door don't hear. And Tobias has never been angry with me.

I shrug so he can't see how much his words sting.

"Do you have any idea how hard it is to watch you get hurt over and over again?" he says, quieter now.

"Why do you even care?"

"Because," he says, pushing open the panel and pulling me into the dark behind him, "unlike a lot of people around here, I'm not an arsehole."

A chuckle ripples along the walls and Alice's fingers brush mine in the darkness. Clair whispers, "About half the Resistance would disagree with that statement, Toby. What took you so long?"

"Nothing." Tobias strikes a match and touches it to a candle. The flame flickers on his mask, lighting one side of his face while on the other, the shadows seem to deepen. He gives Clair a grin. "Come on. You know how irritable she gets if a meeting starts late."

"You'd think," Clair says, following the light of his candle down the stairs and nudging me and Alice ahead of her, "that given the circumstances, she'd be a little understanding."

As we stand outside the same tunnel wall Ella brought me to before, Alice's fingers tighten on mine, and she murmurs right by my ear, "I'm not Alice down here."

"Why?"

"He took my name."

I don't have time to respond before the door slides open and Beatrice slips out into the hallway. She greets Tobias quietly and reaches up to press a hand against his mask. Her eyes sparkle with magic, and the gold turns black, seeping out from her hand like a wave on the beach. The metal melts at the edges, turning fluid and spreading to cover Tobias's face completely. When she's done, she blows Clair a kiss, and vanishes back inside, leaving the door open behind her and Clair blushing at my side.

I'm wholly unprepared for the scene before me. Last time I expected a shadowy underground Resistance and got a tea party. Now, I face a hall filled with figures dressed in black. No chandelier dances light around the marble coffins, and there's not a finger sandwich in sight. A tunnel gapes where a large tapestry had hung before, buzzing with the voices of those gathered beyond.

The figures snap to attention as we enter. "Summon the dark," one says in a voice like gravel shaken in a cup. His features are hidden behind a black stone mask moulded into a caricature of a face. It should be comedic, with its bulbous nose and smooth round cheeks, but the effect is more terrifying than the Gilded's golden half-masks.

Tobias answers for us all: "Surrender the light."

"You weren't followed?"

Clair scoffs. "Stop with all the cloak-and-dagger bullshit. You think we're fresh in the doors? If anyone suspected, we wouldn't be here."

"Enough," Tobias says quietly. "Is she ready for us?"

"It's a full house. They're waiting," Bulbous-Nose answers from behind his mask.

Though I can't see anyone's face, I can see their lifelines. His is flecked with gold like the Gilded's but there are no barbs and it flickers as he speaks. "Everyone turned out to see the Death-Weaver and the Life-Spinner in the flesh."

"My name is Penny." My voice shakes, but I hate being called the Death-Weaver. I might not be able to stop the Warden taking my name, but I'm damned if I'll let the Resistance do it too. "And this is Alice."

Beatrice calls from the doorway where the tapestry was. "We try not to use names. Idiot. Only the council know everyone's identities. Otherwise the masks are pretty pointless—though I suppose there's no mistaking who you two are. Hurry up. She's waiting." She waves a little wave, pulls her mask to one side to shoot me a smile, and vanishes back through the opening.

Clair's whisper slinks down the rocky walls. "Don't let the masks get under your skin. Beatrice makes them. Not all are as hideous as that one—he pissed her off."

I stifle a smile as we walk through the arched tunnel, but I have to force myself not to reach for Alice's hand as the passage opens into a cavern filled with black-cloaked figures in military-precise lines. Grey light dances down the walls, illuminating the aisle, which stretches to an altar made of bones. Ash-black whorls darken gleaming white humeri. Femurs form the base, the protuberances of hip bones supporting a thick slab of pure gold.

This cavern is a temple, packed beyond capacity—and it's bigger than the mausoleum we entered through. Humidity moistens the air with body heat, but I don't push up my sleeves. I don't want the Warden's cuffs on display.

Eyes watch as we walk toward the altar, murmurs trailing behind us. Blocks of black wax are stacked on the altar top and a scorch mark is burned into the gold. A ripple in the metal as if it melted and cooled. And in the centre is a rectangle of grey sand, an iron lid beside it with teeth and tiny wrist bones embedded in the metal to form a whorl. Recognition crawls down my spine.

This is a temple to Death and the one who created it. These are the Sorcerer's halls.

Two pillars stand to either side of the altar. They are carved from black marble, which glitters with silver veins, and slung between them is a platform. A rickety wooden stair zigzags up the rock face to reach it.

I want to shrink as we take the stairs. Each tread seems more unstable than the last, less steady, or maybe my knees shake harder. I feel so exposed. Every person watching is a risk; someone that might inform on me and Alice to the Warden. But I remember trying to talk to Malin about the Resistance, how my mind went blank and I couldn't form the words. I whisper to Clair, "Have they all made the same oath?"

She nods, and some of the tension in my chest releases.

"Couldn't we have done this more privately?"

"That's not how the Resistance works. Everyone is welcome to every meeting."

I skip up a step and slide into the space between Clair and the rock face, grabbing her arm to steady myself. "But there's more people here than can possibly live in the Colligerate. I don't understand!"

"They come up from the city," Clair says.

The sea of stone-masked faces is overwhelming. "But how do they get here? They can't exactly walk in the front gate!"

Clair squeezes my hand, sensing my nerves. "The catacombs go under the city, all the way to the sea. One tunnel opens out into a cave right on the cliff face. It's beautiful at sunset."

"Surely the Gilded guard them?"

"Mostly, that's the palace guards' job. And there's more in the guard than just me aligned with the Resistance." She jerks her chin up to the platform. "Him for example. The big brute is my commanding officer. Careful of him. The witches are powerful too, and—well, Elsweather didn't get here by baking cookies."

Tobias and Clair halt, military sharp, at the edge of a platform with no handrail, nothing to stop someone from stumbling off—or being shoved.

A huge painting of a rose in a silver frame hangs behind the platform, looking very out of place. Six people sit at a long table, unmasked and raised above the masses, and all of them are looking at me. Four witches stare with varying degrees of interest, a representative from each coven except the thorns, the palace guard leans back in his chair and folds his massive arms, glaring as if I'm wasting his time, and Miss Elsweather sips at a porcelain cup of tea, peering above her glasses. There's a teapot beside her, and where the others are tense, she seems relaxed. "Hello, Penny. Lovely to see you, dear. Let's get this started, shall we?"

"The Death-Weaver is here?" a voice echoes from behind her, and I realise that what I thought was a painting hung on the wall is actually a screen. And someone is behind it.

Miss Elsweather pushes her glasses up her nose. "Leave the Spinner there, you can let go of her hand. There's nothing to worry about, the council just has a few questions."

I walk forward alone and face the council, unsure what's expected of me, horribly aware of the drop at my back. "Her name is Alice," I reply, and standing up for Alice, reclaiming her name, strengthens my knees and stops fear sneaking down my spine.

"Is it now?" The question rasps from behind the screen, slightly muffled. It sounds like she's speaking through layers of fabric to disguise her voice. "And you are Penelope Albright?"

"Just Penny." I'm surprised at how steady I sound.

"She joined the Resistance?" This question is not directed at me.

An ore witch with a ruby piercing the dark skin on her shoulder and six more studded down each arm answers. "My niece recruited her."

The ember witch beside her confirms it. "We have storm and tide witches who witnessed the deal. Tobias is assigned as her minder, both for the Resistance and the Warden, which is working well."

The tide witch on the other side of Miss Elsweather jots the report down in a huge ledger, the pages yellowing with age. Water flows from her pale fingertips, across a small ink pad, and into the nib of her pen. The scratch of her writing pauses, nib hovering above the paper, and the voice asks, "Did they explain why we need you?"

I nod, and the storm witch at the end of the table smiles encouragingly. "She can't see you, dear. You'll have to speak up." She raises her voice, making it carry like a distant rumble of thunder rolling in off the sea. "For the record, Penny nodded. She knows why she's here."

I swallow hard. "You want me to find the Grimoire," I say quietly. It's not a question. No one answers. But the palace guard raises a dark eyebrow and glares at Clair. "I've already found it. I have the spell to reforge the knife."

A low murmur ripples through the hall. I wasn't quiet enough. They heard.

"Tobias?" the voice says, rich with anticipation. "Is this true? You've read the spell?"

I scowl at the painting. A lifeline curves up above the screen for a moment before it curls back down, pale grey with no shimmer to it. Alice sees it too; I hear her sharp inhale. Tobias stiffens beside her. I recognise it. I'm sure I've seen it before, but I can't remember where.

Reluctantly, Tobias answers, "I've read it."

I continue, "I'll need help. Magic from each of the covens." I hate that—that the spell risks more than just me.

The storm witch watches me carefully, her eyes darkening. "We have volunteers."

"Penny!" It's Ella. I hear the rustle of her disturbance in the hall below. Mila echoes my name, and the noise swells.

It takes everything I have to ignore my sisters, face the painting, and say what I came here to say: "I can work the magic." I pause before I drop the final piece of information on their table. A page torn from the mythology book—the story with the Ember Queen and her fiery crystal—and a picture of the Sorcerer's knife I copied from the Grimoire, five crystals embedded in the hilt anchored with a single black thread. "I've been reading, and…I think every coven had crystals once, a long time ago."

The council refuse to look at one another. The ore witch digs a coppery nail deep into the table.

I ignore her silent threat. "To forge the knife, you need a crystal from each coven."

Smoke drifts from the table beneath the ember witch's fingers. "There was a legend that the first Ember Queen had a crystal. But as far as I know, no other ember witch has ever had one. Not since the world divided and the Dark Mother wove the magic into our blood."

The ore witch says, "We had the same tale. The first Ore Queen had a yellow crystal on a chain carved into the statue of her in our shrine. I doubt it was the real one or the Gilded wouldn't have burned it to the ground with the rest of our town." Bitterness clings to her confession.

The tide witch isn't writing anymore.

The ore witch shakes her head. "Crystals are a weakness."

The palace guard, unaffected by this new information, asks calmly, "How do you propose we obtain the crystals?"

"A thorn witch would take a drop of blood from each coven into Death and grow a crystal in the sand," I say quietly. "I can do it if you'd like me to, but if you don't trust me, I'm sure Ella or Carlotta would next time they're on patrol. But you'll need a crystal from each coven and a black crystalled-witch to forge the actual knife."

Silence falls. Deep and unsettled.

The voice behind the screen says, "You are sure you can work the spell, Penelope?"

I don't look at Tobias as I answer. "I can."

As one, the council stands and vanishes behind the screen.

Alice moves silently to stand so her shoulder touches mine, her presence reassuring. I have no idea if they'll agree to their blood being taken into Death. I'm not sure I want them to.

The council file silently back to their places with worried eyes and soft shoulders.

The storm witch says, "Magic always has a price. What price is on this spell, Penny?"

I bite my lip hard and shift away from Alice. Unsteadily, I approach the table, stand right in front of Miss Elsweather, and lean close enough that the council will hear my whisper but no one else will. "A lifeline from a black-crystalled witch."

Miss Elsweather's eyes widen behind her glasses. Her hand trembles as she sets down her cup of tea. She goes to speak and shakes her head, swallowing quietly before she begins again. "Are you sure, Penny?"

"I am."

They stare at me a moment, and then the muttering starts, on the platform, behind us in the crowd. I don't know if I can leave or if the meeting is over. The noise, so many people, it's too much to bear. I press my hands into the table, trying to ground myself, but it just gets louder and louder. My knees tremble.

Miss Elsweather saves me. "Go, Penny. You can leave. Think about what you're agreeing to a little longer. No one will hold you to it if you change your mind."

The palace guard scoffs. "I will. She agreed. And I don't see anyone else around here who can."

Is he mocking me? I look to Clair in desperation, and she flaps one hand, gesturing me to leave the platform. Gratefully, I turn away and hear Miss Elsweather say, “Shut up, Dante! What have I told you?”

I don’t hear his reply.

I take Alice’s hand to stop my own shaking, and hurry down the rickety stairs.

Tobias catches my elbow, slowing my pace. “You have to be the most unpredictable—”

“Save it. Get me out of here.”

Ella clambers through the crowds as Tobias hurries me away, trying to shove aside the black-cloaked figures closing in behind us. Mila is right behind her. Fear shines in their silver eyes—and Ella is angry. I’ve never seen either of them look like this before.

I slip my hand from Alice’s as we reach the exit and run.

Chapter Twenty-Nine

Ice slams into my veins as I round the tunnel corner into the wards. The light shutters and I'm alone in the dark, freezing and with no idea which way to go. Running was stupid. But Ella's glare, Mila's expression! I can't handle talking to them now. They're frightened, but so am I. I love my sisters, I'd do anything for them, but without magic, the wastes outside Halstett will never heal from the blight of the Warden, Life will stay dead and grey, and the cherry tree in my village will never blossom again.

I'll talk to them, I will. I'll make sure they understand. But not tonight. If I don't cross into Death soon, I'll miss my appointment with Malin.

I lean into the wall, shivering, as the light of a candle brushes away the dark.

At first, I think Tobias is alone, but Alice steps from his shadow. She's beautiful in the candlelight, blonde hair shimmering as if she's from beyond this world. There's no judgement in her eyes, no anger. She just reaches for my hand and murmurs, "You need to cross?"

What I need is time. Space to breathe. But in Life, even Alice can't give me that. In Death, I might escape it, just for a little while. And she's right, I *do* need to cross. So, I squeeze her hand and move closer to her side, and Tobias stays silent as he leads us, holding the dark at bay. The shadows rolling along the stone walls are gentle.

"You'll come back?" Alice asks when we reach the panel. She sounds unsure, a waver to her question.

"I will," I promise.

"I'll be here," Alice says softly. "Together, Penny. We'll survive it. I'll help you pay the price."

Tobias clicks the panel open. "It's late. We'll talk tomorrow." I open my mouth to argue, but he cuts me off with a hand on my shoulder, pushing me into my rooms. "Tomorrow. You need to burn, Penny, and I'm on night duty in less than an hour."

Tobias helps me cross. He holds my hand as the poison burns me from the inside out. He takes half my pain and recites the words to part the veil. It's a relief to not pass on alone—it's a bigger relief when Malin catches me as I stumble through.

I'm exhausted. My soul shivers as I enter Death. My heartbeat stills, and I barely notice; my body doesn't know if it's alive or dead anymore.

"You saw the Resistance?" he asks as he sets me steady.

I nod. "I've agreed to work the spell."

"Of course you have."

Malin's silence as we walk to the manor is jarring. He's refused to give his opinion on the spell. Completely refused to discuss it beyond checking I'd found it without mishap—that I was fully aware of the cost. I expected him to tell me I can't. That the price is too high. He doesn't. Not even when the portcullis rattles shut.

Mist drapes his gardens, lacing rosebushes with silver glitter and hiding his wall of thorns. Each step down the path swirls the mist deeper, thicker, and dampness clings to my skin with gentle fingers until I can barely see Malin, let alone the steps to the manor doors. It soothes me, somehow, the muffled lack of sound, the absence of birds or wind or sight.

"Penny." Malin says my name carefully—as if it's more than a name. "Do you trust me?"

It's the last thing I expect him to ask, and the answer slips free before I have time to consider it. "Yes."

He sighs and steps back, vanishing into the mist.

The first piece of paper lands on my skirts. A torn scrap no bigger than my pinkie nail. The second falls on my hand, a red line cutting it in two. Paper blizzards from the mist, brushing my skin and swirling around me, dry and whispering. I stand alone in a tornado of fragments covered in broken words.

"Make me a promise." Malin's voice comes from everywhere and nowhere. The gardens beyond the paper storm grow dark and shadows swarm in, slicing through the silvery mist. "Promise, Penny." I shiver as the temperature drops. "Promise you'll never heal the Warden and I'll make all this go away."

"All what?" I'm so damned confused. I wanted to escape tonight, to stop being frightened. Just for a while. Instead, Malin is talking in riddles and making everything worse.

"Our contract," he explains. "The stake I have in your soul. I tried to destroy it, but this is what happened. The pieces of it have been whirling around my grounds all day. Death won't let you go without a price."

I blink, trying to see past the mist to him. He can't be letting me go? "Everything costs something."

"Indeed," he says, a word so quiet it's barely an exhale. All around me, the paper whirls faster and faster until my head spins. "Promise you'll never heal the Warden."

I want to close my eyes, but I don't dare. "I've already said I won't."

"Exactly," he replies, and a piece of parchment slides from the maelstrom of torn contract. A pen hovers beside it. "I can't destroy the original contract without creating a new one. So I did. Sign it." He pauses and the whirl of paper stops, tiny pieces frozen midair. "Please."

"Where's the small print?"

"There is none. Not this time."

I read it carefully. Twice. Thrice. Checking every one of the nine words. *I, Penelope Albright, promise never to heal Reginald Halstett.* I pluck the pen from the air and sign it neatly, *Penny*, written in my blood on the dotted line.

I hear a sigh.

Fire whirls up from the ground, the paper of my contract combusting in a single blaze of heat and smoke, and ash floats down to confetti my skirts. I hold tight to the new contract and blink as light replaces the dark.

It isn't ash drifting from the skies.

It's cherry blossoms.

Swathes of them fill the air and the scent of home wafts on the breeze.

In the centre of the lawn is my cherry tree. Every knot in the wood, every branch, exactly as I remember it. And Malin stands beneath it, a single pale pink petal caught in his hair.

We sit in the grass, leaning against the trunk with our shoulders nearly touching, and don't say a word. Time slips past like the cherry blossom dancing in the afternoon sunshine. Malin's hand rests beside mine, the little black rose of our bargain still marked on his wrist. It's still on mine too, and I'm glad of it. I want to move my fingers to touch his. I pick a petal from my skirt to stop myself and hold it up to the light. Veins branch across soft, translucent pink like lifelines winding together. One pinch of my fingers and it would crumple.

I drop the petal.

Malin stares at it where it falls. A little pink boat sailing on a sea of grass.

"Who are you, Malin? Really? And why are you here?" The peace between us shatters. It doesn't dissolve or fade into quiet. Its shards prickle my nerves as Malin stiffens, his bicep tensing against mine.

"You'll never come back."

I want to lean into him, wind my fingers around his and reassure him nothing will change if he tells me the truth, but I've never been one to lie. "I'll come back." I have unfinished business here, no matter who he is. The library in the woods for one.

He takes my hand as if it's made of glass and I might break or slip away. "The veil is anchored like a fishing net to the seabed. The Sorcerer was the original Guardian of the Veil, his magic fed it and strengthened it, but he wanted to be free of the burden. He found a boy, a farm boy with a magic that was wasted in a barn with the pigs, and offered him a throne and eternal life in exchange for the responsibility of guarding the veil."

"I know all this, Malin. It's in a book of fairy tales on my bedside table. The boy took the deal, became the Warden of Halstett and the new Guardian of the Veil. That doesn't answer who you are or why you're here."

He squeezes my hand. "Each new moon the Warden remade his oath in Death, but after he banished the Sorcerer, he refused to cross, unsure if the veil would let him return if he did. With his oath broken, the Warden weakened. He decayed, so did his lifeline, and the veil began to fail. Unwilling to give up his eternal life or his throne, the Warden needed another lifeline. So...he took mine. He sliced my lifeline free of my crystal and—"

Malin stutters to a halt, staring at the thorny wall guarding the woods. He's slipped away, lost in the past. His fingers tighten on mine. "They bleed. Lifelines. They bleed magic when they're cut like that. And the pain..." He swallows hard, a muscle flickers in his jaw, and my heart catches. My bones protest at his grip, but I'm clinging to him as tightly as he's holding on to me. "When your coven arrived in Halstett—the final piece in the Warden's defence against the Sorcerer—he walked into Death for the last time with an army of Gilded, skewered the end of my lifeline to the veil, and left me here to uphold his oath. With no crystal anchoring me in Life, I couldn't cross back. My magic fuels the veil, and it keeps the Warden alive. I am anchored to it and so is he."

My lungs refuse to work as I turn wide eyes on Malin. "What colour is your crystal?"

"It was black," he says. "Like yours. It shattered when they trapped me here. Even if I could find a path back to Life, I'd lose my mind."

"Malin," I ask, not wanting the answer—but I need it. "Who are you?"

He tries to untangle his fingers, but I hold tight, anchoring him to me. "The Warden is my father. And I'm every bit the monster he is."

My stomach clenches.

The Warden's son? How can the immortal tyrant who destroyed our world, who controls my coven and chained Alice and me in his service, be Malin's father? My eyes prickle and I swallow back my emotions, trying desperately not to react as Malin watches me. He's frozen, tense. Bracing himself for my rejection. My lip wobbles. The Warden used his own son to protect himself. I think I'm going to be sick. "I thought..."

I stare at my hand, still clamped around his.

Maybe Malin is delusional. None of this makes sense.

The tension between us is agonising. I have to say something. Anything. "The Warden doesn't have a son, Malin."

Anything but that.

He shakes me loose and springs to his feet. "You need proof?" In one swift movement, he strips his shirt over his head and slowly turns his back. Ivory-smooth skin gleams in the dappled light through the leaves, shadows marking muscles carved into his shoulders and deepening the dips of his spine.

I want to close my eyes. I don't want to see the gold burned into his skin. Compared to the Gilded's gold desecration, Malin's back is worse. Infinitely, horribly worse. And if what he says is true, his own father did it.

Broken stars lace his shoulders and the gold spire of the High Warden's insignia rises from the dimples of his hips to the base of his neck.

I rise, and he stills as I tentatively reach for his back. Metal flexes with the movement of his ribs, freezing as I trace the raised lines with my fingertips. Tension slowly coils in his muscled shoulders, but he lets me complete my gentle examination before he turns.

"Does anyone in Halstett know you exist?"

His eyes darken into the chill of a storm before it breaks. "I assume my mother is aware."

"The consort..." I trail off at the twitch of his jaw. "Maybe I could undo it? I...I found another spell on the ninth floor—"

"It's not that simple."

"Malin—"

"It won't work." He cuts me off a second time, reclaims his shirt from where he threw it on the ground, and hides the evidence of his imprisonment. The distance he's put between us feels like a chasm I can't cross; with the way he's staring at me, paring me down to my soul beneath, I wouldn't if I could.

A petal floats down and he catches it in his palm for a moment before letting it fall away. "I intended to use you to set myself free. The first night you came here, I meant to take you into the woods, to my library. I meant to the next night, and the next, and the one after that, but I couldn't. Not after what it did to Ella."

"I never believed she looked back."

"She didn't. The woods refused her entry, and the refusal bruised her lifeline. Badly. She didn't even get close to the library; I wasn't sure she'd survive it. It would have let you in, but…I can't let you." He clenches his fists. "Go, Penny. Leave. Before I hurt you more than I already have."

"No."

He prowls toward me. And I should step back. Every part of me screams danger. It hardens every line of him. "I won't watch you destroyed. Not at my hand. Leave Death, escape Halstett, and never look back."

"I'm not leaving you stuck here on your own."

"Do you want to know what I was going to do to you? Exactly what my father did to me. When the Warden first brought me here, I walked easily through every layer of protection the Sorcerer wove around the veil and its source. No wards activated when I stepped into the woods; no vines reached for my lifeline and tried to tear it apart. The book sprites welcomed me to their magical library. I was a child, just a boy, I thought it was an adventure. I felt so special, loved. I'd never felt loved before. My mother gave me up when I was a few hours old, which makes sense on this side of it.

"It wasn't until later that I learned the truth—that my father ordered her to ensure I was never born." He pauses. Pain creases his brow. "Maybe it would have been better if she had. She left me in the lap of luxury, cared for by a merchant family, part of a storm coven on the Western Seaboard, unaware of who I was—what I was. For years I was free of responsibility, court games, and politics. Then the Warden turned his sights on the Western Seaboard. I grew up playing in high-turreted towers, helping with the storm witches' workings, watching them study the climate, shifting wind patterns and positioning rain clouds as the crops demanded until the grey wastes came. Then, I watched them struggle, helpless and useless, as harvest after harvest failed. Sand smothered green fields, fog blotted the sun, and the Warden's twisted army wiped everything good from the land."

His inhale catches, his eyes soften a moment, and blaze silver hard as he composes himself. He catches my shoulders, and my heart hurts for the boy he was, the man he's grown into. Then, he continues and his voice is colder. A man reporting an incident. Impartial. "When the Warden's Gilded finished incinerating the entire Western Seaboard, I was brought in with the last survivors from our city. My adopted mother was executed right in front of me, my adopted father swapped knowledge for power and handed me over in exchange for a seat on the Warden's council."

Malin towers over me, his grip tightens on my shoulders, and he's so close, I feel the chill of his skin against my chest. I want to run my hands through his hair and tell him it's all right, he's not on his own anymore, cup his face and pull him down to me, but I don't quite dare move. He's so lost, drowning in the past, and his eyes are fixed on mine so tight, I can't look away—if I look away, he might be lost forever. "If the book sprites accepted you, I was going to tear myself free of the veil, tie your lifeline there instead and follow it back to Life so I could take your crystal as my own. And then, I was going to kill my father."

Silence falls with his confession. I stare at him, the silver in his eyes. He is a captive who meant to cage me, a man who couldn't. A boy so horribly betrayed by everyone who should have loved him. A tear slides down my cheek. "But you didn't."

"I couldn't. My one chance to destroy the Warden, to take revenge, and I failed." He looks away, to the forest behind me. "When it came to it, I couldn't hurt you." It sounds like an admission of guilt.

"You don't need to hurt me. We can do it together. I think I know how to kill the Warden and protect the veil."

"The spell to forge the Sorcerer's knife requires a lifeline. If you work the spell, Penny, you won't die. You'll just stop existing."

"I know," I say quietly. "But what kind of person would I be if I didn't?"

"As bad as me."

"No." I reach for him. My fingers rest on his chest and I feel the beat of his heart beneath the silk of his shirt. Fast and hard and hurting. "I have a report."

"You don't need a report. You owe me nothing." His hand slides down to the small of my back, pulling me closer into him.

"My sister is alive because of you."

"You're in the Warden's possession because of me." He brushes my jaw with his thumb, fingers trailing down my neck, and inside I melt. I want to offer him the world on a silver platter, promise anything, if he'll just hold me, keep me, kiss me.

Holy Dark Mother, he's distracting. "I'm in the Warden's *possession* because I made a mistake." I try to remember the spell to bind a lifeline, to anchor Malin to me and bring him back to Life. "The Warden intends to destroy magic, Malin. And I can't stop him alone."

He leans closer. Inches separate us. Less. "What do you need?"

I exhale with relief and feel the slight hitch in his inhale.

Malin's breath is soft against mine, his lips so close I can nearly feel them. Nearly. Not quite. I want to push onto tiptoe and meet him in the middle. He whispers my name, and it's like the darkness itself tempts me.

"I found a spell to bind lifelines together," I whisper, determined to get to the end of this conversation.

He groans. "You are infuriating." Gently, he rests his hands on my shoulders and pushes me away. "You're asking me to watch you destroy yourself."

"But it will set you free! Someone needs to be Guardian of the Veil when the Warden is gone. Otherwise everything will crumble."

"Find someone else."

"There *is* no one else."

"I won't let you bind yourself to me."

"You don't get to *let* me do things, Malin."

He smiles and a little of the light returns to his eyes. "No," he says, and softly presses a kiss against my hair. "But I do get to decide what you do to *my* lifeline, Penny. And you *do* need to go."

He's right. Soon, dawn will string my lifeline tight, I can feel it trembling. "I'll come back. I promise."

"I won't let you fall. And if you do, I'll catch you. Don't forget that." He sounds so desperate. He holds my hand all the way to the veil, and when I return to Life, I leave another piece of my soul behind, and a piece of my heart as well. But this time, I'm taking a sliver of hope with me. I can help Malin. I'm sure of it.

Chapter Thirty

It's still dark when I return. Alice is curled into the window seat, the curtains pulled wide, her fingers twitching to get back to her loom. Need flashes in her eyes, and I'm not sure if it's for me or to weave the future she sees. "Penny?" The sharp edge of her whisper sinks me back into the pillows. "You're splitting right down the middle. Half of you is here, with me. Half of you belongs there. I understand."

I stare at her. "You know..." I falter. It was simpler when Malin was a jerk. A seductively handsome one, but a jerk, nonetheless.

Alice shakes her head with a soft smile, reassurance in her eyes. "When you're happy, the air sparkles where your lifeline should be. It shines when you come back."

"I'm sorry," I whisper.

"Don't be. Where do you go in Death? I can't see beyond the walls and I've never asked; you've never told. But the Warden's fate has sunk its teeth into your future, and soon, it will never release you. I don't want to lose you."

I answer with a defence. An unfair one. "You can't see beyond the walls, yet you sent me after Ella. Why?"

Alice's eyes turn ink black like the first time I saw her; the Spinner, perched on her chair like a bitter queen ruling over a fractured realm. She sighs, her shoulders slumping, fingers laced together to stop the future spilling free, and she's Alice again. And I just hurt her. "The paths of the future split. If I hadn't sent you, Ella would have died inside the walls and the Warden's reign would be eternal. I...I couldn't let that happen, even if the price was you."

"You should have warned me."

"I didn't know you then. I saw—" The colour drains from her cheeks. "Would you have gone?"

"Ella's my sister. Of course I'd have gone. Alice, what did you see?"

She closes her eyes and leans back against the windowsill, wrapping her arms around herself. "Our futures tangled. Three threads wove into one. I can't see you, Penny. I can't see me either. I don't know how this ends anymore." She pauses, her lip sucking between her teeth as she drifts from the window seat to my side.

I want to reach for her, hold her, but I pat the bed beside me and answer her question instead. "Behind the walls, there's a manor. I made a deal with the man who's trapped there. He tore our contract up tonight and set me free, Alice. Afterward, I nearly kissed him."

"You're falling for him."

"I've already fallen for you."

"With me," she says softly, but her eyes sharpen. "We fall together. You and he will too. That's why there were three."

She's lost me. "Three what?"

"I see it. I've spun it in silk. Over and over again. Three lifelines twisted and I can't see where they go. Three threads wove together and vanished from my sight." Her black eyes glaze, her focus drifting, and I lace my fingers with hers so her compulsion to weave dances against the back of my hand. "Three lifelines. Yours, mine, his. It has to be."

"He's trapped in Death, Alice. His lifeline's severed—the Warden used it to tie him to the veil—and he won't let me help him. I thought he was the Sorcerer, but he's not."

"Whoever he is, you need him." She leans so close the scent of spring sunshine wraps me in home. "I can't see the threads of your future, but I see you, and you're slipping. If you force yourself to decide between us, he'll take you."

"I'm not something to be taken."

"Tell that to the High Warden." Her eyes hold mine, focused on me now, not the past or the future, and relief hits me in the chest, followed by a pang of guilt; I thought she was talking about Malin. "I know," she whispers. "I understand."

"I'm sorry."

"Don't be. Love isn't weakness. It's strength. There are no limits and honesty is the only rule. Shutting him out isn't being honest. It doesn't take anything away from us if you're with him too."

"I barely know him. Until a few nights ago, I thought he was an arsehole."

Alice chuckles. "But tonight he set you free."

"He did, and he told me everything. Something changed."

"Where are we, Penny? Me and you?"

"We're together, Alice. Aren't we?"

She nods, relief in her eyes, and the hope swelling in my chest matches the shine of her tears. "When I can't see you, it's terrifying," she says softly. "But if he's keeping you safe, if he cares about you, I don't need to worry about you so much. I like that. Where are you, with him? The man in the walls."

I take a moment to consider it before answering. "It's simple with you. When we're alone, I don't want to let anyone in. I can be myself without having to second-guess every word." I trail off. "Are you sure you want to hear about him?" She nods and I bite my lip, trying to work out how to make it make sense.

Alice rests her head on my shoulder. "Just tell the truth, Penny."

With a shaky exhale, I do my best to explain. "He's irresistible. I thought at first it was purely physical. Two magnets, drawn together. I didn't think it meant anything, just a bit of lust, a brush of a hand here, a glance there. He's warm one minute and so cold the next. When I'm with him, he takes up so much space. He's like a single star in a midnight sky. And I thought he was manipulating me. But...well, he wasn't. At heart he's gentle. So careful, and he's been hurt so badly. Everyone has let him down."

Alice smiles. "You've fallen for him."

"I think I have," I admit. "I'm sorry."

"Don't apologise. If he makes you happy, I'm happy. You can't have too many people on your side, and I saw him coming. I care about you, Penny." She sounds so genuinely happy, so sure of herself and her feelings, my heart feels too big to fit in my chest, all full of hope and something that might turn into love one day, if we all live long enough. But then I think about what Malin asked of me, and I feel troubled again.

"He wants me to bring my crystal into Death."

"You should take it." Alice leans in so the tips of our noses touch and murmurs, "We're the same, you and I. And I made a mistake that will break us both."

"You didn't," I try to reassure her. She wraps her arms around me and her cheek presses hot against my neck. "There are times when I've been tempted to stay in Death, you know. But thinking about you here, it helped anchor me. More than any crystal."

"My name is Alice. And you are Penny. Don't forget that. Don't forget me." There's a desperate edge to her words and her fingers whisper a question on my skin as she traces my jaw and brushes her thumb across my bottom lip. Her breath hitches at my answer. I kiss her. Soft at first, then deeper.

She tastes of mint and sunshine and shattering hope. I cling to her as she clings to me. In her arms, it doesn't matter that I left part of myself in Death. I'm half of me and she is half-destroyed by the Warden—and two halves make a whole. Together, we are perfect just as we are.

I run my fingers down her side, feeling the warmth of her beneath her thin cotton nightgown. With a soft gasp, Alice leans into me, her weight slight and warm. "I've got you," she whispers.

This. This is why I cannot stay in Death. "We've got each other."

"Always." The word whispers against my lips. A promise.

I sigh and pull away, breathless and wanting. "I need to talk to him."

She nods. "And when you have, come back to me, Penny."

"Always," I reply.

We curl together in the dark side of the morning, and sleep claims us too fast. I see her in my dreams. We walk together hand in hand across a landscape spun in silk. Malin is with us and I think we're in Death. Sands shift and spiked flowers sprout in our path, thorned roses drawing a line into the impossible light of the Horizon.

Alice wakes me with a gentle hand on my arm. Dawn's relentless fronds are already breaking apart the last of the night beyond the open window and it's so cold outside the eiderdown. Her fingers tap dance on my shoulder. "I dreamed of roses," she whispers. "He was there, Penny. His name is Malin. He used to live here too."

"Alice, I..."

She grins. I've never seen Alice grin. But she's like a cat who got into the cream this morning. "You dreamed the same dream." With a regretful kiss dropped on my lips, she slips from the bed and shivers. "He dreamed it too. Talk to him tonight. Take the light where you find it. It's going to be dark for a while yet. The silk spins it so." And Alice returns to her loom, leaving me alone.

I remain in the warm cocoon of my bed for a little longer. I should be confused, I should be worried about the knife and lifelines and everything else, but this morning, I'm happy. Now, Alice has kissed me, and I want to kiss her again. I want to run my fingers through her hair and—I blink. My breath quickens and I dig my nails into my palms as my imagination plays havoc with my heart.

The panel opening jars me awake again. Clair stares at me, arms folded, expression grim. Her lifeline, sunshine yellow last time I saw her, coils above her head, thin and cold and the palest of blues.

Pillows scatter as I shoot to my feet. "What happened?"

Clair shakes her head and puts a finger to her lips. Silence rings like an alarm bell. I cannot hear Alice. Her loom has been a steady background noise since I was brought here. She can't be away from it long; I've seen her try in the early hours—I watched her nose crinkle with dismay as she reluctantly slipped from my bed this morning.

"Where's Alice?" I whisper, sitting up stiffly.

Clair leans against the table, one dark hand clamped on the wood so tight her knuckles stretch thin. The urgency in her whisper sends ice crackling down my spine. "Toby walked in her door and marched her down to the Gilded Barracks as if he was following orders."

"I don't understand."

"Neither do I," she says. "They caught them in the catacombs."

My brain struggles to catch up. "Toby openly defected?"

She nods, jaw clenched tight. "Apparently, Ella was with them."

"Ella wouldn't leave, not without me."

The table groans against Clair's grip. "The charges are bullshit, Penny. Toby would never risk Ella or Alice. Not with such an idiotic plan. Everyone in the Resistance is offered the chance to escape Halstett when they first join. If Toby wanted to leave, the Resistance would have helped."

"The Warden doesn't need to lie to get what he wants. He takes what he wants!" I pull at the cuff on my wrist. I want to tear it off and I can't. I'm trapped and useless and the Warden has Ella and Alice and Tobias. "Where are they?" I don't want her answer. I don't want to know.

"The Gilded took Toby—" Clair swallows and lowers her eyes. "Ella's in the barracks. Alice is... Alice is with the Warden."

My tongue sticks to the roof of my mouth, sand coats my throat. I force the question. "Alive?"

"Barely. What they did to her—"

I'm too shocked to cry. Too horrified to move.

"Penny, I think..." Clair's voice cracks. "There's a traitor in the Resistance. The Warden knows you found the Grimoire. He wants it."

I feel like the world is falling apart around me. "Why didn't he come for me? Why go after Toby and Ella? Why Alice?"

"I honestly don't know." She shakes her head and slumps into a dining chair. "Dante, my commanding officer, he's on the Resistance council, says they're tiptoeing around the Thorn Queen. That the Warden needed an iron-clad charge to stick to Ella so he created one."

"Grandmother heals his wound."

"But he has you."

"I'm not healing him."

Clair swallows. "We think the traitor is a thorn witch."

I stare at Clair in confusion. Accusation stares back at me. She thinks it's me? Three people I care about are in danger. And I'm the traitor? "You think I've betrayed you?"

She blinks and the accusation fades. Relief replaces it. "*I* don't. Nor do I think it's Ella. Or Mila."

"So who?" The pillow crinkles as I hug it tighter to my chest. I want to bury my face like a child hiding behind a curtain. "You can't suspect Carlotta? She wouldn't, not after what happened with Haylea."

"I don't know. Maybe. She hasn't been herself recently." Clair shakes her head. "We'll find them."

"Toby, will he be—"

"The Warden won't let him die, or Ella. Not yet. They're too valuable as leverage. He's planning something—we just need to find out what." She's less convinced than I am by her reassurance. We both know there are fates far worse than death. She stiffens as boots shuffle outside. "Do you need help to cross tonight?"

I shake my head, glad of the poison stashed beneath our feet. I whisper a goodbye as she makes for the panel in the wall. "Be careful. I can't lose you too."

"And you, Penny. Summon the dark."

I nod but stay silent. I'm not ready to surrender the light, not yet.

Chapter Thirty-One

Gilded boots shuffle outside my door at midnight; the change of the guard that signals it is time to cross into Death.

I roll back the rug, silently exposing my secret hiding place behind the dresser, and stare at the initials carved into the wood on the back of the drawers. *MH.* I trace them with my finger. Malin Halstett. How didn't I see it before? Any credibility missing from Malin's story slips into place. I'm being kept in his old rooms, sleeping in his bed.

I glance over to it, and my throat tightens, thinking of Alice.

I've seen what the Warden does to those who defy him, in vividly graphic detail in the barracks. The Alice who kissed me this morning will be gone. All he'll leave behind is his Spinner bound to a loom.

I yank up the floorboard before panic overwhelms me. My crystal shimmers in the darkness. I slip its chain around my neck and fold Alice's silk squares into my pocket; the one embroidered with the girl bound in gold, shadows reaching for the Warden's throat, and the one with Alice and me holding hands.

Slowly, I unstop the silver vial and listen.

Alice's loom is silent.

The absence wraps ice around my heart and poison sears it away in one fiery swallow. When I reach for the veil, there is no resistance. It yields to my touch, parting beneath magic heightened by my crystal.

Tonight, I stumble into Malin's arms and snatch his hand, tugging him across the sands to the manor. Even in Death, something seems wrong. Fear prickles the nape of my neck as if we're being watched.

The desert shifts as we walk; foggy hands break the crusted sand and broken-nailed fingers reach to pluck at my skirts.

Malin tries to slow my pace, but it only propels me faster until I'm half running, and he has to yank me to a halt. "You need to calm down. You're calling the dead from the dark, Penny."

Colourless mist unfurls across the landscape, fog-wraiths whisper from its depths. "Don't you feel it? We're being watched!"

Malin shakes his head and scans the Horizon. "There's nothing there except what you're bringing into existence."

"Please." I tug at his hand, and he lets me hurry us to the manor. I sigh with relief as the portcullis rattles open, and I don't slow even as it slams down, shutting out the chill of Death.

The parlour is green again today; apple blossoms drift across the wallpaper, the hearth is white marble embellished with pale green flowers. But as I pace to the window and back again, the wallpaper shifts to crimson, blossoms flickering between white and black, swirling as if caught in a storm.

I halt at the window, fingers curled tight in curtains that can't decide if they're white and gauzy or black velvet. The effect is disorientating, the room begins to spin, and I cling to the wall as storm clouds darken the sky. "Stop it!"

"It's not me, Penny," Malin says, his eyes troubled. "You're confusing the manor. You need to calm your emotions."

I've been emotional here before, yet the manor has never reacted like this. "It's *your* manor."

His sigh catches on my hair. "Not anymore. It likes you."

Colour ripples across the walls like the aftermath of a stone thrown in a pond, red to green and back again. "Ask it to stop. I can't think."

He barks an order, "Enough!" The room fades from green to red and settles on scarlet with white blossoms. A compromise. "Has the Warden hurt you?"

Shudders tremble down my back. Malin's hands span my waist and pull me back into the solidness of his chest. I don't resist. I lean into him, my spine pressed into his middle, and tell him everything.

Alice and what she has come to mean to me, how she vanished. How Ella is now imprisoned in the Gilded's dungeon. How I'm terrified of what the High Warden might do to them both. I don't look at Malin as it all spills out of me, about the Warden and his cruelty and how he plans to destroy magic on Samhain Eve. When I'm done, I release my death grip on the curtains and turn in the circle of his arms. "The Warden knows I found the Grimoire."

Malin is quiet for a moment. "You're sure?"

I nod.

"And you couldn't have started with that?" he says, his voice flat.

I ignore him, slipping his hold to cross to the coffee table, and drop to my knees, emptying the contents of my pockets onto its shining ebony surface. Alice's squares of silk and the page with the whorl on it, torn from *A Complete Illustrated Collection of Fables and Myths*. Lined up on the table they look like nothing until I slip my crystal over my head and nestle it carefully on Alice's folded silk. I retreat to the black velvet sofa, sink into it, and wait.

My obsidian crystal consumes the light, but fire flares in Malin's eyes as his hand hovers over it, a gentle caress of the air that sends a shiver down my spine.

He rests his hand flat on the table beside the crystal, not touching it, not quite. "You brought it."

"You asked me to."

Reluctantly, he turns his attention to the other items on the table: the spell, the page, and the silk. Not a flicker of his features betrays his thoughts. I wait in silence, sitting straighter and straighter as the prickly feeling on the back of my neck reforms and amplifies. It shrieks that we are being watched; that someone can see. Rustles of wind in the forest canopy stoke my unease. But Malin's immaculately tended lawns are empty.

I need to shut the window. Fear spikes as I hurry to throw the curtains wide. The wallpaper shifts to ebony black, laced with sickly yellow petals. Malin watches from his crouch by the table as I slam down the sash window, slide home the latch, and swish the curtains shut for good measure.

A silk square is in Malin's hand, the one with me and Alice embroidered across it. The other lies on the table. Tension ripples through his shoulders as he rises to his feet. "Alice wove these?"

"Alice…"

"I knew about Alice, Penny. You talk in your sleep. It isn't an issue for me unless it is for you. From what I know of Alice, she'd say the same about me…us…" Suddenly he seems unsure. "If there is an us?"

"How do you know Alice?"

"She was imprisoned in Halstett, in the room beside mine. She stitched pictures onto little silk squares and passed them through a panel in the wall. She was just a child." Malin taps a perfectly manicured fingernail on the picture of the whorl. "Where did you get this?"

"A book."

"I can see that." He reaches for my crystal.

I don't mean to do it, but a tiny noise of denial slips free from my lips, and pain flitters in his eyes as I take a step backward. I press my spine into the wallpaper, running my finger across the fuzz of flocking to stop myself rushing across the room and snatching it back.

I trust him, I do. I wasn't lying when I told him that. But my crystal—it's a piece of me, a deep and personal part of myself. And I've spent so long without it, it's so hard to let go.

Malin straightens. "Penny, please." He sweeps his offered hand wide to gesture at the table and my crystal. "Take it. I'm not going to hurt you."

"I know."

"So why are you looking so terrified?"

"Just be careful with it."

"When it comes to you, Penny, I have been nothing but careful." He smiles reassuringly, but doesn't move until I offer a jerky nod. I watch how gently he folds the silk around it before he picks it up, how he makes sure it doesn't touch his skin as he rests it in his palm.

I feel his power whisper deep in my chest, seeping through the silk and into my crystal with a pulse that brushes the beat of my heart. I breathe out and I can't breathe in. "Malin," I murmur. "Please."

He looks at me then, silver irises sparkling. "It's real."

"Of course it's real." I don't know what's happening. My head spins, and it's not unpleasant. My veins fizz, and I'm not sure I want it to stop. I blink and lean against the wall. And he's there, right in front of me, offering it to me in an outstretched hand.

I could take it. Make this stop. But when I reach for it, I pause, my hand hovering over his.

"Penny?"

I offer him a shaky smile. "What are you doing?"

He looks confused for a moment, then his eyes darken, pupils dilating. Quietly, he takes my wrist, turns my hand over, and eases my crystal into my palm. When he talks, his words are molten chocolate. "One day, when this is over, if you ask me very nicely, I'll show you exactly what I was doing. But for now, please be assured, I did not intend that to happen."

I tuck my crystal in my pocket, half-relieved, half-disappointed. "Thank you." I'm not entirely sure what else to say.

"You're most welcome." He laughs a sad sort of laugh. "Thank you for trusting me. I'm honoured. But we have more serious issues to deal with this evening. I think it's time I took you to see my library. You need to know where it is, so you can find it when you have the knife."

"I won't survive—"

He cuts me off, taking my hand and marching me out into the hall. "Yes, you will. You *will* survive this. I am not having you simply ceasing to exist. We'll find a way around it. We'll forge the knife, and then you'll bring it here."

"Malin, there is no way around it. You're being ridiculous. Just because you want something to happen, doesn't mean it will!"

"We'll see about that." He hurries me down the front steps and onto the lawn. I skip a step to keep up.

I had forgotten, for a moment, my worry that we were being watched. But as we step away from the safety of the manor, it returns with greater intensity. Shadows trail our steps, and eyes I cannot see are pinned on the nape of my neck. But Malin doesn't falter as he strides toward the forest, his hand clamped around mine.

The wall of thorns disintegrates as we approach, reforming behind us as we enter the woods. In the cool dark beneath the trees, the feeling vanishes, and I breathe a little easier. Light filters through the canopy, dappling the pine-needled ground with shadows that dance to the tune of the wind through the trees. Little red-and-white spotted toadstools circle the tree trunks, and vines bearing clusters of brightly coloured flowers hang down from the branches.

Each tree trunk is cragged with grooves and covered in centuries of moss. I've never been anywhere so deeply, assuredly alive. We walk until my legs ache and my palm grows damp against his. The space between the trees narrows, the light reaching the forest floor grows dim. Moss coats the trunks so thickly here I can't see where one starts and the next begins. This part of the forest is old; the earth beneath us breathes, and the branches whisper secrets in a language I don't understand.

I don't see the wall or the door until Malin draws me to a halt. Pale stone glints between moss-cushioned bark; a faded blue door half-concealed with ivy and twisted vines. Malin snaps his fingers, and the vines unfurl from a brass-curlicued handle.

"What now?"

"Now, you knock."

"That's it? No blood, no knives, no spells?"

Malin exhales shakily. "Only book sprites."

I swallow, remembering what they did to the intruder on the Ninth.

Not giving myself time to think, I raise my hand and knock. The handle turns. The door creaks open. Green eyes wink into existence and the paper-dry whisper of my name repeats in a flood that spills down the stairs and lights them as it goes.

Penny.

The eyes wink out, but the light remains, an eerie glow illuminating the stairwell. I take a deep breath and hold tighter to Malin's hand. "Is this what normally happens when you come here?"

"Not even close." Malin's slight grimace stops me asking more.

Despite the damp of the forest and the crumbling nature of the walls, inside is dry and dusty. I smell the familiar, comforting scent of beeswax and leather and books. Tiny eyes wink along the walls, blue and green and purple hiding in shadowed bookcases. Book sprites cluster around my skirt hems and tug me down a stained-glass staircase spiralling into the library proper. Red glass roses wind around green thorny stems, framing scenes I recognise from the books I've read. Mythology and fables and fairy tales sit side by side. The story of "The Dagger in the Dark" is immortalised in crystal glass halfway down.

Light cascades from glittering gemstones embedded in the walls, washing the library with a rainbowed glow—crystals, hundreds of them, the colours of each coven.

This library is bigger than the one in Halstett, older too. In the centre, where a librarian's desk should be, a raised platform is circled by a moat brimming with black nothingness.

I pause. Blink. It's not a platform, it's a crystal, growing from the bedrock beneath Death. A crystal as black as mine. On top stands the gold spire of the High Warden's crest, a tower with a pinnacle on the top, like the one where the Ember Queen was imprisoned in the book of myths Ella sent me. A waist-height approximation of the one marked across Malin's back.

The pinnacle is so sharp it cuts darkness into ribbons. Entangled around it and anchored to it, the Warden's lifeline pulsates sickly green, swirling away as it fades from my sight. Yellowish ichor oozes from its diseased coils and trickles down the spire. It congeals on the crystal and rivulets slowly drip off the side.

Shadowy book sprites reach for my hand, wrapping my fingers with their cool grip. They lead me step by step across a bridge as insubstantial as starlight but sturdy as stone. I step onto the crystal and power surges from the chasm. It winds around my ankles and fizzes against my skin. Close up, the crystal's surface is hazed with cracks and a light dancing at its heart pulses with a beat that matches my own. A little too fast; a bit too hard. It flickers and magic echoes through my blood.

My crystal chills in a silent answer.

I drop to a crouch and press my hand against the glass-smooth surface. Tendrils of darkness brush my palm from the other side as if a window divides us. It can't reach me, but I feel its power. So much power.

The book sprites sigh and their eyes wink out. The crystals vanish.

Darkness clamps down. And I'm alone.

Malin's whisper breaks the silence, his hand catches mine and pulls me to standing. "The crystal's roots branch beneath the desert. They're everywhere, a network beneath the ground in Life and Death. The veil is attached to it. My father's lifeline fuelled the crystals once. Now he's sick and the veil is dying." He pauses, his fingers tracing my wrist. "Open your eyes, Penny."

"They aren't shut."

"Then you should see."

I blink, and the crystals sparkle back into life up the walls. Right beside me, Malin's lifeline glitters obsidian black, skewered to the spire's spindle.

And mine is as black as his.

Malin is not attached to the veil, he is pinned to it. Brutally.

I fumble for the spell in my pocket. The one to bind lifelines. Alice said three lifelines wound into one. If Alice is to survive, she needs him. I need him. "Come back to Life, Malin. Please. Let me take you away from here."

Malin turns me around and holds me by the shoulders at arm's length. Something that might be regret flickers in his eyes. "I can't." He pulls me close, and here, on top of the crystal in the dead of night, with the book sprites whispering around us, I stop resisting. His arms wrap me, pressing me into his chest. His heartbeat thuds against my cheek. "You want to bind my lifeline to yours, Penny? I told you last night, I won't allow you to do that."

That's not exactly what I intend to do, but if he won't agree to this, he'll never agree with my actual plans. I want to bind his lifeline and anchor it to my crystal. When I give mine up to reforge the knife, his will survive, and it seems pointless to let my crystal go to waste. Malin can have it. "Will unpinning your lifeline damage the veil?"

He inhales slowly, wincing at my word choice: *unpinning*. "Not immediately."

"This side of Samhain?" I intend to reforge the knife before the Warden's planned magic-stealing celebration. Malin reluctantly shakes his head, and I close my eyes, trying to keep the irritation from my tone. "So, you'd rather stay here? A martyr to Death's divide from Life?"

"I'd rather you survived. You're stubborn enough, strong enough. But with a passenger on your lifeline—" His voice catches, his lips press into the top of my head, and a tremble runs through his shoulders. "No."

"Please," I whisper. "Alice said—"

"No," he replies. "Trust me. Whatever comes next, trust me, Penny. Can you do that?"

I drop it—for now. This isn't over. "I trust you."

"I will always find you," he says softly, and I want to ask what he means, but his hands run down my shoulders, not quite touching me. I freeze, unwilling to breathe, unable to move in case he stops. He smoulders at the edges. As if he burns deep within. If I lifted a corner, peeled back the defences he keeps firmly in place, I'd set myself on fire. And this time I'm not sure I'd return. The brightness in his eyes consumes me. His skin is scorching, his fingers hot where they don't quite brush my skin. And I don't care who he is, the danger I might be in, tonight, I want to burn.

Slowly, agonisingly gently, Malin runs a finger down the black sparkling silk of my lifeline. Need darkens his gaze and a sensation of *together* shivers through my soul. I forget where I end. Where he begins. I move into him without taking a step and close my eyes as his lips crash into mine. He tastes of chocolate and midnight rain. He is forever and never and all the time between.

For one moment, this quiet pause in the dark, I am his and he is mine.

His hands splay across my back, moving to my neck, and he cups my face to pull back a little. He whispers my name as if all that exists is him and me. Then he kisses me again, slower this time, harder, deeper, and I lose myself. I melt into him, my back arching, clinging to his shoulders, his neck, winding my fingers into his hair.

Then, he releases me, and what felt endless, ends. I open my eyes and beneath our feet, the crystal pulses harder, faster, brighter.

"Don't let him break you. Come back tomorrow, Penny." There's a disconcerting melancholy to Malin's tone, and his hands are gentle as he guides me away, up the stained-glass library stairs, and back into the woods. I'm still spinning, my heart still pounding as we step into the damp forest. I've never been kissed like that. I want him to do it again. I exhale slowly, shakily, and cling to his arm. Right now, I want him to take me back to his manor, lay me down, and—

Pain stabs deep in my chest, and a tiny whimper slips loose. My lifeline strings tight as the thorn wall disintegrates. Malin wheels toward the gates, wraps an arm around my waist, and half carries me as we hurry for the borders. "I didn't realise the time."

Neither did I. He kisses me again as I whisper the words to part the veil, the soft pressure of his lips regretful and bittersweet. It tastes like goodbye. I blink as he pulls away and start my chant again, his voice joining with mine. My hands are still laced around his neck as the veil parts.

I hesitate.

The feeling of being watched hits me square in the back.

A shout barks across the muffled death-silence, an order of

command. Gold masks shimmer in the grey light. Boots pound across the sand. The words to hold the veil open die on my lips. Another chant whispers through the stillness: the spell to close and seal it.

Malin unpeels me, holding my wrists tight so I can't cling to him. "Go!"

"You won't make it back."

"I don't have to. Go, Penny. I'll find you. I'll always find you, no matter what."

He half pushes, half throws me backward into the veil.

As the roar of mists fills my ears, he turns away, summoning two flame-bright swords into existence. He shifts his grip on their hilts, curved blades dipping to greet the sand as he drops his stance, waiting.

The mists slam shut, sending me screaming into the dark.

Chapter Thirty-Two

I wake in silence. A silence that breathes and nibbles at my nerves. Alice's loom is still, no guards move in the halls. Maybe the Gilded were sent into Death to retrieve me, catch me in the act of an unsanctioned walk in Death. And I left Malin to face them.

The thought crushes the quiet. It crinkles at the edges and blood rushes in my ears.

Curled in my bed, I close my eyes. What if the Gilded overpower Malin?

Every morning, I've healed their prisoners, and I've seen what they do to them after. What, even now, they might be doing to Ella and Tobias and Alice. And I was in Death kissing Malin in his magical library while they did. I screw my eyes shut and bury my head in my arms.

Nightmarish images kaleidoscope behind my eyelids, each worse than the last. Malin bound in chains. Alice broken. Ella screaming. Tobias marked with the Sorcerer's whorl.

I desperately wish Alice was here to help me piece myself back together. I'd give anything to sit quietly with her in the dark, inhale the springtime scent of her—I need her to ground me in Life. And she is hurt.

Morning brightens into afternoon, afternoon bleeds into night, and there is no sound, only my heartbeat and the clock for company. No food is brought to my rooms, no guards change outside or patrol the courtyard beneath the window, and my door is firmly locked so I can't peek out into the corridors to check I'm not the only one left alive.

I want Alice. I need to know my family is all right.

I try to open the panel in the walls, but I can't find the notch.

I lift the floorboard beneath the dresser and pull out the spells. I read them over and over and over again, committing them to memory until I could write each one with my eyes closed. I should be hungry, but fear fills my stomach.

I never wanted to walk in Death. Now, I count down the minutes until the veil weakens with the approach of midnight, desperate to step into the grey deserts and set myself free. Terrified of what I'll find when I do.

Midnight finds me on my knees with my stockpiled poison clutched in one hand, my crystal in the other.

There's no change of the guards outside my door. I'm not sure they're there at all. But they must be. This solitary confinement is playing with my mind.

The poison doesn't burn tonight. It slides down my throat, thawing my soul, which has slowly frosted during the day and frozen solid as night fell.

Tonight, I do not burn. Tonight, I step painlessly into the soft embrace of Death. And it's worse than burning.

Malin is not here to meet me. Alone, Death holds me closer. Tighter. The sand whispers a warning, and fog-wraiths screech in the distance. I should fulfil my duty as a thorn witch and protect the veil, but the urge to find Malin unravels the last threads of responsibility binding me to my coven. I dip to a crouch, sketch a blade with my finger, and summon it into existence with a flush of magic.

I sense the familiarity of my sister's lifeline, all soft and prickly in the same direction as the fog-wraiths, and exhale an airless sigh of relief: Mila is capable of handling a few fog-wraiths alone. But still, guilt bites deep as I leave my sister behind and hurry across the dunes in the direction of the manor.

The darkness that precedes the walls' appearance is faded like a painting left too long in the sun. Emptiness reaches across the sand, clasping at my gut and twisting. Up close, it's worse: the portcullis is raised, shadows drape the black walls, and fissures weep sand down the granite. Beyond the entrance, the manor wears shadows like widows' weeds; gardens normally bathed in magical sunshine are dull beneath a cloud-laden sky.

I adjust my grip on my conjured blade as I step inside. Withered roses line the path, their petals crystallized with ice like the candied fruits in the Warden's court. If I touch one, I think it might shatter. Spider frost cobwebs the gardens, spun through the lawns and lacing desiccated flowers.

Malin didn't meet me in Death because Malin isn't here.

Or he's horribly injured inside.

The door to the manor hangs open, one hinge destroyed. A trail of silver liquid runs up the steps and in through the door.

I call his name and the echo shakes the ceilings. Wallpaper uncurls down the walls like peeling flesh, exposing a skeleton of beams and cracking plaster. The parlour is shrouded in dust and empty of furniture, the window hazed with cobwebs.

Sorrow chills my unbeating heart.

I knew he was gone before I walked in the gate, yet my last tattered shred of hope dies with the confirmation. Defeated, I sink to kneel on the bare floorboards in a puddle of silk skirts and bury my head in my hands, my blade dissolving into sand.

The Warden has Alice, Ella and Tobias are in the Gilded's hands, and I just left Mila to face fog-wraiths alone. I have failed as a sister, as a lover, and as a friend. And I've lost Malin too. I've lost everything. I am weak, helpless, worthless.

I don't know what to do.

My chest aches, my heart pounds in my ears. My tears come in great gulping gasps I can't breathe between.

I don't know how long I lie there on the floor, curled in a ball in the dust. Slowly, my sobs fade to hiccupping gasps, my head hurts, and my eyes sting. I feel a tiny tug on my skirt, a minuscule pressure on my knee, a soft little brush against my hair.

Penny?

I jolt to sitting, but there's no one there. Nothing in the room with me.

The shadows thicken and shift, and I clamber to my feet, wishing I hadn't let my blade dissolve into nothing. Tiny lights flicker across the lawns outside, the chandelier in the parlour glows softly, and three words are written in the sand that was my blade: *Don't give in.*

Book sprites.

I watch the little lights dancing in the cobwebs on the lawn, and slowly, my sorrow, my fear and devastation, gives way to rage. And it burns bright. Today, I didn't lose everything—the Warden stole it. He hurt my friends and family to get at me. He's bent and broken them to meet his own needs. I won't leave them in his hands.

If only I could imagine Ella and cross the veil to where they're holding her. But I need a solid location, not a vague hope. If only it was that easy. I rub my eyes on my skirt. I need a plan. The parlour has drifted into a grey-blue reflection of my emotions. Dove-soft curtains hang limply at the windows; the mirror above the empty hearth is silver framed and frosted with snowflakes. And propped against the mirror is an envelope, my name written across it in Malin's perfect hand. The twirl on the letter *P* catches at my heart.

It thuds once, a flicker of hope, of life. There is still magic in Malin's manor, the changing wallpaper told me that, but the beat of my heart gives me hope he might have survived.

My hands shake as I open the envelope and read.

Penny,

If the Gilded catch you here, they'll deal with you themselves. Stay out of Death until I find you. I will always find you. We've made it this far; we'll make it to the end. We'll face it together, you and Alice and me. I promise. Please try to trust me. I mean you to survive.

Malin

PS: I know what you're thinking. Do not go to the library, Penny. Please. x

Malin knew the attack last night might happen, or suspected enough to write this. He knew my next move too. I wonder if he knew I'd ignore him.

Quietly, I walk out of the manor, which exhales as I leave it behind. I don't look back to see the wallpaper slide down the walls and glass windows haze with cracks. Frozen rosebushes disintegrate as I pass, petals crumbling into ash that swirls and eddies around my skirts.

The thorn wall has shed its roses. The stems are thick and twisted, briars woven together so I cannot pass. The manor likes me, Malin told me that. I hope that extends to his wall of dead roses too. I rest my hand on the stems and whisper, "Let me through. Please."

It doesn't disintegrate as it did for him, but with an almighty groan, it shuffles apart. I murmur a thank you as I slip through a gap and run.

Shadows dart between the trees, tiny eyes light my path, and my name whispers through the leaves. I've never seen a book sprite outside a library—but until last week, I'd never seen a book sprite at all.

They fall silent as I reach the library door. It stands open, lights glittering beyond it. Without Malin, my heart stutters. My pulse melds with the crystal's and I hurry down the stairs before my resolve can falter.

I hit the bridge running, slide to a halt on the crystal as a rumble trembles through the ground. The Warden's sinuous mess of a lifeline is exactly the same as it was yesterday, but Malin's is invisible—or it isn't there. I squeeze my eyes closed, praying that when I open them, I will see. Knowing the spell to bind our lifelines backward and inside out won't help if I can't see his.

Cold fingers take my hand and lift it. I try to open my eyes but they're frozen shut.

Hush, Penny. The whisper makes me startle. I can't breathe. I can't see.

I feel it then, his lifeline beneath my fingertip, and *together* shudders through my soul. Relief hits me. Malin is alive. "I'm sorry," I whisper.

I shouldn't be doing this without his consent. He expressly and explicitly asked me not to. Malin might never forgive me this violation. But Alice saw it, his lifeline joined to ours. I trust her.

And I don't know what else to do.

I recite the spell, and my voice finds a rhythm to the chant. It rises and falls, spins and weaves.

I will find you, he told me over and over. After this, he won't have to look very hard; we'll be bound so tightly, he'll just have to close his eyes and I'll be here—until we forge the knife and I'm not. Maybe he'll be glad when I cease to exist. Maybe I'm doing him a favour, breaking his trust so completely that he'll be relieved when I'm gone.

I force my eyes open, and the spell falters on my tongue. I can see his lifeline, obsidian like mine. Two dark strands of spidersilk intertwining in a breeze. Threads unravel from his and knit into mine, binding them tighter and tighter. Pressure builds behind my breastbone and wraps around my chest. Magic begins to bleed. Sparkles trickle from the obsidian of my lifeline. Slowly at first, then faster and faster. Surging with shadow-black. It settles to a steady stream, an osmosis of magic from Malin to me and back again.

I wasn't expecting this. His magic shared with mine, mine with his.

Malin's lifeline jerks where it's pinned to the veil; mine spasms in sympathy. Gently, so carefully, I ease his lifeline off the spire—and set Malin free.

The spindle pricks my finger. Pain jolts up my arm and spikes deep in my chest. A single bead of my blood splashes onto the crystal. And vanishes into it.

The book sprites sigh.

My knees tremble.

It's done.

The weight of Malin's lifeline settles into a low ache beneath my ribs and heavies my soul. The air thickens in my lungs and my heart pounds harder, fighting to support us both. My magic shudders and stills.

I could sleep for a thousand years and still be exhausted when I woke.

My lifeline ripples, tension muffled by Malin's woven through it.

I need to get back to Life.

I stumble across the bridge, up the stained-glass stairs, and out into the silent forest.

The gap in the thorns releases me into the gardens, and I hurry out the gate, leaving behind a burned-out ruin.

The desert sighs as if with sympathy, the scent of cherry blossoms and candied pears weaves through the stillness, and I wonder as I walk, what memories my soul will bring to paint the desert of

Death. Will I be able to pass on without a lifeline? Where will I go if it can't?

I'm nearly at the veil when it hits me.

Cherry blossoms were not unique to our village, but the blossom festival was. Candied pears were Mila's favourite. If I can scent her memories on the air, she's close. And she's in trouble.

A screech ripples through the sand. A second is louder. The whimper of a thorn witch is quiet.

Mila.

There, at the base of the veil, fog-wraiths swarm around a crumpled form robed in black, red hair fading into the dull grey of Death. The fires of her blade gutter, and I drop to my knees, sketching new weapons of my own. Two blades curve from my hands, flames dripping to the sand, and my crystal turns to ice against my breastbone. Since I came to Halstett, I've trained in swordcraft and memorised spells until I whispered them in my dreams and woke with the taste of magic on my lips.

I am a black-crystalled witch, and even with Malin's lifeline weighing me down, my power is more than theirs.

If these fog-wraiths think they're having my sister, they can meet the Dark Mother.

I inhale a breath of absent air and run toward her. My legs ache and my knees tremble, but magic flares unbidden in my veins—and I'm not sure it's entirely mine.

Four fog-wraiths cage her against the veil, reaching with talons that drip silver poison. It splatters the sand, circling Mila with evidence of her lost fight. A gash runs down her arm, black veins lace around her wrist, and there's a puncture mark on her neck. "Penny," she whispers.

The fog-wraiths freeze. Slowly, they turn.

I smile coldly. "Stay away from my sister."

Chapter Thirty-Three

Silence explodes with a fog-wraith screech.

Grey forms writhe up from the sand. First a finger, then a hand, clawing free one spiny, disjointed limb after another. They pen us in, pushing closer. I can't let them get between us and the veil.

I firm my grip on my blades and soften my knees.

Mila shoves to her feet, inching closer while the fog-wraiths' attention is on me.

I need her hand to pull her through the veil. And I need it fast, or the wraiths will swarm through after us.

I don't move, trying not to watch Mila creeping toward me, not to wince as she stumbles. Fog-wraiths slither across the sand. A steady unstoppable beat to their angular movements. I am bait on a hook waiting to be eaten, praying I'm not. Quietly, I call on my magic and whisper the words to part the veil. If I open it just a little, we can slip through.

A gnarled hand snatches at my arm, and I slice it off at the wrist. It scuttles to clutch at my skirts and clambers to my waist. A flash of magic turns it into a damp splotch on my skirts, but the distraction tears apart my concentration, and the gap I'd made in the veil closes, barring our escape as a second wraith springs, all talons and snarling teeth. Malignant breath brushes the fine hairs on my cheek. I jerk away, wrenching out of its grasp. My skirts whirl as I spin, crossing my blades in an arc above me. I meet no resistance as I slash downward in furious twin strokes, slicing through corrupted mist. A blank-eyed head rolls to my feet and disintegrates.

But as this one falls, three more slink from the dunes to replace it. I need to slow them. Magic tumbles from my fingers, spilling down my blades and splattering the sand with ink-black threads. They weave into a circle that rises up, a net of magic between them and us. My lifeline groans under the pressure. I can't keep this up. Binding Malin's lifeline to mine has weakened me. Reluctantly, I drop one blade and it crumbles into sand. I cling tighter to the other, and force magic rattling down it, fortifying my shield.

Fog-wraiths crash into the web, their furious shrieks sending my heart thundering. My magic ripples and, with the new weight of my lifeline, nearly brings me to my knees.

With the last of her strength, Mila lurches toward me, and I catch her. Magic slips through my fingers as I hold her on her feet. My shield shatters. Desperately, I whisper the words to part the veil. Fog-wraiths surge toward us. Mila's voice joins mine. Our lifelines tangle. Shit! If we get this wrong, Mila and I will get torn apart.

The veil parts.

Mila's eyes are as wide as mine. She's as scared as me. Our lifelines knotted—this is everything we've been warned against. Her fingers curl around my wrist. "We have to cross."

"I'm sorry!" She's right. If it closes now, I won't be able to open it again. I don't have the strength and nor does she.

Our only option is...My heart sinks. Mila confirms it with a defeated whisper: "The Gilded's watchtower."

"No, Mila!"

"If we don't, we risk the whole of Halstett. I can't fight anymore,

Penny. Neither can you. When we cross, the fog-wraiths will break through. We need the Gilded."

If we cross to the Gilded on watch, I'll be exposed. If we cross to anywhere else, we'll commit the ultimate crime and allow fog-wraiths into Life. But we're all out of options. If we stay here any longer, Mila's going to die. Horribly. And so am I. With our lifelines snarled up, we might anyway.

"Together?" Mila whispers.

I squeeze her hand. "Together."

A wraith springs. She yanks me backward, and tangled, we fall. An ice-boned hand grips my wrist. The veil tears my last blade from me. We can't stop the monsters from following.

Mila's fading, her voice trembles. I've never heard her like this. If Mila is scared, we really are screwed. "I'm sorry."

I imagine the watchtower and so does she. My hand is clamped on her wrist, hers on mine. If we slip apart, our tangled lifelines will tear us into pieces. I cling tighter and tighter to my sister and close my eyes.

Stone slams into my back as we reform in the Gilded Barracks' watchtower. A wraith tears through after us, one talon raised, and poison sizzles on my calf. It lurches, and I shuffle backward, pulling Mila with me. Its eyes meet mine, white and bleak and feeding on my fear. Behind it, more claw through the veil, widening the rift we opened to pass.

A golden blade slashes through its neck.

Metal-clad hands shove us away from the rent in the veil. A fissure hangs in the air, an opening into Death. A bone horn sounds and the Colligerate clock tower begins to chime with an incessant, urgent clang.

As the wraiths flood into Life in a silver-poisoned tide, the Gilded spring into action.

This is what they were made for. They thunder into the watchtower.

A wall of gold armour and flashing steel protects us where we huddle against the wall. Mila whimpers. Where I'm bruised, she's bleeding; where I bleed, her skin is torn and gouged. Fingers limp, eyes closed, she lies where the Gilded dropped her. Her lifeline flickers out. Mine unhitches as hers stutters back into existence. She exhales through parted lips—doesn't breathe back in. I press my fingers to her wrist and can't find a pulse.

"Mila!"

She doesn't answer.

I snatch her fading lifeline and with my crystal around my neck it's easy. Too easy. Even with Malin's lifeline anchored to mine.

Magic falls from my fingers, ink black and shining. Mila's lifeline strengthens into an amethyst cord. Her heart thuds in her chest. Once. Twice. A steady beat. Silver poison drifts from her wounds in a bitter haze and her skin knits neatly to heal them.

Mila opens her eyes, and I gasp my relief and look around us.

All that remains of the fog-wraiths is damp patches on the floor. The veil no longer roars, which means—

Grandmother's arthritic fingers unpeel my grip on Mila's lifeline. "Twice in two days, I've healed the veil, thanks to you." She drops her voice to a hiss. "Stupid little witch."

Father hauls me to my feet. "I'll ensure the High Warden is informed of your willing participation, Mila Albright."

Mila shrugs away Grandmother's hand, wincing when she sees who caught me. "Pen!"

I'm hauled away from my sister—the only one of us not in chains.

My head whirls. Someone gave me up to the Gilded; Clair thinks there's a traitor in the Resistance. I suspected Carlotta.

I never once thought Mila would be the one to betray me.

My father's voice rasps against my cheek as he marches me down the stairs, "Honestly, I didn't think you'd fall for it, Penny."

He shoves me into the wall by the shoulders and pushes his face so close to mine, I see the scars where his mask meets skin. "He'll be interested to see this." Cold-gauntleted fingers trace my throat, hook under the chain of my crystal, and tear it from my neck. My heart, already cracked from Mila's betrayal, seems to shatter.

He yanks me the rest of the way down the stairs into the barracks entry hall—and I see a chance.

I take it.

Wrenching free, I duck under his arm and flee, scrabbling for the door handle. Relief hits when I find it unlocked. Crumbles when I crash into a wall of black armour, knocking the breath from my lungs.

These Gilded wear new armour, obsidian dark with a spider-web stamped above their heart. Magical black metal I've never seen before somehow protects their lifelines; they pulse beneath my fingers but I cannot reach them. I have no power over them.

Beyond them, night laces the breeze across the courtyard and the moon shimmers silver blue above the palace. I try to breathe as the Gilded turn me around. I don't resist. There's no point. Their grip tightens on my arms as we walk toward the amphitheatre. Bruises will purple my skin tomorrow, but there might not be much of me left that cares.

I am quiet as they lead me onto the arena sand. I am steady as I face the Warden.

Inside, I scream.

Chapter Thirty-Four

Blue flames blaze in the firepit, casting a malicious glow about the tiered seating. The amphitheatre is empty except for the High Warden and his Gilded guard—and a huge cloth-covered box in the centre of the sand.

Sickening dread curdles in my stomach. The obsidian guard shoves me forward. Fighting is futile. I know this. I fight anyway and there's a grim satisfaction that it takes two of them to keep me moving. I hold my head high as they force me to stand before the skull-masked Warden, and he stares at me long and hard. "Death-Weaver, you defied me." He sounds amused, not angry. Somehow, that's worse.

"My name is Penny."

A cruel smile twists his golden lips, and his eyes don't leave mine as he twitches a finger in command.

The door opens and boots thud across the sand, soft feet padding beside them.

Above the stench of stale execution blood painting the arena, the scent of primroses catches on the breeze of the shutting door.

Alice.

Escorted by two Gilded guards, her head is bowed and white-blonde hair falls around her shoulders, hiding her face. She stumbles as she's led to the Warden's side, bare feet scuffing in the sand. She seems so fragile against the bulk of him.

The Warden gently tucks her hair behind her shoulders and turns Alice to face me.

Bile rises in my throat. I can't breathe.

He has given her a mask, delicately wrought in gold and marked in agonising detail. It surrounds her eyes like the masquerade masks our coven used to wear on Samhain, a butterfly looping over her cheekbones.

It might be pretty if it wasn't so gruesome—if her skin wasn't healing and raw around it. Behind her eyes, no trace of Alice remains, but one corner of her lips wobbles as she meets my tear-filled gaze.

I see then why she has not been weaving. Her fingers are broken, bent and malformed.

Slowly, steadily, my fear hardens. My throat loosens, releasing my ribs so I can breathe. Fury stills the shaking in my muscles, anger tightens my resolve. I remember the spell from the Grimoire.

Alice saw three lifelines meld into one. But maybe she interpreted it wrong. Maybe it was the Warden's lifeline she saw. I could bind it to mine—I know the spell. My soul sags at the idea, but my lifeline is so heavy, so weighed down with Malin's, a third would drag me into Death. The Gilded couldn't stop me crossing. Fog-wraiths would tear the Warden apart, feast on his lifeline. And mine.

And Malin's, which I've bound to mine.

The Warden traces Alice's mask with one finger. "My Spinner needed a little convincing to submit. You, my little Weaver of Death, are in need of the same." The Warden raises one golden eyebrow. "Time to play."

A low growl of rage punctuates his statement. Tobias is dragged into the centre of the arena, fighting every step of the way.

His armour has been stripped and a black-bloodied hole gapes behind his mask where his eye should be.

He throws himself at the Warden, and it takes four Gilded to restrain him.

The Warden smiles, unsheathes his knife, and slowly presses the point to Alice's throat. Tobias goes still. Horribly still. He has the look of a dead man walking, one whose hope just died.

My heart shrivels.

I will find you, Malin said—I wrap his promise around me, a shield against what comes next. No matter what happens he'll find me. He'll find me. He promised.

The Warden snaps at Tobias. "You intended to marry her?"

Tobias's eye flies wide, meeting mine with a desperate plea: *Don't argue. Don't give Ella up*. The Warden's grin splits his mask in two, wrinkling the gold at the corners of his lips. "Did you think I wouldn't find out? Fool. I know everything that happens in my city. Everything is reported to me." The Gilded holding Tobias draws his blade. My heart slows. Time with it. "Now, show me, my pet, just how skilfully you heal after all the practice I've arranged." The dagger flashes. I let out a cry.

The hilt protrudes from Tobias's chest, right where his heart is. Slowly, the Gilded slides it free. Tobias slumps to his knees, lifeblood flowing to the sand.

"Ticktock, Penelope. Your betrothed is dying." The Warden paces toward me, irritation twitching his jaw when I don't cringe away. "Heal him."

I yank desperately at the Gilded still holding me prisoner. "I need to be closer! I can't help him from here." Tears blur my vision, and I swipe them away.

Devious light fills the Warden's eyes as he steps to one side, and the Gilded release me, shadowing my movements as I hurry to Tobias.

The colour has already drained from his face, the light dims in his remaining eye, but I can't see his lifeline at all. I drop to my knees and grab his hand instead. "Please," I whisper. "Please, Toby. Let me help you."

"Let me go," he says. "It's all right, Penny."

It's not all right! How can he say it's all right when he's bleeding out into the sand? This is the man who loves my sister with all his heart. Since we met, he's helped me every step of the way. He trusted me and kept my secrets and met me on the Ninth without question—and offered to reforge the knife in my place knowing it would cost him everything.

"I can't—" I choke on a sob. "I can't let you die. Toby, please. I need you."

He's fading, fast. No Gilded are poised to drag him back, not one. And I still can't see his lifeline. I try to reach for it, to feel it in the air, but it's not there. Nothing is. Tobias catches my wrist, stopping me as he exhales. He's fought so hard to not become what the Warden made him to be. Blood bubbles from his lips, drowning his words. "Play their game. We'll make sure you win."

"We?" His fingers twitch and relax. I grab his hand, cling to it. "Don't you dare leave me."

"Trust him," he says weakly.

"Who?"

But Tobias's eye closes. Sprawled in the sand, his blood soaking my skirts, he dies. I hold his hand as his heart beats its final beat—but I hear no whisper of the veil as he passes. No chill of death in his fingers before the Gilded prise me away.

I'm pulled to my feet and forced to face the Warden, my head a fog of fear and grief and confusion. How did I not feel his lifeline? How was it not there? Who do I need to trust?

The Warden's smile is frozen into a snarl of gritted teeth. My magic jolts and shudders. I feel like I'm fracturing right down the middle. It is unbearable. An agonising stripping of my soul. Nausea wells. The strength siphons from my bones. Slowly, the Warden opens his hand, and I see why. My crystal lies in his palm. With a snap of his fingers, Alice is hauled up onto the platform behind him. "So tricky, the pair of you, with your strange magic. But my Spinner gave up and submitted to my mask. So will you. Or you can cease your childish games and heal me."

"No." He needs my submission to gild me, I think frantically. Isn't that what Tobias said?

The Warden sees my question. Answers it. "Oh, but you already did, Penelope."

"I didn't!"

"I'm afraid that's just not true. You can resist, of course. And I'll have the entertainment of breaking you." The Warden slides my crystal into his pocket and pulls out another. It hangs from his fist on a silver chain. Deep-hued pink sparkles purple in the light of the eternal flames.

Ella's.

Silently, the Gilded bring out a butcher's block mounted on a thick steel frame with an iron mallet on top.

The Warden lays Ella's crystal on the block. "You can stop this before it starts, my pet. Submit, and I'll let your sister go. Heal me, and after Samhain, I'll set you all free."

Freedom is not a concept in Halstett; the High Warden wouldn't recognise freedom if it hit him in the face.

Ella's crystal glitters and winks with life.

I could stop this. Right now. I could save my sister.

I didn't think my shattered heart could shatter again. But slowly, I shake my head.

The Warden picks up the mallet.

"No!" I gasp. Tears are running down my face and dripping into the sand.

The Warden smiles and slams the hammer down.

Shards of precious crystal scatter the air, raining down to spangle the sand. I weep. I want to gather them up with care and put them back together, but their light is already dead; Ella's anchor is destroyed.

I'm frozen. I barely react as the Warden gently traces a mask around my eyes with one finger, the same as Alice's, and turns his back.

The mallet winks from the butcher's block. I grab it and hurl it at the back of his head. It spins once before a Gilded snatches it from the air. Rage clouds my thoughts, and I grab the fetid green lifeline trailing behind the Warden.

It slips from my grasp as the Warden swivels on his heels. He's on me in two strides, his fingers gripping my jaw. "Do you think, for one second, knowing the power you wield, I would leave myself open to your magic? My lifeline is unbreakable. Blades would blunt against it, no steel can sever it, and you couldn't uproot it even with every last scrap of magic buried in your pathetic soul."

"I'll kill you," I snarl.

"No, my little Thorn Princess, you will not. By the time the sun rises, you will dance to my tune like everyone else." He smiles. "However, if that's how you want to play..." He claps his hands, and the Gilded grab my elbows. "Burn the witch!"

Relief hits me like a solid wall. They'll chain me to the stake and keep me alive until I crack and swear myself to the Warden. They won't hurt anyone else. The grip tightens on my arms, and I steel myself for the pain of burning.

I've done it before; I can do it again.

Ella's little cry crashes through my resolve. She struggles as they drag her into the arena and carry her to the pit. Her face is bruised, her eyes are round and wide, lips forming *I love you* when she sees Tobias's crumpled form.

The Warden sees my faltering defiance, leans into it. "I will systematically strip away everyone you love, everyone who might help you, until you fall to your knees and beg me to make you forget."

I'm still reeling from Alice's gilding, from Tobias's death; I cannot watch this happen to Ella. With her crystal shattered, she won't come back. I bargained my soul for her life; she gave herself to Death to protect me.

Ella's gaze is clear and silver as always, even in the Gilded's grip. Even facing the stake with the man she loves dead in the sand at her feet. "Don't, Pen."

Tears burn as I reach for her, my fingers twitch, a gesture of longing. Then, I bow my head and whisper to the Gilded guard restraining me. "Please. Stop."

He holds up one hand, and the Gilded marching Ella toward the stake halt.

The Warden laughs. "So easily, Penelope?"

"Let my sister go."

He smiles. "You heard my Death-Weaver. Let her sister go."

Ella fights now, harder than she did when it was her facing the stake. "Penny, no. Don't give in!"

A Gilded clamps a hand over her mouth and drags her away. In the silence that follows, I am turned to face the purple-draped box. My heart stalls as the cloth is removed. Beneath is a frame with a contraption of gears allowing a huge wooden wheel to swivel and pivot. Metal restraints are attached to the circular section with steel bolts.

The Warden catches my wrists, and walks me backward. His eyes are cold and hard. The wheel nudges my spine, and he lifts my wrist to fit the first manacle, clamping it tight. He repeats the same with my other wrist, and then with my ankles.

The wheel tilts back until I'm lying prone, staring at a ceiling wrapped with smoke from the eternal fires. Rough fingers attach a collar to my throat. I smell woodsmoke and metal heated to boiling.

I wish I was able to die. I wish the Warden would let me.

The amphitheatre doors swing open one final time and the sudden scent of midnight rain on the draught washes over me. Malin! He's here! I twist my head to find him, relief nearly drowning me. He found me. Like he promised. I should never have doubted him.

He sweeps in, his black cloak trailing through the sand, striding right at the Warden. "No!" I cry a warning. My crystal is in the Warden's pocket, and Malin is as vulnerable as I am.

But Malin doesn't look at me. Why isn't he looking at me?

Then he does. And my hope dies. An obsidian mask covers half his face, roses enamelled in ruby-bright lines across one cheekbone and his brow. He clicks his fingers, and my lifeline snaps rigid as he forces it to appear, black sparkling blue in the light of the eternal flames.

His is twined so tight around mine, it will never let me go.

My heart cracks. I did that. Bound us together. He told me not to, and I did it anyway. He told me to trust him, and I did. I was a fool. He showed me precisely how to bring about my own destruction, and I kissed him in return.

I lost this game long before I knew it was being played—beneath a cherry tree in Malin's arms. Maybe before that. The first time I met Malin in his parlour filled with light and hope and colour.

Hollowness shoves at my ribs as the Warden stares down at me like a vulture about to feast on fresh meat. Malin's black-eyed gaze is as cold and calculating as his father's.

He promised to find me, and now he has. I have the horrible desire to laugh.

The Warden's next words chill the marrow of my bones. "I should thank you, *Penny*, for returning my son."

Malin taps the Warden's arm. "A word? In private, if you would?"

With a wave of one hand, the Warden dismisses the Gilded. They step back as one, giving them the privacy Malin requested.

"You promised I'd have her undamaged." His hand clamps on my wrist, just above the restraint, covering the mark of our bargain still staining my skin.

"Consider it a modification. A minor detail. You may have her once she's gilded." The gold lips of the Warden's skull mask curve into a vicious smirk. "Or you may not have her at all. I'll return you to your manor and throw away the key. Build walls so high, you'll never escape, never leave, never speak to another living soul for the remainder of your long, immortal life. Do you think I brought you back to negotiate over this scrap of a witch and her crystal?"

"Negotiations? No, Father. I merely wanted the honour of making the cut in her lifeline myself." His eyes harden as he looks at me, sparking with anger behind the obsidian masking half his face. The red enamel roses glitter on one cheek. Somehow, the roses are my undoing.

Defeat is overwhelming. It fills my lungs, and there's no space for air. I kissed him. I trusted him. I made everything harder for myself so he could have my crystal when my lifeline failed. I thought he cared. And he repaid me like this. "I hate you," I say dully.

"I'm sure you do," Malin says, unflinching.

"Was it all lies?" I hate myself for the question, the kernel of hope that maybe there's an explanation.

"Not all of it."

The Warden scoffs. "Beautiful as this is to watch, have your reunion later. She'll be happier to see you then."

Malin raises a disdainful eyebrow.

"I hate you," I whisper again.

His eyebrow hitches higher. "You've already told me that. I can't say I blame you." He blinks as if he's disinterested in me and my predicament. "Now, sweetheart, you just have to submit, out loud if you would. So everyone can hear it."

My heart slows. My chest hollows. "No contract? No small print?" Sarcasm is an ineffective defence, but what else do I have to throw at him? We all know I'm going to submit. To protect my sister and Alice, I'd give up anything that is mine to give.

"Trust me," Malin says, his sarcasm served cold and underlined with a hard smile that hits right in my sternum. "No one bothers with the small print."

"I did trust you." Never in all of Halstett's history has one witch made so many stupid decisions.

"Then you're a fool," Malin replies.

The Warden bends close. "Now, give me your name." His voice hollows me. "Say you are my Death-Weaver. Say you submit."

Malin's murmur sends shivers down my spine. "Say it."

Defeat tastes bitter. "I submit."

The Warden sneers as he hands a scalpel to Malin. "Make it deep." He strides away. His boots ring on the steps of his platform, and I see Alice at his side, kneeling at the base of his throne. Malin steps between us, keeping his back to the Warden, and hisses, "You couldn't trust me, could you?" He clamps his teeth shut, biting off his accusation, and his voice softens as the Gilded clank toward us, "Close your eyes. Try to trust me, Penny." He says my name like it tastes of honey—tears prickle, but it's too late to cry.

His hand wraps my wrist and holds tight. There's a muted clatter and the boiling metal smell intensifies. I hear the Gilded remove their gauntlets and drop them in the sand. Cold fingers press against my temples and their barbed magic digs into my mind. With my last thought before it begins, I realise just how gentle Tobias was when he worked on the Warden's orders.

I expect burning. I expect searing lines that scorch my flesh.

I get a soft brush of metal painting patterns around my eyes and across my cheeks and brow. I can smell my burning skin, but it doesn't hurt. Malin's breath hitches, his molars grind, and his hand tightens on my wrist.

He's taking my pain. But he can't halt the magic in the gold.

Each delicately painted line buries me deeper, breaking me down and dividing me from myself. Memories peel away, exposing me and laying me bare and blank like a page in a book not yet written. I cling to the pieces as they scatter, but Ella's face blurs and a brush of metal at my temple tears her away. A stroke on my brow and Alice's whispers in the dark side of morning incinerate.

And Malin…His name hurts and I don't know why. Panic hits, and metal cuffs dig into my wrists and throat as I struggle against them.

"Stop," Malin orders. His words slide through my body and pin me still. I go limp. Compliant. I'm locked inside my head and I can't even scream.

Something sharp rests against my breastbone, and Malin's finger brushes my lifeline—our lifeline. *Together* trembles through my soul. Realisation dawns, what he's about to do, what I watched my grandmother do. One tiny cut and I won't be me. I open my eyes and meet Malin's midnight gaze.

He's so close a curl of his hair dances with my exhale. I feel the softness of his words against my ear. "Let go, Penny. I'll find you. I promise."

His fingers twitch and the coldness is gone from my sternum. Confusion spreads me too thin. My thoughts disintegrate. My tears dry.

"Scream," Malin whispers.

I close my eyes. "No."

The final brushstroke of molten metal throws away the key to my new cage.

The Gilded release my consciousness, and I fall down and down and down into an abyss. And when I hit the bottom, I'm trapped in a pit of nothingness so deep, I'll never escape.

Chapter Thirty-Five

I am not myself.

I know this with absolute certainty.

I belong to the Warden.

This is the other thing I know.

Everything else is foggy and hazed at the edges. His words are my will, his wish my desire. When he visits my rooms, he calls me Death-Weaver.

I am his salvation, he tells me.

I think it rains as I drift in and out of the dark. Calloused fingers gently stroke my brow, and the scent of chocolate and almonds drifts through fragmented dreams. When I open my eyes, primrose-scented night greets me, and a girl with white-blonde hair and a golden mask whispers to come back.

I'm not sure I want to. I close my eyes. It is peaceful here, safe and warm and empty.

Another girl visits, one with red hair who murmurs soft pleas for forgiveness, telling me she didn't know, she didn't set the trap, it wasn't her. I whimper, and a male voice tells her gently to leave. I spiral down into dreams filled with sand and candied pears.

I think I scream. And a man wakes me carefully, reassuring me that I'm safe. Telling me to trust him—he'll find me.

And he always does.

Warm fingers hold mine when I stretch out my hand, anchoring me in what is real and what is not.

They don't allow me out of bed for three days after I properly wake; they tell me I slept for three more. The man doesn't leave my room, sleeping in a chair in the corner when I sleep, telling me stories when I'm awake. Tales of a sorcerer who gave a farm boy a throne, and a girl with red hair and silver eyes who set the throne aflame.

I lie on my back, listening to a soft click-clack running through the air with a broken beat.

On the fourth day, I am ordered out of bed. I sit obediently in the porcelain bathtub while two servants wash me and a palace guard stands at the door. She's silent as they pour warm water over my back and lather honeysuckle-scented soap into my hair, but when she thinks I'm not looking, her mouth twists in an odd little quirk. Her eyes are the darkest brown I've ever seen, her hair slicked back in a neat bun, and silver triangles band her wrists, shining bright against her black skin. I think I know her. I clutch at the memory and it scatters.

I am dressed in a gown of white silk with no back and a high straight neckline at the front. My waist is bound with a gold braid and the skirts are strips of silk that flutter and swirl around my feet.

I watch in the mirror as my hair is pinned in a mass of curls on the back of my head, and a gold band finishes it off. My mask shimmers in the last of the afternoon sunshine; curlicues lace my brow like black cobwebs and loop delicately across my cheekbones.

The man inspects me when they are done, and gently places an obsidian crystal around my neck on a fine silver chain. Then, he leaves me alone with the Gilded.

The broken click-clack that has accompanied my days in bed slows to a halt and ceases. The air seems empty without it.

I touch my fingertips to my face, tracing my mask as I am led toward the throne room, and a girl in a black dress similar to mine is brought to stand beside me. Her hair is white-blonde, her mask a butterfly of golden flowers. At her sides, her fingers flutter, bent out of shape and malformed.

A hush falls as we are announced, and I learn that the other girl is called Life-Spinner. We are led to stand before the dais where the Warden and his family sit on their thrones. Two lifelines coil around their feet, poison green and lifeless grey. Absently, I wonder where the third is. The Warden is masked in gold-plated death, his consort with serpents around her eyes, and the dark-eyed heir of Halstett half-masked in rose-enamelled obsidian—the same man who eased me from nightmares and anchored me in reality.

Memories prickle, but the Warden beckons me forward. "Death-Weaver. I trust you will indulge me with a display of your power."

"Your wish, it will be done," I whisper.

I don't blink as the Spinner is pushed to her knees and the Gilded hold out her wrists, displaying her broken fingers for all to see.

"Heal her."

Tentatively, I rest my fingers on top of her broken ones, and guided by instinct, I reach for where her lifeline should be. It sparkles like starshine against my palm, and a bolt of remembering hits me square in the chest. Her skin is familiar, her pain hurts my heart, and the mangled mess of her hands catches deep in my gut. Magic uncoils, tiptoeing down her lifeline to find the fractured edges of her bones and knit them together.

She sighs softly, and something else uncoils inside me, warmer and darker and secret. I've heard her make that noise before. Her name is Alice.

"Excellent." The Warden's voice cracks like a bullwhip. The Gilded snap to attention and unpeel my grip on her lifeline, scattering my thoughts like snowflakes on the wind, leaving me breathless and confused. The Spinner's fingers are straight and perfect.

The Warden inspects them, his smile brightens. I'm waved to the floor then, and the Spinner and I curl like bookends, one to each side of his feet in front of his throne.

Hours pass, motionless on the floor. The Warden gives us grapes and cheese and small sips of wine as he listens to news of his court: A district by the walls rioted last night, the thorn witch brought news of the Resistance, they cannot locate the Grimoire.

Slowly, the court dwindles, and when the consort bids her husband good night, leaving in a swirl of burnt-orange taffeta and turquoise lace, we are alone. The Warden and his son, the Spinner and I.

I stifle a yawn, hoping I might be allowed to sleep soon, but Lord Malin crosses to a grand piano set beneath a golden balcony. He lifts the polished lid and begins to play. A soft, sad song drifts around us. The room is lit by candles in crystal chandeliers, guttering one by one so shadows curl in the corners, flecked with rainbow sparkles. The Spinner's hair shines gold, her perfect fingers clasped in her lap. Behind her mask, her eyes are wholly black. I see myself reflected in them, my mask glittering obsidian in failing candlelight.

The Warden leans forward and speaks above the lilting strains of music. "Tomorrow, my Weaver will begin my healing." He straightens to bark across the throne room. "Have them both brought to my chambers one hour before the noon bell, Malin. I tire of company. Get them out of my sight."

The music cuts off abruptly. The lid of the piano slams shut. Malin stalks to his father's side and takes my wrist in an iron grip. He marches to throw open the doors, pulling me behind him, the Spinner hurrying in our wake.

I don't look back.

I'm not sure why.

He leads us past our rooms and up a grand flight of curving stairs with gleaming gold banisters. At the top is a landing with three doors. The left one is marked *RH* in swirling gold letters, the middle one *AH*, and the one on the right is freshly painted with the initials *MH*. I frown. I've seen those initials before, carved into a dresser, written in ink on a note. He pulls us inside and locks the door. The Spinner he deposits gently on the sofa and he takes me into a bedroom. His bedroom.

He pushes me to sit on the bed, and I smile up at him, wondering what he wants.

"Stop it," he snaps, snatching a soft robe and throwing it at me. "Cover yourself up."

I feel my brows tug together just a little and my mask pulls at my skin, so I make my forehead smooth as I wrap the robe around myself and belt it at the waist.

He gives me a tight-jawed nod. "Stay there. I need to speak with Alice."

Alice? He's gone five minutes, and when he returns, he seems calmer. I curl my knees into my chest and wait for him to speak.

"Penny?"

The word makes me think of freshly minted copper coins stamped with the High Warden's face on one side.

He shakes his head and exhales harshly. "It will wear off," he says, more to himself than me. "It has to wear off."

I blink and give the pillow a longing glance.

Malin sits beside me and turns me by the shoulders so I'm facing away from him. He eases the gold band from my head and lays it on the nightstand, then slides the pins from my hair, placing them beside the band in a neat little line. He smooths my curls with his fingers, releasing them from their twist. "Alice will be through in a moment. You can stay here, tonight. I'll take the sofa."

"Alice?"

He winces a little. "The Spinner." He says her name like it has sharp corners.

Twisting, I reach for him before he stands. "Please," I whisper, "don't leave." He's been with me since I woke. I feel safe with him. Something niggles, suggesting maybe I shouldn't trust him, but the thought slips from my grasp before I can follow it to the end.

"I'm not leaving," he mutters. "I promised I'd find you. I just didn't think it would be this hard."

"I'm right here."

"No, you're not." I am, I think as he pushes me so I lie down, pulls the covers up over my shoulders, and sighs. "I'll be just outside the door."

A moment later, he's gone and the Spinner slips into bed beside me. She curls on her side, so close I feel her breath against my cheek. She doesn't talk, just quietly reaches for my hand and holds tight. "Do you remember?" A silver-blonde strand of hair is caught on the corner of her butterfly mask.

I brush it away, gently unhooking it and tucking it behind her ear. "It all shivers out of reach when I try."

Her lips quirk into a little smile. "You will. I promise."

I like that promise. Slowly, she slips into sleep with her perfect, healed fingers dancing against the back of my hand.

But the first certain thing I know picks at my shifting memories, keeping me awake long after her breathing evens.

I am not myself.

Maybe I am Penny.

Chapter Thirty-Six

Hours blend into days. Autumn sprinkles the courtyard white in the mornings. I've forgotten what normal was, but I know this isn't it, which means there are now three things I know:

I am not myself.

I belong to the Warden.

Normality has forsaken me.

Everything else is a blur, lost in the mist that clouds my mind, anchored there with tiny barbed hooks. The rhythm to our routine is my one familiarity, and I cling to it.

Each morning the Warden summons us to his chambers, all black marble gilded with gold. We stand side by side, the Spinner and I, heads bowed, hands clasped in front of our skirts. Opposites. Dark and light. Death and life.

I don't understand why he smiles when the Spinner hands him the silk; why he brushes a thumb tenderly along her cheek and praises her for her efforts. Every day, the silk is blank.

Then, he comes to me, and where the Spinner succeeds, reliably, I fail. He orders me to heal him, and I cannot. I heal the others he presents for my attention; councillors with ulcerated blisters inflicted by the new fashion of pointed-toe boots, a kitchen maid with a burnt arm from tripping against an oven, even a palace guard with a blade skewering his chest from a training session gone wrong. Magic flows from my fingers down their lifelines, and their skin heals perfect and unblemished.

But when I reach for the Warden's emerald-glistening lifeline, my magic burrows into my bones and hides. I tell him there is strange magic poisoning his wound, but the truth is, I cannot produce a flicker of power to heal him. Each day his frown deepens, anger glinting behind his golden mask.

This morning, he beckons me forward with a click of his fingers. His smile is a promise of a game I cannot win, a question I cannot answer, and a task I cannot complete. The sickly green thread of his lifeline is strung taut. If I flick it, it might vibrate like a harp string.

"Today, my pet, you will succeed?" It isn't a question, but his inflection puts a question mark at the end of it. The Warden does not ask. "Your reluctance concerns me." This requires a reply. And I don't have one.

Soft feet cross the rug, gentle fingers rest on the Warden's hand. The Spinner drops a square of grey silk into his lap. "Give her time. After Samhain. The loom weaves it so."

The Warden turns the silk to face us. "You saw this?"

The Spinner whispers, "Her magic will strengthen. I cannot spin what I do not see."

The silk is blank. She has shown him nothing, and I say nothing.

He leans back, and I breathe the softest sigh of relief as he waves us to the door, dismissing us. As we're escorted silently back to our rooms, the Spinner smiles and the dull glaze in her eyes cracks. Behind them is someone. Someone like me, lost in the dark and unreachable.

Afternoons are spent in my rooms with books Malin brings me from the Warden's private collection. Spell books focused on healing and recipes for potions and tinctures and antidotes to poison. I devour them page by page, desperate to heal the Warden's sulphurous wound whilst the Spinner's loom clicks and clacks next door. Malin normally watches me as I read, but today, he cannot settle, pacing my rooms from one end to the other. Each time he sits, he springs back to his feet, muttering to himself. Occasionally he stares at me, concern creasing his brow, and rubs viciously at his temple.

Carefully marking my place with a ribbon, I set down my grimoire, and watch him. The harder I chase my thoughts, the more they fracture. I've learned to let my mind wander. I'm no closer to remembering, but sometimes I am closer to knowing.

Malin spills nervous energy until it crawls up my arms and itches in my toes. "Stop doing that!" I snap. Horrified, I clamp my hand over my mouth.

Malin freezes mid-stride and spins on his heel.

I bow my head, clasp my hands in my lap, and whisper, "Forgive me."

He's on his knees, reaching for my hand, and I yank it away without thinking. Oh, Holy Dark Mother, what am I doing?

"I know you're there," he says carefully.

"Of course, I'm here."

His finger crooks under my chin, gently making me meet his eyes, and anger shivers down my spine. I open my mouth to tell him to let go, raise my hand to shove him away. But ice hooks into my thoughts. I don't resist. It's easier not to resist. Safer. I smile, and Malin's face falls as he releases me.

The quiet after midnight is when I take the pieces of me and slot them back together.

Malin thinks I am asleep, but I cannot sleep when he or the Spinner are not near. Alone, my dreams fill with feverish images of a black-walled manor and a girl's whispers I can't quite hear. Curled into the window seat in my bedroom, I watch the stars flicker in the dark.

Muttering began in my sitting room an hour ago, not long after Malin brought me back from court. Mentions of the Ninth slip under the door, and a grimoire and a knife. I hear the word *Penny* and cling tighter to the curtains, clutching at a ripple of a memory:

Malin called me Penny.

On silent feet, I tiptoe to crouch by the door and listen.

"She hasn't healed him; she's still there," Malin says.

A deep male voice replies, "But she is not in control of herself, nor is she able to consent to working the magic. We're running out of time."

Malin sighs, exasperated. "I don't understand it. Tobias told her exactly how to resist the gilding. She should be herself."

"Samhain Eve is the day after tomorrow," the deep-voiced stranger replies. Quietly, I crack the door and peek through the gap. A huge man sits opposite Malin, silhouetted against the fire. "We have no choice but to retrieve the Grimoire."

Malin's voice rises and I wince. "The moment it leaves the library, it will be beyond the book sprites' protection. Do you have any idea what the Warden will do with access to a spell book like that?"

"You have to let us take her, Malin. Or you'll have to take her there yourself. They won't let anyone else near." The man takes a swig from a whiskey glass and shakes his head. "Tobias gave us one key, but she has the other one."

"Stop." Malin sounds angry now, and I don't like it. "She'll come back. She has to."

The stranger snaps. "Well she hasn't yet!"

A girl leaning against the hearth, hidden by an armchair, replies in the same lilted tones as the Spinner. "Do you not trust what I spin?" It is the Spinner. Memories crash into me. Her name is Alice. And the key—I know where it is. It's shaped like a rose.

"We need an army, not a wall hanging," the man snarls.

A woman with half-moon glasses perched on her nose whispers in a voice like the turn of a page, "What do you show the Warden, Alice?"

"His arrogance betrays him. He'll never admit he cannot read what I weave; I produce blank silk and he pats me on the head." Alice holds out a square of silk embroidered in black thread. "The sprites accepted her, Malin. We have to release him."

I frown. Release who?

Malin shoots her a sharp-edged smile. "Not yet. Give her time."

The stranger shifts position and picks at the velvet-clad chair arm. "We're out of time, Malin. And you know it. Stop trying to protect her. She agreed to forge the knife before this happened, and tomorrow will be our last chance."

Silence.

Silver triangles sparkle at the wrist of a girl in fatigues. She twirls a spiral of hair escaped from her bun around one finger. "Penny didn't ask for this."

Her name is Clair, I suddenly think. Oh! I remember her. She smells of jasmine and laundry soap and she helped me, before.

"None of us asked for this," Malin replies. Their voices drop lower, their conversation slips below the crackle of the fire, and I don't hear anything except the beat of my heart and the softness of my breath. I close my eyes and slowly put myself back together, sliding around the hooks in my mind.

When I finish, I haul myself to my feet, push open the door, and interrupt their meeting. All eyes swivel to me. Malin springs to standing and steps toward me. I hold up a hand to stop him. Alice meets my eyes and smiles.

"My name," I say quietly, "is Penny."

Chapter Thirty-Seven

Malin tries to convince me back into my room, whispering that we need to talk, and apologising, but it feels safer somehow, not being in my bedroom. I remember everything. Every brutal detail. It's me that needs to apologise to him—I bound his lifeline to mine without his consent. But when I try to talk, the words won't form and the Gilded's hooks in my mind dig deeper, threatening to tear me away from myself all over again.

So, I stand there, one hand clenched around the doorframe, refusing to move until Malin turns to Clair. "Can you fetch him?"

Clair winces slightly and nods.

"Malin?" I mumble. His name feels wrong on my tongue.

"Go, Clair. Please."

My thoughts unravel as Malin guides me to sit in a chair. I snatch them as they slip, weaving them close and keeping them safe. Alice opens the window, and the cold night air helps, a little, but my head hurts, the edges of my vision pulse black, and the soft click of Clair's departure makes me grit my teeth.

Miss Elsweather pats Malin gently on the shoulder. "I'll inform the others. This can't wait, or I'd give her more time. Clair won't be long; he's waiting in the tunnels."

Malin nods, distracted, and Miss Elsweather and the other man vanish through the same panel in the wall that swallowed Clair.

Alice's whisper is low and strained. "Help her."

Malin's fingers wrap my wrist, and the pain eases as his eyes tighten.

Reality has forsaken me for too long; now, I see it, and the grief that accompanies it is blindingly, viciously sharp.

Tobias died. We can't forge the knife. We need to take the other covens' blood into Death and bring back their crystals with their magic contained inside, and now I can't. Panic catches my throat as I try to speak, but Alice answers from the window seat without me having to ask. "The Resistance kept working without you."

"They made the crystals?"

"Not yet. Mila offered."

"But Mila…" I trail off as my mind twists. "Mila betrayed us. If she makes the crystals, the Warden will know everything."

Alice gives me a weak smile. "She isn't the one who turned on us."

The sofa puffs as Malin sits beside me and looks at me long and hard, his expression unreadable. "He needs to hurry."

"Who?" I ask.

"You'll see," Alice whispers without lifting her eyes, and the hard lines of Malin's face soften. "He's here." Her lips give a funny sort of quiver and she turns to the quiet click of the panel in the wall springing open.

A dead man steps through.

I know he is dead because I saw him die.

He stands by the wall, arms folded, tension in every line of his body. He is Gilded, but his mask is gouged with jagged lines, the eye hole a mess of blackened scrapes. His hair stands up at odd angles like he just got out of bed and there's a hint of a frown in the un-gilded half of his forehead.

Tobias.

I remember his death as clearly as I feel the pain of the gilding's hooks still in my mind, trying to drag me back into compliant nothing. I pull away from Malin's grasp and fly across the room. I don't care that it hurts: Tobias is alive.

Tears stream down my cheeks as he opens his arms and I throw myself into them. He's solid and warm and safe. He holds me tight into his chest, and another memory crashes into me. My breath is a wet sort of gasp. All that comes out is one word—a hopeful whisper of a word. "Ella?"

"Her crystal was destroyed. But she's fine. We got her to a safe house."

The relief is like a wave, crashing over me, consuming me. "You died." My whisper is so low I'm surprised Tobias hears.

"I didn't. Malin hid my lifeline from you. If you'd touched it, you'd have healed me and ruined everything. Dying like that hurt like hell, but I'm no stranger to Death, and I've clung to my soul before and survived. He's helping Ella too. He had access to your magic, Penny, thanks to what you did—"

Malin coughs, cutting him off. "That's something Penny and I need to discuss in private if you don't mind, Tobias."

Tobias sighs. "I'm sorry, Penny. There was no time to warn you. We needed the Warden to think you'd let me die. That you wouldn't cave to his threats. We were trying to protect Ella."

"And failed." The gilding's barbs hook deeper in my head and I wince in pain.

Tobias speaks to Malin over my head. "You promised to keep her safe. You said this would work."

"It did work!" Malin snaps. "Look at her!"

I turn in Tobias's hold as Malin's hand twitches toward me and clenches around the edge of a cushion instead.

Malin exhales, steadying his temper before he continues. "If I'd stood in the Warden's way, he'd still have gilded her." He gestures to my face, and I bite hard on my lip. Metallic blood slips over my tongue. "All I could do was protect her lifeline and hope she fought back. He's not touched her since."

A tiny noise a little like a sob comes from where Alice sits in the window seat. Tobias's biceps harden. His silver eyes spark as he eases me away and takes my hands; my fingers vanish in his grip. Calluses on his palms scrape my skin, and shivers tremble down my spine as pain floods from my head into his hands, like Malin did for me when I was gilded—like he did just now.

"She's in pain. Surely you could have helped her with that." Tobias's words are sharp. If they were any sharper, I think Malin might bleed.

Alice's whisper is like a leaf in a winter wind. "He did, Toby. She hasn't been hurting. But Penny needs you. Do what you did for me."

I try to pull away, but Tobias tightens his hold. "Stop talking about me as if I'm not here," I snap. I turn on Alice, my irritation dying as I see the devastation in her eyes. "Alice?"

She smiles a little. "Toby can stop the pain. It hurt when I resurfaced too. The Gilded have their claws so deep in your mind, you won't be able to fight for long alone. But he'll need your help."

"What do I have to do?" I ask quietly.

"Don't resist," Tobias says. "It will make it worse. Sit down, Penny, this is going to hurt." I don't ask how much as I let him walk me backward to sit on the sofa, and he exhales slowly as he adjusts his grip on my hands so one thumb presses into each wrist. "Don't scream."

I nod once.

It's like a knife sliding between the layers of my mind, gouging out hooks embedded in my thoughts. The pain is blinding. Excruciating. But this pain scours me clean.

It's over in minutes. The pulsing throb in my head vanishes, and Tobias squeezes my hand. "I have to go. Hold it together, Penny. Just a bit longer and this will end."

I wrap my arms around myself as Tobias leaves and watch Alice slip through the panel in the wall after him. Leaving me alone with Malin.

He is betrayal and lies and safety and hope all rolled into one confusing muddle. I want him to take me in his arms and tell me it's all right.

I want to push him away and run.

I do nothing except wrap my arms tighter around myself.

Malin doesn't speak. He sits at the dining table and waits in silence for my breathing to calm.

When I manage to look at him, his eyes are so full of apology it sets me gasping anew.

"Breathe, Penny," he says. "Just breathe. It's going to be fine. I promise."

I don't know how he can make promises like that. I don't think I can accept them. "Was it all lies? Was it all a trick to get me to bind our lifelines and make me think it was my idea? Or—" I can't finish. *Did you want me too?* It sounds so weak, pathetic, especially now.

"I didn't mean for this to happen."

I thought my heart couldn't hurt anymore; apparently, it can. He didn't mean for it to happen? I was naive to think I'd been more than a means to an end.

"Penny, don't. I didn't mean to hurt you. I didn't mean to fall for you. I don't regret *us*—I wanted that, more than you can imagine."

"There is no us." My voice is flat.

"No," Malin says sadly. "I don't suppose there is. You couldn't trust me. I intended to give up my lifeline when you forged the knife. It was all arranged, the book sprites were helping. And—" He clicks his fingers and our lifelines appear, melded together. "You did *this.* I asked you not to, and you did it anyway. All on your own. Without my permission."

"I'm so sorry." I hang my head in shame. "I didn't know what else to do. I couldn't lose you." I thought forging the Sorcerer's knife would be the hardest part of this. That giving up my lifeline would hurt. After this conversation, ceasing to exist sounds almost peaceful. "Why didn't you tell me you had a plan?"

"I told you I'd find you, and I told you explicitly that I didn't want my lifeline bound to yours. What you've done—" He stops and presses his hands flat against the table as if trying to calm himself, and I dig my nails into my palm to keep myself still. We need this conversation. But my head hurts. I've been lost in the dark so long, now I'm awake, the truth is blindingly, viciously bright. Malin groans low in his throat and his words soften. "Penny, what you did to our lifelines is permanent. I meant to work the magic and forge the knife. I just needed the spell."

"Malin..."

"Don't." He doesn't move, doesn't come closer. But he explains everything. He tells me how the book sprites helped arrange his escape from Death. After Tobias made it to the Ninth with me, the sprites took messages between the libraries in Life and Death, and coordinated a plan. Mila was bait in a trap sprung on the Warden's orders. But they still don't know who's feeding our plans to the Warden.

As Malin talks, my breathing eases and knots of guilt unravel from my chest. I have let no one down, he tells me—except him, though he doesn't drag me over the coals for that again. "Beatrice,

Evelyn, Gail, and Sybil have volunteered their blood to make new crystals—they fought to be allowed to do it. The knife can still be forged," he says, "but—"

Of course. There had to be a *but.*

He crosses to the window and peeks out through a gap in the curtains.

I stiffen. "But what, Malin? You can't leave it like that!"

The curtains fall to block out the night and he shakes his head. "I meant to set you free. And now I can't give up my lifeline to make the knife without taking yours."

I stare at him, horrified. "You mean—" I can't put it into words. It's too grim. I do anyway. "I thought when I gave up my lifeline, you could have my crystal. Instead, I ruined everything. I didn't know the magic would take your lifeline too."

Malin strides toward me and pulls me to my feet. I'm in his arms. "Penny," he murmurs into my hair. "We'll work it out. You've beaten the odds before. I refuse to lose you now. We'll find a way to fix this." His fingers run up my back to gently tangle in my hair.

For a moment I let myself be held, imagine what might have been, and then ease myself out of his embrace and slump back into the sofa.

"I should have trusted you." He sits stiffly beside me. "When I felt you cross the veil the first time, when I saw you that first night you walked, a red-haired witch alone in the grey deserts, you set my damned soul on fire. I thought I'd lost you, and I've never been so scared. When you were gilded, I didn't touch your lifeline. Didn't you fight it?"

"I..." I try to remember, but it's all fuzzy. "When I saw you... When I thought you were on the Warden's side. It hurt, Malin. I trusted you and I couldn't see how I could stop it. I gave up."

"I'm sorry."

I give him a shaky smile. "Why didn't you warn me?"

"Because the Warden had to believe I was as cold and ruthless as him. He had to think I'd do anything to escape from Death. And for that to work, you had to believe it too. The Warden knew you were coming to my gates each night. The Gilded were following you into Death, watching you disappear and reporting back. We didn't know until it was too late. He'd have hurt you so much worse if I hadn't been here."

"That's why they were so sure our traitor was a thorn witch? The Gilded tear the veil when they cross. They'll have needed thorn magic to repair it."

But the rest of it doesn't make sense. "What I don't understand is why the Warden let you put on a crown like the prodigal son returned when he's the one who locked you in Death in the first place?"

"That was the deal he offered me: you in exchange for royal privileges. On Samhain, he intends to seal the veil. He'll sever his lifeline completely and destroy all magic so it can't be remade." Malin rubs his thumbs in his temples.

"Then we'll be overrun with wraiths! No one will be able to pass the veil."

Malin winces. "They will when he has them thrown into the eternal fires. That gateway will only close if the fires go out. As people die, the Gilded will dispose of them.

"He'd have sealed it already if it wasn't for Alice and her spinning. She convinced him to wait until Samhain night, entirely with blank squares of silk." He laughs a little, but there's admiration in his eyes.

I smile at that. The Warden gave her a loom and she used it to weave a weapon. Alice with her midnight eyes and delicate fingers seems so fragile, but the burden of the future is in her hands and with it she protects us all. But I'm still confused. "How does you being here help the Warden?"

There's strain in his eyes. "Trapped in Death and anchored to the veil, I could have held the veil open. Even with no crystal, I could have taken Guardianship of the veil and lasted long enough for someone else to step in."

I fall silent as the full awfulness of the Warden's plan sinks in. "With you here, it's completely irreversible."

Malin nods. "It will never open again."

"You should have gone back."

"I couldn't leave you here to face the Warden alone." Malin stares at his fingers.

"So, the book sprites are actually on the Warden's side?" If they helped Malin return and his return helped the Warden's plans all fall so neatly in place—but that makes no sense either. The book sprites helped me. They're the most terrifying little things in the whole of Halstett. If they're on the Warden's side, I don't think he'd need the Gilded.

"The book sprites belong to the Sorcerer. Can't leave the libraries. Shame really, the Resistance could use them." He sighs. "All our plans played beautifully into the Warden's hands."

"But surely the Sorcerer could fix the veil..." My words fade at the anger in Malin's eyes. "You know where he is, don't you?"

"Yes." Quietly, Malin comes to sit beside me, and gently untangles a strand of hair caught on my mask. "Again I ask. Can you trust me?"

"I think," I answer, "the question is: Can you trust me?"

"I never stopped." He smiles and raises that infuriating eyebrow. "Penny, the Sorcerer is on the ninth floor of the library."

Honestly, at this point, I'm not surprised. "Fine. Then that's where we'll start."

Malin frowns. "Where we start what?"

"Looking for a way to fix this mess." I lean into him and close my eyes. He waits a moment, then slowly, tentatively, he slides his arm around my shoulders. And we stay there like that, him and me. A little piece of quiet before it begins.

When Mila, the first of the arriving Resistance members, steps through the panel on the wall, I'm ready to face what comes next.

Chapter Thirty-Eight

It turns out, being the unofficial plaything of the heir of Halstett, completely unable to think for myself, has its benefits even if it is utterly mortifying if I think about it too long. The Gilded who guarded my door are gone, Malin can come and go as he pleases, and with no one listening in, my rooms have become the meeting place for Ella's Resistance friends.

Blueprints cover my dining table, old spell books are held open with paperweights on the rug before the hearth, and we're scattered among them, shadowed in shades of exhaustion. Miss Elsweather perches on a stiff-backed dining chair, a seemingly bottomless cup of tea in her hand, talking quietly to the huge palace guard who referred to Alice's spinnings as a wall hanging.

Alice sits with Malin on the sofa, her eyes shining, his shoulders stiff and tense. Clair returned half an hour ago with a black canvas satchel slung over her shoulder. She sits with Mila and me on the floor, twirling a lock of hair around her finger; Mila chews on her lip, scribbling in a notebook, asking me questions about my last trip to the Ninth.

I need to find a way to undo what I've done. And the Sorcerer, the actual Sorcerer who swept out of the woods, cracking the Wayvern Spine mountains up from the earth in his wake, and settled a farm boy on a new-conquered throne, is trapped on the Ninth. "You're sure you want to do this?" Mila asks for the fiftieth time.

I force a smile, half my attention on Malin and Alice, wondering what they're talking about. "I can't see another way."

We've been arguing for the last ten minutes. I'm certain the Sorcerer will talk to me, that we can negotiate with him; Mila is on the fence, saying anyone trapped on the Ninth has to have lost his sanity. Clair thinks the whole idea is ridiculous. She sighs and refolds a library blueprint. "It's Malin you'll have to convince."

Mila shrugs. "He can go with her?"

I pick up my tea, cupping it in my hands to warm them. "I'll go with Alice. He won't stop me. He's the one who said the Sorcerer was up there; even if he disagrees, he doesn't have a leg to stand on."

Clair grins wickedly. "Just like his fetid father."

The gasp of my laugh prickles tea up my nose. "Clair!"

Mila smirks. "The Warden's getting worse. Grandmother suggested amputation, but he offered to amputate her head if she mentioned that idea again." Her smirk softens into a sad sort of smile. "Another year and he'd have been easy to take to his knees."

"We don't have another year," I say, dabbing at a tea spill on my skirt. "We have until Samhain or the Warden's going to destroy magic and the veil all in one horrible night. If we have a hope of stopping him, I need to get to the library."

Mila grimaces, well aware of the price of this spell. Malin helpfully brought them all up to speed on that while I was under the gilding's control. "The others want you to be the one to grow their crystals, Pen. I said I'd ask."

"Of course." If they're prepared to trust me, it's the least I can do. "When?"

"Malin was crossing into Death tomorrow anyway—"

"He's still crossing?"

Mila nods, but there's a shadow in her silver eyes. She's worried. "The Warden has no idea."

I cross my arms and stare at her. "It seems to me, every time we think the Warden knows nothing, he knows every damned thing. Are you sure it's safe?"

"Nothing about this is safe. But I'm walking for the coven tomorrow. I'll do what I can to protect you."

Clair reaches for my wrist, redirecting when I flinch at her sudden movement, and strokes the pile of the rug instead. "I can take you to the library doors, but Malin won't like you going without him."

"He doesn't have to." I scowl at my skirts, diamonds spangled across them, wishing I had something appropriate for sneaking through night-dark corridors to change into. "I can't go like this; I'll light up like a chandelier if I go near a lamp."

Clair laughs. "As though I wouldn't think of that. Really, Penny." She pulls her bag open and lays out two precisely folded piles of black fatigues. "Who's going to tell Malin?"

Judging by Malin's fingers clamped on the sofa arm, I think Alice has already discussed it. "I'll deal with Malin."

Miss Elsweather beckons me over, setting her cup neatly on her saucer with a clink. "Penny, dear. If you're going to the library, please refrain from breaking any more of my windows."

"She won't this time," Alice says over my shoulder.

Peering over her glasses, Miss Elsweather assesses Alice carefully. "How long, dear, before the Gilded notice your absence?"

Alice's smile widens. "Time enough for this."

"Wonderful," Miss Elsweather replies. She clicks her fingers at the man beside her. Without a word, he rises, nudging the table so her teaspoon clatters against her cup, and she tuts. "The future is in your hands now, girls, precisely as it should be. I don't suppose you know how this ends, Alice, love?"

Alice shakes her head, answering Miss Elsweather's question. "The future split the day you found Penny in the library. She was supposed to die. She did. And now she has, I can't see her future anymore. We need a legion, the legion needs a knife, and the knife demands a sacrifice."

Her words have too many meanings to untangle. Miss Elsweather seems to understand, even if no one else does. "Assemble your legions, Alice. They won't spin themselves from nothing. We don't live in a fairy tale. Come along, Dante. If we're reforging this knife, we should prepare." She's still chuckling under her breath at her own joke as Dante, the soldier with the wicked eyes, shuts the panel in the wall behind them.

Alice and I vanish into the bedroom, slip into Clair's fatigues, and when we reappear, Malin is standing by the window, staring into the night as if he's counting the stars. When he turns, a muscle twitches in his jaw. "You're going to the Ninth with Alice?" He shakes his head, exasperated.

"For goodness' sake, Malin. Stop it. You and Alice mean the world to me. I want this to work out between us, but if I don't go and see this Sorcerer hiding out on the Ninth, only one of us is going to survive to see next week and it won't be you or me. I have to try," I say firmly, take Alice's hand, and follow Mila and Clair through the panel into the dark between the walls.

The tunnels spit us out behind the Warden's giant stone boot. Leaving Mila and Clair behind, we creep to the library. We don't speak as we walk; it's enough to be together, alone and with freedom so close we can almost taste it.

We climb the stairs to the Eighth, and in the shadows of the night-time library, I can almost forget Alice and I were gilded by the Warden, that he tried to reduce us to the sum total of our magic.

And we got off lightly in the grander scheme of things. Compared to the Gilded, the people he's killed. All the families he's destroyed, an entire continent laid to waste. "He failed," I say quietly. "He tried to subdue us and he failed. The Resistance will end him."

"He was always going to fail." Alice pauses at the foot of the steps to the Ninth and smiles at the maelstrom of shadows at the top. "Every end I wove, he failed. Except one."

The end where you let her go. The voice trickles down the stairs and echoes silently off the walls. I want to ask Alice what he means, but I'm too scared to talk. *That's when he failed, didn't he, little spinner of futures not yet lived. How does it feel to lay the paths before their feet and watch them walk? Do you wonder, Alice, if they would walk the same way if you did not give them a map?*

The voice of the Sorcerer. Banished to the Ninth by the Warden and forgotten. No wonder the Warden refused to step foot inside the library doors. Caged in a library with nothing but spell books and his rage for company. But the book sprites did not forget.

Alice smiles a spidersilk smile. "He'll fail," she says in her sing-song Spinner's voice. "The Mother shows me what she wants them to see. The paths I weave are hers, not mine."

Is that so, Daughter of Life? Clots of ink ooze down the banisters. Book sprite eyes wink between the railings as the darkness solidifies into a human-like form. Spindled legs sprout from odd angles, glistening white eyes burrow into a misshapen head, features rippling into a face.

My heart shudders. I spoke to this before, this creature made of malformed ink. I thought it was a ward woven by the Sorcerer to protect his spells, not the Sorcerer himself. The creator of all magic.

And you brought the Daughter of Death. Interesting. You came to make a request, Penny, make it.

I swallow and try to talk, but no words come out.

Alice whispers, "Go on, Penny. Ask him."

I stare at the ink seeping from the Sorcerer's feet onto the stairs. Words form as it drips down to the next step: *Ask. Ask. Ask.*

"We want to reforge your knife," I whisper.

You have the spell. You have only to pay the price.

"I... well... I made a mistake and I was wondering..." My words falter and die. Now I am here, facing a deity in the flesh, I feel so stupid. So inconsequential. I can't ask him to make his own knife!

Alice saves me. "She can't pay the price. She bound her lifeline to someone else. It no longer belongs to her. If we bring you the ingredients, might you work the magic?"

Silence trembles as the Sorcerer inhales. The floor shivers. *The knife requires a lifeline.*

The book sprites blink in unison, a snap of pitch-black that sends my heart spiralling for my throat. Their shadowy forms slither down the stairs and gather around us, stroking Alice's silver-blonde hair and tugging gently at my curls. One perches on Alice's shoulder, peeping around her to stare at me; another blinks from the banister.

The Sorcerer's eyes narrow into deathly slits. *Someone must pay the price.*

"But that means he has to pay it too."

Unfortunate. He doesn't sound like he thinks it's unfortunate at all. *But I cannot work the magic. It is no longer my spell to cast. What else did you come here to ask, child? I see another question in your eyes.*

"I... is there a way to unbind our lifelines?" I stutter.

The Sorcerer waves an ink-dripping hand, and there's a tug deep in my chest. It twists, clasps my lungs, and siphons the strength from my knees. I struggle to stay standing as my lifeline appears, black and sparkling. Malin's is woven round it, through it. The Sorcerer laughs. *You bound yourself to his son! Foolish girl.*

Alice says softly, "You call Penny a fool, but you need her. No one else can undo what Reginald Halstett has done. Give her the tools and she will make you a key. Help us. Tell us how to help you."

Three enter, one returns.

Alice stiffens. "I wove three lifelines on my loom."

She tangled them. Three wind around her.

"They vanished in my weaving."

Three go in, one comes out. When she holds the knife, one will be set free. The Sorcerer floats down the stairs. Milk-white eyes bore into mine, pupilless and swirling with barely chained power.

I want to flee, run away and escape out the library doors, but Alice's fingers brush mine, giving me strength. "Please," I say, my voice trembling. "Please help me."

I have no magic, child. I have no power. There is no spell that can undo what you have done. The knife requires a price. I paid it when I forged it; I could not pay it again even if I was free. You must pay or find another who can. Return with the knife, Penelope, release me, and I will lend you a legion to banish Reginald Halstett from the face of the world, but now, I can do nothing.

I knew the odds of the Sorcerer helping were slim. But at his words, a fresh wave of fear hits. The only choice I have is no choice at all: sacrifice Malin and forge the knife to save my friends or watch them fall as the Warden destroys their magic and seals the veil.

Alice cocks her head to one side, and I have a horrible feeling she's listening to something I can't hear. "Fine," she says quietly. "We'll come back when the knife is made, but if you want us to release you, we'll need better terms than that." She takes my hand and turns her back on the Sorcerer. "Come on, Penny." Her fingers twitch where they hold mine and she huffs a little sound of frustration. "I have a loom screaming my name."

She doesn't look back as she walks down the stairs. I don't either, though that's more through fear than Grandmother's meticulous training. I'm not sure many people in the course of Halstett's history have turned their backs on the Sorcerer and survived. Maybe we're the first.

Book sprites skip down the stairs, little inky shadows darting around our skirts and sliding down the banisters. *We miss you, Penny,* they whisper. *Come again, Penny. Come soon. Come to the other side.*

"Hush," I whisper, and their green eyes sparkle.

One vanishes and reappears on Alice's shoulder. *Alice,* they whisper. *We missed you, Alice. We missed you most. Come back.*

"Soon," Alice replies. "Both of us will come back soon."

Their eyes turn amethyst, washing the stairs in a rosy moonlight hue. *Bring the third,* they hiss. *Set us free. Make him let us go.*

Their voices slice into silence. Their eyes turn scarlet and wink out one by one until only two book sprites remain. They block the stairs, forcing us to stop. *Penny,* they say, and their voices are strained. *Please, come back.*

"I don't know—"

Please, they whisper. And then they're gone.

When we get to Malin's sitting rooms, he gives us a single glance to check we're in one piece, shakes his head, and sinks into the sofa. "He won't help?"

I feel my chin wobble. I don't want to admit defeat, yet here I am, defeated. "He can't."

"It's all right," he says quietly. "Tomorrow, when you forge the knife, you won't be alone."

I should refuse, but I can't. I should fight him, tell him there has to be another way, but I don't. I've taken Malin's choices once. I won't do that again. So, I thank him quietly, and he gives me one final gift before our world is torn apart: time with Alice. He holds out a hand to his bedroom door, an offer of peace and safety; a chance to say goodbye. Alice gives him a soft smile, takes my hand, and we leave.

"He's a good man," Alice whispers as we climb into the bed. It is cosy and familiar and safe; we've slept in here before, lost and curled in each other's arms.

"I know," I reply.

Alice kisses me gently. "We'll be together, Penny. Always. Don't forget."

I don't argue with her. I just wish we'd had more time—time to see where this could go and how deep it could be. How far we'd fall…

"Tell me a story," Alice murmurs against my shoulder.

So, I do. I tell her of two girls grown in the dark without a single light to guide them. Or so they thought. I tell her how they led each other into the light. I tell Alice our story, how we met, how we grew and changed. And then, I change our end. "They break free," I whisper against her hair. "Turn their faces to the sun."

"You're my sun, Penny." She sighs in my arms, soft and gentle. She's saying goodbye.

"You're my stars." I breathe her in, exhale a silent farewell I cannot put into words.

Alice's delicate fingers slip under my nightdress, stilling my thoughts. Butterfly kisses follow the path of her touch, and my back arches. My inhale shudders as she shifts slightly so her fingers can trail the top of my thigh. My body responds with a jolt down a fine thread hooked beside my heart. I close my eyes and feel her smile, filling me with warmth and hope, washing the chill of Death away.

Her caresses are soft, so gentle as they dance over my hips. I open my eyes and see her. My link to life. "Together," she whispers.

I gasp as her fingers draw a line to the centre of me, and our gazes lock, her pupils dilating. A smile catches the corner of her mouth as my lips part with a small "oh" on my shaky exhale. We're safe here in the shadows, cradled in the dark and lost in each other. "Alice."

She shivers at the sound of her name and whispers something against my skin. It sounds like *sorry*. It sounds like *don't leave*.

She shifts so she kneels between my knees, and when her kisses take over from her fingers, I clamp a hand over my mouth.

"Let go," she whispers against me, and then she sends me spiralling. Pleasure coils deep inside as she eases me closer and closer to the edge, and I think I might shatter when I reach it. Then, I am lost. I am falling. She falls with me as I break with a shuddering inhale muffled by my hand.

She holds me as I float back to reality. And when I reach for her, my fingers tracing the perfect skin of the inside of her thighs, she makes a tiny noise into my hair.

"Alice." I murmur her name over and over again. She smells of sunshine and primroses, and when I kiss her throat, trailing lower, she tastes of honey and salt. In the dark before dawn, I copy her movements, and she whispers my name with a soft catch to her breath. Heat builds in my core, powerful and strong, I need her. So desperately. She whispers my name as she shatters in waves that threaten to tear me apart all over again.

We lie tangled, sweat-slick limbs and bare skin and soft pulsing warmth that tingles the soles of my feet, forgetting, just for a little while, what new horrors the rise of the sun might bring.

I want to hold this moment, lost in the afterglow, wrapped around each other in the dark. I feel each beat of her heart. We whisper, somethings and nothings and all the things in between. And the time we have together fades into nothing as the stars fade into a morning sky.

Maybe our fates have always been tied, our silk spun as one before the Dark Mother wove our souls and threaded life into our veins. Maybe our choices make no difference and the future is impossible to change. It's an oddly comforting thought, that this—us—was always meant to be.

Chapter Thirty-Nine

I make it all the way through the next day without the Warden noticing something has changed. He's too arrogant to consider that his plan might fail, that I might have found my way out. I strengthen my facade of nothingness by remembering every act he made against us, every injustice and loss. There are so many I lose count by midafternoon. Every step is steady, every blink carefully measured. But as I wait for Malin at the tapestry-covered entrance to the Resistance temple, I falter.

How did we get here? This wasn't how it was supposed to end. This wasn't *when* it was supposed to end either.

I send a silent prayer to the Dark Mother. It's difficult to not believe in her after everything I've seen, but I'm still not sure if she listens or cares. I pray that my family survive what comes next, that Ella is made whole and Mila is safe, that my father is returned to himself and my mother is happy. That my grandmother softens and loves again. I close my eyes and imagine my village, my sisters sitting by the stream making daisy chains in the grass, my mother tending her herb gardens, my father cooking dinner on the stove.

The village is gone, but my coven could rebuild. The mountains still stand, the Wayvern Spine will never break. No man can take down a mountain.

It turns out, one witch can't save the world either.

My father always said it took only one spark to start a fire. This fire needs more than one witch to make it burn. Tonight, I begin to set myself ablaze for the very last time, and this time, Malin burns with me.

Behind this tapestry, my friends are waiting. I never had friends before. Which means I have more to lose if I fail. More on the line if my nerve cracks.

I've accepted my fate. Malin has too. But I'm not sure about Alice. I hope someone will catch her when I leave her behind.

Malin approaches, soft footsteps in the dusty dark, and hands me the collection box Mila gave him. "Ready?" he asks quietly, one hand on the small of my back, lending me his strength and sending butterflies fluttering through my chest.

"I'm not sure I'll ever be ready for this." I force a smile, brace myself, and push aside the tapestry.

Inside the Resistance temple is cold and echoey. No one knows we're here except Miss Elsweather, who gave Clair the key, and us. No one sits behind the rose painting tonight, no council presides from the rickety platform. It smells oddly of Death, a chilled dampness that clings to my nostrils when I inhale, and I'm glad of Malin's hand on my back as I walk.

My friends are gathered around the altar, dressed in black shifts, their coven sashes tied around their waists, lines of colour against the dark. Evelyn perches on the solid gold altar top playing with a candle flame, making it skip from finger to finger. There's a single garnet embedded in the back of her wrist, which can only have been Bea's doing, and her sash is knotted untidily, the ends uneven and frayed, one red thread trailing down her skirts.

Bea leans against the wall behind her, a little smirk curving her mouth. Tiny emeralds run down the inside of her arm and the end of her yellow sash is charred. She's focused on rearranging the stone pillars' decorations with idle waves of her fingers that remind me of Alice weaving on her loom, but she's aware of our approach. A jade spiral of rock swirls down the pillar from the ceiling, a topaz one rises up from the floor, whirling around and around until I feel dizzy just watching. Bea chuckles and makes the quartz form a smiling face on the wall between the pillars. It winks at me, and I can't help but smile back.

Gail sparks lightning from the top of one pillar to the other, illuminating the rock faces in flashes of pink and orange and blue, and her eyes blaze so bright her sapphire irises are almost silver. Sybil just stares at her feet. She's sitting on the floor, back against the femurs holding up the altar, arms wrapped around her knees. Water drips from her finger and trickles across to the floor. It pools beside a scattering of yellow sand on the flagstones like a tiny little beach.

My heart hurts for them. Once the knife is forged, we think they'll lose their magic. There's nothing definitive in the spell wording, but if this works and I manage to grow their crystals from the sand in Death, their magic will be contained inside the gems. It's like having a piece of ourselves forever held outside of our bodies. I don't remember anything different; I was only five when my crystal was grown. I've no idea what it feels like to have my magic completely embedded in my soul.

But they do.

Malin squeezes my shoulder. "I'll wait here."

"Thank you," I reply as he goes to take a seat a few rows back from the altar, giving us a little space. Bea grins, waves a finger in the air, and the floor tiles do a little jig, knocking Malin's chair out from under him as he goes to sit. He jerks straight, flashes Bea a devastating grin, and pins the chair still so he can sit without being dumped to the floor.

Evelyn is still giggling as I put the collection box down on the altar. Stars are carved into the ebony lid and the inside is lined with red velvet. The needles are fresh and sharp. Bea snaps her fingers. "Mila said you went to see the Sorcerer last night! Who'd have thought, all these years and the mystery of the ninth floor was him all along. I take it from your cheerful demeanour you had no joy?"

"Waste of time," I reply, handing her the first needle and holding out a tiny glass vial.

"Sorry, Penny. It was worth a shot." Bea pricks her finger, squeezes a drop of blood into the vial, and Evelyn offers her candle flame. The glass softens and Bea pinches the end shut, sealing the drop of ruby red inside.

Evelyn takes another needle from the box and holds it delicately between a finger and thumb. "Don't mess this up, death-walker."

"When have I messed anything up, fire-girl?"

Evelyn chuckles and pricks her finger, raising an eyebrow to indicate Malin sitting quietly watching. "Rumour has it, you messed up there."

"Rumour has it, you're dating my big sister."

"Then not all the rumours around here are lies." She squeezes her finger and blood beads on the tip, shimmering in the candlelight. "Don't worry, I'll play nicely with her."

"You'd better."

Evelyn tilts her finger and blood slowly runs down her skin. "You think this will work. Growing the crystals. Forging the knife?"

"I hope so."

"You don't need to label them or something?" She gestures at Bea's blood in the thin glass tube lying in my hand.

"Your crystal should grow red. Bea's yellow." I wrinkle my nose and give her a grin. "Even I can tell the difference between two primary colours."

"I misjudged you," Evelyn says, her tone as sharp as ever, but her smile says *sorry.* She drips her blood into the tube, seals it over her flame, and hands it over. "See you at the end, Penny. We'll be right here with you all the way." She stares at me and her irises spark red. Tears sparkle on her lashes. Her smile twitches down at one corner as she sets the flame back on a candlewick and stalks away without looking back.

Sybil is next. Her lower lip trembles as she pricks her finger, and when she hands me the little tube of her blood, she throws her arms around me and squeezes tight. "May the tide flow in your favour," she says. "May the current carry you home." She waits for Gail to take her turn, and the two of them link arms as they leave.

Bea quietly closes the collection case. "Clair said she'll see you later and to be careful."

"I'm sorry," I say. "If there was another way to do this...I wish you didn't have to risk your magic."

"Better than risking all magic." There's sadness in her eyes as she looks at the four little tubes lined up in my palm. Firmly, she curls my fingers around them, and clasps my hand between hers. "This is nothing."

"It's everything, Bea, and you know it."

"Maybe." She glares at Malin over my shoulder. "Look after her. Bring her back. No funny business!" She forces a grin, and when she lets go of my hands, there's a tiny black crystal embedded in the inside of my wrist. She slides the Warden's cuff down over it. "Don't forget, Penny. We're right here like Evelyn said. All the way to the end."

Then she leaves us too, and it's just me and Malin alone in the Resistance temple.

Malin hands me the poison vial, ready to burn at my side. He watches me take a sip, takes a tiny sip himself, then wraps me in his arms. I snake my hands around his neck and bury my face in his shoulder as the fire in my blood ignites. We burn together, him and I. Our ashes left behind on the temple floor.

Tonight the veil is silk on my skin and the desert sand is cool and smooth beneath my toes. Dark chocolate and woodsmoke and cherry blossom are threaded on the windless air. Death welcomes us with open arms, and it feels good to be home. I'm glad Mila got to walk one last time—to say goodbye. It gets under your skin, Death. I'm glad I get to walk again too.

I check everything as I was taught to do: My crystal is at my throat; my lifeline is anchored. My friends' blood is still in my hands. I close my eyes and exhale, breathe in the chill of the sand, and step away from the safety of Malin's side. Everything else, every other step of reforging the Sorcerer's knife, I will do with his hand in mine, but this I do alone.

I walk away from the veil, putting a little space between us, and drop to my knees. My skin feels like it dissolves into the sand, as if here, so close to the end, there's no longer a distinction between the desert and me. I gave no thought to what I might wear tonight, but Death has clad me in pale silver starlight. My skirts shimmer like a full moon where they're spread out in the dark grey sand. It seems appropriate somehow. That I am dressed like a fairy-tale Thorn Queen for this chapter of my story. This is the stuff myths are made of. I wonder if one day a small thorn witch will read stories of me and my friends in the pages of a book—if the colour plate will do justice to reality.

With one finger, I draw a circle in the sand around me, and a flush of magic catches it alight. In Life I cannot work fire, but here, tonight, I could set fire to the rain that's beginning to fall.

Raindrops whirl around me, solidifying into a dome of translucent water that settles over me and the circle of flames. Inside I am perfectly dry and the fire continues to burn. I imagine the sand dimpling and with a single thought four little holes appear. I whisper *thank you* as I take each tube in turn, snap it in half, and let the ruby-red blood drip into the holes.

Then, I smooth sand over the holes, burying the witch blood, and press my hands flat over the top. I begin to pray. I pray to the Dark Mother, who made us all and wove our lifelines from starlight and sunshine, to guide the blood in the sand to grow. I pray to the Sorcerer to accept the magic in the blood and make it solid. I pray to Death itself to accept our offering. Magic runs out of my palms into the sand. The rain stops. The fire dies. The sand beneath my fingers trembles and goes still. And it is done.

I squeeze my eyes shut tight and lift my hands. When I open them, four perfect crystals lie on the sand in front of my knees. I stare at them in awe. However much I wanted to believe that this would work, no matter how many pictures I saw in the books of other covens' crystals, this... seeing a rainbow of crystals sparkling in the half-light of Death... it is impossible. And perfect.

Possibilities are grown with the birth of these crystals. Hope of rescuing lives. Maybe even my father's life.

Bea's crystal is yellow, ore magic swirling gold and bright inside. Evelyn's is scarlet and fires burn in its heart. An entire storm cell seems to be contained inside Gail's sapphire crystal. And Sybil's tide magic is a maelstrom of rushing water, a whirlpool encased in emerald stone.

That something so small has so much power is beyond even my wildest imagination. And I've had a crystal since I was five.

Malin taps me gently on the shoulder and hands me four velvet pouches and four silk squares. Alice's embroidery borders the silk, tiny flowers in a rainbow of gemstone shades. She's written their names on the pouches too, in silk thread that matches the crystals.

Slowly, I pick up each crystal, protecting it from my skin with the silk, and wrap it carefully before tucking it safely in the velvet and tying the ribbons at the top tight. Then, I slip them in my pocket and let Malin help me to my feet.

"What now?" I ask, staring at the veil. I'm not ready to return to Halstett. Not yet. I'm not ready to say goodbye to the desert or the manor or the sand. Or Malin.

Malin's fingers brush the death's head hawkmoth tattooed on my shoulder as he turns me away from the veil. "Penny," he says, "do you like to dance?"

"Do I what?" I blink up at him, utterly confused.

His smile is so warm, so genuine. "Would you like to dance?"

I blush, remembering our kiss in his library on top of the crystal buried beneath the world. My blood fizzes and my heart skips even though it strictly shouldn't skip here. But I don't blame it; the depths of Malin's silver eyes are threatening to drown me. "Here?"

"Come home, Penny. Dance with me under the stars." He bends close and lowers his voice, though there's no one around to hear. "Or, if you like, I'll show you my tower."

"Your tower? Is that a euphemism?"

"The one with the flag on top!" Malin laughs. "If I was propositioning you, I'd come up with something far more romantic than that."

"You're not propositioning me?" I raise an eyebrow and try to look disappointed.

He chuckles again, but it's deeper this time and he doesn't deny it. "One perfect night?"

"Everyone's waiting for us to come back."

He groans low in his throat and exhales hard. "Let them wait, Penny."

I nod and watch the grey expanse of desert, waiting for the manor to form, unable to look at him. "Malin...I'm scared."

"I know," he replies, devastatingly gently. "So am I."

I lift my fingers to my cheeks, tracing the cold metal mask burned into my skin. "I've been scared for so long, I don't remember what it's like to not be frightened anymore. Even when the gilding was working, I was still scared; the blank nothing just lay on top and smothered it. I knew I was afraid of something, the fear was there but I couldn't touch it, couldn't escape it. I wish I could forget everything bad, forget I'm scared, just for a little while."

"I can give you that." He squeezes my hand. "If you'll let me?" I shut my eyes tight, nod, and open them, and together, Malin and I begin to walk as we have so many nights before this one, across the desert toward the portcullis. Behind the black stone walls, the tattered flag dances in the breeze.

The manor is whole again, perfect and filled with magic. The parlour is black tonight. Deep velvet curtains frame the approaching night. Grey wallpaper flocks the walls with a murder of crows in flight, and wrought-iron chandeliers hang on chains, casting smoked-glass shadows across grey marble floors. Stained with Malin's darkness, patterned with my fear. A black-lacquered piano stands by wide-open patio doors.

Malin sits at the piano, lightly tracing the keys with strong fingers. His hands are gentle, his shoulders relaxed, but tension shows in the set of his jaw. I half expect a funeral dirge or a dramatic piece, uplifting like the onset of battle. The first note is quiet and quivering. A teardrop waiting to fall. The second note joins while the first still sounds. And another and another. Building like streams meeting behind a dam wall.

Dark hair curls at the vulnerable nape of his neck, half-hidden by the collar of his black shirt. I want to smooth it. I want to stand behind him and breathe him in. I watch his fingers dance, and I'm envious of the piano keys. I imagine how it would feel to be caressed so softly, so tenderly and gently. To be treated with such intimate respect. Quietly, I cross the parquet floor to the patio doors, skirts swirling around my feet.

Malin shifts tempo, his chin drops, and the very top of his gold branding shines just below the curl. I don't know how I'll make it through tomorrow kneeling at the base of the Warden's throne without giving myself away. I wish we didn't need the knife to destroy the bastard that did this to Malin. If I could, I'd tear the Warden's lifeline from his chest. Shatter it. I stare at the forest across the lawns and shove the thought away.

I open my eyes and lean against the doorframe, staring out into the dusk. If there were stars, it would be perfect. Dew already gathers on the grass beyond the veranda, velvet rose petals shimmer in the light from the parlour, and the path to the forest is sheened silver by a nonexistent moon.

The forest itself is dark and shadowy and coloured in shades of grey.

Malin's music winds around me. The tune is familiar, but one I can't place. Thorn witches have little need for music and the Warden is not known for his indulgence in the arts. I was parched and I had no idea. My father played the violin once, before his fingers were gauntleted in gold. So I drink Malin's music in until I'm intoxicated.

The piano sings without words, paints without canvas in brilliant colour a meandering stream through woodland glens and bluebelled spaces between green leafy trees. And it's so real, I want to cry.

The rhythm changes into a garden with sparkling fountains and orchids lined up in rows. A waltz emerges, the beat taking precedence over the story it tells. I sigh as the magic begins to evaporate, surprised to find my cheeks wet. I didn't mean to cry.

A tap on my shoulder startles me. I whirl around, and Malin is there. Right there. So close I should have sensed him in the movement of his breath on my skin. I blink up at him stupidly, look at the piano on the other side of the parlour, and back at him. "Who's playing?"

"The manor," Malin replies. He's amused by something. There's a warmth to his tone that shines in his eyes. "Dance with me?"

I blink at him again, and he lets out a quiet huff.

"You do know how to dance?"

I do, but I'm still trying to place the music. It conjures memories so clear I can almost taste them, yet I cannot anchor it. I taste sugar-shelled almonds and smell caramelised sugar, toffee apples and marshmallow fluff and spiced cider made from the first summer pears. I see my grandmother wearing her silver-thorned crown, dancing a waltz with my father, beneath a star-laden sky; I hear my own giggles as my father whirls me into a kaleidoscope of jewel-coloured dresses and spins me around the blossom tree that never goes out of flower.

"Penny?" Mal says softly, jerking me out of the past. His hand is offered, palm upturned.

The room spins as he pulls me close, one hand on the small of my back, and I press my fingers against his shoulder. I can feel the beat of his heart, a reminder of what was done to him, how he was chained here, alive and vital and so horribly restrained. There are no steps to our dance. No keeping up with the music or staying in time. The manor dances with us, matching its rhythm to our tentative tempo, and building its song to our silent words.

The lights dim and candles reflect like a thousand stars in silver-framed mirrors that now cover the walls. The furniture has vanished and the curtains are turquoise velvet fringed with silver where they're looped back from the wide-open glass double doors.

We dance until we forget what comes next.

"May I show you something?" Malin whispers.

"Is it your tower?" I grin.

His hand tightens on my waist and butterflies explode in my chest as he presses me harder against him. "Are you going to let me forget that?"

"Unlikely," I gasp.

"If you'll let me, I'd like to show you my home."

A million questions collide into one another, but Malin looks so vulnerable, like he's just dropped a defence I didn't even know was there. I smile and let him lead me away. The piano music fades as we walk down a hallway glittering with magic. There's a door at the end that is old and painted red. Dots of silver and black swirling lines might have made a design once. The paint is faded and little stick figures are scratched into the wood. A man and a woman holding hands, a little person beside them with a huge childish smile.

This door is real, not an illusion like the rest of the manor. This door will not change, no matter Malin's mood. The breath catches in my throat, a subtle hitch in my inhale that shudders through Malin's shoulders.

He unlocks it with a rose-engraved key and holds it open. A spiral stair lies beyond, carved in pale stone as if from one solid rock, seamless and pristine. I step into the dark stairwell; Malin ducks his head to follow, and closes the door, sealing out the light. Coal black blankets my sight, but I hear his movements, the scuff of his feet on stone.

He finds my hand in the pitch dark and begins to climb, up and up to the top of his tower. Outside the window is shrouded in the clouds, concealing the view beyond frost-glazed panes. A fire roars in the hearth, filling the room with cosy warmth. There are no fancy flourishes in here. A desk sits below one window, the cherrywood top so satiny smooth, I want to run my fingers across it. A glass-shaded lamp sits upon a tan leather mat, reflecting the firelight though the oil is not lit. A cloth-bound book sits beside it, his place marked with a red satin ribbon.

Malin watches me take in his room. The bed is shoved against one wall, heavy black velvet drapes tied neatly back to posts at each corner, the wood so dark it might be black. "This was my one safe space for so many years," he says. "When the loneliness got too much, I'd come here and know I was real. This was real. It's what's outside this room that's not." He looks at me with such wonder, such gentle longing, that my breath catches. "Now," he says, "you're real too."

He smiles and pulls me into him, cupping my face, so gently, so carefully, and he kisses me softly, as if I might vanish if he closes his eyes.

"It's a very nice tower, Malin." I smile against his lips.

He groans. Want gives way to need in his gaze. "I was trying to be honest."

"So was I." I push onto tiptoe and press against him. A low growl in Malin's chest vibrates through my core, and my hands tangle in his hair as his lips meet mine.

He tastes like chocolate and hope and a future that cannot be ours. His hold on me tightens as he tips my head back to claim me. Need deepens and darkens, and I want more. More than the kiss on top of the crystal. More than a dance in the dark. So much more. I arch into him as calloused fingers brush along my cheek. He wants me. As badly as I want him.

"Please," I whisper.

He exhales harshly and unpeels my hands from his neck, catching my wrists so I can't reclaim my hold. "Are you sure?"

"I've never been surer of anything. Please, Malin."

"Penny," he says softly, but his eyes, Holy Dark Mother, his eyes are liquid night. Longing fills them—desperate and hungry. Husky words, low and deep, mirror the warning in his gaze. "You coming here every night...it was torture, not telling you how I felt, or asking if you felt it too. When I thought I'd lost you to the gilding, I've never been so terrified. Once you're mine, I won't let go, I won't let anything hurt you again. Tell me you want me too."

He bends to press his lips to the sensitive spot below my ear, his breath caressing my throat as he releases my wrists. The thin fabric of my dress is barely a barrier between us. His mouth lingers so close to mine. "Say you want me," he says again, his words brushing against my lips.

I taste him. Inhale him. Breathe him in.

"Of course I want you. I've wanted you since I first met you."

With a groan, he kisses me, hard and soft and searching. He pushes me gently back toward his bed. Hesitates. My fingers shake as I slip my dress off my shoulders. Warm air hits my skin as it puddles on the floor at my feet.

He swallows hard as he drinks me in, his gaze slowly devouring my curves. "You are the most beautiful thing I've ever seen." He presses my shoulders gently, making me sit on the edge of the bed.

My fingers clench on the bedspread to stop myself wrapping my arms to cover my chest. No one has ever looked at me like this. The expression in his eyes terrifies me and ignites something deep inside. Liquid heat floods my veins with fire and life and yearning. I am terrified but I have never wanted anything more than this.

He strips his shirt over his head, undoes his belt, his pants hit the floor. My eyes travel over his skin, taking him in as he did me. Firelight traces the dips between muscles, shadows dance along the groove running from his hips to his—oh!

My eyes widen slightly. I suck my lip between my teeth at his soft chuckle. The bedspread crinkles tighter in my hands.

He leans over me, his fingers splay to cover mine, tangled in the sheets. Warmth radiates between us. Stubble scuffs against my cheek, and his whisper sends shivers of longing down an invisible thread joining my heart and my navel. “Penny.” He says my name like a prayer, like it tastes of honey on his tongue.

“Please.” It’s barely a word. It’s all I can say.

His exhale is half growl, half purr as he gently untangles my fingers. “I promised myself I wouldn’t do this.” He spreads me on the bed, pressing my hands into the pillow, and kneels over me. “So many nights I told myself I wouldn’t, I couldn’t. That you’d never want me. And now—” He moves closer and brushes his thumb across my bottom lip. “Now, you do.”

A whispered gasp catches in my throat and I reach for him, tangling my fingers in his hair and pulling him down. This kiss isn’t gentle or searching. It takes me. Owns me. I crumble with the depth of it, the stroke of his tongue—the pressure of his hand sliding to my hips.

I can’t breathe. I don’t want to breathe. My fingers dig into his forearm, whimpering softly as his kisses flow down my abdomen.

Then, I’m floating, and Malin anchors me. My fingers clench on his wrists and I shatter with his name on my lips.

He moves so his mouth crushes mine before I recover, bruising and gentle, and I tremble as he eases himself to press against me. His lips inch away and I want them back. “Have you done this before?”

I hesitate and shake my head. “Not like this.”

“Are you sure you want to?”

I nod, unable to form words.

“I’ll be gentle.” He kisses me softly, his fingers tracing my jaw as he moves. I gasp, tensing at the sharpness of the pain, and he freezes, his back granite-hard beneath my fingers. The only sound is our breath, quick and gasping. His heart pounds against his ribs, and I feel it against mine. “Do you want to stop?”

I shake my head and try to breathe but my ribs are caught halfway between wanting, desperately, and the thin edges of fear that this will hurt worse.

"Relax," he murmurs. I do and he waits. Then, brushing a strand of hair off my cheek, he whispers, "It won't hurt anymore."

He smiles, softly lethal.

Oh. My eyes fly wide, locking with his. He's gentle. Careful. Whispers of pleasure coil around us, through us, binding me to him and him to me tighter than our lifelines. He takes me to the edge where I shattered before. Past it. My eyes flutter shut. My nails dig into his back, and I'm falling. He catches me, holding me to his chest as we break together.

Our breathing slows, sweat chilling my skin as he moves off me carefully, pulling the bedcovers up, and I turn so my back presses into his chest. We fit together like we were made to lie like this, designed by some higher being to curl in the flickering firelight. I sigh softly as his fingers trail my arm.

Tired satisfaction weighs my eyes, and as I drift to sleep in the safety of his embrace, he whispers into my hair, "Forgive me."

He wakes me before dawn and climbs from the bed, stooping to reclaim his clothes. Buttoning his shirt, he shrugs his jacket over the top. "We have to go back."

I rub the sleep from my eyes and sit up, watching the way he moves, how the lines of his muscles catch the light and cling to the shadows. "I don't want to."

"Neither do I. It's just one day."

"And we cease to exist."

"And it'll be over. The knife will be forged and no one will hurt you anymore." He sighs, glancing at the clock on the mantelpiece. He looks so worried, I don't have the heart to state the obvious and tell him I'd rather hurt than simply not exist at all. "Hurry or we'll be missed."

"Malin?" He picks up my dress off the floor, checks the crystals are still in the pocket, and hands it to me. I slip it over my head, watching him carefully. "How do you know how much time we have before we're missed?"

"Because," he says, gallantly holding open the door, "I asked Alice. You should really talk to her more."

"Did you tell her you intended to show me your tower?"

He snorts a laugh as he starts down the stairs. "No, Penny. I didn't mention the tower."

"Thank you." I giggle and grab his hand. "For showing me. I very much enjoyed it."

We descend the spiral stairs into the dark, our laughter fading away into silence.

Chapter Forty

We barely make it back before there's a knock on my door. Malin answers, his hair all dishevelled and sticking up at adorably odd angles. He's completely naked except for a sheet! Idiot. Why didn't he imagine clothes as we crossed? This morning I'm wearing a most respectable nightgown with a deep pocket for the crystals we grew in Death. Malin, however, doesn't seem even slightly fazed to be wearing absolutely nothing. I hear him answer the door and try to regain my composure. Anyone glancing at me would know exactly what happened between him and I last night—and what it meant.

I'm supposed to be the Warden's Gilded pet, Malin's plaything, emotionless and empty. There should be nothing behind my eyes. But there is. *I* am behind my eyes, and I don't know how to hide anymore. Malin's voice rises, and I slide my friends' crystals in their velvet bags under the mattress and curl on my side, closing my eyes and pretending to be asleep. The bedroom door slams open and an obsidian-armoured Gilded marches in.

My father.

He hauls me out of bed by the top of the arm. "Warden's orders," he snaps, his voice cold as ice.

Malin grumbles, "She's mine until lunchtime. That was the deal."

"Not today," the Gilded-who-used-to-be-my-father replies. "He said to tell you, you may have her this evening."

Ice slides down my spine, and I pin my eyes on the floor. If anyone is going to notice I am *me* behind my mask, it will be my father. He releases me and barks, "Get dressed."

Malin squares his shoulders and steps between us. "Get out."

The Gilded straightens. My heart stops. He's the same height as Malin. They glare at each other while I try to stare at my feet. I want to tell Malin not to do this, that it doesn't matter, that we're too close to the end to risk the fallout of this altercation. The Gilded snaps first, "The Warden ordered—"

"Right at this moment, I do not give one tiny little rat's shit who ordered what," Malin says coolly. "I am stark-bollock naked, you woke me an hour earlier than I prefer to be woken, and my father will not thank you for bringing him his Death-Weaver dressed in her nightgown before she's brushed her teeth. So get out of my rooms, wait in the hall, and I will bring her to you when I am finished with her. Do you understand me?" I've never heard Malin sound more like his father. I've never been so glad he does.

My father's jaw clenches. He swallows audibly and his hand tightens into a fist at his side. I risk a glance from below my lashes; anger sparks in his eyes as he stares at Malin, but Malin's already turned away and seems to be choosing a shirt from the armoire.

He barks, "Five minutes."

"Get out," Malin replies chirpily.

My father marches out, the hallway door slams, and I sag with relief into the bed. Malin turns, worry written in every line of him. "Alice didn't tell me this," he whispers. "Why didn't she see this?" He pulls a clean white dress off a hanger and throws it on the bed. "What changed? Something must have changed."

His anxiety is rubbing off on me and I can't walk out of here with fear in my eyes. "Stop it!" I hiss softly. "Please, Malin, stop. I need to go and deal with the Warden, and if he sees me like this... It was hard enough yesterday. If the Warden notices a difference, this is over. We should have forged—"

Malin cuts me off with a slice of his hand through the air. "Go to the bathroom."

His jaw clenches, and I hear a scrape of a chair in the sitting room, the sound of someone taking a seat. I hurry into the bathroom and lock the door, rushing through my morning routine. I fight myself calm as I pin my hair neatly back and clean my teeth. When I emerge, my eyes are completely blank and emotionless. Malin gives me a once-over and whispers, "Be careful."

"They're under the mattress," I reply under my breath and tap my chest where my crystal would hang if I was allowed to wear it. Malin nods once in confirmation and pushes me out the door.

My father sits at the dining table. He stands as I stumble in, and without saying a word, he takes the top of my arm and marches me away.

"Bring her back when he's done," Malin growls after us. "I want her returned unharmed."

"Bastard," my father mutters and my eyes snap up. My father stares at me.

I blink at him foolishly.

"Eyes down, little Death-Weaver," he orders, but it's not as cold as before. His hand on my arm doesn't hurt today either. What the heck has happened? It's like I walked into Death last night and the world changed direction without me.

I'm still confused when he shoves me into the Warden's suite of rooms, still reeling when the Warden orders me to his side. Alice is not here, as she normally is. I drop obediently to my knees, folding myself to the floor at his feet, and bow my head, trying not to gag at the smell this close to his wound.

The Warden is terrifyingly cheerful this morning. His mask lies on the sofa beside him, and I try not to look upon his face. "Good morning, Death-Weaver," he says, and his voice is stronger than it normally is when I'm summoned to heal him. "You must forgive me our little change in routine. With our upcoming entertainments, I find myself otherwise engaged for the rest of the day. But I thought, I know my little thorn princess will indulge me. Was I right, my pet?"

"I am yours to command." I hate him. I've never hated anyone as much as I hate him.

"Excellent," he says. The sofa protests as he leans forward, and his fingers catch my chin, making me meet his gaze. I hide my fear in silently reciting the words of the spell—the spell I'll use to forge the knife and end him. It's worth it. Any price is worth toppling this tyrant from his throne. "I'll almost miss you when this is done," he says, his words oily and dark. Fear knifes between my ribs as he inspects my eyes, and I make myself smile softly, the picture of a girl as lost as lost can be. Apparently satisfied, he sits back. He smiles as he hitches his robe up, exposing his wound, which has decayed since yesterday. "Heal me."

I close my eyes. When I rest my hands on his lifeline, I shove hard against the binding deal I made with Malin in Death, searching for a path around my oath to never to heal the Warden. I don't care anymore if my soul belongs to Malin. He's welcome to it. We just have to survive long enough to forge the knife and give the others a chance. Sweat prickles down my spine, my head hurts with the effort, but I find a thread of magic, a spark of power that evaded my grasp when I had the Warden's lifeline in my hands before. By some grace of a deity I wish I could go back to not believing in, I manage to prise enough magic loose to soften the brittleness of his disease. Maybe enough to convince him I am trying. Enough to make him complacent in my gilding.

I sit back on my heels, breath gasping. My hands are shaking. Oh, Holy Dark Mother, let it be enough. We only have to get through today. One day. My chest hurts and my eyes sting and my magic burns in my blood, a painful protest at what I made it do. The Warden pats me on the head, all patronising encouragement, and apologises that I must be returned to my rooms. "Maybe I'll find time for you later," he says and some of the gravel in his tone is gone. He sounds stronger. "Would you like that, my pet?"

I nod and whisper my thanks, and he laughs.

"Return her to my wayward son. Let him enjoy her while he still can."

My blood chills in my veins. My head is spinning too much when my Gilded father hauls me to my feet and half carries me away. I make it out the door before my knees buckle. Darkness closes in at the edges of my vision and the world around me rocks and sways. I've strained myself, forced my magic to work against a promise made in blood.

I feel myself lifted. I'm caught between waking thoughts and dreams. I hear confused words, murmurs in a voice that used to be my father's. Someone tells me to hold on. Just a bit longer.

Then everything goes black.

When I prise open my eyes, I'm in Malin's bed and Alice is sitting beside me. The sky outside the window is a bruised, heavy twilight waiting for stars. Alice's fingers squeeze mine, and I burst into tears.

It is late and I have to forge a knife that will take my life and I have no time left to be me.

My last hours were spent pandering to a diseased monster and recovering from the side effects of it. I swallow hard, push away my tears, and wrap my arms around her neck. "I wish I could have said goodbye to everyone. Mother and Ella and..."

"Penny, it's all right. I promise." Her arms slide around my waist and she holds me close.

I don't want to leave her behind. "I think we've run out of time."

"Tonight isn't the end of us." She sounds so sure. She's never been more wrong. Malin and I can't possibly survive this.

"Don't, Alice. Please. Don't make it worse. There isn't a way out of this."

"There's always another way, Penny."

"Always." It's a hollow promise with no hope of fulfilment. "I'm sorry."

Alice pulls back to kiss me gently and presses her forehead lightly against mine. "Don't be sorry. You were sorry before and it was not your fault. Today is not your fault, either."

I wrap myself in the shawl Alice has put on the end of the bed. "Where's Malin?"

"He'll be here soon." Alice plays with the edge of the shawl, and the fringing tickles my arm. "It will all be fine."

I frown, my thoughts still fuzzy from sleep. I don't want this to be the end. "It's not fair."

"I know you don't believe me," Alice says softly, brushing her fingers along my cheekbone just below the mask where my skin is damp from tears. "But one day, you and I will have all the time in all the worlds to be together. When it gets hard. Tonight. What comes after. Remember that. We *will* survive this. All three of us, I promise."

"Did you weave it?"

She shakes her head. "I can't see you, Penny. I can't see me or Malin either. I have faith in us."

I wish I could believe her, I do.

"Stop it," Alice says and presses another kiss to my lips.

"What comes next? After life. Beyond the Horizon."

"I can't see that either." She sighs, her eyes shining with hope. "Something better than this. There is no end. And tonight is not yours. Or Malin's. Or mine. Come and sit by the window. And breathe."

I sigh and curl with her in the window seat. I stop fighting her and just hold her hand. We watch the Gilded march out for the night patrols. Watch the first star prick the darkening sky. Dante and Clair leave the barracks and cross the courtyard, and Dante trips on the flagstone I watched the rebellious ore witch raise, what seems like years ago.

Clair's lips twitch with hidden laughter and she glances up to our window. We watch them go inside. We watch the last of the twilight descend into night, and then Alice says quietly, "It's nearly time."

I let Alice hang my crystal around my neck as we wait for the bell to chime, for midnight to sound, and for the Resistance to knock on our door.

When they come, it isn't Tobias or Dante or Clair. On the other side of the panel is my mother. And I've never been so relieved or scared at the same time.

Her eyes are exhausted, her skin is so pale, and her hair is dull, braided loosely down her back. She looks like she could sleep for an entire week, but she's as strong as ever when she gathers me into her arms and holds me tight. I close my eyes against my tears. In her embrace, all the tension drains out of me. Just for a moment, I'm a child again. Mother is safety. She is home. The scent of the glass-house clings to her skin, beautifully deadly flowers hiding delicately lethal poisons, all blended with Mother's lavender perfume.

I sob and my shoulders heave.

Mother rubs my back like she did when I was little and I'd scraped my knee. "Oh, Penny." Her voice catches. "Don't cry."

"I'm scared," I confess into her shoulder. Her shift is damp with my tears.

"Don't be." She swallows, and I feel her breath hitch.

"Tell Ella I love her."

"You can tell her yourself." Mother steps back to hold me by the shoulders and looks at me, properly. Pain flashes in her eyes and I try to turn away. I didn't think it would hurt, seeing my mother take in the mask, my gilding. But I forget, she's done this before. "Penelope Albright," she says firmly, "look at me."

I do. And now all I see is her love shining back at me.

She releases me and wipes away my tears with a black lace handkerchief. Her fingers trace the outline of my mask. "You are the bravest, most beautiful witch I have ever seen, and I have never been prouder of you. You've faced the impossible and won. You'll win again."

"I mean to try." I bite my lip to stop myself crying all over again. "Don't go."

She gives me a sad smile. "No, petal. I'll be here right until the end."

And with the next knock on the door, the end begins.

"Penny," she says quietly as Alice goes to let Malin in. Her words are hard, her silver eyes bright with anger. "Let's make that bastard pay."

I cling to my mother's hand through the catacomb tunnels to the Resistance temple, where we'll forge the knife. She tells me again as we reach the Resistance doors that she loves me and not to be scared.

Then, she smiles at Alice. "This isn't the end."

"I told Penny that, but she refuses to listen."

"Penny has always been as stubborn as the day is long. You'll get used to it."

Malin joins us at the entranceway; Mother gives him a respectful nod, then kisses me on the forehead. "Stay strong, my darling. When the time comes, you have to say goodbye and let go. It's all right to let go. Try and remember that." Then, she goes to take her seat, but I see the hard shine in her eyes.

If I wasn't frightened before, I am now.

I push the tapestry aside.

The Resistance temple is half-full tonight; row after row of black-masked members all gathered to watch the reforging of the Sorcerer's knife. I had no idea we'd have an audience. It's not as many as last time I was here, but hundreds fill the rows of seats closest to the altar. It seems twisted to want to watch someone die.

"What if the magic goes wrong?" I whisper to Malin.

"I won't let it." He sounds stern, but he's worried too. "You're not doing this alone."

"But what if—"

Malin takes my hand and holds it tight. "I can tell them I've changed my mind?"

I shake my head.

Alice catches my other hand. "Penny, do you trust me?"

I nod.

"This is the beginning of his end, not yours. You will survive."

"But does everyone else?"

Alice's eyes shine too bright and she looks away. "Everyone who needs to." My heart plummets when she squeezes my hand and presses her lips together.

"Malin!" I look to him for reassurance, he gives me none.

"Just focus on us," he says, his voice gruff. "We do this now, or you say the word and we leave, Penny. I'll take you far away from here where the Warden can never touch you again."

I exhale shakily. That place doesn't exist, but that he believes it does is enough. Turning away from safety feels like a choice, and I will not leave everyone else behind. And I owe the Warden.

"Are we doing this?" Malin asks, and it's a gentle question. If I say no, he'll turn us around and take me away from this—the knife, the Sorcerer, the Resistance. He'll stand between me and them if I ask him to.

I nod, and a hush falls as Malin and I step inside. A grain of sand would echo in the silence as Malin and Alice and I walk down the aisle to the altar. The other witches are already here, each with their crystal.

Dante, the huge palace guard, lays a perfect replica of the Sorcerer's knife carved from black wax in the tray in the centre of the altar. Sand from Death's deserts fills it. A detail missing from their previous attempts. Mila brought this back last night. Beatrice and Evelyn stand to one side of me, Gail and Sybil to the other, and Mila faces me, their crystals resting in their palms.

Five little half-circles are carved into the wax knife's hilt.

Gail lays her crystal in the dip closest to the pommel. Blue as the sky, it flickers with lightning and swirls with white clouds of storm magic. She shudders as she releases it. Her magic is contained inside that crystal. She grips the edge of the altar to stop herself snatching it back.

These witches will survive the forging. Their crystals aren't bound to their lifelines; they cannot anchor them to walk in Death as the Thorn Coven witches do.

But if the crystals shatter, they'll lose their magic. Forever. It seems almost as bad as being cast adrift and anchorless.

Sybil is next. A green crystal, waves crashing in foamy bottomless depths inside.

After she places it, she clings to Gail's arm, her eyes fixed on the handle of the knife.

Beatrice is all business, simply setting her crystal in its spot and folding her arms. But the light in her eyes dims and her lashes sparkle. Copper and gold shimmer in the heart of the yellow crystal.

Evelyn presses hers in so hard she nearly cracks the wax. Hers is fiery like her eyes, flickering as it lies there, innocently waiting.

Mila swallows hard. When this is done there'll be no more walking in Death, no Thorn Throne in her future. Next time she crosses the veil, she'll die like anyone else. She won't be able to return to Life; the only way out will be the bright line of the Horizon.

Something in me eases when I see the look of relief on her face as she sets her crystal neatly in the dip closest to the blade. In some ways, she is shedding a burden she never asked to carry.

Her crystal shines purple, and rainbows swirl as if she walks in Death even here.

We're so close, I can almost taste the cool chill of Death's airless breeze.

My friends' lifelines flicker and spark as they stare at the offerings they've made.

I run my hand over the wax hilt, checking the crystals. Power lurches from each one in unfamiliar waves of magic.

Except Mila's.

I check again.

Nothing.

She frowns. "Penny? What's wrong?"

I stare at her across the altar, horrified. "Your crystal. It's fake! Mila, *what did you do*?"

She steps back, confused. "I took it from Grandmother's glass case, Pen. It can't be fake."

"I don't know how, but it is." I believe her, though. She is not a good enough actress to fake the confusion and shock flickering across her features.

Dante doesn't.

He grabs her arm. "I said you were the traitor. Right from the start!" I lurch toward her, but he yanks her out of reach. "Damned thorn witches."

"Let go of my sister!"

Ella tries to rise from her seat, but Clair grips her wrist. Bea glares at Evelyn in silent warning.

Alice rescues me—and Mila. "It's not her, Dante. We established Mila is loyal to the Resistance. After what she's done, I trust her." Alice drifts to my side, runs her fingers over the crystals, and one by one the other witches shiver at Alice's delicate touch. She stares straight at Mila, who's turned deathly pale. "You got it from the cabinet?"

Mila nods, her eyes filling with tears.

"It is fake," Alice says. "I think..."

"Think what, dear?" Miss Elsweather asks encouragingly.

Alice ignores her. "Penny, I should have seen it before."

"Seen what?" I ask, trying not to panic.

"How the Warden controls your grandmother."

Mila sags in Dante's hold, bracing her hands against the altar, realisation widening her eyes. "*That's* why she handed Penny over without a fight?"

Alice turns black eyes on me. "The Warden has all the thorns' crystals, Penny. They're all fake."

My head spins. I need to sit down. Everything suddenly makes sense: why Grandmother kept the crystals behind warded glass, why she obeyed the Warden without question, why she disowned me so completely. Beatrice tries to comfort me with a pat on the shoulder, but I shrug her off, shoving down my grandmother's decade of secrets and lies. "We need a thorn witch's crystal. We can't forge the knife without one."

Miss Elsweather presses a cold black crystal into my hand. "Here."

I stare at it, confused. Is this mine? But it can't be. My crystal is around my neck on a silver chain with my and Malin's lifelines weighing it down. "How did you...?"

"Don't ask questions, dear," she says. "It's a long and extremely private story. Rest assured, they gave their consent and were in their right mind when they gave it."

"With no thorn witch here to offer their magic, the blackest crystal in the world won't save the spell."

"They're on their way. Dante, release Mila, please. Mila, dear, come sit with me and Alice."

Alice leads a trembling Mila away.

I don't like placing this mysterious black crystal into the hilt. It's deeper than midnight, and swirling darker than the obsidian of mine. Magic sparks inside it, winding threads like the stems of Malin's roses in Death. I wish I knew whose it was, but when I look to Miss Elsweather for answers, she shakes her head. We watch as Beatrice closes the lid of the sandbox, and carefully I pour more of Death's sand into a hole in the top, packing it down with a small metal stick.

"Ready?" Beatrice asks through gritted teeth. Around the altar, the witches nod, one by one. Sybil whispers a quiet goodbye to her crystal and her magic. Evelyn's eyes harden, but her hands shake as she grips the altar edge. Gail sways on her feet as Bea's magic begins to rise.

Panic swirls around my ribs. The gold altar melts around the edges, and I'm terrified I've gotten it wrong. I remember what happened when Haylea tried. If I mess this up, I'll tangle my friends in the veil. Streams of molten gold wind into the hole at the top of the lid and run inside, melting the wax, and the whole temple, the whole Resistance holds their breath.

I watch my friends shiver as the heat hits their crystals. Magic trembles in their eyes. And the gold bubbles out the top of the box.

A chill of magic slides across the space, slipping up the altar and gripping our wrists.

Dante exhales sharply. "We've never gotten this far before."

"We're not there yet," Malin helpfully replies.

Silently, Beatrice unclasps the top and lifts away the box. Gail gently brushes the sand clear and Sybil rinses the blade cool and clean. Evelyn lifts it from the sand, a perfect re-creation of the picture from the Grimoire.

The Sorcerer's elusive knife.

It's the most beautiful thing I've ever seen. The crystals sparkle with a gentle pulsing beat. The blade is already lethally sharp.

All that's left is to forge the magic.

But the thorn witch whose crystal lies in the hilt of the knife is not here.

Miss Elsweather gives us a nod, indicating we should continue, but we can't start without the missing witch.

As if hearing my anxiety, Malin rests a hand on the small of my back. "They'll be here, don't worry."

Alice's hand slips into mine. "Focus, Penny," she whispers. "Together?"

I swallow hard, fight back my tears, and reply, "Always."

There is power in words, for those who know how to wield them and how to listen. And I have lived my life buried in them.

The first are hard. I'm torn between the spell I've memorised until I could chant it backward in my sleep and fear at what comes next. Alice adds her voice to the spell, weaving her gentle magic into mine. I want to tell her to step back, but the spell has gripped me and I can't stop. If I stop, the power welling in my blood, creeping into my lifeline, and brimming in my fingers will latch on to something, something solid, and bring the temple crashing down around us.

I'm running before a flooding tide and I've forgotten how to swim.

Sybil whispers, "Go with it, Penny. Don't fight the current."

Evelyn wraps her fingers around my wrist. Beatrice hands me the knife and grips my forearm. Sybil shivers as she joins hands with Beatrice, Gail exhales and closes the circle around me.

But the thorn witch who gave up their crystal still has not come.

The spell's words crawl from the knife into my hands, they sneak across my skin to wrap my friends, winding up their arms like ink flowing from a pen onto a page, but there's a gap I can't fill.

A door opens with a crash. Two Gilded step out from a door behind the altar. A metal hand clamps on my shoulder.

Mila cries a little cry and rushes forward. Mother is on her feet, Ella at her side, and we recognise the Gilded at the same time.

Father.

His eyes are his—not cold. Not soulless. My father smiles, and this is a warm smile; the hand on my shoulder is gentle. And Tobias is with him. Somehow, that's more reassuring than my father's eyes.

The spell crawls under Father's armour and inks across his cheek.

The black crystal is his.

I want to ask *how*, but I can't. When I look at Alice and then at Malin, they're as shocked as me. Alice did not see this end. My heart squeezes and forgets how to beat as the words of the spell fall from my lips.

My father brushes a thumb against my mother's cheek, and tears stream down her face. *I love you*, she says. An eternity of love in a whisper. Her wedding ring flashes as she wraps Mila and Ella in a hug and pulls them away.

I have a million questions, but magic rages in my veins. Pain stabs in my heart. And I have no words left to ask anything. I want to say hello, tell my father I love him, that I thought I could save him. All I can manage is a wordless goodbye.

This is it. This is where it ends. The first thread of my lifeline unravels from my fingers and into the knife, binding the crystals into the gold. Tendrils of blue fire surge from the centre of the altar, searing my lifeline away as it wraps the hilt, forging the Sorcerer's new knife in fire and pain and magic.

Strand by obsidian strand, my lifeline smoulders and singes, melting into metal and gemstone, and the pain is my undoing.

Burning is excruciating, but it is not endless—that pain loosens my soul so I can step from my body.

This pain anchors me. It binds me and winds through my blood and it will not let me go.

A scream wells, but I can't breathe to set it free. Tears burn my eyes. Malin whispers to let go. I feel the steady weight of his hands on my shoulders. His lifeline falls with mine; bound together, they are destroyed together. My knees buckle, and he wraps me in his arms. I'm slipping, and so is he.

Black threatens my vision, and Tobias pushes it away with a hand pressed against my cheek. But it's not enough. Nothing will be enough to stop this. Numbness floods from my fingers as the last tattered threads of my lifeline fray, disconnecting *me* from myself.

"Fight," Tobias whispers.

I have nothing left to fight with. The pieces of me are scattering to the wind, burning into the embers of Malin for eternity. Pain takes my senses. Pain takes my name.

Alice returns it. "Penny," she whispers. "Let go."

But I can't. I can't. I can't.

I feel nothing. I hear nothing. See nothing. I am nothing. Then, in the nothing is a something. Another lifeline wraps the last thread of mine. Pain softens as the lifeline burrows into my chest. I prise my eyes open, and my hearing returns.

My father says quietly, "Let go, Penny. Let go. It's all right. I've got you."

Tears stream down my cheeks as *me* reforms inside myself. Malin's eyes clear, and my father's dim. The little girl I used to be, the one that wants to go home, to cling to her father, to forget I'm supposed to be a grown witch, whispers, "Daddy?"

He brushes his thumb across my cheeks, wiping away my tears. "I am so proud of you, sweetheart. You, and Mila and Ella. Tell them that for me. Let go, Penny. Let me end this. I love you."

"I wanted to heal you. I thought I could—" But my father, the man who I longed to bring back, unpeels my fingers from the knife. My lifeline winds around Malin's as it reforms and digs so deep in my soul it will never uproot. My father's slides from his chest, replacing mine around the knife. The barbs heal as it does, silver deepening to obsidian black. His lifeline sparkles before it vanishes. He gives it up so I can live.

My father nods at my mother, and Mother says quietly, "Finish the spell, Penny."

But I can't kill my father.

For a moment, I cling to the hope I had, of my father back with us, of home the way it was before. All of us together again. And then, even though I know it will hurt, ever so gently, I let it go. I open my mouth and recite the last words: "Flammae ac fumo."

One hand pressed against his chest, my father drops to his knees. The gold mask falls. I see my father's face, whole and perfect one last time before his outline fades. And I don't know where he's gone. Magic leaves in a rush that drains the strength from my bones. Malin catches me as I crumple, and Alice's fingers run through my hair as she murmurs, "Three threads into one. I thought it was me." There's sorrow in her eyes. Tears on her lashes. "I thought I could save you."

Malin's voice is strained. "You did, Alice. Look." The knife is in Beatrice's hand, shimmering with power, and around it, the air trembles. Bea holds it out, offering it to me, but I don't want to touch it. It stole my father. It should have taken me.

"No," Alice replies, her eyes flying wide. "I didn't. They're coming."

There's a crash in the hall. The tapestry covering the doorway wafts in the wind. The clock chimes midnight.

Chaos reigns.

The first wave of Gilded march into the temple, fire running from their hands and onto the floor. The Resistance guards at the door are cut down before they have time to react. The back rows of the audience are incinerated so precisely their chairs aren't even scorched. I try to step away, but my knees shake and I stagger into the altar. Malin's hand is gone from my back. He steps between me and the approaching carnage.

Tobias shouts, "Get them out of here. For fuck's sake, get them out!"

A hand clamps on my arm as the Resistance try to retaliate. Another row becomes smoke and ash on a wind that rushes into the temple as a second wave of Gilded march inside.

I'm dragged sideways as the wind begins to circle with a roar. The Gilded's eyes flash blue with storm magic. Alice's hand is yanked from mine. I can't see her. I can't see Malin. I try to pull away as the floor ripples. Ore magic. A new regiment of Gilded or the Resistance fighting back? Smoke blinds me, chokes me.

A hard voice snaps in my ear, "Move, now."

"No," I choke out. "The knife."

"Too late," the voice growls. "We need to get you out." The hand tightens on my arm as the first gold sword flashes. The smoke clears in a waft of Gilded magic, and I see him. The Warden. Watching everything with a smile on his lips. And I think there's a thorn witch standing at his side. He doesn't see me. Not yet.

Bea yells, "You bitch."

She chokes into silence.

I scream. Finally, after everything. I scream.

A hand slams over my mouth. I scream into his fingers. In the chaos and confusion, I can't see who wraps an arm around me and picks me up. He takes me away, carrying me behind the altar and out the door my father and Tobias came through only minutes before. Then I'm in a corridor and he's shoving me into the wall. Dante, the brute of a palace guard who threatened my sister. His hand presses hard into my mouth, almost cutting off my air as people run past us, desperate to get away. He leans closer. "You can't help them if you keep screaming."

I nod, and he releases me. "Alice?" I gasp.

"I don't know."

"Malin?"

Dante sneers. "Don't care."

But Malin is alive and unharmed, I feel it in our lifeline. Alice can't be hurt, I won't let her be hurt. I open my mouth to ask about Mila and Ella, Beatrice and Evelyn, Sybil and Gail, Tobias and Clair. An explosion blasts down the tunnel, throwing us into the wall. Dante shields me from the worst of it, holding me on my feet and swearing under his breath.

In the ringing of the aftermath, he says quietly, "If I thought we could help, I'd go back. Believe me, I'd go back. Those are my people in there. But there is nothing I can do, and I swore I'd get you out if anything went wrong."

I want to argue, but thorn magic is no match against the Gilded in Life. As if hearing my thoughts, a shout ends any hope we had left. "The knife is secured. And the witches with it."

The Warden's order echoes down the tunnel. "Seal them in. Let them all burn."

I duck under Dante's arm, slide out of his grip, and run. Back to where I left Malin and Alice and Bea and my sisters and my mother. My family and friends. My legs hurt and my head pounds and I run.

The ore Gilded slam the rock closed. The tunnel is sealed.

Silence falls and I can do nothing.

Everyone in the temple will die for nothing.

I forged the knife and the Warden has taken it.

Strong hands take my shoulders and turn me, walk me down the tunnel away from everything that meant anything in my life.

The Resistance burns tonight. And I cannot help them.

Dante keeps me stumbling along a tunnel that slopes down and down. We pass blank-eyed, horrified Resistance members. The ground is littered with their discarded masks. I look around, desperately trying to see through the dark to work out who escaped.

I failed. I made everything worse.

I stumble again and Dante sets me on my feet. "It's not over," he says quietly.

"How can you say that?"

"Because it's only just begun. We forged the knife."

"A knife the Warden has!"

"For now." The tunnel stops in a dead end. Dante presses a hand against it, and the rock slides back. There's a cave filled with people. Behind them is a sky full of stars, and the crash of the ocean far below echoes around a cavern that opens directly to the sea. "But we have you," he says and nods across the cave. "And we have Alice."

"Alice?" I see her then, her fair hair dark with ash, her eyes glazed with shock. And my heart unclenches just a little. Her hand finds mine in the dark, she squeezes tight.

I see Malin, hurrying toward us through the straggling survivors. He's alive. Blood darkens one cheek, his hands are burned, but he's alive. He reaches for us, Alice and me, and pulls us both into his chest. "I thought…" he chokes out.

"I know," I whisper into his shoulder.

He stiffens. His arms harden around us. "Thank you," Malin says over our heads. "You got her out."

Dante grunts. "I didn't do it for you."

The wall rumbles as it slides back into place behind us. I hear other witches gulping back sobs and one breaks down into shocked and desperate gasping. And Malin releases us as Dante points to the opposite side of the cavern where a Gilded stands with his back to us, staring out into the night. "I did it for them."

At first I think it's Tobias. Then, he turns.

The Gilded is the one I helped to gild. The number 963 is stamped into his breastplate. At his throat is a purple crystal. He is there behind his silver eyes. And talking to him quietly is Mila. She throws me a thin smile, the light in her eyes watered down like the moon behind a cloud.

Mila survived. So did I. I think Ella did too. I don't feel a space where she should be, but I won't breathe properly until I see her again.

Dante gives me a cold grin. "You thorn witches are a force to be reckoned with. And this is far from over."

I take a deep breath of the salt-tinged air.

He's right. Our losses are many. The wound is deep. The Warden has the Sorcerer's knife.

But we have his army in our hands.

Tonight, we lost. Tomorrow, we will rise. And when we do, we'll set his world ablaze.

The story continues in . . .

TONIGHT, I BLEED

Book TWO of the Thorn Witch Trilogy

Acknowledgments

Tonight, I Burn hit me in the middle of the night with those first three lines. I meant to jot some notes down for later and finish drafting another story. Penny had other ideas and spilled out onto the page. I typed *the end* on the first draft a few weeks later. Since then, so many people have gone into transforming it from a sandpit full of ideas and words into this book.

My amazing agent, Ernie Chiara: You rock. Without your endless patience, sense of humour, and support, this publishing thing would have been impossible. You saw me and my words. And I am so glad you did. Penny couldn't ask for a better champion!

My editor, Priyanka Krishnan, thank you for loving Penny, Alice, and Malin and for making me giggle with your edits. You saw what I meant this story to be and made it shine! Working with you, Jenni Hill, and the teams at Orbit US and Orbit UK is the realisation of so many dreams. So many magical moments, from the first time I saw Lisa Marie Pompillio's cover—which my daughter, Tilly, pronounced "the most beautiful thing ever!"—to Kelley Frodel copyediting my mixed-up British x New Zealand spellings into something logical. To everyone else behind the scenes on both sides of the Atlantic: thank you.

Kate Stephenson and everyone at Moa Press, I'm so ridiculously lucky to have you on board with Penny on home soil, and I'm honoured to be a part of Moa's debut year. Jeanmarie Morosin and Hachette Australia, thank you for looking after us over the ditch.

I'm so fortunate to have had support from a fabulous writing community. If I tried to name everyone, I'd miss someone, but you are appreciated. So very much.

Katie, who knew Penny from the moment I sent her a message in the middle of the night with three lines that wouldn't go away, followed an hour later by a chapter of witches and matches and burnings. You held my hand long before the first words of this. "Thank you" doesn't cut it.

Jenn R., I wish I could print octopus emojis on the page! You've saved my sanity (and my romance scenes) more than once. You make this journey brighter, and the rollercoaster is a little less terrifying for riding it with you.

Ashley and Wendy for being some of Penny's very first readers and for your endless support. Dani, Megs, and Jess H., who all read the most appalling first draft of my very first manuscript and didn't laugh when I told them my publishing dreams. Julia, who's listened to my story-related ramblings and woes on our school-run walk, twice a day, five days a week, rain or shine, for many, many years. I'd have lost my way without you.

Mum and Dad, who filled my childhood with boats and adventures and made up stories in the middle of the sea on dark, stormy nights. Dad, the mud beast is all yours. And Sam, the sibling relationships are entirely your fault; Isla and Isobel, your dad is the best.

To my little family. Tilly and Noah, thank you for sharing Mummy with the magical people who live in my head. So many nights you fall asleep to my writing playlists until you know which world I'm in from the order of the songs. I would bargain my soul for you over and over again. And Ben—fancy seeing you here! I don't have space to list all the ways you support me, encourage me, and believe in me. You are my always and forever.

And finally: to anyone who picks up this book and steps through the veil with Penny, thank you for sharing her journey. Without readers, and the booksellers and librarians who help books find their place in the world, none of this would be real. The book sprites thank you too.

extras

meet the author

Tara Lemana Portraiture

KATHARINE J. ADAMS is an English fantasy writer based in New Zealand. You can find her tucked away in her office in the wee small hours of the morning while the rest of the house sleeps. No matter where she is, she's never happier than in those moments when her writing truly takes her away, and she's in a realm where witches burn, the future is spun from silk, and Death is more than it seems.

Find out more about Katharine J. Adams and other Orbit authors by registering for the free monthly newsletter at orbitbooks.net.

if you enjoyed
TONIGHT, I BURN
look out for
THE FOXGLOVE KING
The Nightshade Crown: Book One
by
Hannah Whitten

In this lush, romantic epic fantasy series from a **New York Times** ***bestselling author, a young woman's secret power to raise the dead plunges her into the dangerous and glamorous world of the Sainted King's royal court.***

When Lore was thirteen, she escaped a cult in the catacombs beneath the city of Dellaire. And in the ten years since, she's lived by one rule: Don't let them find you. Easier said than done, when her death magic ties her to the city.

Mortem, the magic born from death, is a high-priced and illicit commodity in Dellaire, and Lore's job running poisons keeps her in food, shelter, and relative security. But when a run goes wrong and Lore's power is revealed, she's taken by the Presque Mort, a group of warrior-monks sanctioned to use Mortem working for the Sainted King. Lore fully expects a pyre, but King August has a different plan. Entire villages on the outskirts of the country have been dying overnight, seemingly at random. Lore can either use her magic to find out what's happening and who in the king's court is responsible, or die.

Lore is thrust into the Sainted King's glittering court, where no one can be believed and even fewer can be trusted. Guarded by Gabriel, a duke-turned-monk, and continually running up against Bastian, August's ne'er-do-well heir, Lore tangles in politics, religion, and forbidden romance as she attempts to navigate a debauched and opulent society.

But the life she left behind in the catacombs is catching up with her. And even as Lore makes her way through the Sainted court above, they might be drawing closer than she thinks.

Chapter One

No one is more patient than the dead.
—Auverrani proverb

Every month, Michal claimed he'd struck a deal with the landlord, and every month, Nicolas sent one of his sons to collect anyway. The sons must've drawn straws—this month's unfortunate was Pierre, the youngest and spottiest of the bunch, and he trudged up the street of Dellaire's Harbor District with the air of one approaching a guillotine.

Lore could work with that.

A dressing gown that had seen better days dripped off one shoulder as Lore leaned against the doorframe and watched him approach. Pierre's eyes kept drifting to where the fabric gaped, and she kept having to bite the inside of her cheek so she didn't laugh. Apparently, a crosshatch of silvery scars from back-alley knife fights didn't deter the man when presented with bare skin.

She had other, more interesting scars. But she kept her palm closed tight.

A cool breeze blew off the ocean, and Lore suppressed a shiver. Pierre didn't seem to spare any thought for why she'd exited the house barely dressed when mornings near the harbor always carried a chill, even in summer. An easy mark in more ways than one.

"Pierre!" Lore shot him a dazzling grin, the same one that made Michal's eyes simultaneously go heated and then narrow before he asked what she wanted. Another twist against the doorframe, another seemingly casual pose, another bite of wind that made a curse bubble behind her teeth. "It's the end of the month already?"

Michal should be dealing with this. It was his damn row house. But the drop he'd made for Gilbert last night had been all the way in the Northwest Ward, so Lore let him sleep.

Besides, waking up early had given her time to go through Michal's pockets for the drop coordinates. She'd taken them to the tavern on the corner and left them with Frederick the bartender, who'd been on Val's payroll for as long as Lore could remember. Val would be sending someone to pick them up before the sun fully rose, and someone else to grab Gilbert's poison drop before his client could.

Lore was good at her job.

Right now, her job was making sure the man she'd been living with for a year so she could spy on his boss didn't get evicted.

"I—um—yes, yes it is." Pierre managed to fix his eyes to her own, through obviously conscious effort. "My father . . . um, he said this time he means it, and . . ."

Lore let her expression fall by careful degrees, first into confusion, then shock, then sorrow. "Oh," she murmured, wrapping her arms around herself and turning her face away to show a length of pale white neck. "This month, of all months."

She didn't elaborate. She didn't need to. If there was anything Lore had learned in twenty-three years alive, ten spent on the streets of Dellaire, it was that men generally preferred you to be a set piece in the story they made up, rather than an active player.

From the corner of her eye, she saw Pierre's pale brows draw together, a deepening blush lighting the skin beneath his freckles. They were all moon-pale, Nicolas's boys. It made their blushes look like something viral.

His gaze went past her to the depths of the dilapidated row house beyond. Sunrise shadows hid everything but the dust motes twisting in light shards. Not that there was much to see back there, anyway. Michal was still asleep upstairs, and his sister, Elle, was sprawled on the couch, a wine bottle in her hand and a slightly musical snore on her lips. It looked like any other row house on this street, coming apart at the seams and full of people who skirted just under the law to get by.

Or very far under it, as the case may be.

"Is there an illness?" Pierre kept his voice hushed, low. His face tried for sympathetic, but it looked more like he'd put bad milk in his coffee. "A child, maybe? I know Michal rents this house, not you. Is it his?"

Lore's brows shot up. In all the stories she'd let men spin about her, *that* was a first—Pierre must have sex on the brain if he jumped straight to pregnancy. But beggars couldn't be choosers. She gently laid a hand on her abdomen and let that be answer enough. It wasn't technically a lie if she let him draw his own conclusions.

She was past caring about lying, anyway. Lore was damned whether or not she kept her spiritual record spotless. Might as well lean into it.

"Oh, you poor girl." Pierre was probably younger than she was, and here he went clucking like a mother hen. Lore managed to keep her eyes from rolling, but only just. "And with a poison runner? You know he won't be able to take care of you."

Lore bit the inside of her cheek again, hard.

Her apparent distress made Pierre bold. "You could come with me," he said. "My father could help you find work, I'm sure." He raised his hand, settled it on her bare shoulder.

And every nerve in Lore's body seized.

It was abrupt and unexpected enough for her to shudder, to shake off his hand in a motion that didn't fit her soft, vulnerable narrative. She'd grown used to feeling this reaction to dead things—stone, metal, cloth. Corpses, when she couldn't avoid them. It was natural to sense Mortem in something dead, no matter how unpleasant, and at this point she could hide her reaction, keep it contained. She'd had enough practice.

But she shouldn't feel Mortem in a *living* man, not one who wasn't at death's door. Her shock was quick and sharp, and chased with something else—the scent of foxglove. So strong, he must've been dosed mere minutes before arriving.

And he wanted to disparage poison runners. Hypocrite.

Her fingers closed around his wrist, twisted, forced him to his knees. It happened quick, quick enough for him to slip on a stray pebble and send one leg out at an awkward angle, for a strangled "*Shit!*" to echo through the morning streets of Dellaire's Harbor District.

Lore crouched so they were level. Now that she knew what to look for, it was obvious in his eyes, bloodshot and glassy; in the heartbeat thumping slow and irregular beneath her palm. He'd gone to one of the cheap deathdealers, one who didn't know how to properly dose their patrons. The veins at the corners of Pierre's eyes were barely touched with gray, so he hadn't been given enough poison for any kind of life extension, and certainly not enough to possibly grasp the power waiting at death's threshold.

He probably wasn't after those things, anyway. Most people his age just wanted the high.

The dark threads of Mortem under Pierre's skin twisted against Lore's grip, stirred to waking by the poison in his system. Mortem was dormant in everyone—the essence of death, the power born of entropy, just waiting to flood your body on the day it failed—but the only way to use it, to bend it to your will, was to nearly die.

If you weren't after the power or the euphoric feeling poison could give you, then you were after the extra years. Properly dosed, poison could balance your body on the cusp of life and death, and that momentary concession to Mortem could, paradoxically, extend your life. Not that the life you got in exchange was one of great quality—half-stone, your veins clotted with rock, making your blood rub through them like a cobblestone skinning a knee.

Whatever Pierre had been after when he visited a deathdealer this morning, he hadn't paid enough to get it. If he'd gotten a true poison high, he'd be slumped in an alley somewhere, not asking her for rent. Rent that was higher than she remembered it being, now that she thought of it.

"Here's what's going to happen," Lore murmured. "You are going to tell Nicolas that we've paid up for the next six months, or I am going to tell him you've been spending his coin on deathdealers."

Fuck Michal's ineffectual bargains with the landlord. She'd just make one of her own.

Pierre's eyes widened, his lids poison-heavy. "How—"

"You stink of foxglove and your eyes look more like windows." Not exactly true, since she hadn't noticed until she'd sensed the Mortem, but by the time he could examine himself, the effect would've worn off anyway. "Anyone can take one look at you and know, Pierre, even though your deathdealer barely gave you enough to make you tingle. I'd be surprised if you got five extra minutes tacked on for *that*, so I hope the high was worth it."

The boy gaped, the open mouth under his window-glass eyes making his face look fishlike. He'd undoubtedly paid a handsome sum for the pinch of foxglove he'd taken. If she wasn't so good at spying for Val, Lore might've become a deathdealer herself. They made a whole lot of money for doing a whole lot of jack shit.

Pierre's unfortunate blush spread down his neck. "I can't—He'll ask where the money is—"

"I'm confident an industrious young man like yourself can come up with it somewhere." A flick of her fingers, and Lore let him go.

Pierre stumbled up on shaky legs and straightened his mussed shirt. The gray veins at the corners of his eyes were already fading back to blue-green. "I'll try," he said, voice just as tremulous as the rest of him. "I can't promise he'll believe me."

Lore gave him a winning smile. Standing, she yanked up the shoulder of her dressing gown. "He better."

Pierre didn't run down the street, but he walked very fast.

As the sun rose higher, the Harbor District slowly woke up—bundles of cloth stirred in dark corners, drunks coaxed awake by light and sea breeze. In the row house across the street, Lore heard the telltale sighs of Madam Brochfort's girls starting their daily squabbles over who got the washtub first, and any minute now at least two straggling patrons would be politely but firmly escorted outside.

"Pierre?" she called when he was halfway down the street. He turned, lips pressed together, clearly considering what other things she might blackmail him with.

"A word of advice." She turned toward Michal's row house in a flutter of faded dressing gown. "The real deathdealers have morgues in the back. Death's scales are easy to tip."

❧

Elle was awake, but only just. She squinted from beneath a pile of gold curls through the light-laden dust, paint still smeared across her lips. "Whassat?"

"As if you don't know." Lore shook out the hand that had touched Pierre's shoulder, trying to banish pins and needles. It'd grown easier for her to sense Mortem recently, and she wasn't fond of the development. She gave her hand one more firm shake before heading into the kitchen. "End of the month, Elle-Flower."

There was barely enough coffee in the chipped ceramic pot for one cup. Lore poured all of it into the stained cloth she used as a strainer and balled it in her fingers as she put the kettle over the fire. If there was only one cup of coffee in this house, she'd be the one drinking it.

"Don't call me that." Elle groaned as she shifted to sit up. She'd fallen asleep in her dancer's tights, and a long run traced up each calf. It'd piss her off once she noticed, but the patrons of the Foghorn and Fiddle down the street wouldn't care. One squinting look into the wine bottle to make sure it was empty and Elle shoved off the couch to stand. "Michal isn't awake, we don't have to pretend we like each other."

Lore snorted. In the year she'd been living with Michal, it'd become very obvious that she'd never get along with his sister. It didn't bother Lore. Her relationship with Michal was built on a lie, a sand foundation with no hope of holding, so why try to make friends? As soon as Val gave the word, she'd be gone.

Elle pushed past her into the kitchen, the spiderweb cracks on the windows refracting veined light on the tattered edges of her tulle skirt. She peered into the pot. "No coffee?"

Lore tightened her hand around the cloth knotted in her fist. "Afraid not."

"Bleeding *God*." Elle flopped onto one of the chairs by the pockmarked kitchen table. For a dancer, she was surprisingly ungraceful when sober. "I'll take tea, then."

"*Surely* you don't expect me to get it for you."

A grumble and a roll of bright-blue eyes as Elle slinked her way toward the cupboard. While her back was turned, Lore tucked the straining cloth into the lip of her mug and poured hot water over it, hoping Elle was too residually drunk to recognize the scent.

Still grumbling, Elle scooped tea that was little more than dust into another mug. "Well?" She took the kettle from Lore without looking at her and apparently without smelling her coffee. "How'd it go? Is Michal finally going to have to spend money on something other than alcohol and betting at the boxing ring?"

"Not on rent, at least." Lore kept her back turned as she tugged the straining cloth and the tiny knot of coffee grounds from her cup and stuffed it in her pocket. "We're paid up for six months."

"Is that why you look so disheveled?" Elle's mouth pulled into a self-satisfied moue. "He could get it cheaper across the street."

"The dishevelment is the fault of your brother, actually." Lore turned and leaned against the counter. "And barbs about Madam's girls don't suit you, Elle-Flower. It's work like any other. To think otherwise just proves you dull."

Another eye roll. Elle made a face when she sipped her weak tea, and sharp satisfaction hitched Lore's smile higher. She took a long, luxurious swallow of coffee and drifted toward the stairs. There'd been a message waiting for her at the tavern—Val needed her help with a drop today. It was risky business, having her work while she was deep undercover with another operation, but hands were low. People kept getting hired out from under them on the docks.

And Lore had skills that no one else did.

She'd have to come up with an excuse for why she'd be gone all day, but if she woke Michal up with some kissing, he wouldn't question her further. She found herself smiling at the idea. She liked kissing Michal. That was dangerous.

The smile dropped.

The stairs of the row house were rickety, like pretty much everything else in the structure, and the fourth one squeaked something awful. Lore winced when her heel ground into it, sloshing coffee over the side of her mug and burning her fingers.

Michal was sitting up when Lore pushed aside the ratty curtain closing off their room, sheets tangled around his waist and dripping off the mattress to pool on the floor. It was unclear whether it was the squeaking stair or her loud curse when she burned herself that had woken him.

He pushed his dark hair out of his eyes, squinted. "Coffee?"

"Last cup, but I'll share if you come get it."

"That's generous, since I assume you need it." He grumbled as he levered himself up from the floor-bound mattress, holding the sheet around his naked hips. "You had another nightmare last night. Thrashed around like the Night Witch herself was after you."

Her cheeks colored, but Lore just shrugged. The nightmares were a recent development, and random. She could never remember much about them, only vague impressions that didn't quite match with the terrified feeling they left behind. Blue, open sky, a churning sea. Some dark shape twisting through the air, like smoke but thicker.

Lore held out the coffee. "Sorry if I kept you awake."

"At least you didn't scream this time." Michal took a long drink from her proffered mug, though his face twisted up when he swallowed. "No milk?"

"Elle used the last of it." Lore shrugged and took the cup back, draining the rest.

Michal ran a hand through his hair to tame it into submission while he bent to pull clothes from the piles on the floor. The sheet fell, and Lore allowed herself a moment to ogle.

"I have another drop today," he said as he got dressed. "So I'll probably be gone until the evening."

That made her life much easier. Lore propped her hips on the windowsill and watched him dress, hoping her relief didn't show on her face. "Gilbert is working you hard."

"Demand has gone up, and the team is dwindling. People keep getting hired on the docks to move cargo, getting paid more than Gilbert can afford to match." Michal gave the room a narrow-eyed survey before spotting his boot beneath a pile of sheets in the corner. "The Presque Mort and the bloodcoats have all been busy getting ready for the Sun Prince's Consecration tomorrow, and everyone is taking advantage of them having their proverbial backs turned."

It seemed like Gilbert was doing far more business during the security lull than was wise, but that wasn't Lore's problem. That's what she told herself, at least, when worry for Michal squeezed a fist around her insides. "Must be some deeply holy Consecration they're planning, if the Presque Mort are invited. They aren't known for being the best party guests."

Michal huffed a laugh as he pulled his boots on. "Especially not if your party includes poison." He rolled his neck, working out stiffness from their rock-hard mattress, and stood.

"Be careful tonight," Lore said, then immediately clenched her teeth. She hadn't meant to say it. She hadn't meant to *mean* it.

A lazy smile lifted his mouth. Michal sauntered over, cupped her face in his hands. "Are you *worried* about me, Lore?"

She scowled but didn't shake him off. "Don't get used to it."

A laugh rumbled through his chest, pressed against her own, and then his lips were on hers. Lore sighed and kissed him back, her hands wrapping around his shoulders, tugging him close.

It'd be over soon, so she might as well enjoy it while it lasted.

Despite Michal's warmth, Lore still felt like shivering. She could feel Mortem everywhere—the cloth of Michal's shirt, the stones in the street outside, the chipped ceramic of the mug on the windowsill. Even as her awareness of it grew, a steady climb over the last few months, she was usually able to ignore it, but Pierre's unexpected foxglove had thrown her off balance. Mortem wasn't as thick here on the outskirts of Dellaire as it was closer to the Citadel—closer to the Buried Goddess's body far beneath it, leaking the magic of death—but it was still enough to make her skin crawl.

The Harbor District, on the southern edge of Dellaire, was as far as Mortem would let her go. She could try to hop a ship, try to trek out on the winding roads that led into the rest of Auverraine, but it'd be pointless. The threads of Mortem would just wind her back, woven into her very marrow. She was tied into this damn city as surely as death was tied into life, as surely as the crescent moon burned into the bottom curve of her palm.

Michal's mouth found her throat, and she arched into him, closing her eyes tight. Her fingers clawed into his hair, and his arm cinched around her waist like he might lift her up, carry her to their mattress on the floor, make her forget that this was something finite.

The fact that she *wanted* to forget was enough to make her push him away, masking it as playful. "You don't want to be late."

He lingered at her lips a moment before stepping back. "I'll see you tonight, then."

She just smiled, though the stretch of her lips felt unnatural.

Michal left, that same step squeaking on his way down, the windows rattling when he closed the door. Lore heard Elle heave a sigh, as if her brother's job were a personal affront, the thin walls making it sound like she was right next to Lore instead of all the way on the first floor.

Lore stood there a moment, the light of the slow-rising sun gleaming on her hair, the worn silk of her gown. Then she dressed in a flowing shirt and tight breeches, made her own way down the stairs. She had a meeting with Val to attend.

Elle was curled up on the couch again, a ragged paperback novel in one hand and another mug of tepid tea in the other. She eyed Lore the way you might look at something unpleasant you'd tracked in from the street. "And where are you going?"

"Oh, you didn't hear? I received an invitation to the Sun Prince's Consecration. I wasn't going to go, but rumor has it there might be an orgy afterward, and I can't very well turn that down."

Elle rolled her eyes so hard Lore was surprised she didn't strain a muscle. "There is something deeply *off* about you."

"You have no idea." Lore opened the door. "Bye, Elle-Flower."

"Rot in your own hell, Lore-dear."

Lore twiddled her fingers in an exaggerated wave as the door closed. Part of her would miss Elle when the spying gig was up, when Val had a different running outfit she wanted watched instead of Gilbert's.

But not as much as she'd miss Michal.

She couldn't miss either of them for long. People came and went; her only constants were her mothers—Val and Mari—and the streets of Dellaire she could never leave.

That, and the memories of a childhood she was always, always trying to forget.

With one last glance at the row house, Lore started down the street.